Books by Lonnie Coleman

ESCAPE THE THUNDER

TIME MOVING WEST

THE SOUND OF SPANISH VOICES

CLARA

ADAM'S WAY

THE SOUTHERN LADY

SAM

THE GOLDEN VANITY

KING

BEULAH LAND

ORPHAN JIM

LOOK AWAY, BEULAH LAND

THE LEGACY OF BEULAH LAND

MARK

SHIP'S COMPANY, short stories

HOT SPELL, play

MARK

by Lonnie Coleman

SIMON AND SCHUSTER

NEW YORK

This novel is a work of fiction. Names, characters, places and incidents are either the product of the author's imagination or are used fictitiously, and any resemblance to actual persons, living or dead, events or locales is entirely coincidental.

Copyright © 1981 by Lonnie Coleman
All rights reserved
including the right of reproduction
in whole or in part in any form
Published by Simon and Schuster
A Division of Gulf & Western Corporation
Simon & Schuster Building
Rockefeller Center
1230 Avenue of the Americas
New York, New York 10020

SIMON and SCHUSTER and colophon are trademarks of
Simon & Schuster

Designed by Irving Perkins and Associates
Manufactured in the United States of America
1   3   5   7   9   10   8   6   4   2

Library of Congress Cataloging in Publication Data
Coleman, Lonnie, date.
Mark.
I.   Title.
PS3505.O27967M3   813'.54   81–1941
                                       AACR2
ISBN 0–671–42785–7

To Gloria and Bernard Beckerman

I

AUNT BELLE was talking to Uncle Grady in the kitchen the night Mama died. My own life hung in the balance and I knew it, so I listened hard.

"We've got to let Mark come back with us," she said.

"You mean keep him?" Uncle Grady sounded grim but unsurprised.

"It's not a matter of big-heart but have-to. Where else can he go?"

"They have homes."

Orphan-fear was common in 1933, when the Depression had taken such a grip nobody thought good times would come again, no matter what President Roosevelt said on the radio. "Homes" were places to put the young and the old, and crazy people.

Aunt Belle said, "He doesn't eat much."

"Only because he's distracted. He's thirteen, and he'll eat like thirteen armies when we get back to Montgomery. It's not that I grudge victuals—after all, I'm in the business. But if we take him, we won't get rid of him till he's grown. Thought of that?"

"One more won't make a lot of difference."

"Roland's nearly eighteen, Beatrice sixteen. In a couple more years—" He paused a long time. "Shit."

Aunt Belle laughed.

I didn't blame Uncle Grady. Why should he want me? They hardly knew me, for one thing. The only time families at any distance got together was weddings and funerals, and nobody acts himself at those. For another thing, my father hadn't wanted me. When I was ten, I heard him tell my mother he wished I hadn't been born.

Aunt Belle and Uncle Grady Benedict had come in their car yesterday from Montgomery to Savannah. They brought Roland and Beatrice because they knew they were coming to a funeral, and whole families came to funerals then. The doctor had told me to send for them by telegram, explaining that Mama had developed pneumonia on top of the cancer she'd had for two years. She died the day after they got there, without knowing them.

"All right?" Aunt Belle asked.

Sigh changed to groan. "Well, she was your only sister."

Having his consent, she allowed, "Of course, it's for you to say."

"All right, Belle. Shit." She laughed again.

Savannah, Georgia, was my birthplace and the only home I knew, but I wasn't sorry to be leaving it, because I'd seen hard times there. My father, Fred Bowman, was a flagman on the railroad until he was killed in an accident. Soon after, my mother got sick. Nobody said what it was, and I didn't think about it much. I'd find her lying down when I came home from school, but I put that to low spirits because we had less to live on. The railroad paid her less than a hundred dollars a month. Later, she went to the hospital for a week, and when she came home the doctor told me and my brother, Tom, she had cancer. Tom was almost four years older than I, and he

8

was actually the one who told me. Everyone else seemed to know it already, the way they do.

Nothing changed much in the old house on Gwinnett Street.

We paid twenty-five dollars a month for the ground floor and rented out three rooms to a Mrs. Harrison, who worked for the city, and her daughter Beryl. They gave Mama eighteen dollars a month, but we paid for lights and gas and water. Tom and I stayed in school. Tom never had a job, said he couldn't find one; but I worked two afternoons a week and all day Saturday for a butcher named Mr. Cramer. He was a big fat man and always wore a dirty, bloody apron and carried an unlit cigar in the left side of his mouth. I never saw him smoke it; he used it like chewing tobacco.

On Thursday afternoon I'd slice bacon for the weekend trade and Friday kill and dress his chickens. Saturday I waited on customers for things out of the case and carried sides or quarters of meat in and out of the cooler for Mr. Cramer to cut into steak and chops and roasts for those more particular. It was heavy work, but Mr. Cramer said it would make a man of me, winking as he said it.

Savannah was old and beautiful, with squares to walk through instead of around, full of flowers and liveoaks and magnolia trees. I loved watching the squirrels. How many hundreds of generations of them had come and gone in those old moss-hung squares? They seemed to own them as they went about their business, seeking and hiding. They'd run quick along the ground and make a sudden Tarzan leap onto a tree trunk, then climb like lightning, stopping high up to look down as if they had all the time in the world.

The birds sang in early morning and early evening and during the day when it had rained and stopped. There was one, though, near our house I hated to hear. He must have lost his mate, for he made an urgent, begging call as he flew back and forth, seeming to say, "Here I am! Where are you?" I could have cried, I felt so sorry for him.

9

After she came out of the hospital, Mama had a Christian Science practitioner to visit twice a week; but when she grew weaker and thinner, the practitioner turned cranky, hardly speaking as she came and went. Finally she stopped coming; maybe Mama told her to. Her name was Mrs. Klein, and she was the only Christian Scientist I ever saw who didn't smile.

One afternoon the spring before, when I came home from school, I was surprised to find Tom. He wasn't going to school any more; he'd been expelled for shooting craps in the toilet with some other boys; but Mama didn't know it. We decided not to tell her, for Tom was her whole heart; and he usually timed his day so she'd think he was at school as usual.

They were eating Jello. I didn't care, but seeing them close together made me say, "I made that lime Jello this morning for our supper!"

"I was hungry," Tom said. " 'Jello, everybody, this is Jack Benny.' You made four. Still two left. One for you and one for Mother, because I won't be here for supper."

"Where'll you be?" she asked.

"I promised a girl. Have you got a dollar that's spoiling? Two would make her think I'm the Prince of Wales."

Mama said, "Marcus, bring me my pocketbook." She seldom left her wheelchair, except to go to bed.

"I know where it is." Tom went to the bureau where she kept it in the top left drawer with hairnets and bobby pins and a box of Coty face powder she seldom used.

She opened it and put her hand in, then held it to her and smiled at him. "Who's this girl you like better than me?"

Taking both arms of the wheelchair, he kissed her on the lips and then all around her neck till he got her laughing. "Give me some sugar! Give me some sugar!—Angel, there's none I'll ever like as much as you, but they run after me, and I have to promise one to get rid of the rest."

"You're always promising!" She gave him two one-dollar bills and snapped the pocketbook shut.

"One day I'll be rich, and you'll sit on a golden throne!" He twirled the wheelchair around like a kiddy car.

She giggled even as she demanded that he stop, until he let go the chair and kissed her again. "There, I leave you beautiful and smiling, the way I always think of you."

When Tom left, there was always a blank. I began to tuck in the edge of the afghan that had come loose in their playing.

"Do leave me alone."

"Sometimes you're cold."

"I've had the windows open all day. It's spring outside—"

"The doctor says your circulation is slow and you might feel cold when other people don't."

"Aren't you due at the store?"

"Do you have something to read?"

"I've a jigsaw puzzle Tom bought me."

"Is there anything I can do, or get you?"

She shook her head and wheeled herself to a table where the puzzle pieces had been dumped out. "Go along, Marcus."

"What do you want me to bring for supper?"

"Anything. It doesn't matter with Tom not here."

When I left, Beryl was on the front porch, slouched low in a rocking chair and looking broody as she turned pages in a *Photoplay* magazine.

I said, "Hey," and she said, "Hey, yourself. How do you like the new way I've fixed my hair? Tom didn't notice."

Neither had I, but I said it sure looked nice.

She studied me as if to test the truth of the statement. "Mark, you're not a bit like Tom."

"So I've been told."

"I like you, though."

"I like you too."

"You never say funny things, and you never try to flirt with me. How come?"

"You're two years older than I am."

She laughed. "I take it back—you do say funny things. I've been reading about Joan Crawford. We think movie stars never have any trouble, but they do. She's had a terrible time lately, I can tell you."

"I thought all she had to do was use Lux soap and kiss Clark Gable."

"I don't think you care—go on to the store and slice bacon." I did.

Beryl always looked sloppy because she did only one thing at a time to herself. If she took a bath, her hair was messy or her dress had a rip. If her dress was all right, *she* looked oily-faced and sweaty. She wasn't pretty, but she was good-hearted and I liked her. Along with everybody else, she was in love with Tom, or thought she was, which is the same thing for all practical purposes. I don't think he cared much about her, but she was there in the house just a wall away, so sometimes when her mother was off at work he took her down to the basement and fucked her. I'd walked in on them that winter when I went to get a scuttle of coal for Mama's grate, and neither one had been embarrassed, just laughed at me because I was.

Without trying, Tom charmed the world and everybody in it. It never rained on Tom, and he never wanted anything he didn't get. He could even charm me, though I was the younger brother and jealous, and knew every trick. He didn't think of them as tricks, just as how to get his way. He certainly wasn't mean; he'd share what he had with anybody, and nobody minded that he hadn't paid for it himself. He'd given me a quarter one day when he had good luck with the dice, because he remembered there was a picture with Katharine Hepburn I wanted to see and it was on for the last day. He didn't like her, but that didn't matter; he knew I did. Some people have charm and some don't. I don't, but at least I know it.

2

WHEN I came home from the butcher shop and found Mrs. Harrison fussing with Mama, it didn't occur to me to excuse myself, and they paid no attention to me. Mrs. Harrison was saying, "You don't answer me by wheeling away. I'm not one of those nigger servants at that big country house you *say* you were born in."

Mama's voice was cold, and anger made it strong. "I was born in town, Mrs. Harrison. We owned several country properties but never lived on them."

"Well, now you live in a twenty-five-dollar-a-month ground floor of an old house on Gwinnett Street, a small part of which you rent to me for eighteen dollars a month, so don't give yourself airs like a fine lady—"

"You are not forced to live here. I assure you I am not becoming rich on your exorbitant rent. You might remember I had to pay the plumber last month when the drain was stopped, evidently by your daughter's carelessness, throwing things down it she shouldn't. The plumber was a Negro, and I was embarrassed when he showed me what had caused the mess."

"That isn't what I'm here to talk about. I want you to promise to speak to Tom. He is to let my daughter alone."

"Mrs. Harrison, my son is amiable to everyone. If your daughter is so silly as to think it means anything if he smiles at her—he smiles at the kettle and the door, tell her."

"She's a good girl, but she's young, and I have to leave her to work. It's a bad situation."

"You should have considered it before you moved here."

"Two years ago she was a child."

"Children grow."

"Tom's grown too quick; he knows too much. He couldn't smile at a saint without the devil showing in his eyes. He even looks at me."

"You disgust me."

"I'm only asking you to help me. I know Beryl appears free and easy, but she doesn't mean it. She just gets it out of those movie magazines."

Mrs. Harrison stared at me, seeming to see me for the first time. Tears popped into her eyes, and she turned and left without another word, slamming the door.

Mama made no reference to her. "What have you got?"

"Pork chops for supper. Mr. Cramer says they're all right but they'd have gone slick by tomorrow. He gave them to me."

"I suppose you hinted. I wish you wouldn't do that."

I held the meat package behind me and handed her the other package I carried. It was a pound box of chocolate-covered cherries; they had been on sale at the store for thirty-nine cents. I placed them on her lap when she didn't take them. She looked at them without picking them up.

"They're so sweet," she said, frowning. "Thank you, Marcus, but you mustn't throw your money away. I don't care much for sweet things any more."

I took the pork chops to the kitchen and came back. I know why I did the next thing, but I don't know why I did it then, perhaps to make her forget Mrs. Harrison and Beryl, but more likely because Tom wasn't there and I wanted to say: Think of me, see what I've done. I went to the small bedroom I shared with Tom, found the loose-leaf notebook, and took it to Mama. She had set the candy box aside without opening it and held two pieces of the jigsaw puzzle in her hands.

"What is it?" She opened the cover and read the title page. " 'Poems by Mark Bowman.' I wish you'd remember to use your full name. Marcus was my father's, Marcus Stafford. Mark is common. What are they about?"

My heart was pounding so hard it seemed to fill my body. "They're not very good, but Miss Perry says for me to keep on."

"She's your English teacher."

I nodded.

"I'm surely not the judge of poetry Miss Perry is. You must take her word."

"If there are any you like, I wish you'd tell me which ones."

She didn't look at me but put the notebook aside and returned to the puzzle. My voice must have sounded as begging as the bird's I tried not to hear.

Next night when I came home from the butcher shop smelling of singed feathers and chicken blood, I found Tom and Mama together. I'd come in by the kitchen door to put down the hamburger we were going to have for supper when I heard Tom saying in the next room, "This one's called 'Coffee Can Flowers.' What does he mean by that?"

"Oh," she answered, "you must have been through the colored quarters and seen them on their porches. They punch holes in the bottom of coffee cans so they'll drain, then fill them with dirt and stick in a geranium cutting hoping it will take root and grow."

"Give me another piece of candy; I need it." Tom began to read in a sissy-poetic voice:

" 'Coffee can flowers, all in a row,

" 'Coffee can flowers, why do you grow?' "

He was reading with his mouth full and almost choked when he laughed. I went in and grabbed the notebook out of his hands and said to Mama, "I gave them to *you* to read!"

Still laughing, Tom clapped me on the shoulder. "Ah, Marcus, don't carry on like a girl. I'm just cutting the fool to make Mother enjoy herself. Isn't it good to hear her laugh?"

I took the candy box from him. "I bought them for *you*, not Tom!"

As coolly as she'd spoken to Mrs. Harrison she said, "When a thing is given to me, it is mine to share as I choose."

"No!" I declared. "When I give you something, it's *my* present and you're to think of me when you eat them, not Tom!"

"You'd better keep the chocolates and eat them yourself."

"I will!"

Tom came into the kitchen when I was cooking the hamburgers and tried to make up in his honey-teasing way. He was surprised I was still mad. When he told me I was another William Shakespeare I took the sharp-pointed cooking fork and told him to get out of the kitchen or I'd kill him. He looked more surprised, but shrugged and smiled and went out the back door. "I'll go find Beryl. She appreciates me."

I cried with misery for what I'd done, but I couldn't stop feeling stubborn and mad.

Saturdays were long, hard days at Mr. Cramer's. I'd get there at six in the morning to grind hamburger meat and sausage, and we'd fill the cases up with other cut meat such as liver and spareribs and stewing beef by seven when customers started coming. We didn't go out to eat but made bologna sandwiches and ate them with a pint of milk at noon and around eight o'clock at night when the business was over.

There'd still be work to do. I had to wash out the meat cases, then clean the glass inside and out with ammonia. Then I'd scrape the two butcher blocks with wire brushes until I was wet with sweat and there wasn't a speck of blood or a stain on them, the wood coming up clean and fresh-smelling. Last thing I did was rake the sawdust that covered the floor to free it of discarded scraps and bits of bone dropped during the day. If I didn't do that, it would stink by Monday morning. Sometimes I took all the sawdust up and put down fresh. After I'd hung up the rake on the back wall, tines up and out, Mr. Cramer would pay me and I was free to go. By then it was usually between ten-thirty and eleven o'clock. He'd have chewed his cigar down to the last smidgen, and

I'd be aching tired. Mr. Cramer always paid me the same way, with two one-dollar bills and two fifty-cent pieces, to make it clear to both of us he was giving me fifty cents for Thursday afternoon when I sliced the bacon, fifty cents for Friday afternoon when I dressed the chickens, and two dollars for all day Saturday. He didn't charge me for the milk and sandwiches, and sometimes he'd tell me to wrap up a piece of leftover meat and take it home.

No matter how tired I was or how late it was when I got home, I'd heat water and take a bath. That night Mama was asleep, or making out to be, and Tom hadn't come in. I took a bath and then remembered the box of chocolates. I got it out of my bureau drawer and ate every piece. I can't say I enjoyed it, but I didn't throw up either.

3

It wasn't all trouble and work. I had school and popular songs and a movie once a week. I could go to a second run for twenty cents, and I reckon to have seen at least fifty movies a year; and those were the times we had Jean Harlow and George O'Brien, the Marx Brothers, Boris Karloff, Marie Dressler, and Mae West. There was no one like any of them, and there hasn't been since. People kept their windows open and radios on, and songs were in the air, wonderful songs from Broadway shows and those Hollywood pictures that were coming out with Alice Faye and Ruby Keeler. Everyone knew them. There were sheets that sold for a nickel with words of popular songs, and I used to buy them. Many did, because the words were good and we wanted to know exactly how they went, not just fill in or think the wrong words as a tune went through our heads. I can remember all the words to some of those songs.

Mr. Cramer was a jokey kind of man in a simple way. If he wasn't busy when he saw a woman in the store he thought was sexy, he'd paw the sawdust like a bull and make bull noises so that sometimes the men working over on the grocery side had to laugh. Sometimes he did it when a woman was ugly; that made them laugh more. It didn't hurt the women, because they didn't know what was going on, and sometimes they even thought somebody had said something funny they hadn't caught, and laughed too.

There was one young fellow fresh from the country, couldn't have been more than sixteen, and for a long time they teased him about getting him bred, as they called it. He said he couldn't afford to take out a girl, and anyway, what if she wouldn't? So the older ones, including Mr. Cramer, chipped in and took him to a whore they knew, paying for him and watching him do it (the whore was in on the joke) so they could tease him afterward at the store. He took it well, just going about his work stocking the shelves or trimming vegetables, looking sheepish but proud, while they carried on. Mr. Cramer held a big bologna sausage down in front of his fly and waved it around. I was too backward to take part in their fun, but I enjoyed it. They said I'd be next, just to wait a couple of years and get a little more growth on me.

At school I had friends, boys and girls, but no "friend," unless I count Leroy. Slam books were popular that year. They were ordinary composition books with a name heading each page, and they were passed around for others to write comments, what he thought of the person. Teachers warred against the books, watching for them and confiscating them when they saw them slipped from desk to desk during a class period. There was a lot of repetition, like "stuck-up" and "pimples" and "good pupil" and "cute but knows it." None of the things written under my name seemed to have anything to do with me, showing we never know how we strike people. Once I tore out a page because I was ashamed to have anybody else see what someone had written: "Wears stick-on half soles from the dime store." For a day or two I tried to walk different to hide the bottoms of my shoes, but somebody asked me if I was practicing to be an English soldier like we saw in the movies.

All grades changed classes every hour, going from one room to another to be instructed by different teachers. The halls during the five minutes of changing were bedlam. Teachers stationed themselves at the doors of their classrooms, and their presence was supposed to show authority. Also, there were student monitors with armbands to help keep order. They were to see that no one smoked in the rest rooms, no one ran in the halls, and no one made unnecessary noise. Nevertheless, there was smoking and some gambling in the rest rooms, and dirty jokes and drawings on the rest room walls.

I was a monitor, and it was during these breaks between classes that I became aware of Leroy that last spring in Savannah. After seeing him several times at the same place and same time, I found myself watching for him, without knowing why. He was a tall, clean, good-looking boy, about fifteen, easy and graceful in his movements the way few are at that age. There were only good things under his name in the slam books.

I remember the day he became aware of me. He frowned, not in displeasure, but showing he realized he'd seen me before. He certainly had. I'd learned his name and his class schedule and knew where he'd be all day, and I wasn't shy about following him or hanging around. He was always with a friend or two, laughing and talking or talking and serious. They were boys his age, and they resented me when he began speaking to me.

Leroy was not a leader exactly, but he was good-natured

1 9

and sure of himself and popular. From his first awareness of me, he accepted me, making nothing special of my attention, but nothing strange either. Sometimes he'd ignore the calls of his other friends to join them. How privileged and honored I felt every second he lingered!

I began to give him things—a candy bar, a tie clip bought at Woolworth's, a new blotter with a funny cartoon on one side. He showed pleasure in my gifts, but would either share them with me or return them after a day or two, as if I had only meant to lend them. He might so easily have been bored or embarrassed, but always had a look of sympathy and liking, a smile of welcome when I approached him. It was the most innocent of loves. I wanted only to see him and be near him, and the most daring of my thoughts was to wish he were my brother. I had learned where he lived and what time he left for school in the morning. I happened by with other friends of his, behaving in such a way that one might think another had suggested my doing so. When, after school, he joined in games, if it wasn't a Thursday or Friday, I was there to watch and wait to the end so I could walk him home.

There was a girl he loved. He spoke of her earnestly to his friends, and I remember praying that she would recognize his worth and reward his devotion. Far from being jealous, I revered her because he did. By the end of May the school year was over and done. The last day I didn't see him, because nothing was scheduled. Everybody was busy getting report cards, clearing out lockers, running and screaming and boasting about what they'd be doing that summer. One boy I knew was going to the Chicago World's Fair, and another was going with his family in their car all the way to Canada and back! I couldn't find Leroy.

The next day I walked by his house, but with school out, I was too shy to ring the bell and ask for him; and although I hung around until it started to rain, he never came out. Mama had a weaker spell about then, and with my working more afternoons at Mr. Cramer's, I didn't go by Leroy's house for two weeks. The porch was bare of furniture, the windows had no shades. Clearly, the family had moved.

4

THE WAY we lived, privacy was not possible, and nothing was secret unless it was whispered in bed. There was never a sneaky side to Tom, so when Mrs. Harrison came to Mama and said Beryl was going to have a baby, Tom admitted everything. Mama didn't cry or get mad, but later I acknowledged that as the hour she made up her mind to die. Mrs. Harrison was carrying on about Tom's having to marry Beryl, but Mama appeared not even to hear her. She looked at Tom, and looked at Tom. It was Tom who began to cry, and then Mama asked Mrs. Harrison to leave and told me to go to the kitchen and get supper ready. I went, but I heard what passed between them.

She didn't blame him. "Are you sure, Tom? Although you may have been seeing her, it's possible she's been with others."

Tom said, "I was the first, I know; and I bet I was the only. She thinks she loves me."

"She's such a common girl."

"I'm a common boy," Tom said. "You rate me too high, Mother, but I'm just as common."

"You are not. I was a Stafford, and you're as much Stafford as Bowman. More, because you're like me."

"Well, Mother, with me maybe the Stafford blood has

thinned out. There's nothing to do but marry, like Mrs. Harrison says. They're Catholic."

"You will not marry her. I won't let you throw yourself away on that tacky creature."

"Beryl's all right." He tried to make his voice comical. "Maybe she's what the Stafford blood needs to thicken up again."

"You'd have to take some low job, and soon there'd be a houseful of her children!"

"If they are hers, I promise you they'll be mine too," he bragged.

"Hush and let me think."

It didn't take her long to decide and plan. He was to get a bus that very night out of Savannah; it didn't matter where, just to be gone. Then tomorrow he was to get another bus to Montgomery. She'd write a letter for him to take to Aunt Belle. He was to stay at Aunt Belle's until she closed her savings account at the bank on Bull Street and sent him money. —Yes, she had, she assured him when he interrupted; it wasn't a lot, but it was enough. Then he was to go by train or bus far away, as far as the money would take him with something left over to live on until he found a job or made his way.

"To California?" he suggested, accepting the plan, even beginning to get excited. "Is there enough for that far? I always wanted to see San Francisco. The Golden Gate."

When I had supper ready, I went to the door and said so. Mama told me she wasn't hungry and Tom would come eat when he was done with her. I filled a plate for Tom and put it in the oven. It was only meat loaf and canned peas and store rolls. Then I sat down to eat.

At one point I heard Tom say, as if it'd just hit him, "Angel, I can't leave you!"

"You can and will. If you stay, you'll have to marry her. There's no other way. And you must *stay* gone, you hear? Whatever happens, under no circumstances are you to come back."

"I won't leave you," he declared, both knowing what they were not saying.

"It's what I want, so you'll do it if you love me." Then she said it. "I'll soon be dead, but I'll end my days knowing you are free. You're the only thing I care about."

There was more, but that was it.

And, oh, didn't Mrs. Harrison rant and rave when she found out! After she'd blessed Mama out, she blessed me out too, and then went back to her side of the house and blessed Beryl out. Beryl must have got tired of it, because she stopped Mrs. Harrison finally and told her *she* knew Tom had run away, because she'd heard him after midnight and gone to the window and watched him go with nothing but one suitcase, walking fast. There was the sound of several slaps and Beryl's crying through the wall and begging her mama for them to move; but Mrs. Harrison said it was too late now and they might as well stay and save the expense. She said again they would not leave the house that had brought them shame. Then she raised her voice so she'd be certain we heard and defied *anybody* to try to move her.

Mrs. Harrison never spoke to Mama again, and she wouldn't speak to me for a week. But Beryl never stopped being friendly, although Mama told her never to enter our part of the house. Beryl was surprisingly cheerful after the big fuss. She even laughed when she said to me, "Wasn't it just like Tom to run off and not face things?"

I had to know. "Are you—sorry, Beryl?"

"You mean ashamed of myself?" She saw that was just what I'd meant and slapped my arm. "When I love somebody, I love them. I bet you don't know what I'm talking about."

"In a different way I do. What are your plans?"

"It looks like I'd better plan to have a baby," she said gaily.

"What I mean—can't you see somebody?" She looked at me blankly. "I've heard there are certain doctors—"

"Mark Bowman, I'm surprised at you. You know Mama and I are Catholics. I don't walk past the church without crossing myself. How dare you suggest such a thing!"

"I'm sorry," I said quickly. "I just thought it would be better for you."

"Catholics don't flush their love down the toilet. It was a dumb question, Mark, and you ought to know better. Did you see that new Barbara Stanwyck movie last week? Why, there wouldn't have been a story if she'd done such a thing, and anyway she wouldn't."

"What *are* you going to do?"

"I won't be going back to school, that's sure. They wouldn't let me, and I'm glad anyway because I hate school. I don't see how you can like it."

"It's just a way to get away from Mr. Cramer's," I said.

She giggled. "Well, it's purgatory for girls like me that hate it, I can tell you. I've got a girl friend Sue Ann that works at the dime store, not one of the good ones, but where all the Nigras go to buy, and she thinks she can get me on. I won't tell them and I'll work till it shows, to save money for my baby. Remember the song that goes, 'I found a million-dollar baby in the five and ten cent store'? Well, that'll be me. I'm going to have it and I'm not going to give it away either, though that's what Mama's trying to talk me into. Anyway, the orphans' homes are full, nobody wants them, although Mama said we could tell them it's got *Stafford* blood. My Mama can sound real mean sometimes." She looked thoughtful and took a crumpled pack of cigarettes out of her dress pocket. "There's two. Smoke with me."

"I wouldn't want to take your last." I'd tried smoking; all boys did, and most girls. Tom had been smoking three years, though he'd never done it at home. I didn't like smoking or not, but I knew how to do it.

She insisted that I take one and lit them for us. "That's the last pack I'm going to buy," she said. "They cost fifteen cents now, and I can save that money for my baby. See what a good mother I'm going to be? Goodbye, dear old nicotine!"

"Did you really smoke a lot?" I asked her.

"Yes." She sounded as worldly as Kay Francis. "Five or six a day sometimes."

5

I WISH I could say that after Tom left, the void between us was bridged, that understanding, if not love, eased the summer of waiting. With Tom gone I thought (hoped, prayed) that Mama would turn to me and use me, but she did not except in the ordinary ways she had long done. Her need of me was only common dependence. I was shameless in the ways I courted her. There was no one to tell me that availability is always a little despised, and if there had been, I should not have heeded him. Love never accepts rejection. The heart never believes its cry will get no answer.

"Stop trying to be Tom," she said. "You're not Tom."

"I know I'm not. I was only trying to entertain you."

"You don't have a talent for entertaining."

"We have to live together, Mother."

She ignored my using Tom's word for her. "We don't have to play games. I'm not good at pretending. I've finished with it."

"You haven't finished with me," I said.

"You're bold, now Tom has gone."

I wasn't to be stopped, "Why don't you love me the way you love him?"

"I always treated you the same."

"No, ma'am."

"You're thinking about your poems and candy and trying to punish me. Well, you can't. No one can."

"I wanted you to love me. I love you."

She gripped the wheels of her chair, but there was nowhere for her to go. She couldn't even go to the bathroom without my helping her.

"I'm sorry, Mama."

"I should think so," she said faintly.

"Is Tom still in San Francisco?" He'd been gone a month, and I knew she'd had letters, because I'd handed them to her; but she had never shown them to me.

She hesitated. "I thought it best that you not know where he is. You've remained friendly with that girl, and she'd get you to tell her."

"She knows where he is," I said. "All she had to do was look in our mailbox and see the postmark."

She sighed. "I hadn't thought of her spying, since they have their own mailbox. It takes a vulgar mind to understand vulgar people."

"I don't think you understand me, Mama."

"Children always fancy themselves misunderstood. I'm sorry if I have offended you, Marcus. That was not my intention."

"Offended me?" I said carefully.

She answered sharply. "Now don't go on. I'm tired. I want to go to the bathroom and then to bed. Go into the hall and see if either of them is using it."

"Please talk to me."

She sat still for so long I was afraid to move. Finally she said, "I'll tell you something, Marcus, and that will be the end of it. When you're young, you think everything is possible. You want everything—love and the world. As you live, you begin to subtract, saying: I can live without this and that and so and so and so. The subtractions go on, and when you've endured every humiliation of compromise and denial, you stop feeling, and you are allowed to die. That's where I am, so don't bother me again."

The end of July, she developed pneumonia. There was no money for a nurse and nothing a nurse could have done I couldn't do; so I sat up all night alone with her after I'd sent the telegram to Aunt Belle.

Beryl and Mrs. Harrison didn't come to the funeral, and Beryl told me why. They didn't think Mama would have liked it. Aunt Belle was friendly with Mrs. Harrison, and they settled household matters between them, while Uncle Grady took care of other arrangements. I went to the school board to get a set of my records to carry with me to Montgomery, and then told Mr. Cramer I thanked him for giving me work, and goodbye.

Beryl still had a job at the dime store. "I figure to make it through September, maybe October. You couldn't tell if you didn't know, could you?"

I shook my head.

"I think it's a joke our moving over to your side. But we do need more space with my baby coming, and it saves *really* moving. Mama will have your mama's old room; she doesn't care. And I'll have yours and Tom's, which will make me feel funny at first, won't it? We're going to rent out rooms just like you did to us and charge them eighteen dollars a month. You remember how Mama used to resent that? Now she says: '*We* have the responsibility.'—Oh, Mark!" We laughed together. "You know, I'm going to miss you. I won't ask you to write, because I'm not a very good letter writer, but don't forget me."

I said I wouldn't.

Uncle Grady was in a hurry to leave, and I was glad. I didn't have a suitcase, because I'd never been anywhere and Tom had taken the only one we owned. All my things went into a couple of cardboard boxes I picked up at the store. One had held pork and beans and the other toilet paper, and Mr. Cramer made a joke about that. Following what Mama

2 7

had made me promise when Tom left, I wrote him only after the funeral, taking the address from his last letter. He answered about a month later, a wild and grieving letter sent to Aunt Belle's house in Montgomery, but never wrote again.

Suddenly we were ready. Mama had died on Friday night and been buried Sunday. There was no reason to wait, and Uncle Grady wanted to get back to his business, which was the wholesale food trade. You had to keep your eye on things and move fast, he said, because of spoilage. Everything went easily into the trunk of the car. They hadn't brought much, coming in a hurry, and my boxes weren't crowded. Uncle Grady and Roland were to take turns and drive all night, or until we got there. We started out with Uncle Grady and Aunt Belle in the front seat and Roland, Beatrice, and me in the back.

Beryl waited on the porch to wave when we pulled off. It was just starting to get dark as we rode through the shady, hot streets and around the old squares. I said to myself: Goodbye, Beryl; goodbye, Mr. Cramer; goodbye, Leroy; goodbye, Savannah. I didn't say goodbye to Mama, because even then I knew it would never be over between us. Then I looked at the other four in the car and it came to me that we were strangers.

6

THE TRIP was nothing to remember. Uncle Grady and Roland took turns driving, and no one talked much, even when we paused to verify directions and use the toilet and consume fried egg sandwiches and Coca-Colas and peanuts. I'd go to sleep sitting straight up, and wake slumped onto Roland or Uncle Grady or Beatrice, as they shifted around. Aunt Belle did not shift.

Roland was the first one I got to know a little, after the house.

The house was on Morgan Avenue in the Five Points area of Montgomery. It was a short avenue, as avenues go, built long ago, its houses ranging from modest to once-grand, its inhabitants all the degrees of middle class. Our house, as I thought of it right away, the young being ever eager to own and to belong, was a bungalow with a small yard between its porch and a sidewalk that tilted and cracked to accommodate the roots of an oak tree that had been there considerably longer than the sidewalk. There was a bigger yard in back. On the front porch were flower boxes and pots of fern, assorted chairs, and a swing that was lower at one end than the other. "Roland's going to take a link out of the chain," Aunt Belle said with a wave of a hand, "one day."

The front door opened directly into the living room, which had sliding doors to the dining room, which had a passage to the kitchen with no door. The living room also opened into a narrow hallway running the length of the house with three bedrooms and a bath off it. The hall was too narrow for any furnishings except a few pictures, and too dim to see them. The front bedroom was Beatrice's, the middle and biggest Aunt Belle and Uncle Grady's, the back one Roland's, which I was to share. The one bathroom was at the back of the hall and house. There was a garage in the backyard and three chinaberry trees but no grass or flowers.

Beatrice's room was dainty with bows and ruffles on the skirt of the vanity table and bench, which she herself had sewed, and a fringed counterpane on the bed, neatly shaped over pillows upon which sat two dolls made of cloth scraps and crepe paper, also by Beatrice. Beatrice, Aunt Belle said, had to have everything "just so." She said it uncritically, and it soon became clear that Beatrice, although only sixteen, ran the house.

"She's domestic," Aunt Belle explained, "which I am not. Lord knows what we'll do when she decides to get married."

"Mama!" Beatrice protested. Roland snickered, and Uncle Grady cleared his throat and looked at everyone except Beatrice, as if he might have to protect her.

"Well, what's the cedar chest in your room for, I'd like to know?"

"Every girl has a hope chest," Beatrice said primly. "I've had mine since I was eleven."

"Tell you one thing," Aunt Belle continued, addressing me as the only one not knowing her sentiments, "I'd rather have her for a daughter than a mama or wife. Oh, she's going to make husband and children jump and toe the line one day. You wait."

Beatrice's blush was fading; she looked thoughtful, as if contemplating her soul. She was, I subsequently discovered, industrious, generally accommodating and mild of manner unless something interfered with the way she thought things ought to be. Do things her way, and she was an angel. She could be prissy and precise, but her heart was as open as her mind was closed. If she appeared a little bossy, it was to get things done. Her only touchiness was in correcting anyone who called her Be-*at*-rice; so with the southern pronunciation she usually found herself called *Bee*-trice. She was never called Bea. "It took me a long while to become reconciled to my name," she confided to me later. "Mama meant it as a joke. Beatrice Benedict, you see?"

Aunt Belle wasn't in the least lazy, although she'd given over the housekeeping to her daughter. She was always doing or saying something, usually the latter, and when a coffee cup wasn't in her hand, it was nearby. "It's my weakness," she proclaimed, "and what keeps me going. I'd die without it. Summer, winter, night and day. I don't sleep a lot—I'm the restless kind. If you wake in the middle of the night and smell coffee, it'll be me. And why not?" She looked around challengingly, although no one opposed her. "Some people drink iced tea all day long. I'm not one of those." The neighbors loved her, for she was always ready to take an interest in what they were doing and thinking; she always had time. Nor would she take offense when they got up to go, saying, "Well, I must get up from here and go do my housework. Wish *I* had a daughter smart as Beatrice."

Uncle Grady was a quiet man, his own man. Looking at him, I often thought his mind was far away from us all. Sometimes I'd catch Aunt Belle's eyes on him, helpless and bewildered. I never heard them quarrel, and I never saw them touch each other.

Roland was the only thin one in the family. His mother and father were solidly built without running to fat, and Beatrice for all her energy had plump cheeks and arms. But Roland, although he ate more than anyone else, remained lean, with corded muscles in his hands and feet and jaws. His hair was blond and coarse and would never stay combed no matter what he put on it, and he tried everything he knew. His nose was aggressively arched and quick to redden from cold or heat or emotion. His eyes were small and dark, wide apart, and so deep-set they seemed to burn both in and out. I have never seen a more intense and watchful look than his.

For as long as I could remember, I'd slept with my brother Tom, and so I felt nothing about sharing; but on the first night, Roland made it clear he resented having to.

"You stay on your side, you hear? If you toss and turn, you can just get out and sleep on the floor. I'm nearly eighteen, and I ought not to have to share with a youngun. You don't wet the bed, I hope?"

"Of course not!"

"Some younguns do."

"I'm not a youngun."

"You're thirteen and I'm eighteen, almost. You remember that. You have to stay clean too, like me, a bath every afternoon after work, or at least before you get into my bed at night. I won't have you smelling."

I told him I liked a bath every day.

He was unconvinced. "Little boys always manage to smell like dogs."

"How do dogs smell? Like boys?"

"You trying to be smart?"

"I'll do my best not to smell bad," I promised.

"That also means no pooting in bed. Don't think if I don't hear it I won't know it; I will. If you think you may have to go to the bathroom during the night, go now. I don't want you waking me up an hour after I get to sleep. I need my full sleep. I'm near a grown man, and a lot of things are going on in my body."

I went to the bathroom and when I came back found him undressing. "I'm used to the left side," he said. "You take the right."

I undressed to my B.V.D.'s and got under the sheet.

"I see you don't kneel and pray. Don't you believe in God?"

"I don't know," I said, "but I don't kneel and say prayers."

"I believe in Huey Long," he said. "If there's a revolution, I'm going to join it."

"You are?"

He sat on a straight chair to take off his socks, shaking them out and blowing into them before hanging them on the back of the chair. "I believe in Technocracy too."

"What's that?"

"Too complicated to explain to a child. I'll tell you when you're older maybe."

In his B.V.D.'s he sat on his side of the bed, his skinny back to me, shoulder blades sharp as fins. "Is it the truth your brother was getting it from that girl next door?"

"Yes," I said, surprised.

He struck his left palm with his right fist. "And her a poor girl, too!"

"What's that got to do with it?"

"He'd have respected her too much if she'd been rich—that's what it's got to do with it."

"Maybe," I allowed, "but Beryl's a nice girl."

Roland shook his head. "No one will have her now."

"She'll be all right."

"That's easy for you and your brother to say after she's left to be reviled."

"I don't think anybody's going to revile Beryl," I objected temperately. "I guess they'll talk about her some, but they'll get used to it and go on to something else."

Roland snorted. "Easy conscience."

"Who is Huey Long?" I asked.

"That shows how ignorant you are. I didn't like your brother when he came here to stay with us. You might as well know that now."

"Well, you're about the only one," I said. "Everybody likes Tom."

"I don't. He thinks he's good-looking."

"Well, he is."

"If he'd looked at my sister, I'd have given him a black eye."

"They're cousins!"

"You don't know much. I suppose it's easy for boys like him."

"What is?"

"Girls."

He pulled the chain of the light on the headrail of the bed, and we were in the dark. I turned on my side, but I couldn't go to sleep. It was hot, and I was afraid to move for fear of disturbing Roland. But I was finally beginning to doze when I heard him whisper, "Mark?" I sighed as if asleep. A few minutes later I felt the bed shake as he began to masturbate.

7

UNCLE GRADY's brokerage business was downtown on North Court Street in the warehouse district. Empty, the place was a big echoing shell with one corner cordoned off as office space, containing two desks, telephone, filing cabinets, a typewriter, and two electric fans with gummy-looking blades. There was no toilet, but there was a filling station nearby whose owner didn't mind our using his "rest rooms." Uncle Grady gave him some produce now and then. There were wire baskets in the office for orders and inventories, but they were never used for their purpose. Instead, all papers were stuck on what appeared to be inverted ice picks mounted on wooden blocks, one for in-coming, the other for out-going goods.

Mrs. Bush, a childless widow of thirty-five or so who appeared older, presided over the office and telephone. It took me about a week to understand that she was almost totally incapable, unknowledgeable, and unreliable. Her neatness and sourness of expression inclined one to trust her, and perhaps that sufficed, for it was not an office in which great efficiency was required. Mrs. Bush was not deaf, but the telephone seemed to make her so. She shouted into it and made all callers repeat themselves. She had no gift for transcribing the sounds her ears received into names and numbers on a pad of paper or an order book. Her typing was labored and inaccurate, her handwriting illegible to all who had not learned its eccentricities. The drawers of her desk, which she had a way of inching open as if she expected snakes to strike from their depths, never yielded a stamp that would adhere to an envelope, an envelope the right size, a rubber band that did not snap when stretched, or a paper clip that did not draw blood with its crooked, rusty prongs.

Yet Uncle Grady and Roland too were always patient with her and even deferential; and Aunt Belle, when I asked how Mrs. Bush had come to work there, only answered, "Poor soul. She was the only applicant when your uncle ran his ad in the paper. How lucky he was to get her! You see, not many ladies like working in that part of town."

Used to a job and not wanting to appear slack, I asked if I could work with Roland in the warehouse. He was in charge of it for the summer, Uncle Grady having "lost" the Negro man whose job it had been back in May. Roland would attend to things until he returned to high school for his last year in September, and even then he would continue to work afternoons and Saturdays.

It was a simple business in that there was no system at all. Uncle Grady boasted that he could and would supply anything needed by small, independent grocers all over town, delivering within a couple of hours. The larger chains—A&P, Piggly Wiggly, and Hill's—had their own suppliers. Uncle Grady dealt in quick-turnover goods such as crates of oranges, apples, and cabbages, great sacks of potatoes and small sacks of onions, as well as the less perishable sugar and rice, canned goods, snuff and cigarettes and chewing tobacco, pepper and salt. He even bought coffee from the chain stores in small lots to resell at a penny profit on a pound to independent stores whose customers wanted the familiar brands. The small stores, unlike the chains, dealt largely with credit customers who were used to paying more for the privilege of credit. Most of them never paid a bill entirely but would put something on account each payday.

There were times the warehouse was full to the doors and rafters and we had to hire extra help from the street to help us move goods. Other times it was empty except for floor grime and a floating of onion skins and paper fruit wrappers with their old-fashioned pictures of smiling children. Watermelons were a quick-turnover item in the summer. A farmer might come to town with a truck or wagon load, and Uncle Grady would buy them, having the farmer wait while he sold them by telephone. Roland and I would then take the load directly to the store that had agreed to buy them and unload the truck, the whole transaction having netted no more than a few dollars. But business was business; whatever came to hand was bought and sold, and any profit was a profit, part of the day's work. In those hard times people rarely paused to ponder the smallness of a profit; that there was any at all was enough reason for work to proceed.

Once satisfied that my willingness to work was not mere show-off humility or a way to ingratiate myself with Uncle Grady, Roland treated me well enough, and I did not resent him. He didn't stand and watch me sweat; he sweated too. I was used to shifting and carrying weights from doing the bidding of Mr. Cramer in Savannah, so for me it was only more of the same and even an improvement. I did not have the monotony of slicing and weighing pound after pound of bacon, the steeling of nerve that had always been necessary for me to kill chickens nor the hand-filth of plucking and dressing them. I did not have to smile and parry the jokes of customers about my age and size and ambitions. And I did not have the cleanup of Saturday nights at the butcher shop with the scraping of blocks, raking sawdust of its disgusting debris, and blinding myself with ammonia to clear and shine the glass cases.

By Saturday noon our work was done. We tidied the storage of whatever was left in the warehouse, swept the floors, and closed the great sliding doors to the loading platforms. Mrs. Bush went home, and Uncle Grady counted out Roland's wage of twelve dollars a week and mine of six. The first Saturday I hadn't known what if anything to expect, and I felt rich. "I'd like to pay board," I told Uncle Grady.

"Save your money for school clothes," Uncle Grady said.

"I don't need much," I said.

"Well, speak to your Aunt Belle," he told me.

Aunt Belle said she didn't know and looked helpless until Beatrice came in to find the scissors. "Beatrice can tell you. Talk to Beatrice about it." She held up her empty cup and went off to the kitchen.

Beatrice listened and was quick to understand. "Why, yes, Mark, I think it's all right. I don't work outside at a job, but I like to make a little money too. Roland gives me four dollars a week to take care of his room and clothes, so why don't you give me two and I'll do the same for you?"

It was settled, and still I was left with four dollars a week of my own. After eating midday dinner and taking a bath, I put on clean clothes and walked down the long hill from Five Points past the Jefferson Davis Hotel and the Paramount and Empire theatres into town. For thirty cents I could go to the Paramount and see a brand-new picture. Across the street at the Empire they charged a quarter, also for a first-run movie but usually one considered less desirable than the Paramount booking. Down a couple of blocks past the Whitley Hotel and the Elite Cafe, then around the corner into Court Square was what became my favorite movie house, the Strand, which charged twenty cents for a second-run only a couple of months after the Paramount. The Tivoli on nearby Commerce Street had third-runs and westerns for fifteen cents, but always smelled of rats and popcorn. However, I remember times I'd see a picture first at the Paramount, then at the Strand, and maybe two or three times at the Tivoli, which was good about bringing popular ones back.

Dexter Avenue climbed a hill from Court Square to the state capitol. Dexter Avenue was the main shopping street with the grand and elegant department store called Montgomery Fair, and Kress's and Woolworth's and Silver's where infinite treasures could be found for a nickel or a quarter. Money in my pocket and feeling king of all creation, I walked the aisles of the stores slowly and consideringly. I bought a blue shirt for seventy-five cents, a bag of hard candy for a nickel. And then, because I had seen her using an ordinary cup to measure sugar and rice in the kitchen, I bought a real measuring cup for Beatrice, with clear red markings on its sides. It seemed only right after that to take something to Aunt Belle. The only thing I knew she liked was coffee, but a bunch of cloth violets caught my eyes, and it was mine for a dime. Croesus unleashed, I marched on. For nineteen cents at Woolworth's I found the first book I was to call my own. It was *Ivanhoe,* and what made me choose it I don't know, for I never had a passion for Walter Scott.

Drunk on possessions and with a glowing sense of my own munificence, I went down the steps at Silver's past the counter that sold popular records and goldfish in bowls with fake coral arches, to a counter and booth where I might have my photograph taken and tinted for thirty-five cents. I hesitated but then presented the sum. It was a great day; I would have a reminder of it to keep forever.

Following directions, I went into the booth, sat, posed, smiled. Then there was the wait. I prowled other aisles, examined counters of trifles that now bored me, but I could not make myself go far from the photograph booth. Back I went before time and waited, listening to a song sung by Russ Columbo from the record counter. At last the picture was ready and mine. I took it without looking at it and walked away, having made up my mind not to examine it until I was outside the store on the sidewalk. The strength was not in me to keep such a resolve. At the foot of the steps I opened the envelope, took out the photograph. There it was: my face a sickly pink and yellow against a watery blue background. Could that nobody's face be mine? Where was the specialness of me? And then I heard a laugh, rude and knowing. Looking up, I saw on the stairs the ugliest boy I have ever seen. His hair was sandy red, his nose, cheeks, and chin bulbous and pimply. He was actually pointing at me and laughing. I knew

instantly he had been watching me. He had observed everything I'd done, read the vanity of my hopes, understood and
ridiculed me. On fire with shame, I raced up the stairs and
onto the sidewalk, hot and glaring in the August heat.

When I knew I'd lost him, I slowed to a walk. Back I went
through Court Square, turned and climbed the long hill of
Montgomery Street to Five Points, into Goldthwaite Street
and finally home to Morgan Avenue. Aunt Belle was surprised when I gave her the violets. I went to find Beatrice,
who looked thoughtfully at the measuring cup I presented
and said, "Come and I'll show you."

I followed into her room, where she raised the lid of the
hope chest. The smell of cedar was sharp and cool. She set the
cup down upon a set of carefully folded, embroidered pillow
cases. "These are my things, and now the cup is part of them.
One day I'll use all of them in my own house and you can
come see me."

8

WE ATE breakfast at the kitchen table in relays. Roland and
I had just sat down and Beatrice was serving us when Aunt
Belle came through the door from the hallway and said, "It's
started." I looked at her, learning nothing from her frown,
and then at Roland and Beatrice. Both had paused but as I
looked at them, resumed what they'd been doing when Aunt
Belle entered, Beatrice pouring coffee, Roland buttering the
three biscuits he'd taken on his plate and split.

Aunt Belle usually had breakfast with Beatrice after we
left in the mornings, but today she sat down with us. "Want

me to fix you a plate?" Beatrice asked. Aunt Belle shook her head but moved a cup toward her daughter, who filled it from the pot she still held.

"Maybe it will be a short one," my aunt then said.

"Maybe," Beatrice agreed quietly and returned to the stove.

"I reckon it was due-time," Aunt Belle said as if trying to be sensible about whatever it was. "But I always hope the last one is truly the last."

Roland and I finished our meal in silence, and I followed him without asking anything until we reached the car and he got into the driver's seat. "Aren't we going to wait for Uncle Grady?" He started the car and was rolling it down the driveway by the time I jumped in and slammed the door. I generally rode in back to and from work, he and Uncle Grady in front, but today I sat beside Roland.

He drove a few blocks before he spoke. "I'll have to stay in the office more till he comes back, but I'll come out and help you as necessary."

"Has Uncle Grady gone somewhere?"

Roland looked at me, surprised. "He's home drunk."

I'd never seen anyone drunk unless I counted actors in movies. I'd heard people did get drunk, but because of Prohibition they did it behind closed doors.

"He'll go five or six, even seven months without a drop, and then he'll start. He doesn't do anything, he just stays in bed and wallows. It's hard on Mama, hard on all of us."

I didn't know what to say, so I kept quiet.

Presently Roland slapped the steering wheel with both hands and his voice rose, not angrily but earnestly, as if he were making a speech. "It's the state of the world. Roosevelt or no Roosevelt, things will never be right until we have a revolution. We can't build a new world on a pile of garbage. The past will have to be wiped out. Until there are new generations who remember only the new, know only good, believe only good, live only good. Revolution! You hear me?"

I nodded politely.

"My daddy's not the worst of men; he's a victim like all of us, me and you—and you and you." He stabbed the front glass with his free index finger. "We must take from the rich and give it to the poor—that's what Huey Long preaches and that's what must happen. Look at *you*. What would have happened to you if we hadn't been there to take you in? The *state* should have taken you, not left you to live on charity!"

I resented that too much to remain silent. "My mother and yours were sisters," I said. "That makes me part of your family, whether you like it or not."

He laughed hollowly. "Family! What I think of *families*. There will be no families—they will all be destroyed."

"Well, I'm glad this one wasn't," I said.

"You're too young and ignorant to talk to."

"I'll be fourteen in February."

We had arrived. "Get in that warehouse and air out the night-stink while I go tell Mrs. Bush."

"Does she know about Uncle Grady?"

"How could she help it? What do you think we've told her—that he goes to Hawaii for his health every six months?"

It was a slack day, Tuesday of the last week of August. By the time things got busy on Thursday, Roland and I—even Mrs. Bush rising to the occasion, however ineptly—were able to manage. Business wasn't as good as usual, because Roland had none of Uncle Grady's gift of selling by telephone. On the other hand, he was shrewd about ordering and pricing. (Uncle Grady sometimes ignored small fluctuations in cost and left prices the same, taking a loss.) Roland tried to discourage small deliveries, which Uncle Grady would not have done, but otherwise he made no changes in the day-to-day operation of the business.

I expected things at home to be quieter than usual, but no such thing. Everyone spoke in normal voices, and no one tiptoed on the hall linoleum. Neighbors came and went, standing a minute or sitting an hour. Everyone close by came to see Aunt Belle at least once a day, to leave a recipe, ask a favor, tell a joke or a lie. One change of plan was Aunt Belle's not being able to have her bridge club at the house. It consisted of eight friends who took turns as hostess every Wednesday. Aunt Belle was matter-of-fact in telephoning the club secretary, Mrs. Judy Brockton, announcing they'd have to skip her this time and she'd make it up later. She explained why without embarrassment.

The only real difference at home was that Aunt Belle shared Beatrice's room, and the hall door to her and Uncle Grady's room stayed closed. I didn't see Uncle Grady until the second night, when he surprised us all by sending for me. I went in nervously, alone. Not only did I have no experience of drunkenness; I did not know Uncle Grady very well, and I remembered he hadn't wanted to take me in. What if he'd called for me now to tell me I must leave?

The room was dark except for late daylight that came under the shades that were drawn three-quarters down. The two windows were open, but only an inch, and although a small electric fan on the mantelpiece was working, the air was heavy with body smell and the odor of whiskey.

"Come here, over here," he directed me with curled index finger. I approached the bed where he lay dressed in shirt, cotton pants, and white socks, his head and shoulders raised on pillows. He needed a shave, but his eyes were clear. "I'm drunk," he said, "and I'm going to stay drunk as long as I can." He lifted a hand as if to touch me, but let it fall to the bed when I edged back. Ashamed that I'd done so, I stepped closer than I had been before. "You're Lillian's boy." I nodded. "Dear God. Poor Lillian. Wouldn't have me, then married worse because of his looks! Never go by a man's looks, you hear me?"

"No sir, I won't."

"I'm sorry to tell you, but your daddy wasn't much man—

that's a fact. Only his looks and his talk made your mama think so, and she soon learned better. It's what turned her—mean, having to admit her own bad judgment." He closed his eyes for such a long time I thought I might slip out, but as if he read my mind, he took hold of my hand. "What's your name, boy?"

"Mark, Uncle Grady."

"Think you can be my friend, Mark?" I nodded, and he pulled me closer to whisper. I could smell his sweat and whiskey breath, but I was no longer afraid of him. "They don't care about me, let me die if they could, because I've failed them. Roland wants the business. Beatrice has seen me this way too often. Poor Belle always knew she was second pick but never blamed me." He closed his eyes, and tears slipped between the lids, catching on the stubble of his face. "Nobody gets what he wants."

"Is there anything I can do, Uncle Grady?"

His eyes opened, and when he spoke it was in the business voice I was used to hearing down on North Court Street. "I want you to get me some whiskey. I've run slap out." He rummaged under his pillow, found his wallet, and extracted a ten-dollar bill from what I saw was several.

"Where do I go to get it?" I asked.

"Ask them. They know."

I hesitated.

"Go on."

They did know. Aunt Belle, when she saw the money, sighed, went directly to the telephone, and gave the operator a number. An hour later as she and I waited on the darkened front porch, a car stopped and a man wearing khaki pants and leggings came up the steps and handed her a package. She gave him the ten dollars. When he'd driven away, she handed the package to me. "He'll want you to take it to him. He gets mad if it's me. He hates Roland these times and is ashamed in front of Beatrice."

I took the whiskey. I could feel there were three bottles.

Two Uncle Grady set under the head of the bed, the other he opened. But he did not guzzle; he took a small sip, carefully, so as not to spill it. Since he did not tell me to stay, I left him.

Uncle Grady's "spell" lasted eight days. He ate during that time, Beatrice taking food in to him. He would not eat while she was there, nor would he eat all of it after she left, but he ate enough for Aunt Belle not to worry about his starving. He did not leave the room those eight days. Aunt Belle provided him with a slop jar with a lid, which she insisted on emptying and returning to him, herself.

On the night of the eighth day, we'd had supper and Roland had gone off to see a girl. For all his agitation for revolution, she did not live in the West End, the poorer section of town, but in Cloverdale where the "rich" lived. I stood talking to Aunt Belle and Beatrice as they washed and dried the supper dishes, when we heard Uncle Grady call my name down the hall. Aunt Belle said, "Well, go on! He hasn't had a drink all day, not since seven o'clock this morning when he finished the last drop he had and I told him I wasn't going to send out for any more."

I knocked on the door before entering. He was still in bed but sitting up smoking. The ceiling light was on. His face stubble was almost a beard. "I'm going to work tomorrow," he said sourly. "Tell your aunt."

"Yes sir."

"You—got liquor for me, time or two, didn't you?"

I nodded.

"You all right?—Everything all right, I mean? I didn't cuss you or anything, did I?"

"No sir."

"That's good. I don't always remember. You been working with Roland right along?"

"Yes sir."

He put out his cigarette. "Don't pay attention to all that— talk of Roland's. His nerves are more active than his mind.

44

Tell your Aunt Belle to heat me some water. I want to get up and take a bath and shave, then have a night's sleep and go to work in the morning."

"She'll be glad," I said.

"I expect so." He almost smiled. "Party's over."

I was at the door before he stopped me. "Boy? Come back a minute." I returned to the bedside, but he wouldn't look at me, pulled a foot up into his lap and peeled the sock off it, stretching the toes with his fingers. "If I said anything to you out of line, forget it."

"No sir, you didn't."

He did smile then, with a little nod. "That's good."

9

I TOOK my Savannah report cards to Baldwin Junior High School the day it opened to register new pupils. The building was old, and its wide hallways with their splintery floors were gloomy with summer silence. I was to enter the eighth grade, and it was settled that my homeroom teacher would be Mrs. Noble, her subject English. I wondered what she was like. How soon might I ask her to read my poems? What would she say? Who would sit in front of me and behind me? They would all know each other; I'd be the new boy. I'd know no one at school, because Beatrice and Roland attended the big senior high school named for the poet Sidney Lanier.

I hadn't long to wait to make my discoveries. On the September morning of first classes I arrived wearing black tennis shoes, gray cotton pants, and the new blue shirt, open at the collar because it was a hot day. Beatrice had washed and ironed the shirt for me, knowing I wanted it to be especially nice, instead of giving it to the washerwoman who did the full family washing for a dollar a week, Beatrice providing her with starch, bluing, and two bars of Octagon soap.

Mrs. Noble stood at the door of her classroom as if at attention but angled somewhat peculiarly at the waist—her idea, I was to discover, of the proper posture for males and females alike: chest up and full of air, shoulders back, feet at an angle of forty-five degrees, rump projecting. The boys later described it to each other as "ass poked out." Mrs. Noble was in that amorphous area called middle age, perhaps fifty. Even to my ignorant eye it was clear that she wore a wig, its color a modest but unconvincing brown. I was to know her for many years, and she never managed to set it quite straight. Perhaps she didn't care, although she did take precautions to protect it. For instance, if a piece of chalk slipped from her fingers when she was making a vehement gesture, she did not bend to pick it up but lowered herself in a direct vertical line. And on one occasion when a free soul named Flossie Fogarty actually attacked her in class, she held her head high and out of reach, it plainly being Flossie's ambition to snatch the wig off. Mrs. Noble quelled the daring Miss Fogarty in less than one minute and had her expelled within five.

That first morning Mrs. Noble peered at me through rimless glasses, and when I gave her my name, found it instantly in the roll book she had already made out. "You're new and from Savannah, Georgia, which exports lumber products and cotton," she announced. "I seat alphabetically, although some exceptions may later alter the seating a bit. I may find a pupil at the back who doesn't belong there—hard of hearing or near-sighted or inclined to be—restless. However, I already know the frailties of most of my class. So far I know little about you beyond your grades in a school system unfamiliar to me, and the fact that your mother and father are no longer living. You are to sit in the fifth seat in the first row. There is only one A. I don't know where all the A's got to. But there are several B's, of whom Bowman, Marcus, is the last. Marshall Blake will sit in front of you, and Celia Cantwell will occupy the desk immediately behind. I should tell you that she particularly resents anyone's leaning his or her elbow on her desk and has been known to strike such offending members with a ruler. You may take your seat." All this was said in a brisk manner, neither friendly nor threatening.

There were perhaps a dozen boys and girls already seated, but none yet in the first row. I went to my place, aware of stares and prepared for them. Looking ahead, I saw written large on the blackboard behind the teacher's desk three words: COURTESY, NEATNESS, ATTENTION. Quickly I folded my hands, endeavoring to illustrate those words by my very attitude. It was not fear that inspired me but a craven desire to ingratiate myself. When Mrs. Noble disappeared for a few moments, stepping down the hallway to greet the teacher of the adjacent classroom, there was a surge of whispering, one sentence of which was directed toward me: "She's the hardest teacher in this school!" As soon as Mrs. Noble returned, so did silence.

The rows filled up. The girl behind me, Celia Cantwell, was a big-boned, tallowy-skinned, blond creature with heavy, languid movements. The boy directly across the aisle from me in the second row was short, even sitting down, and had a pink birthmark on his right cheek that spread halfway down his neck. The seat in front of me remained vacant until the last minute. Indeed, when the boy arrived, Mrs. Noble looked severely at her lapel watch and said, "You have thirty seconds to get to your desk, Marshall Blake." She pointed the way. "Quickly." Into the room and toward the one empty seat left came the boy who had laughed at me the day I had my photograph taken at Silver's. He was as surprised as I, but immediately his eyes gleamed with the kind of delight that said, to my mind anyway, "Ah-ha, caught!"

Marshall Blake he was. He was the only pupil to wear a

tie and jacket that first hot day of school. At some point in his life he must have decided to be conspicuous, for no one could have dressed as he was dressed without deliberation. His shirt was dark purple, with stiff white detachable collar and French cuffs. The jacket he wore was green linen. In an effort to present his best face he had evidently squeezed a few of the more fiery pimples that overran it, and this had necessitated the application of some sort of salve that left a residue like white shoe polish. The effect was grotesque and clownlike. Why then was I afraid of him?—Because he had laughed at me and still enjoyed my embarrassment. When he took his seat, I saw that his neck was red from suppressed mirth; his shoulders trembled in quick spasms.

"Marshall Blake," Mrs. Noble addressed him in a tone I hoped she would never have occasion to use with me, "you will compose yourself by leading us in the Lord's Prayer."

"Sung or spoken?" he queried cheerily.

Every breath was held, but Mrs. Noble said simply, "Spoken will do." She then commanded the class as a whole: "Stand!" When we had completed the required religious observance, she said in a milder voice, "Sit." We settled ourselves, and coughed and swallowed, and giggled at the explosion of a single sneeze. "The Lord does not understand mumblers," she informed us. "He wants to hear us speak up clearly. Henceforth you will e-nun-ci-ate clear-ly. And I do not permit scratching in my classroom, Melna Simmons. If you itch you must suffer the affliction stoically in my presence and rectify it at home." She stood aside to offer a clear view of the blackboard behind her. "If there is anyone present who does not know the meaning of those words, the exact meaning, let him go to the library and consult the dictionary. Their definition will be part of your first written test tomorrow morning. Now, let us begin work. I am aware that some teachers consider the first day of school of no consequence. Not so, I. Although the class today will last only fifteen minutes instead of the usual fifty-five, we shall make a start."

Taking a long new piece of chalk, she wrote on the blackboard: *The dog barked*. "That," she said, "is a simple declarative sentence. I shall show you how to diagram it, and that will help you to learn the parts of speech and the composition of sentences." At the end of the fifteen-minutes class period, Mrs. Noble had, by adding a word here, two there, then more words, constructed and diagramed the sentence: *The small dirty dog barked at a tabby cat and ran alongside the automobile that was starting down the driveway at slow speed.*

The bell rang just as she finished; she had timed the lesson exactly. "Go to your next classrooms quietly," she said. "If a pupil in my homeroom receives a reprimand from another teacher for rude behavior, it means a C in Deportment for the month. Be warned." We rose and filed out soberly. But once free of the room, Marshall Blake jumped ahead of me, wheeled about, and jabbing the air with a finger, laughed at me just as he had done that day at Silver's. I sidestepped him and lost myself in the surge of students from other doors.

Beatrice went with me that afternoon to find the store downtown that sold textbooks secondhand, and I got everything on the list I had brought home from school. They came to less than my savings from working in the warehouse; there was enough left for a loose-leaf notebook, two packages of paper, one plain and one lined, and a box of number-two pencils called Ticonderoga. I spent the evening happily going through the books to erase notes and drawings of previous owners—and all had been through more than one pair of hands. The cleanup work done, I signed my name and address in each of them and felt secure and content.

We were all at home that evening, sitting in the living room after supper, each sufficient unto himself. Aunt Belle made the most noise, slapping cards down for her game of solitaire and frequently talking to them. Roland sat frowning, his sharp features alert and suspicious as he delved into the introduction of a textbook on solid geometry. Beatrice was humming an old song called "Tonight You Belong to Me" as she cut and pasted a dustcover for the secondhand copy of *The Merchant of Venice* she'd bought for her tenth-grade English class. The radio was on, but turned low because the program was one nobody cared about, "The Voice of Firestone," with Richard Crooks. Uncle Grady read the Alabama *Journal,* and once in a while would say aloud, "Imagine that," without explaining. I knew and had memorized from Roland's dictionary the definition of "courtesy," "neatness," and "attention."

The following morning when I got to school, I found the short boy with the birthmark already there arranging books in his desk. We greeted each other, friendly, and talked as he tried different arrangements. He laughed a lot, I don't remember at what, merely being friendly. His name, he told me, was Frank Goodson. The room filled, others employing themselves as we were doing, girls talking mainly with girls and boys with boys. I was glad Marshall Blake had not yet come.

Mrs. Noble was there, but occupied. She had a big chart opened on her new desk blotter and now and then would purse her lips and make a quick, precise mark on it. She showed that she was aware of us though when Flossie Fogarty came in. The big girl slid into her seat, stretching her feet ahead under the next desk, looking around bored and popping chewing gum. Mrs. Noble was off the mark like a champion sprinter. "Flossie Fogarty, my girls do not chew gum. Get rid of it in the rest room and don't ever let me see you chewing again." Flossie sighed but got up.

Melna Simmons was going to be in trouble too, I decided. She wasn't exactly scratching, but she was almost. It was more a sort of purposeful writhing to get traction between flesh and cloth, but if she forgot herself for a minute, you knew the fingers would go to work. She was talking to Margaret Ann Smith about Dick Powell and Bing Crosby and Lanny Ross. They settled it that Bing Crosby was the best-looking in the face but too plump and that Lanny Ross acted sissy. Celia Cantwell sidled up to them as though she might offer an opinion if she didn't go to sleep first.

Although a certain part of me was tense waiting for him to arrive, I didn't actually see him when he came in, not, in fact, until Frank interrupted what he was saying to me to say, "Hey, Marshall."

Marshall Blake nodded at him, then turned on me a look of amazing fury. I simply stared at him, and after a moment he seated himself with a dignity so meticulous as to appear ridiculous. Beside his desk I saw with surprise that he had set down a violin case.

The violin was explained midmorning when the entire school was called to the auditorium in assembly to be welcomed and warned by the principal, Mr. Farriss. After he spoke, a woman appeared on stage and sat down at the piano. There was a ripple of recognition, and Frank Goodson in the row behind me leaned forward to whisper, "Marshall's mother teaches music." Beside me Celia Cantwell turned and hissed, "Shh!" loud enough to earn a cold look from Mrs. Noble, seated on the aisle. Presently we were all on our feet singing "The Star-Spangled Banner" followed by "America the Beautiful," followed by the school song, which I recognized as such because it sounded like every school song, although I was later to learn some alternate words that enlivened it considerably. Next Marshall Blake came on stage, violin in hand. He glared down at us, glared up at the ceiling, set the violen under his chin, and held a taut bow ready. Mrs. Blake played an introduction and then became mere accompanist to her son.

Marshall played well, even to my untrained ears, the sound clear, robust, exactly on pitch. To be one of the large audience allowed me to examine my enemy carefully. He was certainly as ugly as I had considered him at our earlier encounters. He was not fat, but his head was too big for his body, which was narrow at the shoulders and wide at the hips. "Perfect," as he was later to say, "for child bearing." Facial features were bloblike and raw-looking from sweat and acne. He not only ignored us; his absorption in what he was doing dismissed us. His coarse face was rapturous with concentration. When the piece was done, there was polite applause. He bowed impatiently to his mother and to the full auditorium. Then again fixing violin, he played "Pop Goes the Weasel," with more contempt than I have ever seen anyone play anything on any instrument. At its conclusion there was hearty applause, and he hurried from the stage without further acknowledgment.

IO

I COULD not imagine Uncle Grady's ever having loved my mother. To a son and nephew there was something absurd and embarrassing in the idea; yet he was not much over forty, and she had been thirty-seven when she died. I had wondered much at Uncle Grady's confidences, and I was certain he remembered making them. An awkward intimacy existed between us in that house where there seemed to be no intimacies, although my thinking so doubtless had to do with the blindness of youth to what does not directly concern it.

"Mama!" (Roland calling; the world might have been in explosion, such was his urgency.) "Where's my new white shirt?"

"I don't know, son." (Aunt Belle, vague, hardly attending.)

"I got a date with Elizabeth Stringfellow tonight. She turned me down three times before she gave me a date, so I *have* to have my new white shirt! Do you know who her daddy is?"

"We must ask Beatrice.—Beatrice! Where are you, honey? Roland can't find a shirt—where could he have put it?"

"Not *a* shirt, my new, *white* shirt!" (Roland, tormented.)

"I'm coming!" (Quiet. All would be resolved by Beatrice.)

Uncle Grady and I were on the front porch, I in the uneven swing with a textbook on ancient history, he in a rocker with his usual shield, the Alabama *Journal.* The exchange indoors prompted us to look at each other.

"How you getting along in school?"

"Fine, Uncle Grady."

"Not too hard? The change, I mean. Things done different or about the same?"

"All different, but the same."

I was, in fact, getting along well in school. With the cunning of the bright, I had bided my time, paying close attention to Mrs. Noble. She began the semester with a month's hard drill in grammar. She had a passion for diagraming sentences, and it would have been impossible not to catch some of her enthusiasm. With a clear mind and a strong voice, she explained exactly what a noun was and why a pronoun was not one, what a verb did and did not do, the difference between adjectives and adverbs. From there she moved on briskly to commas and semicolons and every other mark of punctuation in the English language. They held no mystery and no terror for Mrs. Noble. I had been taught the rules in earlier school years, but after Mrs. Noble I never forgot them.

Finishing the month of grammar drill, we suddenly found ourselves in a new world: American literature. Disposing of Anne Bradstreet with passing kindness, she threw herself headlong and wig askew into the poetry of William Cullen Bryant. *Here* were subjects worth her mettle—nature and death. Talking about his themes she was as authoritative as she had been with punctuation and parts of speech, but when

53

she actually read a poem to us, her voice changed. It did not hesitate or tremble, but it was wary with respect, almost humble. Something in her seemed to be saying: We are beyond the rules; here is something we may never altogether comprehend. Finishing the poem, she closed the book. "He wrote that when he was seventeen years old." She looked about the classroom challengingly.

I knew the time had come. It was a Friday. After school was dismissed, I waited and asked if she would read some verses I had written. She looked startled but said she would. Monday morning I arrived early, knowing she was always early on Mondays and that I should find her alone. She watched me come in but did not speak when I said, "Good morning." After giving me time to put away my books, she beckoned me to her desk with a lift of the head.

"I've never had a child in my class who wrote poetry," she said. "Oh, a girl now and then who thought she did, and sometimes in spring it's like an epidemic of measles." She shrugged and fixed me with troubled eyes. "I don't know what to tell you." She paused, frowning, as if to test the next words in her mind before speaking them. "I believe you may have a gift. Not as secure as Bryant's, but then he was more than three years your senior when he wrote 'Thanatopsis.'" She held up the dozen sheets I had given her. "They're not original, but they are more than copycatting. They have your own images and feeling, not someone else's."

"I can do better ones" came out of me all at once.

"I expect you will." She nodded encouragingly, but her eyes were still troubled. "Do you *want* to be a poet?"

"Yes ma'am. A writer anyway. Not just poems. Everything."

She looked skeptical; I had said too much. "Poems are excellent discipline. They will teach you to put whatever you want to say directly, unless you mean to try the long narrative forms, like Edwin Arlington Robinson and Lord Tennyson, and I don't advise it. I'm glad to see you haven't taken the easy way of *vers libre*. Girls generally do." She pondered. "It's a serious thing, sometimes dangerous, I believe, to be a writer. A real writer, I mean to say, not just a journalist or someone trying to follow the public taste. But I think nothing can be more important."

"Yes ma'am, I know it."

"Do you? Well, we'll see." She tapped my notebook pages into order and handed them back to me. "I'll be glad to read anything you show me. I don't know how I can help, but I'll try. It's something you'll have to do alone. I expect you know that too."

I nodded. "Thank you, ma'am."

Three girls entered the classroom then and stopped talking as they glanced over to see if I was being reprimanded. Mrs. Noble dismissed me by greeting them, and I returned to my desk. My heart pounded, my head roared, my chest was full to bursting, and I was getting an erection. I had been taken seriously! Not for a second had she talked down to me; there had even been in her voice some of the caution I'd noted when she read William Cullen Bryant aloud. I sat quickly, opening a book and pretending to study. But oh, oh, the joy I felt. I had been acknowledged; I was no longer alone—could earth and heaven hold more?

Many years later Mrs. Noble told me with characteristic lack of sentimentality, "Oh yes, that year I lived for you, I taught to you. Everything I said in class I said with you in mind. By Christmas, Mr. Noble forbade me to mention your name at home."

Mrs. Noble is dead now. I shall, of course, always love her. She was a true teacher, the most generous of women. How lucky I was to find her. Yet I don't know that I thought of her as a blessing then. I don't think I felt the slightest gratitude. With the self-centeredness of the artist, I probably felt that it was only right for her to say what she said and behave as she did. I was glad but not surprised. The artist is constantly surprised and never surprised.

I also advanced on other fronts. I was casually friendly with a dozen boys and girls in class without having strong feelings about any of them. Frank Goodson was, it turned out, a delightful gossip, always merry with a new secret he was wanting to tell. If he invented his tales, I never knew; it was enough to laugh at them. (He swore that a hunchedback boy named Daniel Webster had given Flossie Fogarty a bottle of ink to show him her pussy, but Flossie's wanting a bottle of ink weakens the credibility.)

Celia Cantwell, that great bland calf of a girl, had decided to be in love with me, and having so decided, kept the illusion through the five years of our school days together. She was never my sweetheart, and she knew from the beginning she would not be, but we were friends. She was a comfort during the thousand times I doubted myself. If I could not love her for herself, still I loved her for her loyalty even as I despised her for it. Celia always "believed" in me, and that is something none of us may entirely respect. I think it began with nothing more complicated than the fact of my being placed directly in front of her. She did not have to make the slightest effort to look at me. There I was. It helped too that I never, having been forewarned, put my elbow on her desk.

Marshall Blake and I settled upon ignoring each other—he, me, elaborately—I, him, more or less naturally, I think. He appeared years older than the rest of us, although we were all roughly the same age. Partly, it was the careful but flamboyant way he dressed. I never saw his arms bare or his neck without a tie, no matter how hot the summer day. I had discovered quickly that he was intelligent and scornful of those who were not. Defensive about his looks, he affected sophisticated disdain. Although his mother taught music at the junior high school, I got it into my head that he was rich, or rather that his family was, because of the air he gave himself. Everyone thought of money in those days, of rich and poor.

I had never known anyone rich, and I wondered if they ate the same kind of food others did, and what their bathrooms were like. My ideas of style came from the movies I saw, much more than from any books I read.

And then one Saturday—day of days—Marshall Blake and I met outside the Strand Theatre on Court Square. The attraction, as is said, was *Dancing Lady* starring Joan Crawford and Clark Gable, with Franchot Tone as a rich playboy and Fred Astaire and Nelson Eddy in small parts. I never liked Joan Crawford, but I always felt that I should be on her side because she was the underdog with spirit and half-soled shoes, at least in the early scenes of her pictures.

At four-thirty on that Saturday afternoon in early November, having suffered through to final triumph with Miss Crawford, I came out one door to daylight to find Marshall Blake coming out another, but of the same Strand Theatre. We stopped stock-still. Immediately, without greeting, with no more impulse than the discovery of each other, we began to act the movie, each assuming every character, echoing, mocking, glorying in the gorgeous, gaudy claptrap of what we had just seen. It was, after the long, bad beginning, instant friendship. Two hours later, having walked neither of us noticed where, we parted with the knowledge that from then on, he was my closest friend and I was his.

I I

THE EXPLANATION of Marshall's behavior at our first encounter was simple. He read detective novels, favoring those of Edgar Wallace and Conan Doyle; and when he had nothing better to do, he played Sherlock Holmes, picking out someone on the street to follow. On that day in August he had followed me for an hour and a half before confronting me at Silver's. He had been intrigued by my purchase of a measuring cup, a book, and a bunch of violets (the shirt was dismissed as a red herring), and when he surprised me examining the photograph, he expected me to become part of the game and laugh with him. He revealed that he had his picture taken at least once a month in the same booth at Silver's. He did it, he said, hoping that one day he might see a different face.

"Any but the one I know."

Lately he had tried disguises: false mustache, Halloween eye mask, a workman's cap. In one pose he'd held a ukulele borrowed from the music counter where the clerks knew him. The clerks in all the stores knew him. He made regular rounds to discover what was new, and he liked to be out of his mother's house as much as possible, he said, because she gave private lessons on the piano in addition to teaching music at Baldwin Junior High School.

"Show me your picture," he said one day.

"I threw it away."

"No, you didn't."

I hadn't, so the first time he came home from school with me, I showed it to him.

"It looks like Jackie Cooper with mumps. It isn't you; you're good-looking." Hope gleamed briefly in his eyes. "If you look better than this"—he slapped the photograph down on the dresser top—"I should look better than mine!" We were in the room I shared with Roland, and Marshall turned to the dresser mirror. "No." He waved his hands in front of the glass. "The pimple capital of the world." He took handfuls of both his cheeks. "Also, my head comes to a point."

"It doesn't."

"You'll see when I get bald," he said. "Feel here. No, don't, you'd be sick. I'll go bald before I lose my pimples, because I've got dandruff like leprosy. The more I wash, the more it flakes.—God, why did you make me look like Charles Laughton when I want to be Robert Montgomery? It's not right. The soul of Beethoven, the heart of Strauss, and a face like Porky the Pig. I don't even look *young* ugly. The first picture ever made of me, I looked forty. I started to dress this way to make people look at my clothes instead of me; then I got interested in clothes." He began talking to himself, something he often did, interspersing soliloquy with an occasional remark to me. "I'll order that tabless-tab I saw in *Apparel Arts* and wear my ruby cuff links with it." To me: "You don't know what I'm talking about." I shook my head. "Smooth yellow gloves with pearl buttons. Will that make my hands look bigger or only like Eddie Cantor? My hands are too small. That's why I play the violin. They're not big enough for piano, real piano."

"They'll grow."

"No, they won't. I'll always have little, pale, pansy hands. I hate my hands. Look at yours." He held a hand against one of mine and laughed, vindicated.

"They're bigger because of work."

"Poor boy," he sneered, becoming Basil Rathbone. He was still in front of the mirror. "Maybe I'll be an actor. Lon Chaney's dead.—Marshall Blake, the man with *two* thousand faces, all of them like a baboon's behind."

His voice and gestures changed constantly as he mimicked different people. He was a living catalogue of movie actors and actresses. We rarely saw famous stage actors; perhaps once a year a play would come to Montgomery for a single performance with Katharine Cornell or Tallulah Bankhead or Ethel Barrymore. His mimickry wasn't really accurate, but I always knew whom he meant.

I was Marshall's audience, but it was not a lopsided friendship. In addition to liking me because he thought I was good-looking (and that was a new experience for me), he laughed at things I said, making me feel witty if I was not. Within a week he'd read every line of verse I'd written—he was not one to sample, he must consume all—and pronounced me a genius. If I knew better, it was still a powerful incentive to hear it said. He had chosen me to be his friend; I must be a genius to be worthy. He had genius, he said, although he hadn't yet chosen a channel for it. However low his opinion of his looks, he considered his mind peerless.

The Benedict family disliked Marshall, thinking him ridiculous and wondering why I bothered with him. Roland said he was obviously a sissy and a bad influence for me. The truth was simply that sympathy and understanding existed between us from the beginning, which was often an irritant to friendship as well as a bond.

Another day, Marshall, despondent: "Girls will never take me seriously. I'll die a virgin, except by my own hand. Do you masturbate a lot? You don't have to tell me. I try to keep it down to once a day, but there was a time I found myself doing it three or four times a day until I couldn't. It was like a nasty dead worm. I thought it would never look up again with its Cyclops wink, and after a couple of weeks when it finally gave a wiggle of its own, I had a private service of Thanksgiving at St. John's. Laugh, for God's sake." It was always easy to laugh with Marshall. "Girls our age are just beginning to get titties. I don't count Flossie; she was probably born with them. But the other girls have nothing but nubs. I've got pimples bigger. Who wants to look at pimple-titties? I want to see great, huge titties—fat titties that shake and bounce and gurgle like the volcano in *Bird of Paradise*. Have you read *Gulliver's Travels*? The only thing I liked was the part about the big titties. Imagine—*giant* titties shaking and bouncing—God! I may have to go to the bathroom for a couple of minutes. Will you excuse me?"

"Shut up." I was giggling. "Aunt Belle or Beatrice will hear—"

He was instantly contrite. "Was I loud? Of course! I'm always loud and I forget. They won't let you bring me here again. Should I go out and apologize?"

"No, for God's sake!"

60

"You're sure?" He was whispering.

"I'm *sure*."

His whisper became even softer. "Still, think of it—all those—great—enormous—titties—on all those giantesses! I'd like to be smothered with giantess titties—"

I couldn't control it. My giggles became helpless laughter. He looked at me sadly. "No soul. Great—big—floppy—"

"Stop!—Stop!" I staggered around the room, choking.

If Marshall was extreme in his dejections, he was as extreme in his celebrations. When he read or heard or saw something he liked, he was ecstatic. He swore that he got goose bumps on the soles of his feet. Every superlative had to be repeated and exclaimed. His face went red with admiration. His enthusiasms were as many and as varied as his hates. They included, in addition to music of many kinds, certain detective stories, anything painted or drawn by Daumier or Rembrandt, all comedy from the Our Gang two-reelers to Noel Coward, whose plays he introduced me to. One of his hates was poetry, aside from Kipling's, Poe's, and mine. He also had the capacity to love and ridicule at the same time. One of his favorite targets was Janet Gaynor, whom he also, at moments, adored. He took special delight in Jimmy Durante and Marion Davies, and when they appeared in *Blondie of the Follies* with two other favorites, Robert Montgomery and Billie Dove, he was in paradise. He claimed to have lost count after seeing it a dozen times. He could never have enough of whatever he loved.

Even I, with my hunger for friendship, sometimes grew tired of Marshall, sated with his enthusiasms and hard judgments. Then we would quarrel, parting in dignified rage. We never yelled at each other or abused each other, although Marshall could not help occasionally turning his ridicule upon me, usually for my timidity or uncertainty. He was afraid of no one.

"I used to be scared of the bullies, but that was in grammar school. After dodging them and arranging all my comings and goings not to meet them, one day I forgot and they caught me. I stood there and let them beat me up. I hated it and I hated them, but I never ran again, and they never bothered me again." He became Lionel Barrymore's Rasputin. "One day they will all die, the streets will flow with their blood!"

Marshall had one reticence. He would not take me to his house, although I asked him to, and then teased him to. Nor would he say where he lived. He referred to his mother when it was natural to do so, but he did not talk about her. He mentioned his father once to say that he was dead. He said nothing of brothers or sisters. Finally my curiosity overcame my own reserve and my respect for his. I found out where he lived by the simple procedure of looking for his mother's name in the telephone book. The address was one of the blocks off upper Dexter Avenue near the state capitol building. It was a section of private and rooming houses, with a few small businesses (an electrician, a shoe repair shop) and the old Grand Theatre, not used for movies, going derelict but still rented now and then by a stock company for a few months.

Marshall's address was a store, which puzzled me until I saw a side entrance that led to the second floor, which, I could tell from window shades and curtains, was occupied. Could this be where Marshall lived? I'd made a mistake, found the wrong name in the telephone book. I had always assumed that he lived in Cloverdale and that his family, if not rich, was well off, not from anything he said but from the way he accumulated clothes and anything else he had a notion to buy. They were not days of generous allowances, but Marshall always had money, and he didn't work after school as I did. As I stood wondering, I realized that Marshall had told me nothing. He hadn't misled me; I had made wrong assumptions.

I left quickly that first day, not wanting to be seen and suspected of spying. But as our friendship grew, so did my impatience with his secret. Christmas drew nearer, Marshall and I agreeing (it was his idea) that we not exchange presents; but on the last day of school before the holidays, he handed me a package wrapped in Christmas paper. At home I opened it. It was a fancy, expensive-looking shirt with detachable collar and cuffs, and I needed it as much as I needed a riding crop or a platinum cigarette lighter. "Very elegant, very beautiful," was the way Marshall described such shirts when he wore them, no matter that I thought they looked out of place.

Without pausing to consider further, I went down to The Booklover's Shop on South Perry Street, which I had recently discovered, and bought a copy of stories by Edgar Allan Poe. It was printed in England. Woolworth's would not be good enough for Marshall; he must have something "elegant and beautiful." The woman at the shop wrapped the book nicely when I said it was to be a present, and I walked directly to the address I had scouted off Dexter Avenue.

When I rang the bell, Marshall opened the door. First, astonishment showed on his face, then confusion. "You can't come in." He pushed the door, but I had already taken a step inside.

I said, "It's a beautiful, elegant shirt. I opened it. Holding things for Christmas morning is for children. I brought you this." I made him take the package.

"I don't want you to spend money on me!"

"Well, I did," I said, trying to sound cheerful and natural. A voice called down. "Marshall, who is it?"

"No one, Mother; he's going."

"Hello, Mrs. Blake," I called up to her. Though I had never had reason to make myself known to her at school, I had seen her often at assemblies. "It's Mark Bowman."

"Bring him up, Marshall," she called back.

"He can't stay!"

"I'd like to come in for a minute, Mrs. Blake."

There was nothing he could do but lead the way upstairs. From the landing we went directly into the living room, nicely but ordinarily furnished, an upright piano prominent, beside it a large oblong table covered with stacks of music. The room had a piano smell.

Mrs. Blake shook hands. "I'm glad to meet you, Mark. Marshall talks about you all the time, and I've told him he must bring you here. Can't you stay a little? We cut our fruitcake last night. Marshall likes tea with it because he thinks it's more English." She smiled at her son. "Is that all right with you?"

She left us. Marshall frowned but would not look at me. "How did you find out where we live?"

"Phone book."

"I don't want you here."

"I'd better go then."

"Mother would be upset."

We sat without talking until Mrs. Blake brought in a tray and served cake and tea. "Enjoy yourselves. And do come back, Mark, if I don't see you when you leave."

I thanked her.

Marshall said, "Eat fast," and began to gobble his cake and slurp his tea, which was hot and burned him so that he spilled it into the saucer. He finished before I did and opened the present I'd brought. The binding was dark blue leather with a silk ribbon-marker attached. I watched him run his fingers over it after he looked at the title.

He said, "He was the first—he invented detective stories."

"Yes, I know."

From another room I heard voices, Mrs. Blake's and what I took to be a young child's. When I looked at him, Marshall got up hastily and left me. Returning as I finished my cake, he said, "Let's go walking." He wore an overcoat, and I put on mine, which I'd folded over the back of a chair.

We walked for a long time without speaking to each other. "Why didn't you want me to come to your house?" I finally asked.

"It isn't much to see, is it?"

6 4

"Nothing wrong with it."

"It's not a house, we live over a *store*."

"What difference does it make?"

"You live in a house."

"Orphan of the storm."

"Poor boy," sneered Basil Rathbone.

I bumped into him to make him see I was smiling.

"Why couldn't you let things stay separate?" he said scoldingly.

"You've been to my house," I reminded him.

"So you have to come to mine—like little girls having tea parties for their dollies, first your house, then mine."

"Well?"

He shook his head.

"What's the matter?" I pressed.

"Nothing."

"Was your mother giving someone a lesson today?"

"You saw the piano in the living room. That's where she gives lessons."

"I thought I heard someone else."

"You won't let it alone.—All right, it was my sister you heard."

"You never mentioned having one. How old is she?"

He took time to answer. "Eleven and three."

"Why can't you just say fourteen? She can't be fourteen unless you're twins."

He stopped on the sidewalk, fixing me with his eyes, waiting for me to understand.

"She's eleven years old," I said carefully.

"Her mind hasn't changed since she was three."

"I'm—sorry."

"What do you think *I* feel?" he said furiously. "I hate it! I hate *her* for being like that. She's ugly. She still has to be fed. When she has a cold, her nose just runs, unless somebody's there to wipe it. She doesn't go to the toilet by herself. She can't read and won't even look at picture books. The

6 5

most she'll do is play with a rubber ball like a puppy until it rolls away, and then she doesn't understand what happened to it. That thing is my sister. And look at me. Maybe I'm another kind of freak; maybe that's why I look funny! Don't you want to go home now?" He laughed bitterly and theatrically, but it was Marshall, not some actor. He walked on; I walked beside him.

Presently I said, "How can your mother leave the house to do her teaching at school?"

"We have Ada. An old colored woman who comes every day and stays with Geraldine. She doesn't do anything but take care of her. All day, every day. We get her cheap because she's too old to work in other people's houses." His voice was sullen and reluctant. "I don't hate her. It kills me, but I care about her."

"Will you let me meet her?"

"No!" He stopped again. "Go home, Mark, and leave me alone! You hear?"

He turned and ran, and I didn't follow him.

12

ROLAND CONSIDERED making good grades in school part of the class struggle: "me against them." He worked hard for A's and got them most of the time, but I don't think he much enjoyed the process of learning. I made A's in English and history, which I liked, B's in science, Latin, and mathematics, and a steady C in physical training, a lofty name for the instructor's giving a ball and net to a group of boys at the beginning of a class period. The game was always volley ball, and I was last to be chosen for a side. Although adequately developed, I possessed no muscular coordination and no competitive spirit when it came to games.

Beatrice was, as Aunt Belle put it, "smart at everything except school." To see Beatrice with a book open before her was to witness a study in misery. The sighs she sighed, and not romantic ones either, over *The Merchant of Venice!* A book report brought her to tears. Sometimes she asked me for help, after being turned down by Roland. "Do it yourself the way I did. If you don't, you won't be ready when the time comes to throw off the shackles that have enslaved women down the ages."

Such an argument cut no ice with Beatrice, who replied that she only wanted to learn enough to pass a test tomorrow. If I was able to help her, she'd often say, "I understand when you explain it, but not when they do. Are you sure that's *all?*" And if the help I gave got her a passing grade, she made a batch of candy for me. I had never tasted such fudge before, chocolatey and smooth but with enough grain to please the tongue and set the teeth on edge.

It was Beatrice, of course, who made Christmas at the Benedict house on Morgan Avenue. Aunt Belle was ever ready to admire, to compare, and to judge the preparations of friends and neighbors, but it was Beatrice who resurrected from the upper shelves of closets the folded paper bells, red and green streamers, and boxes of ornaments for the big tree Roland brought home from the warehouse one evening. By then I understood something of Roland's reliance on convention, although he put it down to pleasing his mother and Beatrice. Beatrice hung the bells and strung the streamers, coaxed the tree into steadiness and decorated it so that no bare patches showed. It was she who nailed the wreath to the door and tucked twigs of holly into likely and unlikely places. She baked the cakes, even a special one of fresh coconut for Aunt Belle's last bridge party of the year; she planned and prepared all the more substantial Christmas dishes. Aunt

Belle, coffee cup in hand, praised her to the skies, asking the air if there had ever been such a daughter.

Mother and daughter spent many hours downtown in the stores, although they hadn't much money. Still, everyone must have a gift for and from everyone else, and Uncle Grady and Roland commissioned wife-mother and daughter-sister to decide and buy for them. I did my own shopping, but with a hint or two from Beatrice: size nine-long gun-metal stockings for Aunt Belle, tie clip for Roland, a box of handkerchiefs for Uncle Grady. We tried to choose useful things as gifts. However, when Beatrice suggested that nothing could make her happier than a nested pair of mixing bowls for her cedar chest, I rebelled and bought her a bottle of perfume, something to use too, but not five years from now when, Roland warned us, we might all be dead from bearing the yoke of Capitalism.

In spite of Beatrice's work and planning, the exchange of presents was hasty and awkward, and the enjoyment of her special cooking went routinely unacknowledged, except by Aunt Belle. I guess that was the way it always was, for everyone seemed content. We had observed Christmas and were free to go about our separate affairs. Uncle Grady said he'd better go down to the office and check on things. Roland had been invited (one of seventeen, he told me later) to an afternoon party (fruitcake and punch) on Magnolia Curve in Cloverdale. Aunt Belle insisted that she was going to help Beatrice clear and wash up, then wandered away with her cup of coffee and turned on the radio. I dried the dishes as Beatrice washed them, although she tried to shoo me away when I started. My presents were a tie from Beatrice, two pairs of socks from Roland, a pair of shoes from Uncle Grady, two sets of underwear from Aunt Belle—all doubtless inspired by Beatrice, who still oversaw the state of my clothes, although I paid her proportionately less for doing so, based on my smaller wage earned from working a couple of afternoons, which varied depending on warehouse need, and Saturday morning.

I wondered what Marshall was doing. I couldn't go to his house, though I considered it. I could not even walk by in the hope of meeting him on the street. In those days we did not use the telephone much for conversation, and had I called him, I'd have been at a loss for something to say after the way we'd parted. So on Christmas afternoon I found myself in the Paramount Theatre. I don't remember the movie, but I do recall a lot of seasonal trappings in the local ads flashed onto the screen between feature and newsreel, and that the newsreel tried to be funny with a scene of Santa Claus and half a dozen girls parading around in bathing suits, with their hands on their hips. Everything on the screen told me I was busy and joyous, and I was neither; I was killing time. I didn't consider that I had the right to be sad. My new family was taking care of me. Free of the old cares, I was able to assert myself at school as I'd never been able to do in Savannah, to make friends too. But where was poor Tom—shivering at an outdoor fire in some hobo jungle (like the one also shown in the newsreel) —or had he, being Tom, perhaps eloped with an heiress? Heiresses were part of our common lore during the Depression, and I think Roland thought of them more than he thought of Huey Long. How was Beryl, I wondered. What were Mrs. Noble and Frank Goodson and all the others doing?

The day passed, the holidays ended. We told each other it was 1934, and so it was. School started again. I listened fidgeting as my classmates exchanged experiences. They had done wonderful things and hated returning to school; or so they said, even Marshall, who greeted me buoyantly and told me he'd read all the Poe stories, some of them twice. Had I read "The Gold Bug"? It was a marvel.

Only Celia admitted to having had a bad Christmas. She'd been in bed with flu for eight days and still looked tired. She said, without specifying, that she hadn't liked anything she'd been given. My heart warmed to her, and I might have begun to fall in love with her, except that when Mrs. Noble brought us down to earth with a grammar review, Celia answered that prepositions modified nouns. Even Flossie Fogarty laughed.

13

IF MARSHALL had little patience with his audience at school assemblies, his good humor with his sister, Geraldine, was limitless. He'd fiddle for as long as she would attend him, and that is the way I most liked to hear him play. When we met again after the holidays, I insisted that he allow me to meet his sister, putting our friendship as the stake.

"If you don't let me meet her, it means you don't trust me and we're not friends. After all, *you* know all about *me*."

He could not deny it; no detail was too ordinary to interest him. "Even how your brother Tom used to trim his fingernails before a date. And you never guessed why."

"I don't have your dirty mind."

"Nobody has. If I did all the things I think, I wouldn't last out the day."

Although he allowed my visits, he was never comfortable seeing me in his mother's house, and I went seldom. The first time was after school, a Monday in January. It was only a short walk from Baldwin; we found Geraldine and Ada alone. He told them who I was. Old Ada nodded politely but observed me with a beadiness that made me remember I was the first friend Marshall had brought home. When Geraldine looked anxious, he smiled to reassure her, and she ran to him and hugged him around the neck. She was a plain girl with a sleepy-looking face except when she turned it to Marshall. His behavior was natural, although he treated her like a three-year-old. They apparently forgot me as he talked to her admiring her dress, including Ada in their chat in an unforced manner. Ada seemed to me as childlike as her charge, the way people who deal mainly with the very young may become. When he took his violin out of its case, both Geraldine and Ada jounced with anticipation. Marshall laughed and after checking the tuning of the strings, began to play simple melodies. He continued for three-quarters of an hour, stopping only when Geraldine's head began to droop and Ada put a crooked finger before her lips and whispered, "Nap."

We didn't talk about Geraldine then or later, but she was included in our being friends. Once in a while when Ada was at home sick and Mrs. Blake busy with lessons, Marshall and I stayed with Geraldine, inventing and acting scenes to amuse her.

Spring comes early in the deep South, and the second school semester was little more than begun when we found ourselves looking upon milder weather with complaisance and accepting the greening of trees without remark.

With spring, love came to Marshall Blake.

When I pointed out that his response was as common an illustration of conditioning as the salivating of Pavlov's dog, he groaned acknowledgment. But in love he was, and for the first time, he said. "I never thought it would happen until I met Dorothy Mackaill." He was as surprised and pleased with himself as every lover.

The girl was Sylvia Patterson, and she entered Baldwin Junior High School when the new semester was a month old, her father, who was highly placed with a chain of stores selling women's apparel, having been transferred to Montgomery to open shops there and in other towns nearby. Her mother was dead; she and her father lived in (this caused a buzz) an apartment. A new apartment building, one of the first in Montgomery planned as such, had recently been completed, and the Patterson father and daughter occupied a set of its rooms. A white housekeeper (another sensation in a society where household servants were usually Negro) took care of them but did not live with them. They had come from Atlanta and were therefore more cosmopolitan than we. All these details were known the first day Sylvia appeared, and if they were not enough, the girl herself looked *foreign*, with a faint oriental cast to her eyes. Because of the Army Air Force base at Maxwell Field on the western edge of town, we were not unaccustomed to classmates with exotic features, officers having sometimes married when stationed abroad, or their American wives having been unfaithful; but Sylvia Patterson was nothing to do with the Air Force.

The first thing about her to catch Marshall's attention was her clothes. They were simple but rich and more adult than those of her classmates. When on the third day she wore dark green velvet, Marshall was lost. There was no more talk of smothering in titties. A lily would have appeared profane held to the holy light of Marshall's eyes when he looked upon his love.

And she, what of the damsel? Discreet in manner, she sat at her desk with eyes lowered. When asked a question, she knew the answer, giving it modestly but with assurance. She was at ease with the other girls, all of whom tried to rush into acquaintance with her; but they were soon disappointed because: "She's got nothing to say for herself, or about living in Atlanta, or how she dresses, and isn't a bit interested in boys."

As for the boys, only a few were yet interested in girls, and these evidently found Sylvia Patterson daunting. Not, however, Marshall. He studied her for several days, uncharacteristically prudent, except with me. "Quasimodo's in love," he confided. "Ring out, wild bells!" It was not in him to keep his love hidden, and somewhere in the second week he began to follow her in the hallways when we changed classes. One day she dropped a book. He almost trampled her getting to it first, returning it with a courtly bow and a smile that would have stopped hens laying, I told him. I cautioned him to go slower. "Faint heart," he scoffed. Other evidences of his partiality followed, and soon his passion became a joke with his fellows. Honestly believing that his behavior had been circumspect, he was again surprised. How did they know? He accepted their banter without resentment; it even gave him confidence. But one day when he dared ask her if he might walk her home from school, Sylvia showed distress. "Please," she begged, "you must not embarrass me further!"

"That's the very last thing—"

She didn't wait, but joined another girl and hurried away. Stung, ardor damped but still alight, he appealed to me.

"Leave her alone," advised the lover's worldly friend. "Be nice to her, but let it happen; don't make it happen. Don't set her on fire just so you can turn a hose on her."

"How will she know I worship her?"

"They always know. Look at Madge Evans in the picture at the Empire last week. What happened in the end?"

"That old ice wagon horse!"

"I've heard you praise her ten minutes running."

"Only because she looks normal. Who wants a normal girl when an Arabian princess rides her ebony steed into the desert of my heart?"

"Poor Madge."

" 'Who is Sylvia?' " he sang, improvising a tune. " 'Let me count the ways—' "

"You use a lot of quotations for someone who doesn't like poetry."

"I never knew before what it was for. Maybe if I got sick, she'd nurse me like Helen Hayes. No, she'd let me die.—Maybe if I died, she'd love me then? Lot of good that'd do me. She thinks I'm ugly. No wonder she's embarrassed."

"Let her find out your good qualities gradually."

"What are they?"

"You can play the violin like nobody else. She hasn't heard you—there hasn't been an assembly since she came."

"Probably hates music," he despaired.

"She'll discover you're a genius. Women always love geniuses."

"They don't. Geniuses love women. Besides, I haven't decided which way I'm going to be a genius. It's no use. I could never marry her even if she'd have me. My blood is tainted."

"You can't get married at your age anyway. Why talk about it?"

"Poe's cousin wasn't much older than us when he married her."

"Look what happened."

"I bet everyone that knew him hated old Poe and when they saw him coming, nudged each other: 'Here comes eerie Edgar. Run before he shoves a poem in your pocket.' I think I'll kill myself. What time is it?"

We had walked ourselves, as so often, down Dexter Avenue into Court Square, and I pointed to the clock. After school, unless I was going to work at the warehouse, I'd walk Marshall to his house without going in, and he'd leave his books and walk me through town as far as the movie houses, and sometimes all the way home. We walked thousands of miles together. Outside the Strand Theatre we studied the photographs. The current feature was *Dinner at Eight*.

"Like to see it again?" I trailed the cape.

"Not when my heart is breaking."

"Madge Evans is in it."

"Who is Madge?"

"And Jean Harlow. Remember those tits and feathers? That'll cheer you up. You said the tits were for you and I could have the chicken feathers."

"What a coarse fellow you are. Why haven't you fallen in love?"

"Who with, Celia?"

"You could fall in love with Sylvia and we could fight a

74

duel." He looked at me suspiciously. "You *are* in love with her. Admit it. You're waiting for me to make a fool of myself, and then old Masterful Marcus steps in and waltzes off with the princess."

"While you waltz off with her horse."

We laughed, foolishly and long.

"I'll not forgive you," he said, wiping his eyes and blowing his nose, and starting again. "Her horse!"

"If I ever do fall in love with anybody," I said, "I'm not going to tell you. You might try to help me."

He drew himself up in serious outrage. "You mean that. I'm not your best friend, not someone you trust, just someone to laugh at. That's so, isn't it? You can't deny it! Goodnight, *Damon!*" He laughed cynically and without another word crossed Court Square and began to walk briskly up the long hill of Dexter Avenue. I again inspected the photographs of the actors in front of the Strand, and then I went home too.

Marshall in love. If requited love is better, unrequited love is not so bad either, at fourteen anyway.

14

"I HAVE to lower my standards and expectations."

Sometimes Roland talked of personal matters to me, because he had no friends. The most likely time was when we were preparing to go to bed, the routine of adjusting windows and shades, winding the clock, arranging bedclothes making it easier for him.

"Why *don't* you go to college? You know you want to. You've got the grades, and I've seen you looking at the uni-

versity catalogue for hours at a time. I bet you know it by
heart."

"How could I do it?"

I knew he wasn't asking me, but I answered as if he were.
"Just go, get there, sign up for what you want—then find a
way to stay. Uncle Grady might change his mind and send
you some money." (Uncle Grady had flatly refused to help
him.) "Mow grass and wait on tables."

"I went up to look around during A.E.A. holidays. Mow-
ing grass doesn't pay enough to keep a cat alive, and there
are a hundred boys to wait on tables for every one they need.
All you get is meals, and I'd have to pay for dormitory and
fees and tuition and books. College books are expensive."

I pretended exasperation as a spur. "All I know is if you
start, you'll stay!" I added flattery. "You don't give up."

"Says you."

"Says me."

He opened the fresh shirt he would wear to school tomorrow and fitted it over the back of a straight chair to let it lose
its creases. I'd have thought he was calm if I hadn't got to
know him. "First place: where's my daddy this minute?"

"In his and Aunt Belle's room."

"Drunk.—Isn't he? You ought to know; you're the one
fetches his liquor."

"He'll be up in three or four days."

"Who takes care of the business until he is?—Go down
there at six o'clock in the morning and do all I can and then
get to school late, and soon's it's over, *run* back to North
Court Street."

"Mrs. Bush and I would hold things together for a week or
so a year. That's all it happens, twice a year. His sprees
could be diagramed like one of Mrs. Noble's sentences."

"The business would go down, be lost; and I've worked
for it as hard as he has. Mama and Beatrice would have to
take in washing and ironing from the neighbors, or go onto
the street as common whores!"

76

"I don't think either one would do that," I protested.

"*You'd* take charge of things? You'd be writing a poem. You're fourteen years old, so who's going to take you seriously to do business with? You've only just learned to hang up a stalk of bananas the right way. As for Mrs. Bush, poor exploited soul, we can't ask her to shoulder all the burden."

"I don't think you really want to go."

"You said I did."

"What about Huey Long? Why doesn't he help?"

"You making fun of me? Because if you are, I might slap the shit out of you."

I shrugged, giving it up. "Marry one of your rich girls."

"You think they'd marry a man that didn't go to college?" His small, deep-set eyes burned into me, but I wasn't their real target, and I knew it.

Roland didn't talk about it any more to Uncle Grady and Aunt Belle. He did, a little, to Beatrice, and she'd listen and look sympathetic, but she didn't understand how much he wanted to go. No one admitted wanting anything for himself, but gave a reason, as if practical considerations were all that mattered and anything else was a sign of weakness. So Roland claimed to want to go to college because it was the way to get ahead. College graduates would run everything in business and government, and those without a diploma would be left out of the good jobs and turned down by the best girls. I think he believed all that, but he wanted to go to college with a hunger that had nothing to do with getting ahead.

The first of June, we went together to the graduation exercises in the Sidney Lanier High School auditorium, Aunt Belle, Uncle Grady, Beatrice and I. There was Roland in his cap and gown on stage with the senior class. It was hard to find him because they all looked alike at a distance. When I discovered him, I told Beatrice, and she counted off the row and seat he occupied for his mother, who then told his father, who said shortly, "I know." It was hot, and everybody sweated in the close auditorium, even though the doors and windows were open. The flowers were wilted, and people pleated their flimsy programs to use as fans. When it was over, we drove home and nobody had much to say. It was a relief when Aunt Belle, after telling Roland she surely was proud of him, complained she'd been dying for a cup of coffee all evening long. Beatrice tried indirect comfort. "I wish it was *me* who'd graduated and was through with school."

Roland went to the class dance that night, but he hadn't been able to get a date with one of what he considered the important girls. The best he could do was a doctor's daughter named Helen something who was vice president of the Latin Club. Roland had done all the proper things: paid for his class ring, cap and gown rental, picture in the yearbook, the yearbook itself, and announcements that elicited the usual gifts from neighbors and business acquaintances of the family. The space under the picture in the yearbok where they list characteristics and predictions and extracurricular activities was blank under Roland's, as if he'd had no life and was to have none.

The next morning we got up and went to work as usual. School was over for the year for me too. Tying a shoelace, Roland said, "From now on I'm a man." There was no joking in his voice, and I was careful what I said to him that day.

15

THAT SUMMER was a time of growing. My shirt sleeves and pants legs were too short a week after Beatrice let them down. Collars didn't fit but didn't matter; I wore them open except for an hour each Sunday when the Benedict family, although not religious, went to eleven o'clock service at the nearby

Methodist church to be sociable. Even Roland went, and Uncle Grady said he looked forward to it, for it was the only time of the week he saw Aunt Belle without a coffee cup in hand.

Beatrice teased me for eating so much (one of her rare jokes), but praised me in the next breath, allowing that she never had the concern of leftovers. Roland, leaner than ever, watched me at the table as he loaded his own fork with rice and field peas or squash and snap beans, occasionally saying I ate enough to keep a sharecropper's litter, but more often just jamming fork into mouth and shrugging grandly as he released the empty tines against his teeth.

Marshall was judicious. "You have a sensitive face," he would observe. "I used to believe when you looked faraway you were making up a poem. Now I know it's only your gut on your mind, and the more soulful you look, the hungrier you are. How can you eat food in this heat? Do you realize it's ninety-eight degrees as you stand there eating a greasy barbecue sandwich? You don't eat, you fuck food. I bet when you jerk off you're thinking about peach pie."

"Blackberry."

Although I laughed with him, I was uncomfortable when Marshall talked about masturbation. I didn't want to joke about it, because I was trying to stop it. I didn't think of girls the way he said he did, nor pretend that I was sharing the experience with anyone. As to the eating, I paid no attention to any of them. I was hungry, and I needed every scrap and scrape I put into myself.

I didn't feel clumsy and awkward with the added inches and pounds. When Roland wasn't around, I studied my image in the mirror, the way adolescents do, examining body and face with wonder and suspicion and trying some of the poses I'd seen in copies of *Strength and Health*. Vanity had little to do with it; it was self-discovery, as if before then I had existed only in relation to Tom and Mama. I was finding out who I was, and I felt suddenly, uniquely valuable.

79

The only time I minded working at the warehouse was when it was empty and we had nothing to do, because then Roland made me fight him. His punching and squeezing and tripping were always more than was required to best me, and when in fear and anger I accused him of taking out his disappointments on me, he was unrepentant. "Somebody's going to make it up to me." Most of the marks he left on me were hidden by clothes, only a few showing on my arms with rolled-up sleeves. Face scratches healed quickly. But at night in my bath when I noted the uglier bruises, I hated Roland. My hate, though violent, was not lasting. I don't mean that I forgave him because I understood him, for I understood him only later and then only to a degree; but for whatever reason, and I cannot offer a simple one, my anger was inconstant. I despised and pitied him, but I found something funny in him too. I can't live closely with others without attaching myself to them. I've often wished I could.

I didn't complain to Uncle Grady, and Roland picked at me only when his father was away in the car taking orders from the stores we serviced. It was Beatrice who revealed what was going on by stating one night at supper that she had her hands full sewing for my growing without having constantly to mend tears in Roland's and my clothes from our "wrestling on that dirty warehouse floor." Uncle Grady didn't say anything, but next day I heard him questioning Roland outside the office. Roland declared that he was only teaching me to fight to make a man of me and keep me from growing into a sissy like my friend Marshall. "Just leave him alone—hear?" After that, Roland only tested me when we were loading or unloading heavy goods like watermelons or sacks of flour, throwing them at me hard enough to make me stagger. I told him it made me strong and one day I'd be stronger than he.

Marshall came to see me at the warehouse only once, Roland making it clear it was a place for working, not talking. Talk we did other places and times aplenty, except that plenty never seemed enough for me, and I'd often wake at night with voices in my dreams sounding out new arguments and judging new discoveries, more than once in words of a language I did not know waking. I might never have talked before knowing Marshall, and he said it was the same for him. There were danger areas on both sides, which we understood and did not always honor. We were like young cats learning life-lessons in their play, although we did not look upon our exchange as play. No one might have thought before we did; we reinvented or redefined everything in the world that touched us. We read competitively without niceness of discrimination; and if the book belonged to one of us, we marked passages to reread and to read aloud, thrilling to any felicity of phrasing as much as to the meaning of the words.

Sometimes when I insisted on my right to visit him, Marshall played phonograph records belonging to his mother. We wept over Wagner and averred that no one ever again could be as great as Beethoven. Art we did without, for there was no supply of it beyond a few books at the Carnegie Library behind glass doors and a few reproductions on the walls, the most prominent of which was Michelangelo's *Creation of Adam*. The museum, although it designated itself to be "of fine arts," relied heavily upon Indian artifacts that had been unearthed in the state of Alabama and discards of an older generation's European travels. But the main meal we sat to was reading: Victor Hugo and Gene Stratton Porter, Walt Whitman and Eugene Field and, without self-consciousness, Shakespeare. Marshall claimed that he was weak from masturbating after his first reading of "Venus and Adonis." We might make fun of Scott's verses, but we loved quoting them in imitation of Mrs. Noble. " 'Some sat, some stood, some slowly strayed.'—*That*, children, is alliteration."

Nor did we neglect movies; we went two or three times a week, Marshall more often than I because he went some afternoons when I was working and he was tired of practicing the violin or imitating Sherlock Holmes. There was time for everything, even for being bored as we wandered the streets at night cursing the heat and yearning for the day (would it ever come?) when we were men. But if life for me was ever expanding, it was not for the Benedicts. One weekday afternoon Uncle Grady sent me home because there was nothing to do at the warehouse, and I arrived as Aunt Belle was receiving one of her frequent callers.

"See how Roland has shortened the chain?" she said in greeting, nodding toward the porch swing. "I ought to give him a prize, although I'm not certain he hasn't shortened it too much, so now the other end's low. What do you think? I'm dying to sit in it and see, but he painted it when he did the chain and it's taking forever to dry. I asked him what in the world they put in the paint or left out to make it that way, but he didn't deign to answer. Partly the humidity, I suppose. The Sahara desert would mildew in weather like this." She sat down in a rocker, and Mrs. Quentin sat down beside her.

Gazing at the still-tacky swing, Mrs. Quentin frowned. "Reminds me of the time Elton painted our toilet seat. You know how they flake. I sat down not knowing until I tried to get up. He had to send for the doctor, and they had to unscrew the seat before they could work me loose. Later in private Dr. Benn said to Elton it was the first time he'd ever seen a fanny framed. I'll never forgive either of them."

Laughing, Aunt Belle called through the open door into the house. "Beatrice, honey! If you're not too busy, will you bring out a Coca-Cola for Mrs. Quentin? I've still got my coffee."

When Mrs. Quentin had her Coca-Cola, Aunt Belle said, "I wish I could drink them, but they give me gas."

"They give everybody gas," said Mrs. Quentin. "That's what I like about them. A swallow or two and up comes a bubble that lets me breathe again instead of this terrible tightness I get sometimes."

Aunt Belle nodded. "Lordy, Lord, do you reckon things are going on the same old way forever and this is *life?*"

The Lord does not, evidently, care for such speculation, because the next day Uncle Grady went to bed and got drunk, and Beatrice found the courage to announce that she wanted to look for a job instead of returning to school in September.

It was the middle of August, when unlikely things are likely to occur.

16

DURING THE summer, Beatrice had picked up acquaintance with a girl her own age who was visiting the Griffins across the street. She was an unlikely intimate for Beatrice, who'd never had girl friends, or boyfriends for that matter. The Griffin niece was Helene Kirby (her mother and Mrs. Griffin were sisters), and she might have posed for a picture of Silly Seventeen. She had blond hair in a frizzy permanent wave. She fussed with her clothes constantly and wanted to try on everything of Beatrice's, which Beatrice surprisingly allowed her to do. She changed her makeup every hour, adding—never that I saw subtracting—powder, rouge, and lipstick, as if hoarding them for a siege. Her eyelashes looked sticky because she wetted them with finger-spit so often the gesture had become unconscious. (Girls considered mascara "cheap" and "older.")

Besides clothes and cosmetics, she talked of nothing but boys, although she didn't know any in Montgomery. One might have thought that Wetumpka, Alabama, her home, was the paramount preserve of male excellence. She followed Beatrice about as Beatrice did the housework, but without offering to help. Helene indeed knew nothing of such work and boasted that she had never washed a dish. Everyone called her Helen except Beatrice, who was sensitive about names.

Helene was at our house most of every day of her three-weeks visit, because there were no other girls exactly her age in the neighborhood and she had been snubbed by the eighteen-year-old Grizzle twins, Jessie and Jackie, who were so content with each other's company they were referred to as the Siamese Twins. At first Beatrice tolerated her for manners' sake, but when she became used to her, she found her sympathetic. Their strong bond was a shared loathing of school. Helene had been initially interested in Roland, the fact of him rather than Roland himself, although it never occurred to anyone else that he would look at her twice. Nor did he except to disapprove. Having seen so many movies, I thought this might lead to something, but I was to learn that friction does not always end in fatal passion.

When her interest in her own face was temporarily assuaged, Helene experimented with Beatrice's, and Beatrice, who had never paid more than modest attention to her looks, consented to the role of guinea pig. We had Beatrice with plucked and penciled eyebrows, Beatrice with different shades of face powder and lipstick, Beatrice with wet lashes. Although her naturally wavy brown hair had been considered satisfactory in a simple style, Helene urged her to "get a permanent," or to cut some of it off, or to grow it longer. Such extreme improvements Beatrice vetoed, but she succumbed to Helene's urges that she part it differently, try it in braids, and fasten it back starkly, pinning it behind her ears. Roland, of course, told her she looked like a skinned rabbit, and Beatrice scorched the cuff of a new shirt she was ironing for him.

Helene was an amiable girl and no one could dislike her

(Roland perhaps excepted), any more than one could like her very much. Roland's disinterest, which had become disapproval only when she'd forced him at the beginning of her visit to pay attention to her, had other causes. He still wanted a rich girl who lived in Cloverdale. Any would do, evidently, because he fancied himself in love for a few days with one after another, phoning persistently until even his determinaation gave way to continued excuses. They were going away to visit, had just come home from visiting, were suffering from sunburn and peeling—finally, and always the real stopper, they were getting their things ready to go off to college and wasn't he going too?

Aunt Belle, of course, enjoyed Helene vastly and encouraged her visits until they became routine. Uncle Grady was polite, only lifting his own eyebrows at some of the more bizarre experiments with Helene's. I liked her because she was easy and relaxed and funny. It never occurred to her that there was anything of interest beyond girls' looks and boys' weaknesses. Boys were said by her to "have a weakness" for long hair, or blond hair, or curly hair, or hair behind the ears, or hair lifted from the neck, etc., etc. Helene seemed pleased, if a little puzzled, when I laughed at things she said, and once she slapped me playfully on the arm and said, "You're going to be cute one day!"

I would never have thought of Helene as a catalyst for one of Beatrice's character, but so it happened on the evening of the day Helene returned to the impatient swains of Wetumpka. It was the day Uncle Grady stayed in bed with the first bottle of his late-summer spree. As we finished supper, Beatrice said quietly that she couldn't face the idea of another year at Sidney Lanier and that, in fact, she wanted to quit school and get a job.

Aunt Belle looked at her with interest.

Roland exclaimed, "No! Impossible!"

Even I paused over my last corn stick to consider what she was suggesting.

Better prepared than we, Beatrice set forth her argument. "I'm not learning anything that'll ever be one bit of use to me, and I certainly have no idea of going to college, which is what all these courses are for. I'm dumb in those ways."

"You're not," Roland assured her unflatteringly. "You don't work hard enough and you don't concentrate."

"I try," Beatrice insisted, "but if you threatened to push me off a cliff, I couldn't give you three examples of metaphors in *The Merchant of Venice*. I hate *The Merchant of Venice!*"

"You won't have it again. This year you'll have *Macbeth*."

"I'll hate *Macbeth* too, don't you see?"

"She will," I said.

Beatrice said, "I'm glad somebody at this table understands what I mean."

Roland turned on me. " 'Somebody' can shut up. His opinions are not wanted."

"They are by me," Beatrice said.

"He's just trying to get you to give him the biggest piece of pie."

"I am not!" I half rose in my chair in protest.

Aunt Belle, who had bided her time, said, "You can all just stop hollering at each other, for the one to say yes or no is your father. Now, Beatrice honey, you wait patiently. We'll think it over and talk it over, and when your father decides to get up, we'll ask him what you are to do."

"I'm not going to have *my* sister not finish high school!" Roland declared.

"Pretend you don't know me and we're not kin," Beatrice said.

"I may do that and you'll be sorry when I'm an important man."

"What! Has Mr. Roosevelt asked you to join his cabinet?"

"What kind of pie is it, Beatrice?" I said.

"It's not pie," she said, "it's banana pudding, and I made enough so you can have all you want."

"You must have made it in the washtub," Roland said.

"Mama, are you going to let your son insult Mark?" Beatrice said.

"I'm going to leave home if you don't give me some more coffee."

Beatrice rose hastily, her eyes having gone to Aunt Belle's cup, which was not only empty but dry as well. "I'm sorry, Mama—I'm just as selfish as Roland."

As Beatrice stepped into the kitchen for the coffeepot, Aunt Belle looked at Roland and raised her voice. "You're nothing of the kind; you're my good, sweet girl, and we are *all* lucky to have you!"

"Amen," I said.

Frustrated, Roland sneered at me. "Turning religious?"

A week later Uncle Grady was himself again. An aspect of his sprees that struck me only in later years as odd but characteristic was that after a week of drinking, when he sobered up and returned to life, Uncle Grady did not shake or tremble, did not have bloodshot eyes, and did not appear to feel any remorse. Instead he looked calm and rested, a little sad perhaps, but then he always looked that way; it seemed a part of his preoccupation.

Aunt Belle made Beatrice wait until Sunday after church to talk to her father, and she forbade Roland and me to speak until Beatrice had her full say.

Uncle Grady did not seem surprised or sorry. He listened with an openness that was almost eager, and when she completed her presentation, said, "I see how strongly you feel, and I won't stand in your way. What you say is so; no one can deny it. You're not suited for any more school than you've already had. Now you must think of what you *are* suited for."

"I think it's a mistake." Roland spat out the words, unable longer to contain himself.

Uncle Grady ignored him. "What about taking a course downtown in shorthand and typing? They're always a good place to start, and when people ask you what you can do, you can tell them. I'd even say you could come be office secretary for us, but poor Mrs. Bush has been so faithful."

"Shorthand and typing would mean *more* school," Beatrice almost wailed.

"Nobody listens to me," Roland said.

"Well, you tell me then," Uncle Grady said gently to his daughter. "What do you want to do?"

Beatrice appeared to ponder. "I've asked myself what I can do that I already know. The only answer is"—she took a breath— "work in a restaurant."

"My sister, a Benedict, *waiting* on people? Never!"

"What do you think I do here?"

We all looked at her.

She blushed but went on. "I don't mean I don't like it—I do. That's why I think I'd be good in a restaurant. I like to feed people."

I voiced what was in all our hearts. "What will *we* do?"

Only Beatrice laughed.

17

WITH UNCLE GRADY's business contacts it was not long before Beatrice had a job. The restaurant was on Commerce Street, and it was named Beau Monde although it was not French, not beautiful, and not worldly. It was owned and run by a man named Herbert Vail, and his wife, Gertrude, did the plain southern cooking that made it favored as a luncheon place for businessmen. Mrs. Vail had two Negro girls helping her in the kitchen, and her unmarried sister Ethel, who served the meals, had long complained that the work was too much for one person. The Beau Monde was not open for breakfast and attracted little business for dinner—or supper, as it was called. Beatrice was wanted mainly for the midday trade, which meant her working from eleven until two, and two evenings a week to give poor Ethel's feet a rest. Her reward was to be seven dollars a week and tips.

Because her father was known to them and because she was young and obviously innocent, Beatrice was spared the jokes and jibes of the regulars, although she reported with admiration Ethel's larky exchanges with her customers. Ethel was always ready with a funny word; the only time she was serious was when she talked about her feet. Once Beatrice slipped on splashed ice tea, dropping a tray. Nothing broke, for the glasses and dishes were thick almost to indestructibility, but they made a great clatter, and Ethel was ready with, "Drop the stone out of your ring, dearie?" to the huge enjoyment of the lunchers present. Ethel was a dyed blonde of forty-some-odd-years, which in those days looked older than it does now; and she indulged her talent for innocent vulgarity with all the men who pretended to flirt with her. Most of them did; it was a game they shared. She was forever threatening to tell their wives if they went "one step further," and anyone who actually put a hand on her, however casual or comical the intention, was warned shrilly that it would cost him a quarter tip.

The standard tip was a dime a customer; percentages of the bill were not customary, and indeed no meal cost more than seventy-five cents for, in Ethel's words, "the six-bits deluxe," which was fried steak. Favorites were the meat loaf and fried pork chop plates with three vegetables and dessert, tea, coffee, or milk: fifty-five cents, all included, with bread plate, butter dish, and water pitcher on every table.

Roland fussed and Roland fumed. "We're disgraced. No family stands still generation to generation, and it's plain to see this one's headed down, down, down."

When I pointed out that in the classless society he intended to build that wouldn't matter, he kicked me. But no one minded Roland, and he subsided when just before Christmas Uncle Grady grudgingly consented to his adding in new paint *& Son* to the old, faded sign on the side of the warehouse that proclaimed: *Grady S. Benedict, Food Broker.*

Beatrice's leaving school and going to work as a waitress did actually cause a brief flurry in a neighborhood where most of the young women had jobs as shop clerks or secretaries, but the Benedicts had never given themselves airs, and everyone liked Aunt Belle because she was so agreeably good at nothing. Wasn't there a Depression? A job was a job, and the great Recovery which President Roosevelt promised if only we stopped fearing fear was a long time coming. So no one thought worse of Beatrice; she was never popular, but she was praised.

And how did the family fare without Beatrice as cook and housekeeper? We fared well, for Beatrice continued to be cook and housekeeper. She rose early to clean the house, shop for food, and start the noon dinner before leaving the house at ten-thirty to take the bus to Commerce Street and the Beau Monde. Aunt Belle, with reminder notes from her daughter which she sometimes forgot to consult, managed somehow to put a meal on the table for Uncle Grady and Roland when they came home at twelve. She even occasionally cleared away and washed the dishes, and when she did not, Beatrice did it when she returned at two-thirty. Beatrice also then cooked whatever was needed to round out the leftovers for our supper. Yet we missed her and complained to each other that things were not the same.

On the nights she returned to the restaurant to serve the never more than half a dozen evening patrons (usually one at a table), I often went down to wait until she was done and to escort her home. We walked unless she was too tired, otherwise took the bus for a nickel. Beatrice usually preferred walking to spending a nickel. She was miserly with her dime tips, keeping them in a painted china cup on top of her dresser. When there were fifty, she made a roll of them and exchanged them at the bank for a five-dollar bill, and once a week she deposited whatever she'd saved in a post office savings account. She distrusted banks because they had failed within recent memory, whereas the United States Federal Government was thought by her to be more reliable. Now and then she'd spend a few dollars on a new item for her hope chest.

How many times we climbed the hill up Montgomery Street to Five Points, complaining of the heat in summer, the cold in winter! It made getting home at last a victory. Beatrice was never one to run on with words, but she talked to me those nights, as I talked to her, of what we wanted of life. Sometimes it was as specific a thing as a new shirt or a new skirt. Sometimes it was as nebulous as, "Happy," she'd say a little sulkily. "I just want to be happy, that's all I ask," as if happiness were the least and easiest of God's gifts.

In the dark and walking it was easy to talk. I didn't understand Beatrice, and she didn't understand me, but we listened to each other and thought about what was said. We even spoke carefully about the family and were astonished to find that we saw its members entirely differently. She felt close to her mother and distant from her father. She thought her brother brilliant and thwarted and was afraid that he might one day kill himself in a rage against the world. Sometimes, if it was a clear night and we were not hurrying to get out of the cold, we'd stop, look up, find a star, and make a silent wish, then smile and walk on as if the wish had already come true.

18

As SENIORS, Marshall and I behaved like lords at Baldwin that year. Everything was easy for us. We had mastered its rules and understood exactly how far we could bend them to our own ways and means. It was easier for two of us to assert ourselves as superior beings than it might have been for one. We had given each other confidence that was in some danger of becoming arrogance. We were even forgiven flippancies and irregularities, including a scorn for sports and those who indulged in them, because we had contrived to get ourselves acknowledged as superior. We who had been afraid to walk past a playing field lest a ball go astray and we be asked to throw it back, now safely ignored the athletes. Here, Marshall relied on my presence—I was as hefty as the bully boys.

When we condescended to pass the time of day with our old teacher Mrs. Noble, she who had routed the ignoble Flossie Fogarty and continued to deserve her reputation as the hardest teacher at Baldwin Junior High School, she made much of us, for she looked upon us as her successes. We paid her with trust and affection. She might praise us for being artistic, but she was not foolish, and she brought much shrewdness to the judgments she made. Advice did not then have a bad name, and contrary to the general belief, young people like being advised. Mrs. Noble was so free with directions, we were bound to follow some of them. Indeed, so urgently did she speak when we visited her, she might have been offering last words as we set forth on a long journey, although we would know her for many years.

She told me to continue writing poems because they were good discipline, but to start thinking about stories and plays, and she managed to say this without suggesting that her belief in my verses was less than it had been. But she saw in new work, which I always showed her, a talent for narration and a disposition to dramatize. "Put them to use," she ordered earnestly.

Outside Marshall himself, she was the first to wonder if his future lay with music. Certainly his mother assumed that he would one day earn his way by performing or, failing that, teaching as she did. Mrs. Noble saw Marshall's gift for another kind of performing. He liked debating, to which she had introduced him and at which no one at school now bested him. He might, she said, become anything—a courtroom lawyer, governor of the state, even a senator—if he ever got over being silly. She did not smile as she said it. If she permitted us to take liberties in friendship, she did not forget that as our former teacher she was still our mentor.

It was observed by many that Marshall and I talked alike, and I suppose we did. Talking together so much of the time, it would have been surprising if we did not copy each other's choice of words and tone. In this I think I followed Marshall's lead. He was more daring than I, less afraid of being laughed at; and he had taken to heart Mrs. Noble's early advice to e-nun-ci-ate. Aunt Belle said that when she heard our voices in another room, it was like one voice. Although the accent remained southern, it had been overlaid by the conscious-becoming-unconscious imitation of certain Hollywood actors. Marshall particularly admired Charles Laughton, whom he rather resembled, and Basil Rathbone, whom he would have liked to resemble. Rathbone specialized in chill, articulate villains, but had not yet become his own caricature, and had fairly recently played Romeo on Broadway to Katharine Cornell's Juliet.

And what, what of love?

Marshall persevered in his passion for Sylvia Patterson,

and the lady, flattered by his constancy and noting his increasing worth in the eyes of others, was no longer as unwilling as she had been. They had become better acquainted, although Sylvia still would not allow Marshall to walk her home after school. Her father was very strict, perhaps because he was her only parent. She was not known to have dates. Few our age did, although the proportions would reverse themselves the following year when we began senior high school.

There was no pattern in pairing. Some couples were couples for no more than a single occasion. But one boy and one girl I knew, country dwellers who went back and forth in the same bus, became a couple then, remained so during all of high school, married the day after graduation, and are still a couple, their children middle-aged and grandchildren grown, confounding the disparagers of the constancy of young love. When I discovered the poem of Robert Burns that begins: "John Anderson, my jo, John—" I thought he must have had a pair very like them in his mind.

I longed to be in love but could find no suitable object. Wanting the unusual, I fixed upon one and another of the more exotic daughters of the Air Force officers at Maxwell Field, but nothing came of it. Either they were not interested in me because, having lived all over the world (or so I thought), they considered me a hick, or they were too cordial and frightened me by suggesting that I come to their parents' cocktail parties, as many Air Force children apparently did. Much as I wanted to be worldly, I knew I shouldn't be able to pass myself off as one of them. I went to one party at Maxwell Field, and although the younger guests kept to themselves for the most part, the punch we were given was spiked with rum and had the effect of making me both agitated and sleepy. Worse, I asked if a young Air Force acquaintance would be coming and was told coldly that he would not; he was a sergeant's son—my first encounter with military rank and its extensions into family.

Of course, there was Celia, who persisted in a devotion that was hopeless, perhaps because she knew it was. If she could not have me, she seemed to feel that to be in my group would suffice. Mothers of girls my age were beginning to prod them into a more active social role, and Celia was the first to invite half a dozen of her classmates to a spaghetti supper, a form of entertaining that rapidly became popular. I was always to be one of those invited to Celia's, and so was Marshall, because he was my best friend. Celia, a romantic girl, would often include Sylvia Patterson, aware that Marshall favored her and that I did not. Her doing so, in fact, set Marshall firmly on her side for a while, and he urged me to fall in love with Celia because she deserved it, perhaps the most impotent argument of all. I had considered Celia too phlegmatic to be social, but on the first evening we arrived at her house in Cloverdale the force behind her was revealed. Her mother was a large, fair woman with an implacable smile. She wanted her child to be popular and was ready to exert herself to that end.

There was a new phonograph, there were records. We were invited to dance on the side porch, although none of us did so on that first occasion. The dining room and table were splendid. There was a huge center bowl of spaghetti, enough to gratify even my gluttony, a platter of veal cutlets, a genuine salad instead of one of the sweet dishes most southerners served as salads, French bread, lighted candles, and grape juice in wine glasses, which brought out the antic in Marshall's exhibitionism. (Suave William Powell with a Groucho crouch and a Harpo honk or two.) If I could have been won by worldly considerations, I should then and there have thrown myself at Celia's feet, for my dreams of sophisticated foreign food were realized. But it all came back to Celia, and there she sat smiling uncertainly, hair sweating at the roots, complexion mottled by nervousness. I liked Celia but could not, alas, love her.

Another frequent guest of Celia's was a girl absurdly

named Posy Valentine, the only child of grandparent-aged mother and father, the father being a judge. Posy was plain, which recommended her to her sex; she was bright, which did not; she was funny, which disarmed all. Her humor did not sting, it bubbled; and without making fun of herself any more than she did others, she clearly considered herself part of the fun. She and I became friends quickly, our thoughts sparking each other's. She and Marshall were not so easy together, the timing of their thinking and speaking being just that beat different which makes awkwardness between people who would seem to be compatible.

They were noisy parties with much laughter, some of it nervous, most of it happy. All of us showed off a little or a lot except Celia, whose presence seemed incidental. Mrs. Cantwell would often gaze at her daughter with encouragement that finally blurred to disappointment, although she was wise enough to leave us to ourselves most of the evening. When it was time to go, we were surprised to remember whom we had to thank, and our goodbyes were too effusive, embarrassing Celia. We might have arrived separately, but we left in a body to find our various buses, the exception being Sylvia, who was under instructions to telephone her father to come for her when she was ready to go home. I wondered what Mrs. Cantwell said to Celia when we had gone, and what Celia answered. Were there tears and resolutions, or did they enjoy the comfort of silence? When I came to know Mrs. Cantwell, I decided that Celia had a hard time of it.

I continued to work at the warehouse on North Court Street, while Roland spent more of his time in the office, thereby freeing his father to make calls on the stores in his car. The mainstay of the stockkeeping now was a forty-year-old Negro man named Clive Johnson, who kept a pint milk bottle with gin in it on a high shelf. I never saw him drink or drunk, but the level of his bottle rose and fell regularly. Most often when I was at the warehouse I worked with Clive, grunting and heaving, catching and stacking, loading goods, storing goods, with a smell in the air of sweat and onions and oranges, of coffee and tobacco. But sometimes when work was slow, Uncle Grady would invite me to accompany him on his rounds.

Then I saw a Grady Benedict unknown to his family. Nervous and edgy in the office with Roland, withdrawn at home, he relaxed into affability when paying calls on customers. Not much concerned with his own wife and children, he had a good knowledge of the lives and quirks of those of the storekeepers, making frequent reference to them. He was willing to match anyone for a Coca-Cola, the usual opening gambit on entering a store, but just as willing to buy a round without the gamble—a good sport who would tell a joke not too well nor too badly, a man who was liked and had the air of a man who expected to be liked. Nor was it put on. When we returned to the car, he continued to talk of those we had left or of those we were to meet at the next store.

I remember the pleased shock of realizing that he included me in his thinking about them, instead of his family. Only once in a while would I recall the first overheard exchange between him and Aunt Belle, in which he'd complained that if they took me in, they'd have to keep me until I was grown. One afternoon we were going home directly after stopping at two stores on Day Street, a predominantly Negro area of the city. With no lead-in he said, "Don't you marry, Mark— or if you do, think about it a long time before. It's not every man's nature." Then after a long thought he added, "Not my nature."

"Yes sir," I acknowledged, feeling as safe from middle-aged despair as I did from childhood uncertainty. Savannah was long ago and far away. Grady Benedict had loved my mother, but she would not have him; so I would love him.

19

ON THE evening of September 8, 1935, when he heard on the radio the first report that Huey Long had been shot, Roland began an emotional death vigil. "The people will rise at last, every man a king!" But when Louisiana's Kingfish died on September 10, the poor he had championed did not rise. Roland wanted to go to the funeral. "*Then* will be the time!" But his idol was buried without Roland there to mourn, although he did not lack mourners. I didn't doubt Roland's grief, for I slept with him and heard him. He cried by night, and by day raged against the rich, who, he said, had ordered the assassination. But the storm passed, and I never again heard him speak of revolution.

I had, in truth, paid little attention to Roland during this time, because I was beginning the tenth grade and my first year at Sidney Lanier Senior High School. Considered a child until then, if not by me, I was now acknowledged to be growing up. The end of the tunnel, light or dark, was within conceivable reach. Meantime, I had new problems. In the course of the summer I had acquired pimples. Marshall, who'd had them as long as I'd known him, jeered at mine as a timid few that could be mistaken for fly shit three feet away.

"What if I want to get closer to somebody than that?"

"Who? Why didn't you say? Has she got tits yet? How big? Is she real or a movie star? Tell me!"

"No one particular."

"You're lying, Mr. Christian! I'll have you keel-hauled for this!"

"I'd tell you if there was."

"Swear?"

Another problem was erections. They came swiftly and often without provocation. I had one when my new home-room teacher, Miss Cranford, called on me to read a chapter from the Bible. It was the custom to begin the school day in that manner. Some teachers got it over by quickly reading a few verses themselves, others by having the class rise as a body and recite the Lord's Prayer. Miss Cranford asked each of us in rotation to read to the others.

It was Monday, and I had forgotten over the weekend that the boy in front of me had read on Friday. I now remembered that as he finished and came and sat down, Miss Cranford pronounced it "a psalm of praise," as she did every reading whether from Job or Galatians. Although a proficient teacher of algebra, Miss Cranford was not celebrated for her sweet temper. She spoke my name again, sharply. Far from subsiding, the erection grew with my alarm. I dared not rise. I could not walk to the front and take the Bible she now held in her hand and face the classroom.

When I kept my place, making no reply, every head swiveled in my direction. "Marcus Bowman, you will read a chapter of the Bible to us. We are waiting."

"No."

"What do you say?" Her voice was more puzzled than angry.

"No ma'am," I said feebly.

"Come, Marcus, no nonsense."

"I can't."

There was cold silence. "You are saying you will not?"

"I don't believe in it."

I don't know why those words came. I neither believed nor disbelieved in the Bible, and I had never before considered whether or not a brief religious observance was a good or bad way to start the school day.

She hesitated. "If you are Jewish, you may read from the Old Testament, you know. A psalm of praise?"

"I'm not Jewish, but I can't read it."

There was a longer silence. I stared ahead at no one, but I could not miss Celia's face looking back at me in unbelieving terror. We were separated because I was at the end of a row of seats and she at the front of the next row. She clearly thought she was fated to see the Lord strike me dead as I sat.

Whether Miss Cranford suffered a revelation of the reason for my refusal or simply wanted to get on with her teaching, she said with dignity, "Celia, will you read to us? It seems that Marcus will not." She opened the Bible and handed it to Celia, who had risen from her seat to do as she was bidden. "I've found you a nice psalm of praise."

Celia read, but her voice trembled and at the last broke into a single muffled sob. Miss Cranford took the book from her and nodded her kindly to her seat, after which we proceeded to explore the logic of A plus B equaling C.

As soon as class ended, Marshall was at my side. "What happened?"

"Nothing to talk about." I tried to go around him, in control of myself again. Equations had long since vanquished sexual impulse.

He caught up with me. "You're going to tell me."

"I'll see you at lunchtime. I think I'll have the banana salad with peanuts sprinkled over it and the chocolate cupcake and a glass of milk."

"You always have that." We were to go different ways. Marshall had elected speech as his minor subject, and I was headed for the drill field to join my ROTC unit. I had chosen military training as a minor subject because uniforms were supplied to be worn two days a week and I could save on clothes buying.

"Now," Marshall insisted.

I told him.

Not since the day in Silver's when I first saw him had I heard him laugh so. After a moment I was able to laugh with him. However, the problem remained to haunt me. The immediate result of the day's incident was that Miss Cranford never again called on me to read the Bible. When it came my turn, she skipped to Celia without comment. It was whispered by some that I no longer believed in God.

20

ANOTHER MONDAY, Marshall was absent from school.

We'd met last on Saturday when we went to see Mae West in *Goin' to Town*. Afterward, when we had frozen malted milk at the cool marble counter in Kress's (the weather would continue hot into October), Marshall had been amazed that I had not paid any attention to Paul Cavanaugh's clothes, which he'd admired.

"How can you think about tailoring with Mae West up there?" I teased him. The truth was we both thought Mae a motherly, funny sort of lady and nothing to do with sex.

"You'll never be able to wear clothes like that, even when you can afford beautiful ones instead of those things. You have to be thin for clothes to hang well. You don't care, do you?"

"No."

"When I can afford really good clothes, not just the best Montgomery can do, I'm going to pare myself down. No more frozen malted. I may stop seeing you. You wouldn't go with new clothes and the way I'll be living. I'll only know people like Cary Grant and Fred Astaire who understand clothes. Just watching you eat makes me feel fat. Why don't you get fat?"

"I work. I don't stand around playing the fiddle and speaking from the diaphragm."

"Boloney."

We parted in front of Kress's, he to make his way home and I mine, with no reference to a next meeting because we almost never planned one. Meetings happened. We got tired of each other sometimes, despising each other for being familiar and available. We usually avoided each other on Sunday anyway, because it was a day we both hated.

But if one of us was sick on a school day, he telephoned the other to take notes for him and get assignments. Marshall had not called, and when I went home from school after classes and called him, there was no answer. I tried again before going to bed, but again there was no answer.

Next morning before breakfast I gave the number to the operator and waited. After a dozen rings a voice said, "Hello."

"Marshall?" It had to be, but he sounded different.

"I was asleep."

"Aren't you going to school?"

His loud yawn protested and evaded the question.

"Marshall!—I said: Is anything wrong?"

"That isn't what you said. Geraldine's sick."

"Oh. I'm sorry."

Each waited for the other to say more.

"We took her to the hospital yesterday morning. Mama's with her. I was until late last night."

"Anything I can do?"

He sounded suddenly angry. "She's got pneumonia! Can you cure pneumonia?" The line went dead. He'd hung up. He'd never done that before, no matter how cross with each other we'd been. I gave the number to the operator again, although Beatrice was calling me to breakfast. The operator rang, but Marshall didn't answer.

When I went to school, I told Miss Cranford that Marshall was absent because his sister was sick and she looked at me in her suspicious way; but Celia and Sylvia, who overheard, expressed concern, and we agreed that it was too bad but that he was a good brother to stay out because of his sister. I almost told them about Geraldine, because I wanted to talk. After school I phoned Marshall's house and nobody answered, so I phoned the two hospitals where they might be and went to Fitzhill Hospital when they said they had Geraldine.

When I got there, I wished I hadn't come—or rather, I was afraid of being in the way. I fidgeted outside, then went in and asked a nurse where Geraldine Blake was and if her mother and brother were there. All she said was, "Oh, no, you can't see her!" and hurried away, even when I tried to explain that it was Marshall I'd come to see. Nobody stopped me, so I went along a hall, presently finding a waiting room with chairs, and pictures on the walls, and magazines and a potted plant on a low table. The only person there was an old lady sitting in a corner chair looking down at her hands and the closed pocketbook she held on her lap. I couldn't tell whether she was thinking or going to sleep, but she didn't know I was there. I picked up a copy of *Liberty* magazine and sat down. *Liberty* gave reading time for its pieces, and I liked to test myself with it, but there was no clock in the room.

Sometime later I looked up, my eye attracted by a motionless form, although a dozen people had come in and out of the room since I'd been there. Marshall was glaring at me.

"What are you doing?" he said. The old woman in the corner chair was so startled by his tone she got up and went out of the room.

"How is she?"

"Did you bring flowers?"

"I just happened by." Fitzhill Hospital was, in fact, not far from home.

"Go away and leave us alone."

Mrs. Blake came up beside him. "Hello, Mark."

"I'm just going, Mrs. Blake. I'm sorry if I'm—"

"Wait a minute please."

Marshall had turned and was walking down the corridor. "Marshall," she called, "you stop right there!" I couldn't see him, but he must have stopped, because she turned to me again. "It's nice of you to come, Mark, and I want you to help me. Take him to a picture show and bring him home later. I need a few hours without Marshall. All right? Now stay, while I go speak to him."

Again I wished I hadn't come, but I had, so I stayed. Maybe ten minutes later, which is a long time when you're waiting and don't want to, Marshall came back alone. "I promised to go with you," he said.

"Let's see a movie."

"I've seen everything."

"*China Seas* is at the Tivoli. We've seen it only twice and you like it."

We left the hospital and walked the few blocks to the theatre. At a drugstore on the way I went in and bought two rolls of Life Savers, one orange and one lime; but each of us bought his own ticket as we went into the Tivoli. The picture was on. We saw it to the end and then the news and coming attractions. The picture started again. I tried to concentrate, but it didn't work, so we just sat there. I'd given the roll of orange Life Savers to Marshall. We usually made them last out a whole movie, but he'd already finished his, crunching them with his teeth. When Jean Harlow acted rough at the table because she was afraid Rosalind Russell was going to steal Clark Gable, I said, "We came in here." He got up and followed me.

Outside I said, "I'll walk you part way."

"No, that's enough. I did what I promised." He said it so firmly I didn't argue or try to go with him. It was beginning to get dark as I climbed the hill to Five Points. The evening was clear, and the first star was bright as ice. I thought of the times I walked home with Beatrice and we wished on any star, and I remembered the superstition that when a child dies a new one appears.

I thought about Geraldine and Mrs. Blake and Marshall all next day. There hadn't been any death or funeral notice in the *Advertiser* that morning. I'd told Beatrice last night about Geraldine, and when I got home, she was back from the restaurant. I found her in the kitchen because I was hungry and always went there first when I came in the front door. She was looking at what was left over from noon dinner to judge what she needed to cook to make up our supper. She had a cup of coffee and smoked a cigarette (that was new; she said the restaurant made her nervous sometimes and tobacco quieted her) while I ate an apple tart. Aunt Belle was out with her bridge club because it was Wednesday. I almost never worked Wednesdays—it was a slow afternoon at the warehouse.

She talked about this and that. Ethel had a new boyfriend she'd met at the Beau Monde, only he was from out of town and she wondered if he was married. He traveled for Hellman's mayonnaise. I asked Beatrice when she was going to get a fellow, and she smiled.

I was pressing up the last greasy crumbs with my fingers and licking them when she said, "Marshall's mama called this morning, and I talked to her. They were having the funeral this afternoon."

"So quick?"

"That's what I thought, but there was no one to wait for, and it seemed better."

"I wanted to go."

She nodded. "They didn't want anybody, just them and that Ada woman that took care of her. That's what she

phoned to say. She was nice, didn't want you to feel hurt.
—Where are you going?"

"To see Marshall."

"Wait till tomorrow."

"Did she tell you that too?"

"Yes, she did."

My relief next morning was considerable when I found Marshall already at his desk in Miss Cranford's homeroom. Sylvia and Celia were kneeling side by side on the seat of the desk in front of him to face him, and the three appeared to be talking easily. Celia smiled an invitation for me to join them, and I did, cautiously, to discover that they were discussing a forthcoming book report on *The Talisman*. It wasn't hard to fall into their play, and we kept it up until the warning bell rang and Marshall said he had to look over the algebra lesson before Miss Cranford sent us to the blackboard to do problems.

There was no chance to see Marshall alone all that day; he was with somebody. It was suddenly as if everyone else knew him better than I did and conspired to show me so. At the end of the regular class periods he didn't come to the homeroom for the customary five minutes of announcements before we were dismissed for the day. The following morning— I had been too offended to telephone him after the way he'd avoided me—it was easy for everyone to act as if nothing had happened and life was normal. Any lie comes easier the second time said and seems almost true to the speaker the third time. But I was determined not to be shaken off and kept watch on him so he couldn't slip away after school. Seeing what I was up to, he didn't try, but he had a boy named Walter Whitlock with him when we left, and Walter walked all the way down South Court Street with us, turning over to Hull Street where he lived only when we got to the cross street with the Christian Science church.

When he left, Marshall surprised me by laughing. "You're mule-stubborn, aren't you?"

"I guess so," I said, the wind out of my sails.

"There's no reason to look so grim."

"No," I agreed uncertainly.

He began to speak quickly, with assurance, as if from a rehearsed speech, the way he'd practice the opening argument of a debate at Baldwin last year. "When they're like that, they often die before they grow up. She lived longer than many do. Anything, they say, any of the childhood diseases like measles or whooping cough and they're gone. With pneumonia there wasn't a chance. She didn't suffer. Dr. Drew said she didn't and that she was lucky, and in a way we were lucky too. It was the best thing, he said, since it had to happen."

"I don't believe you."

"Well, then you don't believe doctors. Mama says he's right, and even Ada says it was the Lord's will."

"I don't believe you feel that way."

"You want me to beat on my chest with both fists and cry, 'Woe is me!' "

"I want you to tell me the truth."

He flushed. "Leave me some privacy."

"You haven't wanted it before, and you never left me any," I reminded him.

"Things are different now."

"All right, just say it: We're not friends."

"Good—old—Mark," he said softly but caustically. "I think you're sore because you missed the funeral. It wasn't much to miss—it wouldn't have made a poem."

"This is the first time I've wanted to hit you."

"Go ahead. I won't try to hit you back."

"I'm going to get the bus to the warehouse. I should have been there by now."

"See you Monday."

Monday it was the same again: Marshall in a fever of unconvincing casualness. I was beyond feeling sorry for him. Now I wanted really to hurt him. I tried a hard-boiled, deliberate attack with words. Hearing one callous-seeming remark I made, Celia began to cry and ran away to the girls' toilet. Sylvia watched me, puzzled and cold. Marshall pretended to be amused, so I left him, disgusted.

I ignored him the rest of the week. At first he assumed a tolerant and superior pose, to show me and others he hardly noticed such childishness on my part. Then he forgot the others and when I looked his way put on a mocking *"Et tu, Brute?"* expression. Finally, he was looking at me with no expression at all.

On Friday at the end of the short interval in the homeroom ending the school day, when Miss Cranford dismissed us for the day and the week, he dropped a note on my desk and exited quickly. Unfolding it as soon as I got outside, I read: "If you want to, meet me at Kress at 2 tomorrow."

I was there.

"You want to go with me?"

"Where?" I asked.

"Don't talk. Okay?"

I was puzzled, and I was annoyed with Marshall for making a mystery, suspecting him of enjoying it, even though I knew now he was disturbed beyond anything to do with grief. We crossed Dexter Avenue, I following his lead, and took the bus out to Cloverdale, getting off at Fairview Avenue. I was the more puzzled. We hadn't come anywhere we usually went. He stood on the corner a minute before he did something I'd never seen him do: lifted his hand to a passing car. We considered ourselves superior to hitchhiking.

"You don't look much like Claudette Colbert," I said.

"Nor Clark Gable."

I was cheered only because it was the first thing he'd said since Geraldine got sick that sounded like him. We were soon in a car, and Marshall revealed to the old-man driver that we were going to Memorial Cemetery. The old man was sympathetic. Had anyone died *close* to one of us? Yes, Marshall answered, his sister. Thereupon, to my astonishment, Marshall told our host-driver in detail what had happened. I listened and learned. We were let out on the main road, and there was still a dirty walk along the side road to get inside. Memorial Cemetery was new then. The grass hadn't taken hold. Trees and shrubs were close to the ground. It was bleak and raw-looking, so very different from the only cemeteries I remembered in Savannah, the old Colonial, more like a town square than a burying ground, and Bonaventure, which had a gloomy glamour I associated with Frankenstein movies.

Most barren of all was the new grave he led me to. "Here she is."

"It's a pretty place," I lied.

"You know it's not."

He took three or four deep breaths of air, walking around as if to show me he felt at home. "I've been almost every day."

"Why?"

"I don't want to forget."

"You don't have to come here to remember Geraldine, do you?"

"I don't see why I have to explain it to you."

"Don't do it then."

He shook his head. "You're so bound and determined to be my friend, I had to show you."

I bristled. "Stop making a Eugene O'Neill play out of it."

He looked angry, but after a minute said soberly, "I am vile." He squatted beside the grave and stared at what I took to be the head, although there was as yet no stone to mark it. Teetering, he sat down on the ground and continued to sit. I remained standing, a few feet away. Without taking his eyes from the grave, he told me.

"I wish I knew whether or not there's any afterlife. Last year we decided there wasn't, but how can you be sure? Nietzsche says man is not great enough not to believe in God. Suppose there's not only God but an afterlife as well. If that's so, there's no reason to think Geraldine will be the same as she was here. She could now be as old as her years. You see what I mean." I didn't answer; it hadn't been a question. "If Geraldine has her full mind, then she understands what I did and hates me."

"They wouldn't hate in heaven, would they?" I offered when he was silent; and I wondered if he was going on with it, or leaving it there.

He exploded with fury. "I'm not talking about heaven!— Just don't say anything trying to help, will you, please?" It took him another minute to order his thoughts and resume. "It was almost a year before I knew you. It was a rainy afternoon. Mama was out. Ada wasn't there. I was with her." He was speaking reasonably, almost without emotion. "You know how she loved me. She'd do anything I wanted her to, if she could. I don't know what fiend possessed me. I was crazy, thinking about sex, and I'd never seen a female—organ. I undressed Geraldine and looked at her.—She trusted me, She didn't know, she didn't understand. She just smiled at me when I looked at her and tried to hug me.—I wouldn't let her." He spoke hastily now, almost breathlessly. "Nothing else happened, I swear to God. I'm not that vile. I touched her only enough to put her clothes back on. And then I played the violin until she went to sleep. Mama came home and gave me a quarter for staying with her and for being so good to her." He still had not looked at me. "Isn't it an awful thing?"

"Yes," I said.

"Now you can stop being my friend, but you know why."

I gave him a minute before I said, "We should both leave, and you ought not to come back here for a while."

"You want me to forget it," he said.

"Living, or dead forever, or alive somewhere in a different way, Geraldine could never hate you, whatever she knows."

"Next you'll be forgiving me and absolving me of blame."

"I've nothing to forgive you for."

"I want you to judge me, since she can't."

"No." I turned away from the burial plot and began to walk toward the cemetery entrance. I didn't look around, so I didn't know if he was coming until he caught up with me.

When we reached the main road that would take us back into the city, he said, "You wouldn't have done anything like that."

"I don't know," I said. "I might have." I considered it. "I think of Beatrice as my sister, but one day I opened the door of her room when I knew she'd just taken a bath, hoping to see her naked."

"*Did* you?" It was Marshall's old, thrilled voice.

"Almost. She grabbed her slip with one hand and slammed the door with the other. There was a lot of talcum powder in the air."

"But she knew what you were doing, and Geraldine didn't."

I held up my thumb to an approaching car, and when it slowed, added, "Leave it to Geraldine and God and—Nietzsche—if there is a Nietzsche."

21

"I'M GOING to be president."

"Impossible. F.D.R.'s an easy winner for a second term. I saw it in my crystal balls!" Marshall laughed wildly, as he did when he made a weak joke and never when he made a strong one. It was the spring of the year 1936, and we were sixteen. The school day was over, and as we left by the side entrance, the warm air was sweet with the scent of gardenias from bushes that bordered the front parade ground.

"You're going to be vice president."

"And oust tobacco-spitting Nancy Garner? Never!"

"Of the Ushers Club, fool. You saw Jack stop me. It was to tell me, before the announcement next week." Jack Hendrix was the graduating president of the Ushers Club. At midterm of our first year at Sidney Lanier, Marshall and I had been elected to membership in the Ushers Club because of "outstanding scholastic achievement and upstanding character," whereupon we had said as one that we wished it wouldn't stand up and out so much. We didn't bother even to smile at our common jokes.

There were a number of social and hobby clubs, but the Ushers was the only one making an excellent school record the basis for inclusion. No one could join; no one refused election. It was the one club ambitious parents urged their sons to qualify for. Marshall and I had been elected before we knew what it was, for we scorned all clubs and lumped them together, as we scorned all exclusivity not instituted by ourselves. The only function of the Ushers Club that interested us was that of ushering for performances held in the high school auditorium, where most of the touring plays and concerts that came to town were booked. The well-off citizens of Montgomery subscribed to what was called "the concert course," which usually included three or four recitals during the winter and spring months. Plays were few and rarely sold out. Only actors as famous as Katharine Cornell, the Lunts, and Ethel Barrymore drew large audiences. Ushers were not paid, but could see the performances from any seats left unoccupied, and it was not uncommon for subscribers to the concert course to miss an event.

"Why us?" Marshall asked when he'd thought it over. I shrugged, and he answered himself. "Because we're the best, of course. Who else is as brilliant and as good?—But we're members and didn't vote."

"There's no voting. We were chosen by Jack and the vice president and secretary-treasurer. And Miss Hannah." Miss

Hannah Hamilton, who taught English history, was the club sponsor.

"You mean to say Miss Hannah likes us?"

"I wonder if Miss Cranford told her about my not reading the Bible in class."

"Maybe she's a Rosicrucian. She looks like she might be something funny."

"Oh, she's harmless enough."

"They always say that when they find a farm family of seven axed in the barn and the only survivor is a big-eyed dumpling of a woman who eats cream with a spoon and crochets antimacassars. The only time Miss Hannah ever spoke to me was one day in the library and she asked had I read *Black Beauty*."

"Why would she ask that?"

"I thought it was sinister, too. She must be all of fifty. Her face is the color of laundry soap, and her hair is like old rope. She's got eyes like Bela Lugosi, and when she walks, she creaks like the inn sign in *Treasure Island*. I bet she seeps like cellar walls."

"We're going to be important," I said, a little in awe.

Marshall sighed uncomfortably. "We are important."

"What were you doing in the library to make Miss Hannah ask you about *Black Beauty?*"

"Reading a Birmingham newspaper about one of those sugar daddies. Tommy Manville was getting a divorce from wife number who-knows, and this wife of the week was suing for a million dollars' alimony. Figure it out: if he fucked her three times a day while they were married—and he doesn't look to me like he could—that's a mighty high price for nookie."

"More than you'll ever be able to afford," I said.

Marshall was quiet for a block. "Do you reckon Miss Hannah has a pussy?"

"Only you would think of such a thing."

"Maybe she just has a drain like a bathtub and keeps a

stopper in it when she isn't using it." We laughed until we were red in the face, we the newly elected, of outstanding scholastic achievement and upstanding character.

We had got through the winter. Geraldine's death was behind Marshall. He never spoke to me about her, but now and then when we were at his house, he might take up his violin and play it as he walked around the room and we talked, and suddenly get a look on his face that told me he was remembering the times he'd played for her.

If we had been stately lords our last year at Baldwin, we were scrambling peasants our first year at Lanier, determined to make our mark. But as winter passed and we endured, we became surer of ourselves. From a comment of Mrs. Noble's when we went back one day to visit her, we knew our new teachers were talking about us as "promising." I had contributed two essays to the school's literary paper and was assured of being on its staff the following year. Marshall had won a large part in a play presented in general assembly and made up his mind to become an actor. The speech classes were full of wistful girls who'd read movie magazines and wanted to become Norma Shearers and Loretta Youngs, but boys were harder come by, and Miss Porter, the speech teacher, fell on Marshall like a wolf upon the fold. When he made a strong impression by fearless overacting, Miss Porter praised him for his excesses and promised he could play Rochester when she got around to the production of *Jane Eyre* she'd dreamed of the entire decade she'd been teaching.

Our grades were better than they'd been at Baldwin, and they'd been high there. We'd earned the right to feel pleased with ourselves, although not perhaps as pleased as we were, considering ourselves as we did to be practically among the immortals. That is why the distinction of being made president and vice president of the Ushers Club at the end of our first year of senior high school seemed, after we'd thought about it, no more than our due.

We had worked hard, and few parties were offered. Girls

who, like Celia, had given parties last year to prime the pump, now turned coy, waiting to be asked to school dances, which Marshall and I did not attend, and wanting to go out on dates. I shied from dating, telling myself I couldn't afford it, although I earned more money by working at the warehouse than I spent. But I thought of that money selfishly, in terms of what a book cost, or a new pair of shoes, and reminded myself that I could go to two movies alone for less than the price of taking a girl to one, because no one would think of taking a girl to a second-run theatre. I had begun a savings account with the post office. Marshall called me the Hetty Green of the tenth grade.

Celia and I remained friendly, but I found her dull, and it was to Posy Valentine I turned for boy-girl games of fun. They began with the accident of our meeting downtown one day. Posy was looking into a window of Webber's general store off Dexter Avenue. I stepped up beside her and began to talk about the cups and saucers in the window as if we were considering buying them together. She quickly fell into the patter as we went into the store and pretended to be an ignorant, poor, quarreling couple, engaged to be married and trying to choose housewares. As we disagreed about each item, Posy pretended to burst into tears and ran out of the store. I met her immediately after, and we laughed at our wit and the face of the startled middle-aged clerk we had just left, and wound up having fountain-made Coca-Colas at a drugstore. I don't think we really fooled anyone, but we played and refined the game on other occasions and thought ourselves wonderfully clever.

Marshall was dating, occasionally at any rate, Sylvia Patterson, whose father allowed an evening visit once a week if he was himself to be out and the housekeeper stayed in attendance. Marshall was quick to make a friend of the woman and reported to me that Sylvia could now close the door to the kitchen where the housekeeper sat with radio and cat. He said little, for Marshall, of what went on during those evenings, and only now and then did he actually quote to me anything that Sylvia said. I will add that Sylvia, with her precocious clothes sense, looked virtually grown-up, to us anyway; and what stranger could tell the difference between her and Myrna Loy?

Still, for every drop of self-assurance, we carried a gallon of doubt, but we also carried a secret inside us. It was this: All our work was yet to do, but we knew surely that it would come, be done, be good; and all the world would celebrate our triumphs and strive to touch us, hold us, love us. To have nothing was a blessing; it would make achievement the greater.

22

LET NO one take the mild manner of the Beatrices of this world for meekness. Of all unlikely people to be the center of a neighborhood sensation, Beatrice put herself in the way of being just that in June. When she decided a thing, it was decided; there was no changing her mind or stopping her from a course she'd chosen. Certainly I should never have tried. The Benedicts did.

Working at the Beau Monde had given Beatrice confidence in herself and knowledge of the world. She was nineteen and no longer a homebody. Poor Ethel's feet had got no better with time, although she spent a big portion of her earnings on new treatments, and Beatrice now worked most evenings. One night after we became friendly, Ethel sat down in the empty back booth, usually reserved for making menus and storing spare sugars, salts, and peppers, took off her left shoe and stocking and put foot and foreleg on the table, inviting me to study the geography of her complaint. My shock at the sight gratified her and made me another confidant. Ethel had hundreds; no one's sympathy was despised.

Since Beatrice worked most of the supper shifts now, I was no longer her regular escort, although I'd still walk down to meet her when the spirit moved me. I had never been under the illusion that she needed my protection. However, because I did go now and then to bring her home, I was first of the family to learn that her life had taken a new course. On that particular evening she was pleased to see me but a little embarrassed and amused at herself; and when she came out from the back ready to go, she said, "A friend is taking us home in his car." As we went out the door, a man got out of a car and approached. "Harvey," she said, "I want you to meet my cousin, Mark Bowman. Mark, this is Mr. Harvey Briggs."

"Harvey," he said, extending his hand to shake mine. "Glad to meet you, Mark."

I was thunderstruck. Beatrice was acting as if he was her sweetheart, but how, I asked myself, could he be? He was middle-aged. His curly black hair was already graying, and only when he smiled did his face look young; it was distinguished by deep dimples in cheeks and chin. Perhaps it was his clothes that gave the impression of age, for he wore a full suit with tie, not simply shirt and trousers as did most Montgomery businessmen in warm weather. I took a back seat quickly as he opened the front door for Beatrice, and then he took his own seat. When he'd done so and slammed the door, he hesitated, and as if I weren't there, leaned his head and kissed her.

When we arrived at the house on Morgan Avenue, I got out of the car even quicker than I'd got in and said, "Well, goodnight, sir, and thank you for the lift."

"Goodnight, Mark. *Harvey.*"

Beatrice didn't come in for half an hour, but although Aunt Belle and Uncle Grady and Roland were all in the living room and knew I'd gone to walk her home, no one asked where she was. That was how they took Beatrice for granted.

The next afternoon when I came home from school, Beatrice and I had our usual few minutes alone in the kitchen. Having fixed me a plate of food—although I ate in the lunchroom at school, I was starving again by the time I came home —she sat down across the table from me. She spoke firmly but kept her voice low. "I'm going to get married."

"Are you sure?"

She laughed in a girlish way I'd never before heard her laugh and wasn't certain I liked. "I've known for a long time; last night we decided to tell everybody. He's been after me to meet the family, but I wanted to be certain first."

"Isn't he too old for you?" I ventured.

"He's thirty-five." That didn't bother her, although it seemed to me an age when people ought to be considering green pastures and still waters rather than making a new life for themselves.

"You've never been out with boys."

"I don't like boys."

"Don't you think you ought to know a few before you make up your mind?"

"No."

"How come this one?" I swallowed. "Why—Harvey?"

"I love him." She said it so reasonably I felt tears sting my eyes, although I continued eating raisin-bread pudding. "There's going to be a lot of fuss. Will you be on our side?" I nodded dumbly. She lighted a cigarette, and when she'd blown out a first deep breath of smoke, said, "I'm going to need you. There's more to tell."

She proceeded. She had first seen Harvey Briggs a year ago when he began to have an occasional lunch or supper at the restaurant. He was a lawyer, but that was all she'd known, hardly noticing him beyond registering the fact that he was "nice" and "polite," and that he never tried any of the automatic "freshness" the male customers (and most of them were male) felt obliged to try. She realized he'd been noticing her only when he asked her to go out with him. She had few free evenings, so they met for an hour or two when they both had a loose day. Mainly, they drove out into the country. Very soon ("Oh, Mark, he's such a good man!") they had known they wanted to marry.

Age difference had been no barrier in her mind, nor in his when he was sure of her feelings, but there were other problems that would look insuperable to others. He had been married. After five years his wife left him to live with another man and to marry him after divorcing Harvey. She had willingly given up custody of their two sons, Lucius, aged ten, and Roy, aged nine. Divorce was bad enough, but he was a Roman Catholic, and as such he had been unable to think of remarrying. Meeting Beatrice and falling in love with her, he had despaired until a month ago when his former wife died in an automobile crash.

When she waited, I knew that was all she had to tell me. "What's the problem?"

She jumped from her chair and hugged me as I sat. "Wait till you hear *them*." She pulled her chair around beside mine and sat down again. "A funny thing: I won't need all those things I've been collecting in my hope chest. I've been to his house; he wanted me to see it. It's out on Narrow Lane Road."

"That's in Cloverdale," I knew.

"Farther out," she said. "He has fifteen acres, mostly pine trees, but clear space too with flower beds and borders that get the sun. He's even made a lake on it. The house is all furnished, but I'm going to take my things anyway."

"You won't need that old measuring cup, I guess."

"I'm going to change our bedroom—"

"You've been in that, have you?"

She slapped my arm. "He showed me all over and told me I could throw everything out and start over if I wanted to; but I won't, except things that were obviously *her* taste. I'll get new curtains everywhere and new wallpaper in the dining room and our bedroom. But I'm not going to touch his library."

"He's got a library?"

"Mostly law books in cases. Not the kind of books you read. Will you come to see me anyway?"

"You're going to make him happy, aren't you?"

She nodded matter-of-factly. "I've met his boys and his old mother. She's nearly seventy and very cold about my not being a Catholic. His first wife was until the divorce. I told her I wouldn't change or be married in the Catholic church."

"Why won't you?"

She frowned. "I don't know, I just won't. I'm what I was born. But I told her I'd help raise his boys as Catholics if that was what they all wanted. However, I won't agree to raise any children we have that way, which means we'll *have* to get married outside his church."

"When are you telling the family?"

"Tonight when I come home from work. Will you be here?"

"I wouldn't miss it."

Aunt Belle chose that moment to enter the kitchen. "You sounded like you were having such a good time back here." We laughed. "Some secret or other?"

"You'd be surprised, Mama!"

"Then don't tell me. I never had a good surprise in my life."

23

THAT EVENING and during the days that followed, Aunt Belle had no reason to change her attitude toward unexpected revelations. When she came in at nine o'clock, Beatrice made a fresh pot of coffee, as she usually did, before joining the family in the living hoom. Roland's attention was on a book in his lap. For a week he had alternated a manual on book-keeping for small businesses with Dale Carnegie's *How to Win Friends and Influence People*, which all the ambitious young men were reading that year. Accepting a fresh cup of coffee from her daughter, Aunt Belle closed the copy of *Woman's Home Companion* she'd been reading with the satisfied remark, "Married him—knew she would." Beatrice and I exchanged looks. Uncle Grady was fussing with the radio, and when he snapped it off, Beatrice took it as a signal.

"I have something to say," she began in an uncharacter-istically speechy tone. "You may not like it, but that won't change anything." Having their puzzled attention, she dis-closed clearly and straight-forwardly, although not unemo-tionally, what she had earlier told me. After a few exclama-tions, which she ignored and talked over, they listened quietly enough.

Roland was first to voice an objection. "A lawyer?—Car-rion crows of capitalism, that's all they are!"

"Catholic?" Aunt Belle wailed.

Uncle Grady mused aloud, "Thirty-five isn't much younger than I am."

Putting aside his books as if he understood their inadequacy in his attack on Big Money, Roland said, "I'll tell you right now: No sister of mine is going to marry a rotten Catholic lawyer old enough to be her father! You don't have to sell yourself like that."

"I remember some nice Catholics when I was a girl in Savannah, but we didn't know them the same way we knew other people," Aunt Belle said.

Roland went further. "Catholicism is only one notch above voodoo."

Keeping her control, Beatrice said, "I'm not going to be a Catholic, but if Harvey and his sons want to be, that's their business."

Uncle Grady was doubtful. "As soon as they got you, they'd begin to work on you. His mother, his sons, *him.*"

"I've never," Beatrice said temperately, "heard people criticized just because they follow a religion they're born with."

"Nobody cares what anybody is," Aunt Belle explained, "but there's a lot of hocus-pocus about Catholics and the things they are made to do. It's not just sitting in church hearing a nice sermon once a week and singing a few old hymns the way we do. When people start running their lives along religious lines, you have to watch out. They believe everything the priest tells them, and they have to tell him everything. How would you like your husband and stepsons telling a perfect stranger things about you? It makes my flesh crawl."

Uncle Grady took an impersonal, fatherly tone. "You see how we all feel, Beatrice. I advise you not to go against your family in this."

"Harvey is going to be my family."

"And his Catholic offspring?" Roland asked. "God! He'll make you have a baby every year and turn them all into Catholics!"

Aunt Belle cautioned him, "Don't say indelicate things to your sister, Roland."

Uncle Grady said, "Boys that age—nine and ten, you say? In a few years they'll be in their teens, and you'll be living in the same house with them, grown men to all intents and purposes and no real kin—using the same bathroom—"

"Harvey's house has three bathrooms. He and I will have our own."

"Three?" Aunt Belle was suspicious. "I can see two as a convenience where there are children like that, but what on earth can anyone want with three, unless something peculiar's going on?"

Roland said, "When he showed you this great fancy house —in Cloverdale!—to lure you, did he go into the bathrooms with you?"

Beatrice's temper broke. "You make me tired!"

Uncle Grady said, "That's no way to speak to your brother. He's concerned for your good name—"

Surprised at finding his father on his side on any question, Roland pressed ahead. "She's already infected with popery. I thought the fate of Al Smith would be a lesson to all Catholics."

"Children always resent, if they don't downright hate, a stepmother."

Beatrice said to me, but for them, "Do you hate Mama, Mark?"

"I'm not his stepmother," Aunt Belle said. "He is my dear dead sister's boy."

Feeling that I had let Beatrice down by keeping silent, I said, "I think Beatrice is right to marry whoever she loves, regardless of his age or religion."

"You shut up," Roland said, pointing a long finger at me. "You're not one of the family."

"He's one of my family," Beatrice assured him, "and just about the only one that has any sense, it sounds to me like."

"Mind what you say to your mother and father!" Uncle Grady shouted. I had never before heard him shout.

Aunt Belle said, "I don't know what you could have done

that would have struck me a harder blow, Beatrice, and that's the truth. You're an innocent girl, and you don't know about Life. We're not going to forbid anything—." She flashed her eyes warningly at her son and husband, seeing that they were about to object. "You can ask Mr. Briggs here and let us meet him, if you like, but there can be no question of an engagement."

"We *are* engaged, Mama, and we're going to get married two weeks from Sunday."

"Oh, no, dear, that's impossible."

"We forbid it!" Roland declared.

"Just you keep still and let me and your mother handle this, Roland."

Aunt Belle tried another approach, her voice doleful with the wisdom of the ages. "It's a mistake to believe you can build happiness on the tragedy of others. When I think of that poor woman, wife and mother, killed only a month ago, and you and her husband ready to dance on her grave—"

"That woman left Harvey and her own children to go and live a selfish life of sin."

"It's not for us to judge others," Aunt Belle said.

"Middle-class morality," Roland sneered.

"Do what your mother says, Beatrice," Uncle Grady advised. "Bring the young—or not so young"—(wry smile) — "gentleman here and let us look him over, get to know him, decide for ourselves if he comes in a mile of being worthy of you. If you haven't changed your mind, say six months from now, we can talk it over again."

"I promise you we'll be nice to him," Aunt Belle said.

"Two weeks from Sunday," Beatrice said.

"Why the hurry?" Aunt Belle began to plead.

"Harvey doesn't want to wait, and I don't either. We waited when we thought there was no hope."

Roland said, "Oh, he's *impatient*. A man like that who's been married, *used* to certain things, misses them, doesn't he?

You watch out, Beatrice, a married man knows all about women and can play on their nerves in ways that—"

"Which one of your books did you learn that from, the one under the green sweater in your bureau?"

"Never mind him; why are *you* in such a hurry?" Uncle Grady wanted to know. "He hasn't—you're not—"

"No, I'm not pregnant."

"What a word to use in front of a young boy!" Aunt Belle had decided to protect me.

"All the neighbors will think you are," Roland told her, "if we let you run off and get married like that."

"They'll know they're wrong in a few months, won't they?"

"You've certainly thought of everything," Uncle Grady said accusingly.

"With this family, I have to."

"But the talk there'll be!" Aunt Belle said deploringly. "We were all so happy, and now this." She shrugged with self-pity.

I entered the ranks again. "I like him, and I'm the only one besides Beatrice that knows him. He's a fine-looking man and speaks well-educated too." Having heard him utter fewer than a dozen words and seen him only at night, I considered that a generous endorsement.

"All he wants," Aunt Belle mourned, "is a nurse for his children and a maid of all work. I see the whole thing."

Roland said to me, "What have you had to do with this? Did you sneak around and help them meet secretly while you were pretending to go down and walk Beatrice home from work?"

Unable to say more, I thumbed my nose at him, and it did not seem inappropriate.

To his father Roland said, "Let me hit him—once."

"Behave yourself—both of you. A little peace and quiet after the day, that's all I want. God knows, I don't ask more from any of you, do I?"

Beatrice went to the door. "I've said all I'm going to say, and now I'm going to bed. All of you, except Mark, are being mean and hateful." She went out of the living room, and a few seconds later her door closed. She didn't slam it, but she closed it with finality.

Aunt Belle called after her, "I don't intend to get one wink of sleep tonight! I'll just lie awake studying it over and worrying myself to death. It won't surprise me if my hair has turned white by morning."

"You knew all about it," Roland said to me. "Why didn't you warn us?"

"I didn't know anything until I met him last night, and Beatrice didn't tell me until today when I came home from school."

"You're lying. After all this family's done for you."

"Leave him alone," Uncle Grady said.

Aunt Belle turned to her husband. "You aren't going to let her do it, are you?"

"She'll see things differently tomorrow," he said.

"Just went off to bed like that," Aunt Belle marveled. "She always asks if I want more coffee. You all see how she's changing?"

24

POPULAR AS she was in the neighborhood for her amiability and indolence, Aunt Belle did not wait long for commiseration. When I left next morning at seven-thirty, she was calling, "My heart is broken!" from the back steps to Mrs. Watson who lived next door and had gone into the yard to feed breakfast scraps to her bulldog, Bouncer. I returned from school at three-thirty to find the house full, as if there'd been a death in the family, and Aunt Belle greeted me, hands raised, with "See how quick everybody has found out?" as though she herself had not been chief informer.

Picking my way through the callers, I found Beatrice in the kitchen as usual. "It has *been* a day," she said grimly. "I made a banana pudding, knowing how you love it. I had to keep doing something." We were seldom demonstrative, and it was an awkward hug I gave her before sitting down to the plate she set at my place. "When I left for the Beau Monde, the porch was full, and when I got back at two, porch *and* living room. I had to phone for more Coca-Colas to be delivered, and this is the third pot of coffee I've watched percolate this afternoon."

"You've got to stop waiting on them, Beatrice," I said as I peeled a baked sweet potato to go with the cold roast pork and cabbage she'd served me.

"I will soon, but I see no way of changing as long as I'm here."

"What have they said to you?"

"Not so much to me, but so I could hear, worded as sympathy for Mama. 'Catholic—old man—divorce—stepchildren.' Didn't it seem simple when I told you yesterday? There should have been nothing to it but us getting married and everybody minding their business."

"Have you talked to Harvey?"

"Just for a few minutes when he had his lunch. Ethel's so thrilled about us she thinks her new corn-remedy is working."

"How's Harvey?"

"His ma has decided to act up. Says she won't come to the ceremony since it isn't Catholic."

"Does Harvey mind?"

She shook her head. "Tells me not to worry. The only thing—" Frowning, she hesitated until I knew she wasn't going to finish what she'd started.

"The only thing that's important is you and Harvey. For once in your life, think of yourself."

She was holding her head so still it trembled. "I'm going to. I'm not smart, but I know what's important. How's that banana pudding?" The question was an effort to lighten our mood, as if she was shy of sharing her trouble with me.

"I'm going to miss it."

"I don't see why. I can still make banana pudding on Narrow Lane Road, and you can come eat it, unless you're too proud to mingle with Catholics."

"Who was first to say: 'Change the name and not the letter, change for worse and not for better'?"

She meant to laugh, but it was a choked sound. "They all said it, and every damned one of them as if it was an original saying she'd just made up in her head. The first was Sue Brown."

"Who is she?"

"Lives two doors from the corner of Mildred and Mobile streets, on Mildred, this side. Hair so yellow it looks like it was meant to spread on butter, and finger-waved within an inch of its life."

Placing her, I nodded and sucked the spoon after scraping up the last of the pudding from my bowl. "Nose twitches like a rabbit's and walks like she's holding a walnut between her knees."

"Poor Mama, she honestly believes I am deliberately setting out to break her heart."

"Nobody here's likely to starve. We just won't do as well as you do for us. On the other hand, Harvey and his boys will do better. They may become Methodists after they've tasted banana pudding."

Aunt Belle called Beatrice and asked in her most pitiful voice if there was any more coffee and could she scare up three Coca-Colas because Cora Greenway looked like she was perishing of thirst, and there were others to think of too. I helped her take the things in to the callers, who ignored us until we were directly in front of them, whereupon they fixed us with glazed smiles and asked how we were getting along in the same way they did acquaintances met at the church steps on Sunday morning. The subject had swung from the particular to the general; they were talking about divorce.

Divorce was more talked about than done in our neighborhood; but everyone knew someone, or knew someone who knew someone, who had a sister or a brother or a cousin who'd been divorced, although such a relative was always said to be the innocent party, indeed the unwilling victim. "Grass widows," as divorced women were called, were thought to be hardly better than harlots. Children were piously said to be the worst victims of all and likely to turn bad from the influence.

Then of course there was discussion of stepchildren, and Cora Greenway, revived by her Coca-Cola, declared that she knew a case where a stepson of a perfect *angel* of a lady who had been *more* than a mother to him had stabbed her and his father in the middle of the night with a *butcher* knife!

If, during the following two weeks, Beatrice was not happy, she never faltered in her determination to marry Harvey Briggs. Had I not known them, been one of them, the situation would have seemed comical. The heartbroken mother, the offended father, the forbidding brother never spoke a warm word to the one who kept their house, saw that their clothes were decent, and cooked and served their meals. Their common attitude was that of waiting for her to come to her senses and apologize. The first day or two she tried to give them news of her plans by telling me in front of them the arrangements she and Harvey were making.

A Methodist clergyman (not the one at the church we attended) and his parlor were reserved for three o'clock, Sunday week. Old Mrs. Briggs still refused to attend the ceremony. Beatrice thought that by saying this to me in front of the family, one or all of them would rally around to show up the Catholic side, but no such thing occurred. Mrs. Briggs was to keep Roy and Lucius (by repeating the names, she hoped to make them familiar) while their father and Beatrice were on their wedding trip. After they were married, they were to drive to Birmingham, where they would spend the first night at the Tutwiler Hotel. The day after, they would go by train to New York City, to stay at the Commodore Hotel on East Forty-second Street for a week, returning to Birmingham by train, claiming Harvey's car from the garage where he'd leave it, and so come home to Montgomery.

Nothing she said to me was acknowledged by them. They kept their utterances to each other and with uncustomary courtesy begged each other to forgive them for the trouble of passing the biscuits, or the butter, or the chowchow. One night as we were undressing for bed, Roland asked me what kind of car Harvey had, and when I said it was a Buick, he said acidly, "Of course."

Beatrice bought clothes and brought them home, but when she asked if anyone wanted to see them, she was left unanswered. I was, however, able to report to her that on two evenings when she was out with Harvey after work, her mother and Mrs. Watson had slipped into her room and looked into the clothes closet. Beatrice said she knew someone had, for they'd left the sliding doors reversed.

In the event, Uncle Grady was drunk, and Aunt Belle said her duty was to stay at home with her husband. Roland refused to go on the ground of political conscience, although his political conscience had lain fairly dormant since the death of Huey Long. I went and stood up with Harvey Brigg's junior partner at the preacher's house where the wedding ceremony was held, and when it was over, I kissed Beatrice and shook hands with Harvey, and cried going home on the bus by myself.

As soon as the thing was done, everyone came to life again. I was scolded as a traitor and conspirator but questioned closely. Every detail I divulged was criticized. Neighbors gathered to be given news. The couple was even blamed for not having run away to be married. It was declared that Beatrice might have spared her mother the knowledge of a quiet wedding in Montgomery. It was said that he married her to have a mother for his sons, a keeper for his house, a comfort for his body—as if these motives, had they been the sole truth, were reprehensible. It was said that she married him because she wanted to leave home (as did all ungrateful girls), because she was tired of working and thought him rich, because (most charitable) she "knew no better." They would not see and could not accept that "cold" Beatrice, who had never had a boyfriend, and "old" Harvey loved each other. To do so would have been to acknowledge the lack of love in their own lives. They were not apes or ogres; they were ordinary, and that is the best and the worst to be said of them.

25

BEATRICE WROTE me a postcard every day she was in New York. The first had a picture of the Empire State Building and was delivered on Wednesday. Subsequent ones showed a street corner in Chinatown, the Statue of Liberty with a ferry in the foreground on its way to Staten Island, the new ocean liner *Queen Mary,* Times Square, and—I hoped she meant it wickedly but learned later that it was merely one of a packet she'd bought—St. Patrick's Cathedral. The messages were brief and not very informative. "Saw a play." (I longed to know which and phoned Marshall; we speculated.) "Harvey made me go to the top and I'm glad I guess." (This, written on the one of the Empire State Building.) "It's fun to eat in restaurants when you don't have to wait on tables, but I think of poor Ethel's feet!" (I was pleased with the abandon suggested by the exclamation point.)

When they returned on Monday, she telephoned and talked briefly with her mother, and on Tuesday evening she and Harvey came for their first visit. It was not yet dark, but we'd finished supper, and I'd washed the dishes. I was just joining the family on the porch, where everyone sat for coolness and news of neighbors during the summer months, when the Buick stopped in front of the house. For a moment nothing more happened. Every eye on the porch, and neighboring porches too, was on them as Harvey got out of the car. Beatrice let herself out on the other side before he could reach her, but he helped her with packages she took from the back seat. I was glad to see that he was wearing an open collar and no jacket, for it made him look younger; and it was the first time any of them had seen him.

Greetings and introductions were nervous. Uncle Grady suggested that we go indoors. There followed polite but awkward exchanges about the train trip and the weather in New York, and Beatrice handed each of us a present. For Aunt Belle there was a hat. Beatrice told her it came from a store called Saks. Holding it up from the inside and turning it, her mother wondered where she would wear it. Beatrice answered, "Church." Aunt Belle said, "Too cheery." Beatrice said, "Not for a wedding," and Aunt Belle flushed. Also from Saks there was a silk necktie and matching handkerchief for Uncle Grady, which Beatrice said Harvey had helped choose. The billfold for Roland came from Macy's Department Store, as did the Sheaffer fountain pen I was given. I thanked them so profusely the others were forced to murmur their own polite acceptances. Roland unbent enough to ask Harvey how many miles to a gallon the Buick got, which Harvey answered in more detail than anyone could have appreciated except the manufacturer. A quarter of an hour passed, and they got up to go, saying they hoped we would come-see them soon.

Uncle Grady had sobered up and gone back to work two days after Beatrice married. With school out, I was working full time in the warehouse with Clive Johnson; and Roland, with Mrs. Bush in attendance, managed the office. Roland may have known more about food brokerage than did his father, but he was not a salesman, and during Uncle Grady's absences the volume of business was always smaller. One day, accompanying my uncle, I heard one of the storekeepers explain it: "It's not your boy don't work hard or come to take my order; but you look around and see what I need before I can tell you, and Roland expects me to have a list waiting so he can get on to the next store."

Mrs. Bush, soul of virtue and ineptitude, had taken it into her head to have a real vacation, going by Greyhound bus all the way to a town called Maryville in Tennessee to visit her newly widowed sister, Mrs. Minnie Whipple. Ordinarily, she took her vacation in odd days and was little missed. This year she was to enjoy her two weeks all at once and, in addition, take another week unpaid, making it, she told us, "the trip of a lifetime." To do without her for such a span was, Uncle Grady declared, bad enough; to replace her, impossible; but we must have someone for the weeks she'd be gone, if only to answer the phone and write down messages. That is how Georgette Heaven Beasley came into our lives.

There were not many applicants for the job. Mrs. Bush, who interviewed them, chose Georgette because she "looked steady," explaining that she wore glasses and new stockings and a dress with white collar and cuffs. She had finished "a secretarial course," but not held a job; she was a high school graduate from the nearby town of Prattville, and lived in Montgomery's YWCA.

I didn't meet her until she came in on Mrs. Bush's last day to have the office routine, such as it was, explained to her. I should like to have heard that, but my work was almost entirely in the warehouse. However, I contrived to need an order pad and went to the office for it, discovering Georgette with Roland and Mrs. Bush. Uncle Grady was out making calls on customers. Neither Roland nor Mrs. Bush paid any attention to me until they became aware that Georgette was no longer listening to them, but staring at me with a questioning frown. I was introduced, or rather, she was told who I was. She offered her hand hesitantly and withdrew it when I showed her mine was dirty. I said I was glad to meet her, found the order pad, and as I went out heard Roland explaining me. "Orphan cousin, lives with us. We give him work when he's not in school."

"Since then," as I told Beatrice, "every time I have to go in the office for anything, she looks at me as if I was a stray dog that wandered in off the street. One day she picked up the flyswatter. Do I have B.O.? Halitosis? Still a few pimples, but they're fading, aren't they?"

"How soon did you know she was after Roland?"

"The day after Mrs. Bush left."

"What did she do?"

"It was more how *he* behaved. Helpful and understanding. Hero of the working girl. He even told her the toilet Uncle Grady put in last winter was all hers and we'd use the filling station. Uncle Grady got mad when he found out and said he wasn't going to any filling station and didn't understand why he had to, when Mrs. Bush had never complained about sharing and there was a latch inside. Roland explained that Georgette was an innocent girl and finally got him to promise to pee in a bucket in the warehouse and do the other at home."

We laughed.

It was my first private visit with Beatrice at her and Harvey's house and the second Wednesday afternoon they'd been back from the honeymoon. Some grocery stores closed half a day Wednesdays during the summer, so we did too, the middle of the week being a slack time anyhow. Harvey was at his office, catching up on work he'd missed while he was away, and the two boys had ridden their bicycles to the swimming pool farther out on Narrow Lane Road. We had the place to ourselves, and she showed me all over before we settled in canvas chairs under the trees with a pitcher of iced tea, a jar of peanut butter and saltine crackers. I was to stay for supper.

Our exchanges were frank.

"How are you eating?"

"Terrible. I help in the kitchen when I can, but I haven't had to cook since Savannah, and you forget how if you don't do it regular." She nodded agreement. "Your mama said right after you left she was 'determined to make every effort,' but she'll put something on the stove and forget, or she'll take it up too soon, having forgot to put it on in time for a meal. Everything's mushy or raw. Sometimes a neighbor lends a hand. We don't have breakfast at home any more, except coffee. Roland and Uncle Grady eat at that diner near the office, and I buy a quart of milk and half a dozen sweet rolls to have in the warehouse. How do you get on with the boys?"

"Their grandma comes and gets them sometimes for an afternoon so she can ask them about me. She's sweet as honey *to* me but talks about me behind my back; and she's taken to phoning some evenings to talk to them. Roy's the youngest, and he's all right, loves banana pudding just the way you do." (I felt a twinge of jealousy.) "Lucius is sly. Sometimes I feel like snatching that old woman baldheaded, she makes me so mad, but I've kept my temper so far. If she left them alone, they'd be all right."

"What about you and Eulabelle?" Eulabelle was the Negro woman who'd kept house for Harvey between his marriages. She had been hired by his mother.

Beatrice was frowning. "Well, I never had to boss a Negro before, and I don't know how. She's lazy like all of them, and she'll sass if you let her; but she likes the fact that I do all the cooking. Oh, she brags on me for my cooking—you ought to hear her, trying to flatter me into being easy. She cleans pretty well, but when I ask her to do things *my* way, she acts ugly. The day I showed her the proper way to tuck sheets, she went around with her lips stuck out in a pout until I bragged on *her* way of polishing the staircase. Since then we've got along pretty well, but I have to watch her when she leaves. She carries a paper sack. They all think it's their right and privilege, you know, but Eulabelle can get half the kitchen in that sack she carries, and more than once she's taken something I've made special for our supper. She generally leaves after she's done the noon dishes. Harvey comes home for his dinner now!" She was smiling as she said that, but as she sat thinking, she frowned again. "Harvey pays her *ten dollars a week!* Of course, no Negro is worth that, and I'm determined to make her work for it, I can tell you."

"How are your neighbors?"

"None close enough to be a nuisance, thank goodness. I hated that forever-dropping-in on Morgan Avenue, and they all knew it."

In the same tone I'd asked the other questions I said, "How's Harvey?"

"Perfect." She looked at me intently and went on in contained outrage. "I don't think he's ever known a woman, including his mother, who didn't take advantage of him. Well, they won't any more." I knew enough not to tease her then. "Tell me more about Georgette. Is she really named 'Heaven' in the middle?"

"Just like one of Father Divine's angels. Roland says it's an old family name."

"Why does she use it? You don't have to use a middle name."

"She's proud of it."

"Oh me, oh my."

Roy and Lucius, racing to show off, rode their bicycles down the driveway and circled back to the house out of sight. A few minutes later they joined us, wanting peanut butter and crackers and asking for Coca-Cola instead of iced tea. The ice had melted anyway. Beatrice got up. "Come on to the kitchen."

"What are you going to cook, Beatrice?" Roy begged to know.

"Help Mark with those things," she said. "You've both got eyes as red as bats. You must have stayed in the water too long."

"Roy sneaked up behind me and ducked me," Lucius said.

Roy countered with, "Only after he held me under so long I was like to choke."

"Did you rinse out your bathing suits and hang them to dry?"

"Yes," Lucius said with bored patience.

Beatrice handed them empty glasses, spoons, knives, and sugar bowl. They straggled after us giggling, using their behinds to bump and impede each other because their hands were full.

Harvey found us in the kitchen an hour later. Beatrice had started supper, and I stood in the doorway to the dining room talking and watching her work, as I'd done so many times on Morgan Avenue. But when she heard the side door slam and he called, "Where are you?" she left what she was doing and went running. The boys looked at each other self-consciously, and I asked when they were going to camp, although Beatrice had already told me they were leaving on Sunday and would be away for three weeks.

She chose the first week they were absent to have the Benedicts out for supper. It was the first time any of them had been to Harvey's house. I was at the age to be bored by all formal family visits, but that one was worse than most. It came about because Aunt Belle told Beatrice she'd like to have her and Harvey over for supper but was shy about cooking a meal for him until she had more practice. So, Beatrice promptly asked them, still hoping to create a semblance of family unity. Knowing Harvey would need her more beside him than in the kitchen, she paid Eulabelle an extra dollar to stay late to serve the table and clean up in the kitchen, although she herself had done all the preparation ahead of time.

Everyone behaved nicey-nice, no one saying what he thought and endeavoring to hide what he felt by wearing a fixed smile. Aunt Belle said it was so quiet "out here" she couldn't hear herself think and wondered how anybody could get to sleep with the sound of those crickets. She also deplored the lack of close neighbors and speculated on what would happen if Beatrice got sick suddenly and needed help or a doctor and the telephone was out of order, or she couldn't get to it somehow. Uncle Grady asked if they got a lot of mosquitoes from the artificial lake. Roland fidgeted, mostly silent, but once in a while he'd make a statement. "If they keep on building out this way, you'll make a big profit selling off some of this land by cutting it up into lots."

The size and comfort of the house were ignored, as if to speak of them would betray social inferiority. When Eulabelle served the meal—a custom never followed at home, where everything was set on the table to be passed—Aunt Belle observed that having a maid do the passing reminded her of when she was a girl in Savannah. Since she had not been trained to ignore general conversation, Eulabelle replied, "Yes'm. You make me remember what it was like when I was a girl myself."

Poor Harvey couldn't do anything right and knew it. As host he could not be quiet lest he be considered proud and superior; yet everything he said was being construed as boast or another kind of pride. The only successful ingredient of the evening was Beatrice's cooking, and that had the effect of reminding her brother and parents that they were now deprived of it except for such an occasion as this.

A direct result of the event, I always believed, was that the next night Roland came home at ten o'clock from his date with Georgette to say he had asked her to marry him and what did they think of that?

It didn't occur to any of us that she might have refused, so Uncle Grady said, "Fine! Now can I use my own toilet again?"

26

IF BEATRICE's marriage had been the occasion for hands upped in horror, it was soon evident that Roland's was to be one of smiling benedictions. The principal actors may have lacked the romantic dimension, but their drama made a direct appeal to all who knew of it: small-town girl with first job marries boss's son after whirlwind courtship.

Marshall asked me what she was like.

"A tough ZaSu Pitts."

"And he looks like a cattle rustler in a Republic picture, the first one they catch and hang."

"Right casting would be Loretta Young and Robert Taylor."

"*C'est la vie.*"

"You said it."

Marshall had his first job that summer too, but without a hope, as he pointed out, of marrying the boss's daughter, a spinster of thirty-seven whose clothes were more manly than those of her father. He was part-time clerk in a store selling menswear, working two afternoons a week and all day Saturdays. He never drew a penny of his wages and, indeed, finished the summer in debt to his employer, a chirpy old dandy who encouraged his greed for yet more shirts with French cuffs and pleated bosoms. Marshall's mother declared that it was "all good experience," without specifying for whom.

Summers tended to be lost months for both Marshall and me. It was hot; a banner outside the Paramount Theatre boasted: *20 degrees cooler inside.* We had nowhere to go and nothing to look forward to before the resumption of school in September. Sylvia was spending July and August with an aunt near Asheville, North Carolina, she and Marshall keeping their love affair alive by daily letters so intense, he told me, they would make Greta Garbo and Clark Gable look like loafers. I had no one even to imagine myself in love with, so I imagined myself in love with a girl who died and wrote a dozen sonnets using the Shakespearean rhyme scheme and ringing no new changes on bravery and heartbreak. Body and soul, I hungered for a great passion, scorning the scraps that fell from my cousins' tables.

Roland would have married almost anyone that summer, I think. He had been affronted more by Beatrice's marrying before him than by her choice. If Georgette Heaven Beasley had not been ready at hand, it would have been another. It was time for Roland to marry; it was the next thing to do. He might have been without will, so easily did he acquiesce to destiny.

Georgette was made one of the family, Aunt Belle welcoming her with all the warmth that had been missing in her reception of a son-in-law. That Georgette showed herself eager to help in the kitchen did her no disservice. The neighbors met her and approved. There was nothing to envy in beauty or wit, and so she was pronounced "a fine girl" of the sort they hoped their sons would have sense enough to marry "eventually," for no mother was in a hurry to lose a son, although daughters might do as they pleased as long as they did not marry Catholics or Jews. No one quoted the old saw "Change the name and not the letter, change for worse and not for better."

I did not question that Georgette was a girl of some sense. She kept herself neat, made herself pleasant, and appeared ambitious of nothing more than to fit into her sweetheart's hopes and dreams. Her mother and father and younger sister made the trip from Prattville to meet Aunt Belle and Uncle Grady, who, the following week, returned the compliment by driving to Prattville one evening for supper. (I was excused. On their visit to Morgan Avenue, when Mrs. Beasley simperingly observed that Georgette's secretarial course looked like a dead loss, I said, "Not if she makes a young widow.")

Everything was arranged quickly and sensibly. The wedding would be in the second week of August at the Methodist church in Prattville. Georgette's sister gave a bridal-shower tea the last week in July. After the wedding the couple was to spend three days in Birmingham, returning to live at the house on Morgan Avenue. There was no question of their having their own house or apartment. Aunt Belle urged them to live "at home with us," and Roland couldn't have afforded anything else. I had already shifted to Beatrice's smaller room, and they were to have Roland's room, but everything would be new. Uncle Grady handsomely offered to pay for their choice of "a complete bedroom suite" at Haverty's August furniture sale: double bed, dresser, chest of drawers, vanity table and bench. Georgette declared herself overwhelmed. Aunt Belle begged her to feel at home, "For this is your home from now on," and to treat the kitchen as her own.

Georgette's attitude toward me, insofar as she revealed it, was one of wait-and-see. I once heard her describe me as "in the family but not immediate," with which I could not quarrel. She was shrewd enough to see that although I got along with Aunt Belle and Uncle Grady and was even a favorite with Beatrice, no strong tie existed between Roland and me. The fact that I was male seemed to her a vague threat. I was vain enough to want to assure her she had nothing to fear but had the gumption to keep myself to myself.

Roland was as happy as Roland could be. He was a man, he was busy, and suddenly he had a future. Mrs. Bush had been amazed at events when she returned from her sister's in Tennessee. For an hour she looked nettled, as if she might receive blame for what had transpired in her absence, but as soon as it was clear that everyone rejoiced in happy prospects, she lapsed again into absentmindedness. Georgette was to stay on for a week after Mrs. Bush's return, "until she got her bearings," and I began to notice the small ways in which the younger woman patronized the older and the older accepted it. Roland was bold in the assumption that marriage enhanced his consequence in the business, which he no longer referred to as his father's but as "the family business."

The happy day came. The sun shone on the bride, as it did on all of us. The many photographs taken show faces shiny with sweat, eyes squinting as if into a hundred suns, clothes hanging limp as Spanish moss. There was no reception. Georgette's wedding dress was suitable for travel, and the married pair left for Birmingham immediately after pictures were taken on the steps. Beatrice and Harvey were present; I sat with them in the pew behind Aunt Belle and Uncle Grady. The gathering was small. It was what they called "a quiet church wedding," hence no bridal gown and no attendants. When we went home, Aunt Belle said as if she thought she ought to say something of the kind, "The empty nest."

Looking at me, Uncle Grady corrected her. "Not quite."

I lay awake a long time after I turned out the light, hearing Uncle Grady in the next room go through his first siege of snoring slumber, aware of a door opening and closing as Aunt Belle crept out to the kitchen to make a pot of coffee. It was, I told myself, the breaking up of my second family. Thinking of Roland and Georgette in Birmingham and of Beatrice and Harvey on Narrow Lane Road, I shifted uncomfortably, remembering Uncle Grady's first complaint in Savannah the night my mother died that if they took me in, they'd have to keep me until I was grown.

27

ALTHOUGH OF intense local interest, the love stories of Beatrice and Roland enjoyed warm competition from that of Edward Windsor and Wallis Warfield Simpson during the summer of 1936, the latter providing infinite discussion to chair rockers and fern waterers on hundreds of porches. And when school opened, even the most scornful of democrats had a gracious joke about the royal romance, the only demur being, "But they're both so *old*."

Of more immediate concern to me was a girl named Judith Cohen in my history class. Although I had known her slightly the year before, I'd taken little notice of her. However, summer had ripened her figure while thinning the plumpness from her cheeks. I decided that her black hair and dark eyes were like a Gypsy's, and when she returned my lingering glance, I made up my mind to be in love with her. For a week I enjoyed merely looking at her in the new eager way, and then I approached and asked if she'd go to a movie with me on Saturday night. She said yes.

It would be my first real date. A number of times I had escorted Celia Cantwell or Posy Valentine to and from a party, but group affairs didn't count. I was now to be one boy with one girl. I thought about it during the intervening days, settling what I was to wear, trying on ties and smiles in front of the mirror. I knew where Judith lived and discovered the easiest bus route to use. But on Friday, Judith looked ill and was certainly ill at ease when I spoke to her. Feeling uncertainties of my own, I put it down to shyness and left her alone. At lunchtime, however, she found me and without preamble exclaimed, "I can't go!"

I took a moment to register what she'd said. "You mean you don't want to?"

"I do, but I can't."

"I was looking forward to it."

"You have a right to know why."

I wasn't sure I wanted to. "We can do it some other time."

"My father wouldn't let me."

"You mean he doesn't want you to date yet? Most girls your age are dating."

"It isn't that. It's you."

I was instantly angry. "He doesn't know me!"

"It's because you're not Jewish." Beginning to cry, she turned and ran away.

Marshall, who had been watching us, joined me immediately. "What'd you say to Judith to make her cry?"

"I'm not Jewish," I said, still astonished at what she had revealed.

"You mean you've got a dirty foreskin?" he said in mock horror. "Disgusting! Police!"

I explained what had happened, and he listened quietly, not even complaining that I hadn't confided in him. "I'll go to the movie with you if you pay."

"You'll go if I don't, but not on Saturday night." It was by then a settled thing that he went to Sylvia's apartment every Saturday night. "Why don't you ever take Sylvia anywhere except parties? Are you still in debt for all your new shirts?"

"Her father likes her to stay home, so we stay home, or at most walk around the block if it's a hot night."

"You mean he stands guard?"

"Usually he isn't even there, just the housekeeper, but he's got the idea she's safe at home."

144

"What do you and Sylvia do, just talk?"

"We talk," he hedged, "but not all the time." He hesitated, and then continued. "We hug and kiss. We've done everything except *it*. I can put my hand under her dress up top but not down below.—That's a lie. I put my hands everywhere and so does she. I go crazy, but I'm a gentleman."

"What does that mean?"

"It means I'm a man of honor. I don't take advantage of her."

"Oh."

On Saturday night I stayed at home and reread the parts of *Ivanhoe* having to do with Rebecca. I had never felt anything about Jews. I knew they had their own holidays and practices which the majority of people looked upon as foreign. I knew they had their own religious and social organizations, including a country club. I'd heard it said all my life that they stuck together, but yesterday's was my first experience of being excluded by them. I found nothing in Scott to soothe my hurt pride. The only Jews I knew were a few storekeepers and some boys and girls in school. Only two of these stood out, a girl named Esther because she made the best grades, and a boy named Morris who was always bragging about how much money his father had. If Morris saw you unwrapping a candy bar, he wanted it and he'd say, "If you'll give me that, I'll bring you six tomorrow." And he would. Naturally, no one liked him, but not because he was a Jew.

As for Esther, we'd got over resenting her and were proud of her. All the teachers said she would go far, and we accepted their belief in her without jealousy. Judith was the first Jew to mean anything to me. For an hour or so I brooded over the possibility of our being star-crossed lovers, but finally admitted that what I felt would not bear the weight of such a supposition. I liked Judith because she was pretty and because she liked me. It went no deeper than that. But she had cried, I remembered with satisfaction, until I reminded myself that Judith laughed or cried over almost everything. To be indifferent was not in her. She even loved the serfs and hated the nobles when Miss Mathews, to illustrate a point in history, divided the class into two categories, and I turned out to be one of the serfs and Morris one of the nobles.

Another shock yesterday had been what Marshall told me, and it was more profound. I'd never considered that being in love had anything to do with sexual desire. I understood that it must have, but I didn't know it from experience. Although I respected Marshall's love for Sylvia as pure and true, because he was my friend, I was also aware of his sexual feelings from his constant reference to them. This is what troubled me: his lust always had a tangible, immediate object, and mine did not. I couldn't doubt that Marshall was normal, for his feelings were shared by the many, so I must doubt myself. What else was all the laughter about in movies when the wind blew up a woman's skirt? Why else did men behave (or pretend to?) so puppy-doggy when a pretty girl went wiggling by? We couldn't even stroll past the brassiere counter at Woolworth's without Marshall's rolling his eyes and panting. Something had been left out of me; I didn't feel that way; and that was why I had never been in love, only wanted to be. That was why poems about love meant nothing to me unless they were also about death—or, at the very least, denial and loss.

During the summer I had often gone to the public swimming pool on Bell Street. I went alone because Marshall refused to bare his body in public and couldn't swim anyway, and there I became friendly with a girl named Pearl who lived farther out on Bell Street in the poor section of Montgomery called the West End. Pearl was no beauty, but her apparent availability attracted boys of all ages, and I became one of the pack that surrounded her. The idea of Pearl's rumored earthiness emboldened me one day to follow her as she left the pool after dressing. (When she put her clothes on, "Pearl's pack," as we were known, melted away.) She saw me and invited me to walk with her. Brave with desperation, I found myself bluntly telling her I'd never been with a girl and that I "needed some" in the worst way. Pearl was kind. Thoughtfully, she sympathized. But when I asked, "Will you let me?" she shook her head. "I like you, but I don't want to." She said it simply but with finality.

The week before school began, Marshall and his mother had visited a sister of hers in the Gulf town of Pascagoula, and when Marshall returned, he brought certain trophies he'd bought from an older cousin. One was a handwritten copy of a story I later discovered to be something of a porno-graphic classic entitled "Only a Boy." The other was a dirty comic book using the familiar characters of Maggie and Jiggs in a series of explicit if crudely drawn positions of sexual conjunction. Both these items excited me so that merely thinking about them later roused me sexually. Surely that made me normal, I reasoned. The memory of the story and the crude cartoons was aphrodisiac; yet the idea made flesh was not. I could not follow the transition. I was ashamed and doubted myself; and yet I do not think I was very different, if different at all, from other boys.

After school I sometimes, if I was not with Marshall or working at the warehouse, went for long walks by myself. The walks were not for exploration. Montgomery was not large enough to provide that, and I knew what there was to know of it from riding his rounds with Uncle Grady. I walked for the movement itself, not liking games and never trained to them, and my mind ranged free. I pondered my reading, which was vast and varied, more discriminating now than it had been but not restricted. I would try to read anything, and my curiosity usually led me to finish it, however little it meant to me. I also thought out ideas for stories and plays and poems of my own, stealing outrageously and unselfcon-sciously from what had most recently impressed me in my reading.

One of my favorite areas for walking was the Negro section called Day Street, although that wide, straight thoroughfare only gave it a name without defining or limiting it. There were many lanes and alleys off and around it that I found interesting to wander.

Late in the day there was the smoke of wood fires or charcoal and the smell of frying meat and boiling vegetables. Children ran and played. Old men and women stood talking and watching. Clothes flapped on lines in many of the yards I passed, giving a clean, starchy scent to the air; for a number of the women "took in washing." Dogs trotted about, polite and unthreatening, for they depended for food on the kindness of people too poor to provide garbage for forage.

On such a walk one day in October I paused at the end of a lane, surprised to discover there was no way through. There was a shack at the dead end that looked to be deserted, but as I hesitated, a female voice called softly, "Hey!" Seeing no one, I went closer. A door swung open, and I moved cautiously to it. It was late afternoon, not yet dark. An ordinary-looking Negro girl, older than I, stood watching me from inside. When I saw her, she said, "You looking for pussy, white boy?"

Dumbly, I nodded.

"Slip in here quick."

I did as she said and we stood facing.

"How much you got?"

Reaching into my pocket, I brought out my change. "Sixty cents."

"You give me fifty."

I counted the coins into her hand, and she quickly knotted them into a dirty handkerchief she took from her cloth belt. Dropping belt and handkerchief behind her, she lifted her dress over her head and dropped it too. When I made no move, she said, "Well, ain't you?"

I unbuttoned myself and she took my penis in her hand. I didn't want to touch her, or know how; but when she began to pump me, I moved closer and she pushed the head of my penis between her legs but without making entry. I came, and she pushed me aside to drip on the bare wooden floor. Then as quickly as she had removed it, she put her dress on and fastened the belt, leaving without speaking again or looking at me.

28

THERE WERE successes to set against these failures. It was pleasant to be president of the Ushers Club and preside over its monthly meetings, to choose teams of ushers for such plays and concerts as were taking place. Ethel Barrymore was touring in Maugham's *The Constant Wife;* Tallulah Bankhead —"Montgomery's Own," the *Advertiser* claimed—would bring George Kelly's *Reflected Glory;* and concert events included recitals by Helen Jepson, the Metropolitan Opera star, and Fritz Kreisler, and the Ballet Russe de Monte Carlo. Twenty to thirty ushers were used for each event, and there was competition to be chosen for the more popular attractions. I superintended the downstairs seating, and Marshall was in charge of the balcony ushers. Members seldom used the club room that had been assigned to us, so it became a private lounge and book locker Marshall and I shared. I continued to get high marks in the subjects I cared about, although I was not one of the four or five top students (led by Esther). I enjoyed the company of old acquaintances, the loyalty of Celia, the jokey friendship of Posy. I found time to write almost as much as I read, aimlessly prodigal.

Marshall flourished as the confirmed star of the speech department. It was a rare assembly to which he did not read the announcements, or a monologue (sometimes written by me), or perform in a short skit or one-act play. He was popular; laughter greeted his every appearance on stage. He never played the violin publicly, and his mother grieved about it, waiting for him to change his mind. But success did not satisfy Marshall; he wanted to be the complete Renaissance man. We bought *Life* magazine each week, finding it both exciting and inciting. For Marshall to read about the young Orson Welles, then achieving fame in New York as producer, actor, and director, made him want to out-Welles Welles. He would do everything Noel Coward did, but better, for Coward by then carried the taint of acceptance. There was another side to his ambition: if I did something, he wanted to do it too. I wrote; therefore, he would write.

"I'm going to be a writer-director-actor, but for movies, not the stage. With Broadway"—a hand gesture swept aside the years of getting there—"you get bogged down in a year's run. With movies you do one after another. I may do the musical backgrounds too. With my training it will be easy, and it's really part of the editing process. Listen: picture a long corridor, empty. Sunlight filters through dirty glass windows. Two nuns appear, don't talk to each other, walk purposefully toward a door at the end, whisper a moment—we don't hear what—open the door into a large room in which there's nothing but an old upright piano, like the one my mother uses for teaching. They open the piano, look around nervously, sit side by side on the bench, hands in the air like they're dripping with blood. Then!—they begin to play 'Chopsticks.'" He collapsed with laughter over a scarred old desk in the club room.

"What happens next?" I said politely.

He stopped laughing and scowled at me. "You've no imagination, no soul. Listen again: scene opens with a woman ringing a doorbell."

"House or apartment?"

"Apartment," he decided.

"Where?"

"You're not to know—yet! Rings again. No answer. Pushes door, finds it unlatched, goes in. We follow, camera on her back. Sound of a shower bath. She calls a name, but we don't understand what it is because of the running water. Phone suddenly rings, very loud, camera on phone, big. She hesitates. Man's voice from shower: 'Answer it!' "

"How does he know she's there?"

"She picks up the phone and says hello."

He paused, waiting for invention to catch up. I filled in with one of our old jokes. "Instead of 'Yes, this is the Paragon Laundry, and we do wash paragons.' "

"Just shut up. Over the phone there's a shot—"

"It's all sound effects: doorbell, creaking door, shower bath, phone ringing, gunshot—"

"Do you like it?"

"I think it needs work."

He snapped his fingers. "I could think of enough things before ten o'clock every morning to keep all the studios of Hollywood humming for a year."

"Back to this woman who comes in," I said. "Has she got big titties?"

He considered. "One is the size of a chinaberry, the other more like a volley ball."

"What are you doing in Friday's assembly?"

"Haven't decided."

"You can't read Poe's 'Bells' again—you've done it twice."

"Ignorant turds," he said, remembering what had happened the second reading. "Chiming in when I got to 'the bells, bells, bells, bells, bells, bells, bells!' "

"The good thing about movie audiences is, if they talk back to you, you're not there to hear them."

"Phooey."

"There goes the bell for our next class. The bell, bell, bell, bell, bell, bell, bell—"

He hit me on the back with a book as I ran out ahead of

him. "You're never late for *this* class, are you? Teacher's pet! Teacher's pet!"

We were on our way to Miss Torrence's English class. It was the only one of several classes we shared in which we forgot each other—or rather, I forgot Marshall in my absorption with whatever Miss Torrence was saying or reading. He admitted her genius but remained heart-whole.

Margaret Torrence taught eleventh-grade English. It was not a survey course and ranged over both English and American literature. The first semester concentrated on the Prologue of *Canterbury Tales,* Emerson, Hawthorne, and Melville, with brief readings of lesser writers. The long set piece of the second semester would be *Macbeth,* with time for Dickinson, Whitman, Poe, and Kipling, and an end-of-term sampling of "moderns" such as Sandburg, Millay, Lindsay, and Frost. Past forty now, Miss Torrence was careless of her person in a way that no one who admired her considered important. A shoulder strap of her slip might have broken and been pinned instead of mended. She wore no cosmetic except face powder, and that only when she thought of it, usually applying so much so absently that her face was like a clown's mask, emphasizing the stark, intense eyes which could be as disconcerting as an owl's. She was feared by many of her students because she was impatient of slowness and intolerant of pretense and dishonesty. Nothing was important to her except the subject under discussion, and although it was mainly literature, a question or comment from the class might lead her into remarks on the theatre, music, morals, manners—anything.

She talked of politics as if it was a normal interest, not part of a subject called civics. There was about her face a haunted, listening look, even when she was speaking, such as one sees sometimes in photographs of actresses of an earlier age in scenes from Ibsen's plays. It was said that she had in her youth given brilliant performances in plays at the Little

Theatre, that she'd stopped acting because of the nervous strain.

Her voice was clear and deep. She sat at her desk most of the time, but when she left it, she moved with assurance and control, like a dancer you know will not fail at a crucial moment of performance. Although she did not, of course, smoke in the sight of students, her fingers bore strong stains of nicotine, and if you stood close, her coarse hair, which was black but going gray, smelled of tobacco. She was not a popular teacher except, oddly, with other teachers, who stood in some awe of her, and a few of the stronger students, usually female, who vied for the front desks from which to worship her. She ignored them. She had no pets, in spite of what Marshall had said.

But from the moment of the first day's encounter (I had not known her the year before when Lanier was the new school, vast and unknowable) we had recognized each other. I knew instantly that what she was, was what my life had to be about, that we were kin. Uncertainties fell away when I looked at her and listened to her. I felt that everything she said, she said to me; and I knew this before we ever spoke privately. It was nothing like my old friendship with Mrs. Noble, that good woman who had first led me out of darkness.

I still went to see Mrs. Noble, but the visits were hardly more than ceremonies. I seldom showed her new work, because I didn't want to offend her. I had abandoned earlier subjects and begun to write about whores and murderers without knowing any, and about youth betrayed into war, a subject I anticipated knowing soon enough. History has been rewritten, as always happens, and we are supposed then to have been innocent and isolationist. I don't remember it that way. Everyone believed there would be a big war and that we'd be in it; the only question was when, for we were still living through the Depression and it was hard to imagine ourselves involved in two crises at the same time. Having grown up with pacifism the common doctrine, I was not ready for bayonet drill, no matter the cause. Wanting to blame someone, I blamed the older generation, as we always do until we become the older generation. So, for her sake and mine, I kept my new self to myself when I saw Mrs. Noble. Furthermore, in the brutal way of the young, I knew she had given me as much as she could and was no further use to me; Miss Torrence was the new light.

Miss Torrence gave her opinions without hesitation and usually without qualification, but she never seemed arrogant to me, because I knew she had worried and weighed a thing before making up her mind about it. Nor did I see in her honesty any intention of currying favor with her students. It would not have occurred to her to do so. But because they were not used to candor in their elders and did not like it unless they could guess the motive, many of them resented her.

On all subjects I came to value her opinions more than anyone else's. It was not a matter of hero worship, for I did not set her views above my own if they differed. Although I did not feel for her the personal affection I had for Mrs. Noble (something in her would not have allowed it), still I was concerned when she was out of school with one of her long headaches, as she sometimes was for a couple of days. There was never rumor or mystery about those absences; the reason was stated frankly and accepted, the principal being a man of understanding in spite of his reputation for coldness.

I knew, as did everyone else, that Miss Torrence owned a house on Cloverdale Road left by her father when he died. There was said to be a full-time housekeeper who lived in, which was rare in our society. Two other teachers lived there as friends and shared the expenses of the household. Miss Bartley and Miss Friede were older than Miss Torrence. Having learned where the house was, I walked past it and decided that it was old-fashioned and rather ugly. Its trees and shrubberies were kept thick to shade its porches and grounds from the summer sun, so the place had a somber, secret appearance. I wondered if behind the doors and walls and curtained windows they were lonely or companionable, four women together.

One week in late November, Miss Torrence was out of school both Thursday and Friday. With nothing to do on Saturday night and her on my mind, I took a bus after supper to Cloverdale. Leaving it at Fairview Avenue, I walked back along winding Cloverdale Road to the house. There was no night light on the front porch as there was on most of the houses, but light showed at one upstairs window and from another downstairs at the back of the house. I stared for a time without conjuring up any further sign of life. There was only the sound of the dark, towering pine trees as they moved in the early winter wind, although now and then a car passed as slow and silent as a hearse. Shivering, I turned up the collar of my heavy sweater and walked on. At the next bend of the road I came face to face with Margaret Torrence. A dog was with her. They both stopped, staring at me.

"Miss Torrence!" I managed. "Are you well again?"

Her face looked haggard under the streetlight. "Yes. Do you live nearby?"

"No ma'am." I felt myself blushing and was glad it was night and the light was dim.

Whether she was puzzled by my confusion or guessed the reason, she said, "My dog and I love our evening walks, but we are going home. Walk a little way with us." There were few sidewalks in that part of town, and we walked along the side of the road, the dog trotting ahead but often looking around at his mistress. "The headaches are a nuisance," she declared easily, as one might complain of a cut thumb. "Apparently there's nothing to do but endure them. I particularly resent them during the school year, because they put me behind, and I need more time, not less. What has the class done while I've been out?" I told her about the substitute teacher who had taken us through a Hawthorne story.

"I'll have to do it again," she said impatiently. "It's one of my favorites. If you understand that story, you'll understand Hawthorne; if you don't, you won't.—Do you know I never get one of my headaches when I'm teaching *Macbeth*? I'm sure it's the ham in me. I haven't told you my dog's name, have I? It's Spot."

"I hoped it would be Boris, or at least Prince," I protested. "I expected nothing as commonplace as Spot." We had reached the house. The dog sat at her feet, waiting for me to leave and for them to go in.

"I wanted to be able to say: 'Out, damned Spot.' "

I laughed joyously, enchanted by the revelation.

"It's silly."

"Of course it is!"

"Come in for a cup of tea."

I followed her and the dog along the path. A light was now on in what I supposed was the living room, but she paused at the top of the steps. "Listen." There was only the sound of the trees. "That's the most beautiful sound in the world, and I can't hear it when I'm ill."

I left before midnight. By then I had told her most of what I have put down in these pages, and she had listened without showing anything more than interest. She had told me a little about her father, whom she had loved, and her mother, whom she had not, both dead, and about her brother, two years her junior, who was a lieutenant in the Navy. She was proud of him and the record he'd made at Annapolis. He was married and stationed at Newport News, Virginia. She also talked about the war she was certain would come, scolding the French and British for their complaisance and railing against Mussolini and Hitler. "They are wicked men," she said, slapping the table in front of the sofa on which we sat together. "It's as plain as the nose on your face. Why won't they see they're not to be trusted? They will take us all into war again—war twice in my lifetime!"

Miss Friede and Miss Bartley came from their rooms to

have tea with us. The tray was brought in by the house-keeper, who was introduced as Aunt Sally. I guessed that it was the evening custom and Miss Friede and Miss Bartley resented my presence, but I was too happy to care. They left us before Aunt Sally took away the tea tray. There was a dying fire in the fireplace, and the dog slept before it on his belly with legs stretched fore and aft, jowls resting on paws. We talked and were silent, talked and were silent again.

"I should have gone long ago."

The dog roused himself when we moved and followed us, stretching and yawning, to the door. "Come and see me when you want to."

"I won't be a nuisance," I promised.

"I'll tell you if you are; friends don't have to bargain."

I knew the last bus had gone, but didn't mind the long walk home as I remembered things she had said—and things I'd said! Not even with Marshall was I able to talk so, without fear of being misunderstood. I thought of Marshall with Sylvia, or just leaving her, and felt no envy, only separation. The streets were quiet; the air was cold. I might have been the one living soul. Words I'd known all my life came back to me:

"And the earth was without form, and void; and darkness was upon the face of the deep. And the spirit of God moved upon the face of the waters. And God said, Let there be light: and there was light."

They sounded in my head without the pious shading I was used to hearing, and for the first time they held meaning for me. What would Miss Cranford have made of that? Laughing for myself alone, I began to run. To walk was not enough. I could not hold myself, drunk as I was on night and discovery.

29

It was as well that most of my life was now lived away from the house on Morgan Avenue, for it was possessed of a new spirit that there was no doubting would prevail over the old, not unhappy one of hopeful discontent. That spirit belonged to Georgette Heaven Benedict, the former Miss Beasley of Prattville. The eager girl we had waved on her honeymoon to the Tutwiler Hotel in Birmingham had, by the magic of love and its consummation, returned to her husband's family a sober matron. Roland too was more pensive than he had been, as if delight had not blinded him to the realization that he had met and made his match.

The back bedroom did not long contain them. Meeting no resistance, Georgette brought out the dime store china shepherdesses showered upon her at the bridal party sponsored by her sister. Setting them modestly here and there, she asked Aunt Belle if she minded, and when Aunt Belle answered, "No," she asked how she liked them. When Aunt Belle said they were pretty, there were more of them, more boldly placed; and older knickknacks were consigned to dismal little groupings at the ends of shelves and mantels, until they somehow fell off; and the bride's treasures enjoyed pride of place.

Never was housewife more willing to yield authority than Aunt Belle to her industrious daughter-in-law. Georgette was not a good cook, but she read the women's magazines and held opinions about nutrition. Seasonings were bad for us, and so meals became bland. We did not, it seemed, consume enough "roughage." Determined that we benefit from what she was pleased to call "fuller colonic irrigation," Georgette presented us with thin soups and raw vegetables. She discovered that meat was expensive and told us we ate too much of it. Portions shrank. Homemade biscuits and corn bread were greasy, as well as trouble to make, so we had sliced white bakery loaves. Cold breakfast cereals and an occasional soft-boiled egg were substituted for the fried meat and eggs with which Beatrice once poisoned our systems. Of the old kitchen customs, only Aunt Belle's endless coffee making survived, but it was she who now kept the pot hot and her cup filled.

No one had thought of Georgette as religious, but she asked Roland to buy a shelf radio for the kitchen where she spent so many hours on our behalf. As we fortified ourselves for the day with Shredded Wheat and raw egg, our souls were nourished by Georgette's favorite radio program, a Bible Hour her mother had taught her to love, its star a preacher of no stated denomination who exhorted us to be good and to send a contribution for "the vast work of saving souls yet to be done." Before and after his message, four sisters mournfully flagellated us with hymns.

Georgette's culinary reform did not stop with the aim of better nutrition; she wanted to be admired for refinement of presentation. To this end she found new ways of folding napkins and gave us "sculptured" dishes inspired, we were told, by one of her magazines. One supper showpiece was what Georgette called Candle Salad. Each of us had one beside his plate. The salad consisted of a ring of canned pineapple with half a banana set erect in its hole. The tip of banana was capped with a cherry and dotted with mayonnaise. Georgette held Roland's hand and rattled off a childhood prayer, as was her wont. I kept my eyes respectfully closed, but Uncle Grady evidently kept his on the salad. Suddenly his laughter broke over us like unexpected thunder. As we followed his gaze to the salads, realization came to Georgette. Pushing back her chair, she ran from the room, and ten minutes were required for Roland to persuade her to return, by which time Aunt Belle, slow to see the joke, had chopped up the banana and pineapple and mixed them together.

Aunt Belle's neighborhood friends who had been so keen to approve the new Mrs. Benedict were as quick to judge her and find her lacking. She was "country." (Prattville was a small town.) "Roland might have done better for himself if he'd looked closer to home." (This was said by mothers of unmarried daughters with an of-course-I-don't-care shrug.) When they stopped in casually in the old way, they were not offered Coca-Colas, and they might hardly settle themselves for an exchange of news and views before Georgette decided she must sweep or dust the room they were in, and they were shifted to another. If Aunt Belle voiced a mild protest, Georgette answered, "No ma'am; I have been lazy, and I promised myself I'd do it today." It was too cold now for porch sitting. When, as rarely happened, Aunt Belle thought to offer refreshment, there was no place to put it down. "Not on my new table!" Georgette would beg with a firm smile, but offer no alternative, so that the guest often sat with cup or glass in hand until she got up to go.

Georgette was partial to having things match, to buying what she called "suits," whether it was linens or utensils or furniture. Considering the unmatched pieces of the living room common, she induced Roland to "surprise" her at Christmas with a down payment on a new living room "suit," which was delivered to the house on Christmas Eve. It was hard to believe that anything as large and bulging as the sofa and two chairs could be so comfortless. They did not give to a body; they rejected it with a surface that bristled and stung. There was not much in the way of Christmas decoration that year, for Georgette frowned upon it as "pagan." A somber wreath nailed to the front door was the only admission that we celebrated our Saviour's birth, and it was artificial so that it might be used another year.

If the new family member brought changes into our lives, we doubtless provided some surprises for her, the chief of which was Uncle Grady's semi-annual drinking bouts. When the first occurred, she refused to believe that Aunt Belle and Roland meant to put up with it and wanted to forbid the services I was used to performing for my uncle. It was "a disgrace," not just shameful for the family but a sin against his own body ("the vessel of God"). She wept and threatened until she drove Uncle Grady out of the house. Thereafter, when he felt one of his bouts coming on, he retired to the quarters of a storekeeper named John Brown. Mr. Brown had a small general store on the road to Tuskegee. A quiet man in his thirties, he had been content to live alone in rooms over his store after his wife died during an epidemic of infantile paralysis. He and Uncle Grady had long been friendly, and there was the advantage of his always being there, upstairs or down, when Aunt Belle or I telephoned to ask how Uncle Grady was. There was further reassurance in knowing that Mr. Brown himself never touched strong spirits, although he was philosophical about providing them for Uncle Grady when the need was upon him.

Georgette's family did not visit her often. We were glad, without wondering why.

As for Georgette and me, it was clear from the moment of her return from the honeymoon that I was marked in her mind "to go." I ignored her as much as I could and was carefully polite when I could not. I offered to wash dishes a couple of times, but she told me boys didn't know how. The only one to whom I spoke my mind was Beatrice, and we were of one mind about the new sister. We despised her, Beatrice I think mainly for her bad cooking. I claimed to hate her hypocrisy; yet I complained at greater length about the meals she concocted. Harvey laughed at both of us until we were in good humor again. In time, we even had our favorite Georgette stories, enjoying them like old jokes.

Georgette's verdict on Marshall was swift. He was "some kind of freak." His on her was equally unsympathetic. "I had mumps bigger than her titties."

The one most directly affected was, of course, Roland, and his choice of wife appeared to suit him. Roland had always needed a focus for his attention and energies. Now her ambitions became his. He was no longer alone and floating through life.

I was, in spite of school and work and friends. I studied in my room; I read and wrote there. We no longer sat, evenings, as a family group in the living room—engaged in separate activities, to be sure, but together. After supper Uncle Grady more often than not went off in his car without saying anything to anyone. As her friends visited her less, Aunt Belle visited them more. I took to my room, or went to movies, or walked.

On my walks I had long noted a man described in the area as "a character, but harmless." It was not uncommon for such men to appear, become familiar for a time, and drift on as they had come, without our knowing anything about them. He looked old, but it was hard to tell his age because he went dirty, dressed in assorted throwaways, and wore his gray-blond hair long and ragged at a time it was not the custom to do so. If any knew his name, I never heard it. Against the cold he wore a thin, shapeless overcoat. He carried one or two paper bags containing, we assumed, all his belongings, for he was not seen to live anywhere. He talked to himself sometimes; sometimes he whistled a strain he obviously made up as he went along.

I don't know when I realized that he knew me. He did not appear to observe anyone, but now and then I saw a slyness in his downward glance when we passed on the sidewalk, although I'd trained myself not to look directly at him, as children were taught never to meet a Gypsy's eyes. One night in January during a stretch of warm weather that often came after Christmas, I walked home from a movie instead of waiting for a bus. I was breathing hard from the long climb up Montgomery Street to Five Points when the man stepped from behind a billboard near the top of the hill. He was there before I knew it and said, "Want me to suck you?" I looked at him with horror; and as he began to laugh, I ran.

At home I bolted the bathroom door and turned on the bright light over the mirror. What had he seen to let him ask me that question? Did I look queer? Trembling, I examined my face but found nothing I did not already know. I didn't see the man again, but I never passed the spot where he'd stopped me without remembering him. Later, I guessed that I may have frightened him as much as he had me.

30

FIRST LOVE, if happy, may be forgotten. If it stays in the mind, it is generally to be recalled with wonder and indulgence. But when unhappy, it is not forgotten, nor remembered with complaisance. I was seventeen in February and in love in the worst way: because of a resemblance. Alice Remington looked like a young Katharine Hepburn, child becoming woman, with spirit and will to be both and neither, depending upon the hour and day.

Aside from her features and her northeastern accent, to my southern ear infinitely romantic, I was drawn by her indifference. Used to the notice of both peers and elders, I wasn't prepared for Alice's look that did not even at first acknowledge my existence; and when it did, seemed to doubt the worth of it. I later learned that this skeptical neutrality had a base in nearsightedness as well as reserve.

Alice entered high school at the beginning of the second semester. Her father, Captain Clare Remington, was an Air Force doctor posted to Maxwell Field for a tour of duty. Alice took her place among us with the assurance of one accustomed to change who cannot be surprised or easily delighted by anything new. Her manner was politely uneager, and she kept a furrowed brow even as she smiled, the frown declaring, "This is how I feel," the curve of lips, "This is how I have learned to behave." The first, for a time the only real, smiles she produced were for Posy Valentine. No one except Marshall resisted Posy. The two girls were friends directly, walking arm in arm as classes changed, sitting side by side in the lunchroom, together strolling the grounds during the recess that followed lunch. Air Force children mingled with town children as they pleased, but the shyer ones kept together as if they were certain of being understood only by others of their background. Alice sought no haven in general alliance, old or new.

It was through my friendship with Posy that I brought myself to Alice's attention. Since Alice did not "know" me, she showed no response when I began to greet her in the hallways. Students did not introduce themselves to each other; acquaintance was assumed. Finding myself ignored, I joined her and Posy at recess one day, inventing a reason to speak to my friend of a hundred spaghetti suppers and a thousand shared jokes. For once, Posy gave no welcoming smile, but appeared puzzled at the question I put to her (which I forget, so inconsequential was it) . Leaving them a minute later, I fancied that I heard them whisper and laugh at my retreat.

It was a beginning, I told myself. Alice could no longer deny my existence. Thereafter, when I spoke to her, she looked directly at me, neither smiling nor frowning. She seldom replied, teaching me that there is little one says that may be considered to require an answer. Vain and spoiled I may have been by general credit, but I expected nothing from Alice. I knew I must earn a character with her, as if I had done nothing before and had no reputation.

Marshall was, of course, clamorously amused. "You finally did it!—In love with Morning Glory and Sylvia Scarlett and Josephine March!—Do you dream of her every night and wake sweating and weak? Do you hear her Yankee voice tinkling like ice in tea? Do you imagine what she's doing every second she's out of sight?" He had seen the Hepburn resemblance immediately. Subsequently, when we were all smitten by the actress's performance in *Stage Door*, he repeated the calla lily speech with exaggerated Hepburn mannerisms in Alice's presence, expecting to embarrass and entertain her. " 'The calla lilies are in bloom again. Such a strange flower—suitable to any occasion. I carried them on my wedding day; now I place them here in memory of something that has died.' " Alice looked at him, as he afterward complained, "Like I was a performing dog that might pee on her leg."

Celia hated her with resignation, seeing how it was with me. I doubt that Alice was aware of her at all. Her only friend, really, was Posy; and suddenly Posy was no longer my friend, or at any rate not one I could count upon. School days are days of constant encounters and no encounters. Everything might change in an hour. Anything that endured a week seemed permanent; a month was forever. In love with Alice, I felt deserted by all. I lurked and shadowed; I bumbled and bored everyone except myself, irresolute, dazed, undone by love, without even knowing the girl.

The world rarely loves a lover. It may tolerate, envy, enjoy ridiculing him; but if he is unsuccessful, it will certainly despise him. "Fool and double fool!" my best friend called me. "Can't you see she doesn't care about you?"

"It was a year before Sylvia would look at you."

"She still doesn't; we turn out the light."

"Alice is from Up North."

"Makes no difference: east, west, Seminole Indian."

"Southerners want to rush into things."

"Forget her. She doesn't know you're alive. If you died in front of her, she'd walk around you."

"I don't care."

"You've got no pride. I hate you humble! Nobody likes her."

"Nobody knows her yet."

"You don't understand girls."

"She isn't 'girls.' "

"Stuck-up, too."

"Because she doesn't think you're funny? I love her."

Marshall was the first I'd said it to except myself, and the words broke my heart. My tears astonished, appalled, and impressed both of us.

"What can I say?" he asked the gods. He lifted the end of a foot ruler on the battered desk of our club room and let it go, making a satisfying smack of wood on wood. Getting up, he sauntered out. "When you come to your senses, throw a note over the door of the third booth in the toilet, the one with the limerick about Dolores del Rio. I'll be fucking my fist to relax for the geometry test."

The next day after classes I was writing a book report on *Pride and Prejudice* in the club room when he came in. "I only made eighty-two. Maybe I was too relaxed. I kept hearing birds singing."

" 'And no birds sing,' " I said, continuing to write.

He stuck out his tongue and slobbered it at me. "Do you know she has a car?"

"Lots of rich ones drive to school."

"Not from Maxwell Field. They have buses. A captain doesn't make so much."

"Come the Revolution, the streets will run with blood; no one will be hungry, Comrade."

He explained it to himself. "He must be a rotten doctor or he wouldn't have joined the Air Force. I expect he's rich and likes position without much work. Who gets sick in the Air Force?"

"What kind of car?" I said.

"White," he said. Marshall and I were perhaps the only boys our age who'd have answered the question so, disdaining as we did the expertise of schoolmates. "White for the snow-maiden. Why don't you ask her for a date?"

"I did," I said.

"When?" he doubted.

"Her father doesn't want her to go with boys."

"Incestuous attachment."

What she'd said was simply, "No," but I knew Marshall would pour scorn on me if I told him.

He sat down in a straight chair as scarred and scuffed as the old desk. Opening a book, he began to study. I finished the report and capped my pen. We often lingered after school; the club room was a better place to work than either of us had at home.

"You staying or going?" I said.

He closed his book as dramatically as a preacher closing the Bible after reading the text for his sermon. "You poor, forlorn bastard. I bet you've even stopped masturbating."

"Don't talk like that," I said quietly.

"I'm sorry," he surprised me by saying. "When a woman interferes with a man's sex life, it's serious."

"It's just that I've been writing about Jane Austen and I'm still in her world."

"Oh, yeah?" He gathered his books. "Let's go to a show. I'll treat to Life Savers."

Unable to talk to her, I comforted myself by talking about her, directly to Marshall, until he told me to shut up, by sigh and suggestion to others.

Miss Torrence gave back my sigh impatiently. "Don't tell me who she is if she's a student of mine; it might affect my attitude. Is she pretty?"

"Not everyone thinks so."

"Is she brave and good?"

"I don't know."

"Bright and witty."

"Not with me."

"Is her family very rich, very poor, very anything?"

I shrugged.

"Has she *any* distinction?"

"She's not southern."

"If you'd given me reasons, I'd have said it would pass in a week, but you are evidently in love and I pity you." She lighted a cigarette; she smoked before me out of school, and we were in her living room. "Whatever comes of it, including nothing, it will feed your writing, so it's not a complete loss."

I was even callous enough to speak of Alice to Celia, who contented herself with the uncivil remark, "She's not neat. Her petticoat hangs below her dress half the time."

Beatrice offered support of a kind. "I can't think much of *any* girl," she said stoutly, "who isn't thrilled by your attention. Stay and have supper. I'll make a banana pudding or a lemon pie, whichever you say."

I decided not to, to impress her. She had become pregnant, and it had put a distance between us. I fancied that Lucius and Roy, as well as their father, now behaved as if she belonged entirely to them. On Morgan Avenue, Georgette Heaven Benedict had wondered aloud one night over a supper of dry salmon croquettes if Beatrice would send out Pope cards at Easter.

At first Posy was reluctant to answer questions.

"Do you think she misses the North?"

"Who?"

"Alice!"

"Never says so."

"She probably has a lot of friends up there who understand her better than we can."

She giggled as if I meant a joke, although she knew well enough I didn't.

"What's her mother like?"

"Pale. Big feet. Small ears, no lobes, wax in them."

I refused to smile. "Tell me."

She coughed. "Christian Scientist."

"With Captain Remington a doctor?"

"It's her way of fighting back. The daddy makes jokes. The mama is spiritual. They both refer to Southerners perfectly seriously as 'the natives.' I think maybe they wanted a boy instead and blame each other."

"How does Alice get along with them?"

"She doesn't speak to them."

"Keep it up, Edna-Mae, and I won't pay for your permanent wave next Christmas."

"I don't know how Alice gets along with them, Mark. I don't see them much when I'm there; and you don't watch a friend, do you?"

"I watch Marshall."

Up to then Posy had had friends but no friend. Now she and Alice were as much coupled in people's minds as Marshall and I had been since early days at Baldwin Junior High School. Alice sometimes brought Posy to school in the white car and took her home unless Posy had a club meeting, which was often, because Posy belonged to everything that could be joined, from the Latin Club to the Doodlers' Club. The latter had been organized as a social club with the secondary aim of "helping less fortunate girls."

Not a joiner, Alice had found that she must compromise to keep Posy as companion, so she joined a couple of Posy's less active clubs and then tried to persuade her not to attend meetings. Alice had no musical interests, no artistic ambitions; she was not athletic. She moved, indeed, in a nervous, rather tentative way I found endearing, although I knew it had nothing to do with lack of assurance. Yet one day, surprised by a bell and far from the classroom it called her to, I saw her leap over a gardenia bush and run across the parade ground into the school, like a bird skimming the surface of the sea. I had never seen movement so confident and beautiful.

If Alice did not make friends, she at least, through Posy, came to be known and accepted and could talk easily in a group when she chose to do so, although Celia Cantwell made the unchristian observation that she wasn't really sincere. I took satisfaction in noting that she had little or nothing to do with boys, a fact that made her as acceptable to the other girls as giggles and a willingness to share cosmetics and swap fluffy sweaters would have done.

Inevitably, however gradually, Alice and I became better acquainted, and now and then I had the pleasure of hearing her laugh at something I said, even if often as not it was nothing I considered funny. A few times, as spring progressed, I had the soul-stirring awareness that she was studying me in an open, puzzled manner. I told myself I'd win her yet, for there are few things as flattering at seventeen as not being understood.

We both attended Margaret Torrence's class, and because she made good grades I decided that Alice cared as much about Whitman and Dickinson as I. Miss Torrence never showed she knew me better than the others, but she had low days immediately before and after her long headaches when she would call upon me to answer a question or discuss a point she knew I understood. One day I saw in her quick lowering of eyes that she realized "the girl" was present, because I was showing off, letting my mind and words prance a little to impress her. Miss Torrence frowned and did not call on me again for a week.

3 1

JUDITH COHEN gave me a meaningful glance now and then, as if we shared a tragic memory, although I marveled that I had been even briefly in love with her. She was only Rosaline to Alice's Juliet. Knowing, as all did, of my new attachment, Judith had sensibly bent her mind toward appreciating Morris Beckman, he having discovered attractions in her and been approved by her father. I could admit that Morris behaved less arrogantly under Judith's influence than he used to. He spoke softly when he spoke to her and often waited, patient but manly, beside her locker at the end of a school day to take her home in his new blue convertible. She must have hinted something about me, for one day he fixed me with an expression of smug pity that presently became a winner's smile.

Marshall, of course, had Sylvia. Frank Goodson, my first friend at Baldwin in Mrs. Noble's class, cast his heart at the feet of Melna Simmons (she whose scratching had early offended Mrs. Noble), and Melna did not kick it aside. Everywhere I looked, boys found girls willing to love them. I walked alone in a world of pairs. True, others walked alone, but *I* was not one of those gray people who form lines and fill an auditorium to watch the performance. I was Mark Bowman, a chief actor.

I had other worries. Summer was coming, when I would no longer have the satisfaction of seeing Alice at school. She was to go to an aunt in Canada to escape the hot weather. I was also to lose Miss Torrence. She had been invited by her brother to spend a month or two with his wife while he went to sea on a training cruise. It was not the kind of thing Miss Torrence might be expected to do, but the novelty of it appealed to her, and she wanted to please her brother. Even Marshall, with no prospect of a job this year, was to go for a visit to the cousins on the Gulf Coast, as he and his mother had done before. He sneered, but he would go. Anything was better than staying at home, and however bored he might be, I'd envy him when I read his complaining postcards.

The anticipation of long, hot days of work and long, hot nights of nothing to do and no one to talk to cast me down. Uncle Grady passed most evenings with his storekeeper friend John Brown, no longer using drinking bouts to excuse absences from home. They went to wrestling matches and other sports events at Crampton Bowl, he said, or drove "round and about." Aunt Belle spent uncounted and sometimes unattended hours on the porches of neighbors Georgette had successfully discouraged from coming to her. Georgette and Roland were mistress and master of the house on Morgan Avenue, although Roland did not yet presume to act the boss at the brokerage on North Court Street. I ached to get away; I dreamed childish fantasies of escape, knowing there was nothing for me but to work in the warehouse with Clive Johnson and watch Mrs. Bush grow a summer older, and wait for the posters to change outside the Paramount, Empire, Strand, and Tivoli theatres.

Beatrice was getting big and uncomfortable, and as soon as school was out planned to go with Harvey's boys to their house on the lake to be private and cool. I grudged Lucius and Roy's having her so much to themselves. She urged me to come-see them. There was plenty of room, and I could get a ride with Harvey every weekend and any week night he decided to leave work in time to go to the lake. I would surely go, but I didn't enjoy the boys' company, and I couldn't be with Beatrice now without staring at her pregnancy, as though I expected her to explode. Her child was due to be born late June or early July, confounding those who "had their suspicions" at the time of her marriage last summer.

How was I to survive?

I would read.

I told myself sullenly I had already read "everything."

I would write—but one of the lures of writing was to have an immediate audience, and I'd have no one whose opinion I valued.

Despair has a dead, damp smell, and that is how I smelled to myself even in the midst of the school scents I loved: chalk and ink and flowers the girls picked from yards on their way to school, and wore in buttonholes or carried about from classroom to classroom. I was so low that when a cat mewed at me, I felt a king. But sometimes my thoughts turned angry. Alice—all ice! As I made the unfunny joke, I despised myself, even as I despised the dusty, cracked window shades of the room where I stayed so many hours every evening to avoid Georgette. She wanted me out as much as I wanted to be away, so I sat alone and memorized the details of the grudged room that had once, when Beatrice's, been pretty. One day, I told myself, I'd live in a room as cool and clean and mine as a new bar of soap.

The poems I still wrote were about Alice. I did not ask Miss Torrence to read them, but I did show one to Marshall. His reaction was quick. "Oh, God, the pain!" I showed him no more, but in May, exempt from taking most final examinations because of high grades, I had little to do but despair and rime, while teachers drilled students in reviews of the semester's work. The desperation that had compelled me to write the poems decided me to show them (the best of them) to Alice. Recollection of my mother's response to childhood poems did not deter me. These were written to Alice, and instinct told me no girl can be altogether indifferent to verses written for love of her.

Posy was almost always with Alice, so I picked an afternoon I knew the Latin Club was meeting (Posy was "scribe") for the last time until September. Alice took French, not Latin, and spoke it, Posy said, as well as the teacher. I hung about after school and followed Alice to her car. Although she must have been aware of my doing so, she put on surprise when I walked up to her and thrust a dozen folded notebook pages into her hands. "These are for you, you alone!" Turning, I ran as fast as I could, feeling childish but good too. She would know by my own words how perfect I considered her.

The next day I watched her during the two classes we shared. More than once she looked at me with troubled, wondering eyes. I kept my face and body rigid when she finally spoke to me after the second class, but my heart pounded. "Meet me at the car after school?" She sounded off-hand, giving a servant an order posed as a question.

I nodded. "Will Posy be with you?"

She frowned but answered with constraint, "I'm afraid she has something to do."

I was there before she was. Her smile was not a friendly one, but she said as if on the spur of the moment, "I'll drive you home."

I was going to work and should hurry, but took a seat beside her. I carried no books because I had no studying to do.

"Where do you live?"

Ashamed of the ordinariness of Morgan Avenue—what if Georgette was on the porch in one of her big-print cotton house dresses?—I considered directing her to Harvey's, but Posy would tell her the truth of that. I said, "Morgan Avenue. It's on the way to Maxwell Field—not in the West End—this side."

Other cars were leaving the school grounds with the speed of racers, but Alice drove slowly. I wondered if anyone who knew us saw us together, and sat high in the seat.

"I read them."

I made no reply, thinking to teach her the lesson she'd taught me, that response is not always an obligation.

"I read your note too," she added after a moment.

I had to answer that, remembering how I'd weighed every word in its place. "I meant it."

She almost hit a dog that was crossing Court Street. "The poems are good. Very sensitive for a boy down here. Posy had told me you're a good writer."

I turned my head to stare at her profile. "What do you mean 'a boy down here'?"

"It doesn't make any difference. I'm flattered, I suppose."

"You turn left two blocks further."

She frowned until she had made the turn. "What I said. I'll never feel that way about you."

"How do you know? You haven't given me a chance."

She laughed politely. "It wouldn't matter."

I waited a little, although aware every turn of wheels took us nearer the house on Morgan Avenue. "Is that all you can say?"

"Do I have to say more?"

"You haven't said much!"

"As much as I intend to."

"I want you to like me."

"You've made that clear."

I remembered Sylvia's embarrassment at Marshall's first attentions. "I'm sorry if I was too obvious."

"It was rude of you," she said.

"I don't care!"

"I won't talk to you."

"Then why did you ask me to come with you in the car?"

"I didn't want others to see us standing talking alone."

"Why can't you like me?"

"I don't owe you an explanation."

"I think about you all the time."

"Is this where?"

"It doesn't matter."

"It does to me," she said sharply. "Is this the house?"

"It's across the street. Let me out here."

She stopped the car without turning off the motor, but I didn't get out. I had run yesterday; I wouldn't today, and it could be the last time I'd see her alone. "Do you want them back?"

"They were done for you," I said.

"You don't mind losing them?"

"I have copies."

"Oh." It was her first awareness that I set a value on them beyond their message to her.

"I wrote them to you, but I *wrote* them."

Her laugh was tentative and made me feel I had the upper hand for the first time. "Do you write poems to a lot of people?"

"Oh yes, and God too.—I meant every word in the note. I love you."

She relaxed. "You ought not to say that."

"Was it *rude?*"

"I have to go."

"I'm not good enough for you. That's what you're not saying." I got out of the car and slammed the door, but it didn't catch, so I had to open and slam it again. "I'm not just anybody. Think about me in Canada this summer!"

"I won't," she said coldly.

"I'm not giving up."

"It isn't to be." Glaring ahead, she edged the car away from the curb.

I watched her go. I said to myself, At least I finally talked to her; she knows how I feel.

As I went up the steps, Georgette came out on the porch. "You're supposed to be at work. What are you doing home?"

"I had to get something."

I went in to telephone for a taxi. Montgomery then had what were called Dime Taxis, because for a dime they'd carry you anywhere within city limits; but they could take a long time because they might carry several people to separate destinations on the same trip. Since I was already late and didn't want a quarrel with Roland, I called a real cab, knowing it would cost me as much as I'd earn by the afternoon's work. Passing through the living room, Georgette said, "There's nothing for you to eat. That smell is a pie I'm baking for an Epworth League raffle." I said I wasn't hungry, which was a lie, and went out on the porch to wait for the taxi.

32

MARSHALL SAID, "Like *Alice Adams,* only you're Katharine Hepburn and she's Fred MacMurray." It had been too big an event to keep to myself. I was not unproud of the way I'd handled it, but gave myself better dialogue in the relating than I had actually spoken. "What's the next move?"

"Summer rot."

"You suppose they allow summer to happen in New York?" he said after he'd thought a moment.

"It wouldn't matter to me," I said. "Everything is better in New York."

"Think you'll get there?" he taunted bleakly.

"Of course we will," I said to smother doubt.

When I looked at him again, he yawned. "Testing you."

"*I'll* be there one day," I vowed.

"Meantime." His smile broadened and fixed itself for the last row of circus bleachers as he raised his arms. "Ladies and gentlemen!—Montgomery—Alabama—summer—1937!"

We were in the club room. " 'I heard a fly buzz when I died.' "

"Am I talking to you or some dead writer?"

"None of them is dead."

The last day of school was misery, as it always was for me, although not everyone I cared about was going away yet. Still, the things and people I lived by would stop or be dispersed for three months. Miss Torrence was to leave next Wednesday, Marshall next month; but Alice was to go *tomorrow*. Not knowing the time and place of her departure, I was denied the torture of watching car or train or plane bear her away. Since she lived at Maxwell Field in one of the houses assigned officers' families, I would not even during the summer months have the occasional comfort of strolling dolefully where she lived.

I tried to reread *Anthony Adverse*, which had gripped me two summers ago, but gave it up after a hundred pages. I set a task of studying Shakespeare's histories, which had daunted me, and gave up confused after reading the first scenes of three of them. I saw every movie that came to town, some more than once. I bought a tennis racket, and Celia, who played as poorly as I did, picked me up in her family's car two mornings a week and drove us to the courts in Oak Park to play for an hour and swim in the pool before I went to work at the warehouse. (I still have photographs she took of me in Oak Park talking to a deer through a wire fence.) I bought *Strength and Health* magazine, studying pictures of oily muscles and following a set of exercises in my room with the door bolted, until I found them as dull as Shakespeare's histories.

One day off from work I took a long bus ride and walked in an unfamiliar neighborhood, but gave it up when dogs barked at me, the stranger; for being barked at is unnerving even when the dog presents no danger.

I went alone to the swimming pool on Bell Street, but the girl named Pearl whom all the boys had watched last summer never came. Someone said she'd got married. Posy suddenly left, to my surprise, for a denominational summer camp, explaining that it was "cheap and fun." Marshall went to Pascagoula. Miss Torrence sent a postcard from Norfolk, Virginia, that might have been from anybody to anybody. It was a summer I seemed always to be getting caught outdoors in thunderstorms, which was scary as well as uncomfortable, for the newspapers carried stories about people being blinded or killed by lightning.

One day when I'd run from the rain and sheltered under the canopy of a gas station, a car drove in, and the driver, after ordering five gallons of gas, discovered me. I had already recognized her: Pearl, the girl I used to see at the Bell Street pool. She looked different, no longer a girl but a woman sure of herself. As the attendant wiped her windshield, I caught her studying me and looked directly at her. I smiled and she did too.

"I know you!" she exclaimed, paying the attendant with a dollar bill.

"Sure do," I agreed. "Swimming pool last year."

"You work here now?"

The question treated me too much like a boy. "No," I said vehemently, "just sheltering."

She took change from the attendant, who blew a large bubble with his chewing gum and held it voluptuously for a few seconds before it burst. "You have to be somewhere?"

"Nowhere in a hurry."

"I could drive you there. Nowhere-in-a-hurry sounds like a nice place."

"Well, much obliged."

She drove us out of the filling station. "I heard somewhere you got married," I said.

She smiled wisely. "Did. Bet you heard I had to. Didn't. Too smart for that. Only, I didn't like him, I decided, and quit him after a month. Got me a job and this car."

"Good for you," I praised her smoothly.

"Where you going?"

"Leave me anywhere dry."

"I know several dry places." She laughed. I thought of beds and put on a dumb-innocent look. She sucked in her cheeks and arched an eyebrow the way Joan Crawford did sometimes. "You ever figure out that problem of yours?"

My folded hands clenched on my lap. "Didn't have to. Might say I've promised myself to someone."

"You mean you've got a girl?"

I nodded, deciding to leave it at that, knowing I was out of my depth.

"So where do you want to be let off?"

"Yonder all right?" I said, relieved and disappointed. "Under the Paramount marquee?"

"How come you going to the picture show if you got a girl?"

"Meeting her." I winked. "Her mama doesn't know about us."

"Oh-oh. Hope you know what you're doing."

"I hope so too!"

We laughed together as she stopped the car. I got out and closed the door. "Sure nice to see you again." Even to me the words sounded as final as a deathbed goodbye.

"You filled out some more, didn't you?"

She drove away, and I watched her until she turned off Montgomery Street. Hell and damn, damn and hell!—what a fool I was; she was practically offering!—I got an erection and put my hand in my pants pocket to hide it, but that only made it worse; so I bought a ticket and saw *Topper* with Constance Bennett and Cary Grant for the second time.

Beatrice's baby was a girl, born on the fifth of July. Georgette said she probably brought it on by eating "too much rich stuff" on the Fourth; and when the child was given a name, she guessed it had to be for *Saint* Margaret because there weren't any other Margarets in the family she'd heard of. We all went to see Beatrice in the hospital. It was embarrassing. Harvey was boy-proud, not fitting at his age, giggling and handing out cigars. Lucius and Roy acted biggety, Lucius bragging, "We've got half a sister." Roy corrected him. "Half-sister, dumbbell."

Aunt Belle said she was bad with children and didn't want to hold her because she'd cry, and Beatrice said she wasn't supposed to be held yet anyway. Uncle Grady shocked me by getting watery-eyed when he went to the bed to take a close look. He kept absentmindedly rolling his cigar in his hands until the cellophane wrapper came loose and dropped to the floor. Roland looked affronted and refused to say anything until we all left together. Then it was, "Another Catholic."

"We may be sure of that," Georgette replied in a spiteful monotone. "I don't want to bring a poor mite into this wicked world until we know we can afford it."

Postcards from Marshall came regularly, some with blurred color photographs, some the plain, penny kind. One was covered with the word BORED and exclamation points thick as porcupine quills. At the end of July, Celia put an end to our tennis games, nothing to my regret, by going on a car trip with her mother and father to Natchez and New Orleans. Laughing, she said, "I'm always the last thing through the gate like the cow's tail."

On a Wednesday afternoon when the warehouse was closed, I was so lonely I went out to Memorial Cemetery and looked at Geraldine's grave, but didn't feel anything, only wonder at why I'd come. Many times when I climbed the long hill from downtown to Five Points I thought of the nights I'd walked Beatrice home from the Beau Monde and we talked and made wishes on the stars. I missed Beatrice. I missed everybody who wasn't there. I even missed bad times because I was living through a no-time. God, I thought with resentment and self-pity, will life ever be good? It was the time I learned that I was everything and nothing, all I had.

Beatrice took the baby to the house on the lake to be cooler, Eulabelle going along for a month to wash diapers and "accommodate." I went out with Harvey in his Buick a few times but never stayed long because they seemed such a family now. Lucius and Roy even called Beatrice "Mama." It was a joke when it started, but habit took hold. They were uglier than ever, I considered, their foreheads sun-reddened and noses constantly peeling. They couldn't leave dead skin alone, so it looked as though they were always picking their noses.

I tried to think ahead to winter when I'd be a senior at Lanier, but it was too far to seem real, until the stores began to show fall clothes in their windows. One night at supper Georgette looked at me and looked at me, until I finally asked her if my hair was on fire. Pulling her mouth down to show she didn't think I was funny, she said, "I was just wondering what you hope to make of yourself."

"A writer. Not make. I am."

"You mean you'll keep writing on the side after you get a diploma and work regular at the warehouse," she explained, as if to get it clear for me.

"I'm not going to work regular at the warehouse ever," I said. "I'm going to college."

I was as surprised as everyone else. Only Roland offered a response. "You're crazy if you think you'll get anything from the Benedict family."

"I don't expect anything."

33

If time would hurry!

It never does when you want it to, only when you don't. I was angry with everyone for forgetting and leaving me. I was angry because they had things to do and I didn't. I was angry because I was without importance. I was angriest with Georgette. Knowing her as I did, I generally managed to feel no more than contempt for her, until one night toward the end of August when I was in my room reading with the door closed. Uncle Grady was drunk and staying with John Brown. After supper (canned-salmon salad, a favorite with Georgette) Aunt Belle had drifted out carrying a cup of coffee to make her customary calls in the neighborhood. I'd left Roland and Georgette in possession of the living room, he with a magazine, she with a dress on her lap she was "letting out" for her sister Lorraine, who had begun to get fat at the age most girls starve themselves to be thin. With the door closed I could hear only Georgette's voice clearly; Roland's was a mutter. She went through a list of familiar grievances to which I paid no attention until she said, "Well, I for one hope your cousin does go to college, or somewhere. Anywhere, long as it's not to stay here in my home."

Roland said, my mind filling in words I couldn't distinguish, "—always understood he'd only stay with the family through high school."

"I call that Christian charity and more; it's imposition on his part. He's certainly big enough to take care of himself, or thinks he is. I shudder when I watch him eat, knowing what everything costs. He sneaks into the kitchen sometimes when he thinks I won't notice and pinches edges off my creations. It just ruins the effect." Roland contented himself with a grunt. "Furthermore, he's got nasty habits."

I waited and could feel Roland waiting for her to continue. When she didn't, he asked, "What kind of habits?"

"I don't like to guess."

"Has he ever said anything to you suggestive?" She made no reply. "Have you heard any funny talk between him and that friend on the telephone?"

"Sheets," she pronounced emphatically.

"Huh?"

"His sheets. Spots. You might almost call them scabs."

"I told you never to go in his room. He's supposed to take care of it and put his dirty clothes directly in the laundry for the washwoman. All that was understood."

"Oh, he does—sneaks them in, you might say, like he's ashamed, which he well may be. But I decided I ought to count everything together to make sure that old woman don't steal from us; and that means I have to handle his things. When I opened up those sheets and saw what he'd been doing, honestly—"

Roland coughed and cleared his throat. "You never had any brothers, Heaven, so there's no reason you'd know, but that happens when a boy is asleep after he's passed his twelfth birthday."

"Well, if you want to believe anything so silly. There. That seam's fixed."

There was a short silence. "From now on you make him count his things and put them in a pillowcase before he puts them with the rest of the dirty clothes. I don't want you ever to touch anything he's worn or slept on, you hear me?"

"You mean you're not going to tell him to stop doing it?"

"I'll tell him just what I'm telling you!"

"I certainly am thankful I never had any brothers," she said, "if that's what they do. There's nothing to compare with a boy his age when it comes to nasty minds. I don't like being in the same house with a mind like his. Thank goodness we haven't started our family yet. An innocent child exposed to all that."

"He's leaving next year," Roland said. "I promise."

After another long pause she said, "So he's to have what you were denied. There's no justice in this world, is there? I try to bear with what the Lord sends and show a cheerful face, but I just don't know why He profits the wicked."

I wanted to shout with rage, although I was sitting so still a mosquito settled on my leg and bit through cloth. Slapping my book down on it, I not only killed it but reduced it to a smear on my pants. Whether the noise I made reminded Georgette that I was near or her thoughts wandered on naturally, she said, "If Lorraine took lessons, she could be as big as Kate Smith. Sings all the time, Mama says, mostly hymns she hears on our Bible Hour. She could pick up popular songs if anybody encouraged her. But I reckon it's who you know that gets people ahead in the world and not true talent. What do you think?"

—*I* think you're full of shit, Georgette Heaven Beasley Benedict! said I to myself as I scraped mosquito mess from my leg.—Damn and goddamn you! It's my sheets and my cum!—Should I tell Roland if he said anything to me, that I already, every Monday, put my dirty clothes into last week's pillow cases when I made up my bed with fresh sheets and always handed Georgette a list, so there had never been any reason for her to do what she'd said?

I sat hot with anger, unable to read, August on my head and heart like a tombstone.

One by one, too late for me to care, they came back to town and dared to blame me because I'd stayed there and not endured their boring vacations.

Posy: "We slept in these big shed things that held the heat, twenty cots to a shed, twenty girls on those cots *twisting* and *turning* all night long, *giggling* and *smelling!* I know it isn't nice to say, but they did. I tell you, Abner Jukes, I wished many a time to be back on the farm with you and the chillun. The food was nothing to cheer about either, which made the fact that everybody looked forward to meals even more depressing. Jello made out of old tires would have been a treat. Lots of boiled vegetables, everything needing salt to have any taste at all. And here you were in a nice cool movie theatre eating popcorn and watching Sylvia Sidney be gallant."

Marshall: "I thought hell would be getting married and going to bed on your wedding night to find out your wife had no titties and no pussy, everything flat or sewed up. I was wrong. Hell is Pascagoula."

Celia: "If you think Montgomery's hot, you ought to try New Orleans. Boy howdy!"

Miss Torrence: "I thought I could do anything for Charles, but he was at sea most of the time, and his wife Cora hasn't the mind of a rabbit. No conversation except clothes, whereas I don't care a hang what I wear. And worrying about Charles's safety. What could happen to him on a nice boat on the ocean? It was much better when he got back. He and I can talk a mile a minute, as you and I do. You'll meet him one day. What did you do with yourself?"

"Nothing."

"All summer? I can hardly believe that. What about the girl?"

"She wasn't here."

"Don't let Spot put his paws on your leg. Out, damned Spot!" The dog look offended and trotted into the living room. "He knows he isn't to be here when we're at the table. He tries it only because you're a man." She called through the closed door into the kitchen. "We're done, Aunt Sally. We'll take our tea out to the front porch where it's a little cooler."

I had been invited to dinner with Miss Torrence and Miss Friede and Miss Bartley. The latter two did not go with us to the porch. Miss Torrence set her glass down on a table and sank into a misshapen wicker chair. I took the swing

next to her chair. "And Beatrice had her child. I suppose
that was interesting to you, although I don't know why I say
so, not liking children. I do not consider my students children. Why Margaret? I'm used to it and neither like or dislike it, but I always thought it a little prim and off-putting.
Of course, they may call her Maggie. I'd kill anyone who
called me Maggie. Both my father and Charles always called
me Margaret. What have you written?"

"I brought everything."

"Tomorrow I'll read. I hope you've overcome the wordi-
ness I felt in your last sketch. Leave rolling phrases alone.
Remember Poe. He begins with the first word, and when he
gets to the end he stops. You can learn no more valuable
lesson just now. You're quiet. Was it a wretched summer?"

"Not good."

"I'm sorry." The way she said it, she *was* sorry, if only for
a moment. "I thought about you. One more year for you at
Lanier. It's time you decide where you're going to college."

"I can't afford college."

"You must go."

I said I was trying to find a way.

"I hate the long daylight. Night should come at six o'clock
the year round. What plays are we getting this winter? I'm
out of touch."

I had saved it. "The Lunts in *Idiot's Delight.*"

"You don't mean it! Oh, you do. We'll see them. You have
the Ushers Club; I'll have to buy a ticket. They are a marvel.
You've never seen such acting as theirs, no matter what
they're playing."

"Robert Sherwood's good."

"Not much."

"Why?"

"Big ideas, glib words."

"I liked *The Petrified Forest.*"

"It was the Villon bits that caught you. You won't like it
a year from now. What did we have last year?"

187

"Ethel Barrymore in *The Constant Wife*."

"I've never seen anyone as drunk as she was during the first act. They must have poured gallons of coffee into her at intermission."

"Tallulah Bankhead in *Reflected Glory*."

"What was it she said when you took that note backstage?"

I quoted, " 'Some of Daddy's goddamn friends!' "

She shook her head as we laughed. "We were a little acquainted when she was a girl and stayed with her Aunt Marie, but I was older."

"You knew Scott and Zelda too."

"Everyone knew them. They were public property. I'm the only person in Montgomery who won't 'tell you all about them.' I liked neither.—You simply can't comprehend how famous Tallulah was in England. Much more than here. The summer I was over, her name was everywhere you looked. London buses carried TALLULAH—hugely on their sides."

Aunt Sally appeared at the door with a piece of cake on a plate. "There's just this left, Mr. Bowman. Won't you finish it? You didn't eat so much of dinner."

Miss Torrence said, "He ate like a dinosaur, but give it to him—I can see he wants it."

"It's good to see somebody eat," she defended me, "not just pick and peck like my lady-girls."

When she'd gone and I'd begun to eat, Miss Torrence said, "Why were you unhappy this summer?"

"Nobody to talk to."

"Get used to it. That's going to be a problem all your life.—I didn't mean to speak slightingly of Miss Barrymore. She had gifts, but mislaid them. Now, Tallulah is different; she may come through yet. There's time, and I envy her."

"They say you could have been her if it weren't for your headaches."

" 'My headaches' had nothing to do with it. They began after I gave up acting to concentrate on teaching. We don't have to be students of Dr. Freud to understand that connection, do we? I stopped acting because I lost my nerve, although I told myself I had to look after my father, who had begun to fail. But I was afraid. Tallulah isn't afraid of the devil, and that's as important as her talent."

"You could still do it."

"I like my life well enough, and I'm too old."

"You're not. Look at how old they all are, Cornell and Anderson and Ruth Gordon—"

"Too old to start. Sometimes it's a strain trying to live up to you. Always remember: I don't know any more than you do. One piece of casting I shouldn't like is Mother. You had a mother and hated her."

"I did not!"

"You still hate her for not loving you, and so you should; but look at it her way. Why should she have? Blame her for selfishness if you must, but she thought of herself not merely as your mother. I'd hate to be anyone's mother." She frowned, finishing her tea. "I might allow you now and then to think of me as your father. That would be not so bad. Train yourself not to worry about people. Use them. I'm not advising you to step on every neck laid at your feet—you needn't be callous. But you have work to do. Work is the important thing, in the end the only thing. Still, we must live it out. God may know why; I don't."

"What about love?"

She shrugged. "If you must, but leave charm out of it."

"I've got no charm."

"That almost defines charm."

"You make fun of me."

"Only when you deserve it. I thought I heard a little Sara Teasdale something in your voice. Make fun of me, if you like. You take me too seriously."

"You're the strongest person I know."

"Your cousin Beatrice is stronger than I. She has true courage, not mere theatrical bravado."

189

"What are the Lunts like?"

"Perfection."

"What is perfection?"

"Spot! Rescue me!"

Finally, she and Spot walked me to my bus stop, but they didn't wait. She had been thoughtful a long time when she said, "What do you suppose Bernard Shaw is thinking of tonight, Mozart or money?"

"I don't know, but I'm thinking about money. I've thought about money all my life."

"Your life isn't over. Goodnight."

"I'll see you the first day of school."

"Spot, stop dragging me; it isn't polite."

The bus was a long time coming, and after I got on, the driver dawdled, talking to a man who sat up front about Hitler and Mussolini, as if I cared about Hitler and Mussolini.

34

THERE ARE nights I wake from bad dreams to tell myself: You're not a little boy, you don't have to be afraid. Not that age is immune to fear, but the fears are likely to be different. I no longer fear poverty, although if you've been poor, you never feel altogether safe. I no longer live without love. I say so gratefully and with pride. Being poor and unloved were the keenest hurts of youth, but I have since been luckier than most.

That amiable woman, my Aunt Belle, was lost to love. I was sorry for her, but since I couldn't help her, I turned my face away. She may have been blind in her reaching out, but her heart was good. She'd had to learn first not to expect, and then not to want, close attachment. But the Aunt Belles smooth away some of the world's wrinkles, if only for a little while, whereas the Georgettes kill with placid ill-will. They will stand and watch martyrs burn one year and the next applaud the downfall of the torch bearers, all without caring.

I saw them then as clearly as I do now, but I had little understanding of myself. I divined, but I did not accept my discoveries if they displeased me, or trust my instincts. Conditioned to denial, I cooperated in self-deception.

How different Alice Remington appeared to me when I saw her again. Separation of even a quarter-year alters tricks of speech and dress. Surely she was taller. Had her hands been as big-knuckled last May? I felt impatient at the sight of an untied saddle-shoe lace. She was not the way she'd been and I expected her still to be. She looked at me in another way from her old way too, as if waiting for something to happen. I wondered, not without a trace of disdain, if she had been rereading those poems I'd done for her, which now made me uncomfortable because I acknowledged their thoughts and images to be secondhand. I told myself it was the shock of meeting after absence, that I felt as much for her, indeed more. And presently, if not on Friday, then certainly on Monday, I did. I gazed upon the bare cheek with its thin glaze of sweat in the hot September classroom with adoration.

Marshall saw differences in her too. "She's coming around. She even laughs at the things I say. Sylvia says she's wrong to wear sweaters; jackets would suit her better."

"Sylvia," I told him, "has been influenced too much by the fact that clothes are her father's business."

"Or 'How to Defend Dowdy.' I think she's yours if you still want her. I wrote her a note yesterday just as a test, saying I had fallen in love with her and was there any hope. She said no."

It was too much like him not to be true, but I hollered, "You didn't do that!"

He took a folded sheet of notebook paper from his pocket and handed it to me. In his handwriting were the words: "I have fallen in love with you. Is there a chance for me?" In her hand was the word "No."

"It's not the act of a friend—"

He laughed rudely. "I wanted to see what she'd say."

"What if she'd said yes?"

"We'd have fought a duel. Not she and I, you and I."

I handed the note back to him, and without looking at it again, he tore it in two and dropped it not quite into the club room wastebasket. "That 'no' of hers is pretty cool," I said.

"She's probably used to flattery. Father a Captain, mother the Mary Baker Eddy of Maxwell Field. And looking like Katharine Hepburn, she can't even set foot in Hollywood without being chased all over by Douglas Fairbanks, Jr., Douglass Montgomery, Ralph Bellamy, Charles Boyer, Fred Stone, Paul Lukas, and John Beal, like the Keystone Cops."

"Fred Stone played her father, you bastard."

"Would that I were. *Quelle romantique!*—'Now, gods, stand up for bastards!'"

I said more, but it was ineffectual, so I give him and Shakespeare the last word.

Things did not change easily with Alice. She refused when I asked her to go to a movie with me alone and countered by offering a ride in her car. Posy came along, and we became an occasional threesome. When Alice was busy, Posy and I did things together as we had in old days. Less often, never comfortably, Alice and I passed the time with each other when Posy was busy; but Posy was too loyal to often disoblige her friend. How pleased I was to walk and be seen walking with Alice, even though our exchanges were seldom more personal than a discussion of an English assignment.

Gradually, however, my being in love with Alice became an accepted near-joke among us, by which I mean that I allowed myself lighthearted sophisticated references to my feelings in the manner of movie banter, and they tittered or grimaced and said I was awful. We were what surely now would be considered young for our years.

I had left Miss Torrence's tutelage at the right time. We were friends in a way that would have made difficult a further relationship as teacher and pupil. It was a relief for me to be open in my admiration of her without being called teacher's pet. My senior-year English instructor was an old man with clicking false teeth and a passion for Tennyson and Shakespeare. He was much liked, although not by me. However, I have never since been able to read *Hamlet,* or see it performed, without remembering details of Mr. Cawley's Polonius, the best I know. It was true, funny yet not absurd, so that Hamlet's killing Polonius was more than a mistake, it was a shocking event.

Posy led me to horseback riding, as we called it. (Riding to us usually meant in cars.) She had discovered a stable on a country road near where she lived that rented horses for fifty cents an hour. The week she did so, Alice was occupied with other matters, so Posy and I went riding together twice. I'd never been in a saddle before, and my only lesson consisted of the elderly stableman's telling us, "You *putt* your left foot in this here stirrup and swing your butt over; then when you got your other foot in the other stirrup—go!" The horses were shabby animals whose pace quickened to more than an amble only when their heads were turned toward home. They were good for no better than the skittish initiation of the ignorant, such as we; but we enjoyed taking them out for an hour, which was all we could afford to do. We considered ourselves sporting and complained proudly of sore muscles.

Suddenly I was famous.

In the same month of November, *Scholastic,* a school magazine distributed country-wide, and the *Advertiser,* Montgomery's morning newspaper, accepted and published poems I'd sent them. An announcement was made by the principal at a full school assembly, and I was asked to stand to acknowledge the applause of the student body and teachers. The only people who showed no surprise were Marshall and Miss Torrence.

She was pleased. "The beginning."

He was pleased. "Recognition at last!" And jealous. "When will my turn come?"

"The *Advertiser* will write up the senior play; they always do."

"Next April!" he protested.

The play was to be *Jane Eyre*, and Marshall, as long promised, would act Rochester. He was the only one definitely cast before Christmas. To create interest and maintain suspense, Miss Porter took her time making the other assignments. Many senior students were suddenly eager for the distinction of appearing in the play. Because of the country house party scenes there would be enough dress-up roles to satisfy a fair number.

At home the news of my glory was received variously. Aunt Belle was "Proud as can be!" and carried the good news to every porch and parlor in walking distance. Uncle Grady shook me by the hand vigorously. John Brown sent a congratulatory word. Roland suggested that it had taken me a long time to get printed, and Georgette said, "Do they pay anything? I reckon you have to be really somebody for that. What possessed you to write about niggers?" The poem in *Scholastic* had been a word picture of a ramshackle house on Day Street. I had, in fact, written several poems based on my observation of the Negro district. Miss Torrence called them my "songs of social significance."

Georgette continued: "If I sat down to write a poem, which I certainly don't have the time for, it would not be about anything as common as colored people."

Harvey congratulated me genuinely and generously, as if trying to make up for his sons' lack of comprehension that anyone would want to write a poem when there were already too many. Beatrice almost forgot the drooling Margaret for a minute as she repeatedly assured me, "You deserve it!"

And when all was said and done and I lay in the dark, I told myself that Fame was surely an insufficient reward for the loneliness I felt.

35

During Christmas vacation there was a rush of party giving, enough to make that lean year seem almost a fat one. Mrs. Cantwell, dogged as ever in her determination to make a popular hostess of her daughter, managed two parties, one for the small number of regulars (Celia's idea; we graduated from spaghetti and meatballs to chicken Tetrazzini), and the other for a throng bullied into playing new games Mrs. Cantwell had discovered in magazines and party books. The old guessing games and list-writing games were no longer good enough. On entering the house, all were given crepe-paper costumes and noise makers and made to sport with them. No one was allowed to be still, nor to eat more than a taste of one thing, for there were so many platters and bowls. Variety and superfluity were the order of the evening. The Depression was canceled, and all of us stepped to a quicker march. Poor Celia was presently as exhausted as she was confused, and I think only Posy pretended to have a good time. Alice, who had been asked to the large gathering but not the more intimate one, looked about with undisguised astonishment.

Of the parties, the one Posy's mother gave for her was the best. Mr. and Mrs. Valentine welcomed the guests with genuine interest and then retired to the back of the house for the rest of the evening. Yet even in the twenty minutes they were present, it was clear that Posy was the center of the old couple's existence. I had never seen child-parent love so apparent and so understated. When the time came, Alice helped Posy serve food and drink, and I was charmed by the sight of her pouring coffee and cream. The simpler the action, the more remarkable it seemed to me.

Alice herself did not give a party, but her parents did, on New Year's Eve; and Alice asked some of her friends. Posy and I were the only ones from town; everyone else, young and old, was Army Air Force. It was to be a large party with dancing. Posy had promised to spend the night.

I was nervous about everything. How to get back and forth?—I had no car and couldn't drive anyway. Harvey, prompted by Beatrice, offered to drive Posy and me to Maxwell Field and to pick me up at one o'clock. I was too relieved to argue, but when I politely protested that I'd be keeping him up late, he looked at Beatrice and laughed.

What to wear was no problem. I had one pretty good blue serge suit I'd bought at Stein's. It would do. I bought a pair of black shoes, proud to have the money for them, but I grudged spending money on black ones. Beatrice had given me a shirt and tie for Christmas, so I was set. Dressed and ready for the night, I went into the living room to wait for Harvey; and when she saw me, Aunt Belle cried, "If only poor Sister could see her child now—so handsome!" I couldn't imagine my mother's feeling anything about me, and Georgette's response helped me through the moment. "Maybe she's watching from heaven." Georgette nice was harder to take than Georgette bad-tempered.

Harvey drove us through the post's check-gate directly to Captain Remington's house, Posy in the front seat serving as guide. I had not been there before and clenched trembling hands deep in pants pockets as I sat on the back seat with Posy's overnight bag beside me. The party had begun; and so had dancing and drinking. Social drinking was a thing I knew nothing about; I knew only about getting drunk. Everyone seemed cheerful and easy, not movie-sophisticated as I'd expected. A uniformed Negro maid took Posy's bag away, and Alice led us to her mother for Posy to be welcomed and for me to be introduced.

Mrs. Remington patted Posy's cheek before turning to me with a tired smile. "I hear you have no mother."

I stammered that my parents were dead and that I lived with an aunt and uncle.

"So sad, and you write poetry."

"Less than I used to," I apologized, wondering if she had read any of the verses to Alice.

"Quite famous, in fact." I knew then she'd merely been told of my November publications. "I too am interested in spiritual things, so I'm pleased to know Alice has new friends with a Higher Nature. You don't have the accent of the natives. Are you from other parts?"

"Savannah," I croaked, "Georgia." She looked vague and a little worried, so I added, "On the east coast."

Her eyes wandered. I guessed I was taking too much of her time. "Where is Clare? I'm afraid he's dancing with Major Buckley's wife, so you'll meet him later."

Posy pulled me along with her. In a corner of the square room a trio of enlisted men played "These Foolish Things" on piano, violin, and snare drum. Through an archway the dining room had been cleared for the younger guests. I greeted the Air Force progeny generally, because although all were known to me by sight, none of their names came to mind. Two couples danced a jumpy parody of their elders in the next room. There was a difference in their manner here; they were on home ground, I was the stranger. Posy was accepted, but I was stared at. To reassure myself, I tried to engage Posy in one of our comic exchanges. She went along, but it sounded forced to my own ears.

Alice was in and out, not ignoring us but mingling with her parents' guests as much as with her own. I danced with

Posy. Beatrice had taught me how and made me practice last week. When I asked Alice, she said she couldn't just now, maybe later, and wandered away. We had never really touched each other, and my awareness of it reminded her. Posy became popular, as she was bound to in any group. People always took to her, at first automatically, then discovering and telling each other that she was "wonderful." Through the crowd I later saw her dancing with Alice's father.

I had nothing to say to anyone. The more I tried, the less they cared. A girl the others called Pete was laughing at me as she encouraged me to make a fool of myself. The subject of riding had come up, and I remembered too late how ignorant I was about it. "We have marvelous horses here at the Field," Pete said. "Ask Alice to invite you out to try them."

"I don't ride horseback much," I said.

"Prefer piggyback? Why are you getting red?"

"It's warm in here."

"Ah, it looks pretty with your nice white shirt and your nice blue suit. What saddle do you use?"

"McClellan."

"I bet you prefer a western. They're both like rocking chairs. We all use what you'd call the English."

"How do you like George Eliot?"

"What does he ride?"

"Side saddle."

"I could have you shot. My father's a colonel." She gave a quick hard laugh and turned her back as haughtily as a dowager.

The suit I considered respectable was shiny at knees and elbows, while their clothes, carelessly worn, looked new and expensive. They spoke of foreign assignments with their parents, giggled about visits to New York, and challenged me to deny that Montgomery was the most boring place in the world. When I agreed with them, they smirked at what they took to be sycophancy, and I hated them and myself.

At midnight there was the demanded hush and countdown as someone manipulated a radio carrying the broadcast from Times Square. I tried to look normal and sing Auld Lang Syne with them. When I kissed Posy on the cheek, she gaped at me as if I were crazy, so I didn't dare kiss Alice. Alice's father came and poured a bottle of wine into the "children's" punch bowl, which had already been spiked with dregs from glasses of the officers and their wives. Later I watched Alice dance with a flushed-faced lieutenant who was holding her close as they talked in a familiar, teasing way.

I sat down on the floor against the wall and stayed a long time, nobody noticing. I felt that I might sit there until the party was over and no one would bother me. Alice finally saw me. "You're not about to pass out, I hope."

"No," I said, and suddenly remembering Noel Coward in a party scene of *The Scoundrel,* continued, "I'm just teddibly teddibly bored."

"I'm sorry you're not having a good time," she said coldly. "Posy wanted me to ask you."

The Negro maid stood in the doorway, hands on hips, asking if anyone here was named Mark Bowman. I said I was. She said, "Somebody come for you."

36

"MOTHER-FUCKING upstarts!—Snub you? They aren't good enough to wash your socks. Morons! Philistines! Ass-kissing, rank-conscious, horse-riding—I told you no good would come of that horse business, didn't I?"

It had taken Marshall only a few questions to learn the

way the party had gone and how I felt about it. He had a saying: he didn't know how to celebrate good luck with me, but nobody was better to bitch with.

"How did yours go?"

"We had the place to ourselves. Hamburgers, candlelight, a bottle of muscatel. Her provisions. I brought the cigarettes and matches. She smoked three; I smoked five. We blew the candle out together and kissed over its blackened wick. I was Clive Brook; she, Diana Wynyard. Then we clasped hands and went down on the *Titanic*."

"You stayed home and didn't do anything? You didn't even go walking in Court Square at midnight?"

"We almost did *it*. God! I hate myself for getting so close and not losing my head. I'd rather drown in turtle shit than have this nut ache I've got today. She was ready. When I stopped, she even offered to finish me, but I couldn't let her do a filthy thing like that."

"You ought to wash it sometimes. Remember the Boy Scout motto."

"While you were getting bombed by the Air Force. I hope it teaches you not to mingle with the lower classes. What you ought to do is find a nice, ignorant girl with big titties who's already lost her cherry and fuck her to death. That would do you more good than all your military contacts. I know the one you call Pete; she takes speech. An asshole trying to pass herself off as a glory hole. I'm surprised Alice asked her. What's her old man like?"

I didn't want to say we hadn't been introduced, so I shrugged and lied a little. "We only shook hands and said howdy."

"Very Ken Maynard. Is he a pansy?"

"How can he be? Wife and daughter."

"There are more things in heaven and earth, Horatio, than are dreamt of in your physiology class. I'm suspicious of all doctors. What do they want to be doctors for? It's like grave-diggers and sewage workers—you have to like stink. If a man is a woman doctor, I can understand: he likes being face to face with pussy. But if he's a for-God's-sake Air Force doctor, all he can hope to see is hairy asses and saggy scrotums. It follows: maybe he's a pansy in the garden of love."

"I don't think so. He danced a lot. He even danced with Posy."

"A big thrill, I bet. Listen: those boys who are always snapping their fingers and doing the Charleston in the big musical numbers, they're all certified cock-suckers."

"Where do you hear these things?"

"They get to me. So what's your next move?"

"*A Star Is Born* is back at the Strand."

"Let's go."

That was a Saturday. On Monday when I saw Alice at school, she was all smiles. "What *did* you say to Pete at the party Friday night?"

"What does she say I said?"

"She won't tell me, but she thinks you're awful!" Alice looked pleased about it.

"I'm not her hottest fan either."

"You can't expect me to drop friends on your account."

"No." It was a lie. Nothing would have made me happier than for her to say she wasn't going to waste any more time with the Air Force crowd.

"Who was the lieutenant you were dancing with?"

She knew whom I meant. "Jerry O'Brien."

"Is he someone you've known a long time?"

She smiled warningly. "He's marvelous with horses. Pete tells me I should ask you to ride with us sometimes."

"No thanks."

"Suit yourself. Posy's coming Saturday."

I went too, but decided beforehand not to get on a horse. I worked Saturday morning at the warehouse, and Beatrice, mindful of the kind of table Georgette set, invited me to have lunch at her house and be picked up there, since it was close to Posy's. It was a warm day. I wore old pants and a cardigan unbuttoned. So did Posy. Alice wore riding clothes. I'd never seen anyone I knew wearing them, only people in movies. After lunch I watched for them and went into the yard before Alice stopped the car. Beatrice wanted to meet her but hadn't come out for fear of appearing curious. Besides, she'd already made up her mind not to like Alice and not to let me know it. Posy, she'd met long ago.

I was gratified to see Alice noticing everything. At least she'd know all my background wasn't po'-folks. I asked if they'd like to get out. Alice said, "No thanks, get in," but Posy had the door open.

"I promised Mama to get Beatrice's recipe for lemon cake next time I saw her."

Posy was quick and would know how I felt and want to help me. Alice got out of the car too when I opened the door on her side. She was frowning and silent, although polite enough. They stayed just five minutes, but Posy got her recipe, Beatrice had a look at Alice, and I beamed foolishly at the three girls I liked most in the world as they made talk together. When we left, Posy said we could all fit in front, but she didn't push my luck by suggesting that I sit between them. Still, it was nice to be in the car with them, to feel us close together.

Lieutenant Gerald O'Brien was in riding pants and wore a thin black sweater that molded his chest and shoulders. He was relaxed and familiar with Alice, and I asked myself if he was in love with her. He remembered Posy from the party, and he shook hands firmly with me. We'd met at the gate of the large exercise yard. Others were sitting on the fence watching the horses being paraded around and put through their paces.

"Our steeds are saddled," O'Brien said with a little shimmy of his head and started toward the stables.

"Mark?"

I had remained where I was when they followed him, and Posy turned to call me.

"I don't think I'll ride today."

"Why?" The lieutenant looked puzzled.

"I'm not much for riding."

"Oh, come on," Posy urged.

"I don't feel like it. You all go on."

"Not sick?" Alice asked. When I shook my head but made no other answer, O'Brien shrugged and the girls followed him.

I climbed to the top of the fence away from the other watchers and balanced myself. Once in a while they would applaud some maneuver they approved; so I paid attention to them, trying to see what they saw. Presently, the lieutenant and the two girls trotted their horses into the yard. O'Brien rode a big black stallion and, of course, handled him expertly. I thanked my stars I hadn't put myself beside him. For Alice and Posy he had chosen similar chestnut mares with white throat and ankle markings. They made a few rounds of the yard together; then Alice and O'Brien rode together with Posy taking a slower pace behind them. Alice would drop back and go from one to the other. They appeared to be enjoying themselves, ignoring me in a natural way except for Posy, who now and then sent a glance or quick wave of the hand in my direction. I looked at other riders, but I couldn't for long keep my eyes off Alice and O'Brien. I strained to appear casual and detached, and maybe I did.

I didn't see her until she'd climbed up beside me: Pete. She too was in riding clothes. "You ought to be down there to show us how!" she exclaimed gaily.

"I'm all right here, thanks."

"Doesn't he work that animal splendidly?"

"He certainly does."

"He's a beauty, isn't he?"

"The horse, you mean?"

"Both." She laughed. "All the girls have a great passion for Jerry.—I found out who George Eliot was. You're a bit of a shit, aren't you?"

"Some know about horses, some know about writers," I said.

"They look grand together. Alice is one of my best friends, you know."

"No, I didn't."

"Then you can't know Alice well."

"I'm trying to."

"You'll never make it.—Look! *Look* at *him!*" Her attention had been recalled by a loud round of applause from the other onlookers. We were too late to catch the lieutenant's trick, but as a grace note he suddenly upended himself and did a handstand on the stallion's back before dropping to the ground. Patting the horse on his flanks, he turned in time to hug Alice, who'd flung herself at him in a fit of idolatrous enthusiasm. Beside me Pete smiled wickedly. "All the officers' wives are after him; they say he has balls like coconuts. He could have any of them, and maybe has, but I think he's getting serious about Alice."

Lieutenant O'Brien left the field of glory without our becoming further acquainted. I said to Pete, "Duty, I reckon, beckons."

"You're a poet and don't know it. What were you in— *Scholastic,* is it called? Is that like *The New Yorker?*"

Alice and Posy met me at the gate when they turned in their horses, and the three of us walked to the Remington house. Mrs. Remington did not appear until the colored maid summoned her downstairs for tea. We were joined by Captain Remington, who had a drink instead of tea, and I was finally introduced to him. He looked me over as openly as if I'd been in a cage, and when he'd done so, forgot me. The afternoon that had started so well ended when Alice drove us back to town, letting me out first at the house on Morgan Avenue. As that day's luck would have it, Aunt Belle was on the front porch wearing a torn dress and shouting across to Mrs. Quentin, who was on her front porch. Georgette, who had just set her hair in sculptural waves ("for church tomorrow," as she always explained) was repotting a half-dead begonia.

37

ON MY birthday in February I was eighteen, as magic an age for most of us to achieve as twenty and forty and seventy. When Uncle Grady took me aside at the warehouse and told me he and "Uncle John," as I had come to call his friend, wanted to take me out that night, I was surprised, pleased, and apprehensive. It started all right. Uncle Grady drove me to Uncle John's store; and when they closed it and turned out all but one light they called the Burglar, we went upstairs. I'd been there only a few times when Uncle Grady was drunk, or getting over being drunk, never as a guest. It was nothing fancy, but comfortable and neatly kept. Uncle Grady acted freer than he did at home, and I took my cue from his behavior. We all went into the kitchen, where Uncle Grady opened three bottles of cold beer. Back in the sitting room he drank all of his and half of ours, because neither Uncle John nor I cared about it; we had taken it only to be sociable. I knew they were leading up to something because both, especially Uncle Grady, had a look of smiling-waiting. Whatever was coming, I hoped I could honestly look glad.

At what he considered the right moment, Uncle Grady, on his way back from opening another bottle of beer in the kitchen, brought in a suitcase, set it down on the floor in front of me, and said, "It's yours, Mark." It was a big suitcase that would hold more clothes than I owned, except my old overcoat and leaky slicker, neither of which I'd ever want to pack anyway. Uncle Grady watched me closely as I undid the

straps and examined the inside, which held the smell of new-
ness, the sweetest perfume of the Depression. Uncle John
said, "Isn't that nice leather? It's for when you go to college."

I smiled. I'd thought a lot about it but hadn't got that far
in planning; but they said I would go, and I was beginning to
believe I would, against reason and arithmetic. I laughed and
they laughed too. A little of it was the beer I'd drunk—I'd
never had more than a few sips before—but mostly it was the
gift and our feeling friendly together, liking and trusting
each other. I thanked them so many times our mutual approval became embarrassing; so about then, Uncle John said,
"Shouldn't we go eat supper?" Uncle Grady said, "Sure,"
and we went.

We rode in Uncle John's car out to a roadhouse called the
Paradise. There Uncle Grady ordered beer and again drank
all of his and some of ours, then ordered more for himself
while we waited for our fried chicken dinners, the specialty
of the place. They were slow, he said with a wink, because
they wanted us to drink a lot of beer; and he'd be happy to
oblige them. The place was dark and smelled of beer and
cigarette smoke. I doubt if daylight or fresh air had pene-
trated it since it was opened. The jukebox was kept going by
the manager who was partial to a song called "I Can Dream,
Can't I?" The customers were mostly middle-aged men with
younger women who looked sullen and bored. Just after our
chicken platters came, the jukebox was turned off, and a
woman came out to the dance floor, bowed to us to claim our
attention, and then sat down at the piano and began to play
"The World Is Waiting for the Sunrise" in a quick tempo. I
wondered, what in the world? and was answered by the appearance of a young man and a girl who ran to the center of
the dance floor wearing red balloons tied to their shoulders
and glassy smiles set on their faces. From a darkened side of
the floor the manager called out, "For a special treat, we give
you Fred and Ginger!" and the couple thereupon executed
a combination ballroom and tap-dancing routine. It was too

tacky to be funny. That scared, determined pair had persuaded themselves they could be entertainers, and it was sad. The young women at the tables and the middle-aged men pressing cheeks and thighs against them gave the dancers the unthinking kindness of inattention and no applause.

I had been aware of the waitress's bringing drinks to Uncle Grady; yet I was surprised when I realized that he was saying everything two or three times, none of it making much sense, although his thoughts were easy enough to guess. When Uncle John said, "We'd better get on home, Grady; this boy has to go to school tomorrow," Uncle Grady began to cry, at first quietly, but as sorrow begat sorrow, more loudly, until he sobbed, "I love this boy! I loved his mama! He's not my son, but I wish he had been! I want all of you to know that—hear me?"

The other customers ignored him mainly, but one of the younger women, about my age, looked over at me with a sour smile. The manager was nervous and moving around a lot. Uncle John told me he'd take care of the check and for me to try to get Uncle Grady out to the car. Uncle Grady was willing to go until he was at the door, but there he wrenched away from me and shouted over the sound of the jukebox, "You're all rotten, common sinners! That's what my daughter-in-law would call you, and for once in her rotten, common life she'd be right! Her name is Heaven, like one of Father Divine's angels!"

The manager's polite embarrassment changed to mean threat, and I pulled Uncle Grady out the door while Uncle John apologized to everybody and then came to help me. Uncle Grady had fallen, so we picked him up. He clung to me for a minute to get his balance and then staggered to a tree, throwing his arms around it like a lover. It took a fair amount of coaxing to get him into the car, but Uncle John was patient, and I'd had some practice before then when he was like that. Uncle John got into the driver's seat and slammed his door, and I got in the other side. That way we could keep Uncle Grady safe between us, or he might open the door and try to get out when the car was moving. He began to cry again when we got going.

"Mark, do you hate me?"

"No sir." (Too vehement.)

"You do! You hate me!"

"No, sir, I don't." (Almost begging him to believe me now.)

"I'm glad you like the suitcase." He sounded quite sober then. "I always wanted a suitcase and never got one.—You fill it and *go,* hear me?"

"Yes sir."

"Leave every last one of us.—I couldn't even tell you how proud I was—your poems published! Wasn't I proud, Johnny?"

Uncle John said, "Certainly were," and we were quiet again.

I hoped he'd go to sleep and didn't dare turn my head to look directly at him, because I could feel him looking at me again. "You hate me! You know you do!"

He was right, as people are sometimes when they're drunk. I hated him because he embarrassed and confused me; but that wasn't all I felt. I put an arm around him and said, "No, I don't, Uncle Grady." Then he really cried, and I did too. It was funny, and it was not. I didn't understand him or me. After a while he stopped crying, shivered, and said the night air was cold on him. We all three immediately began to talk sensibly, even cheerfully.

By the time Uncle John stopped the car in front of the darkened house on Morgan Avenue, we had achieved a conspiracy of good humor. Uncle Grady whispered that he wasn't getting out because Heaven didn't approve of his going past her room to the bathroom so late. He said I could pick up the suitcase at the store any time. I got out of the car, thanking them again, and they drove off slowly, as if they were slipping away. It was very still with them gone.

I went into the house and to my room, undressed, and got into bed. The shade was up, and moonlight came in the window. I belched beer taste, worried a little about Uncle Grady, and then decided I had to go pee. When I passed her and Roland's door on my way back to bed, Georgette coughed deliberately to let me know I had disturbed her. In bed again, I had a short fit of hiccups and then went to sleep thinking about my new suitcase.

38

THERE was no way to go. As Roland had done before me, I ordered the new catalogue from the University in Tuscaloosa and studied it until I knew sections of it by heart. I applied for admission in the fall, which was granted. Among the myriad government agencies and authorities created by President Roosevelt, there was one for the nation's youth known by its initials NYA, which paid poor students for work such as cutting grass, tending furnaces, etc. There were no student subsidies or allowances then. It was easy enough to prove the qualifying low income of my family, because I was my family; so I got the promise of a job, nature to be determined, that would pay me fifteen dollars a month for fifty hours of work.

Over the years I had accumulated in my post office savings account $138. The amount rose and fell, fell when I bought a seventeen-dollar suit, fell when I paid twenty dollars for a secondhand typewriter. I had come to that time in every writer's life when I had to have a typewriter. Never before or since has a possession given me such a feeling of satisfaction and power as that portable Underwood. I taught myself to type on it and used it for more than ten years; I can still close my eyes and feel it under my fingers.

However mean I promised to be to myself through the summer, certain expenses were irreducible. I had to shave and brush my teeth and be decently shod, shirted, and pantsed. Socks and underwear might be darned or holey, but what showed must be respectable. I had to pay half what I earned at the warehouse to Georgette for "board." I *had* to go to the movies. With all I'd saved and could save, and with the promised NYA job, there would not be enough to keep body and soul together. I had figured every way, the cheapest everything, ignoring the pitiless, ironic look on Roland's face when he saw me with catalogue, pencil, and paper.

Marshall was running a parallel course. He had registered his intention of being a student at the university in the fall. He had acquired an NYA job. And there he stuck, unable to budge, no savings, no prospects better than mine that I knew of, until one morning he came into the Ushers Club room, plunked books down on the desk we shared, sat chair tilted back on its hind legs, and said, "My mother's going to college with me."

"I thought she'd been."

"This time she's going to run a boardinghouse."

"Will you like going to college with your mother?"

"Why not? I'm used to her."

At my solemn nod, he burst into one of his near-hysterical fits of laughter. I waited for it to subside, whereupon he explained.

Mrs. Blake had worried along with her son about how to manage college for him. During the Christmas vacation she'd spent three days with a friend, Miss Nora Eustace, in Tuscaloosa, where Miss Eustace was house mother for one of the university sororities. Miss Eustace had friends and suggestions. After a long interview with Mrs. Blake and a demonstration of her work with a piano and a student, Dr. Arthur

Shelley of the music department offered to refer to her certain piano students who wanted special coaching and to allow her to use the university's practice rooms.

Together Miss Eustace and Mrs. Blake discovered a house only six blocks from the college grounds which could be rented for a reasonable amount of money. There were four bedrooms. Marshall and Mrs. Blake would each have one of the two small ones. The other two were large enough to accommodate twin beds, twin desks, and four boys. "Boys," Miss Eustace pointed out, "are neater than girls and easier to clean up after. I love my dear girls, but if you saw their rooms you'd think pigs lived in them." There were even two bathrooms, unusual in such an old house. If each boy paid fifty dollars a month for room and board, Mrs. Blake thought she could manage. She would have a job as well as the rooming house. Marshall would have a job and go to school twelve months a year instead of nine, so that he might finish in three years instead of four. One roof instead of two would shelter mother and son. She would pay a local woman (Miss Eustace had half a dozen candidates) to come in for four hours a day to make beds and do heavy cleaning. She herself would do the cooking. All this had been presented to Marshall the evening before, only after Mrs. Blake had secured a loan that would make the venture possible. They were to leave Montgomery, possibly forever. What was there to come back to except one grave?

"I can go to school!"

I congratulated him but was quick to see there was no help for me in their solution. We discussed and discarded the idea of my living with them as one of the four boarders. I had already reserved dormitory accommodation at five dollars a month and hoped to spend no more than twenty-five a month to feed myself at the college restaurant called Pug's. The gap between thirty dollars and fifty dollars for room and board was unbridgeable, and Mrs. Blake could not afford to give me a lower rate in exchange for my helping to serve meals and clean up afterward. I should need at least thirty-five dollars a month to exist. My savings would pay for tuition, fees, and textbooks. I was twenty dollars a month short, and I thought with bitterness of the boys I knew who complained at recess that their parents were making them go to college.

There was no way for me to go, but I hoped for a miracle. It was a time people, against experience, believed in miracles, and hope was what we breathed.

After the riding episode I'd stopped bothering Alice but not thinking about her. She was always there, in the classrooms and corridors, and in my mind. But I didn't know the "what happened next" Marshall was forever urging upon me. I had been daunted by the lieutenant and by Pete's taunts. I could dismiss her, but I remembered what she'd said. I could privately persuade myself that he was an ordinary fellow who only happened to be a little older than I—and better-looking, and masterful with horses, presumably with planes, and by reputation with girls. I might sneer at the way he arched an eyebrow as if his every utterance was witty, but I had to admit that he was an officer in the Army Air Force, whereas I was what almost anybody would consider nobody. So I had let Alice alone since January 1, and that proved the way to her attention.

Alice had a vacant class period directly after lunch, as I did. She spent hers in the library in what was called a study hour, although no one supervised it. I usually spent mine in the club room. One day she and Posy and I were talking in the hallway outside the club room when the bell rang. After a last rush of words Posy went running, and Alice said, "Which way do you go?" I said, "In here," nodding to the open door behind me. "May I see?" she asked and walked in without waiting for me to say yes or no, used to assuming privilege.

For a moment I was struck dumb with surprise and delight. Alice alone! I closed the door behind us, and she wandered about, loose-leaf notebook and dictionary cradled in an elbow, looking at everything with curiosity. There wasn't much of it: desk, a few chairs, the same dusty, unfinished portrait of George Washington that presided over every class-room, a blackboard with nothing on it, a crowded bulletin board from which old items were removed only to make room for new ones. There were cutouts from *Life* magazine of the Mercury Theatre production of *Julius Caesar* with Orson Welles in uniform, and Maurice Evans noble in robes for *Richard II*—Marshall's contributions, as well as the sentence he had copied from somewhere: "A lie is an intellectual way of avoiding a difficulty." There were programs from plays and concerts the club members had ushered for that year, including the recent *Idiot's Delight* that had occasioned a rare disagreement between Miss Torrence and me. In thrall to the Lunts, I had declared the play a masterpiece, and she had retorted, "Fiddlesticks," with a look that said worse.

In no hurry, Alice read everything on the board, neither smiling nor frowning; and when she had done, she said, "May I study here today instead of the library? I hate to go in late." I couldn't speak, but nodded and shook my head by turn to indicate agreement with whatever she had in mind. "We won't talk," she said, drawing a chair up to the desk and opening the notebook. "You have work to do; we won't disturb each other."

Wanting above all to talk, I complied. How could she know the charm of the situation for me? I sat down on the other side of the desk and acted the part of someone studying, keeping still, only now and then scratching an ear or rubbing my nose as if lost in thought, careful not to overplay any gesture. Only when I judged her to be absorbed in what she was doing did I glance at her. She was copying a history outline from Posy's notes (I knew the handwriting), and I marveled as I watched her set down Roman numerals, capital letters, Arabic numbers, small letters, Arabic numbers in parentheses, and so on. Here she is, I marveled, and fantasized: we might be sitting alone with no one to interrupt us for the rest of our lives. I was in another world when without warning of knock or call, the door was opened and the Ushers Club sponsor, Miss Hannah Hamilton, stood there red-faced.

Long finger pointing at Alice, she said, "Get out of this room. It is a boys' club, and you have no right or reason to be here. You must not be a girl with any self-respect, for no good girl would be in a room with a boy with the door closed."

Alice and I looked at her in consternation. Alice was first to recover. "How dare you speak to me in such a way!"

"Out!"

Alice, as crimson with rage now as Miss Hamilton, took notebook and dictionary and bolted through the open door. When I called after her and started to follow, Miss Hamilton said, "Marcus Bowman, I've not done with you! You are a great disappointment to me. You have betrayed my trust and the honor of the Ushers. Do you have anything to say?"

I had a lot to say about her misunderstanding an innocent situation and about the superiority of Alice Remington, but she only shook her head at me. "You would naturally make excuses and say whatever came to mind. I have read your bulletin board, you see." She pointed to the sentence Marshall had pinned up. "I must go to my class, but you will report to me immediately after school."

39

I WENT to the library to find Alice. She was furious, but not with me, and indeed, I began to think of the incident as a possible bond between us. Marshall insisted on going with me to Miss Hamilton after school, and he told her he had pinned the sentence about a lie on the bulletin board because he thought it witty. She heard him with distrust and, cutting him short, included him in the abuse she had readied in her mind for me. No boy, according to her, was to be trusted out of sight, and girls weren't much better. "Particularly those whose families follow the martial way of life. I have heard that many cocktails are drunk at Maxwell Field."

I didn't argue; Marshall tried to and was told to shut up. Yet when we were both mute, her rage boiled up, and she ordered us to march ahead of her to the principal's office. Catching my eye in a side glance as he imitated my ROTC walk, Marshall winked and I giggled, which didn't help.

Elbows on desk, boney fingers making a steeple, the principal listened to Miss Hamilton, and when she was done, he sighed heavily. "This is a serious matter. On the one hand it is serious in itself, and on the other it bolsters a graver charge that has been brought to my attention this very morning. I was going to speak to you, Miss Hamilton." He picked up a letter, read it silently, and paraphrased it.

The local manager who booked touring plays into Montgomery had written to accuse the Ushers Club of allowing people to see plays without tickets. It took a time for me to understand. On the night of *Idiot's Delight* it had not occurred to me that I was doing anything questionable. When a play or concert sounded like being dull, it was hard to get boys to usher for it. They had to study for a test; their parents wanted them to spend evenings at home that week—they begged to be excused. I made do with a small crew. But when an event was looked forward to, everyone in the club offered his services for the night. Such had been the case with the Robert Sherwood play. The Lunts were a lure even for the ignorant.

I have a peasant's sense of the practical: Use what's there. I guessed there would be unoccupied seats; there always were, even when the auditorium was said to be sold out. I allowed more ushers to work the performance of *Idiot's Delight* than were needed, and they sat in the empty seats when the play began. Two were forced to leave seats claimed by latecomers. The boys always worked without pay, although the enterprise was commercial, not charitable. I'd seen no harm; I saw none now and was surprised to hear myself accused of dishonesty. The boys were members of a club. If they worked for nothing, I reasoned that they were entitled to watch the performance without paying, which most of them could not have done anyway.

I was shocked to hear the principal talk of expelling Marshall and me from school. Incredulity gave way to panic. I knew I needed character recommendations to get an NYA job, and I had to have an NYA job if I was to think of going to college. So did Marshall. We looked at each other; we looked at them. Clumsily, we began to beg to be given another chance. Hating them, we groveled. Miss Hamilton was soon smiling. The principal, keeping a straight face, was slow to acknowledge our apologies. He carefully and with a show of great reluctance calculated the moment of mercy. The charges would be set down on our records, we were told, but he hesitated to mark us for life by an expulsion. He realized, he said, that we—hoped to go to college? Perhaps he was being foolishly lenient, but if we were reckless enough to get into any more trouble, we'd regret it. Come to it, he hadn't thought much of the last poem I'd published in the school paper. It was indelicate. Perhaps that should have put him on his guard.

We promised to be good boys. We were doggishly grateful. Finally we were let go.—But how we resented them for that humiliation and for the fact that they had made us witnesses to each other's shame.

Leaving them, we were angry and embarrassed. It was a whole day before we could talk naturally to each other.

When I told her about it, Miss Torrence said, "Actually, he likes boys, so sometimes he is cruel to them; and of course he had to be in front of that crabby old maid. In many ways he is a kind man. You are not to worry about it. You were not dishonest. I'll look at your record one day in the office when no one is there, and if there's anything bad on it, I'll ink it out." No wonder I loved Margaret Torrence.

Marshall wasn't worrying. He had at last what he wanted. He was soon to play Rochester in the senior class play, *Jane Eyre.* "Well, strut mah stuff!" he said jazzily when he knew it was certain. The speech teacher had named him before Christmas, and now she announced other members of the cast. "She's got guts," Marshall said, "letting me play a hero. Do you think the audience will laugh?"

Miss Porter's boldness went further: she cast a Yankee girl as Jane. When we learned who it was to be, Marshall whin-nied with surprise. "The Air Force brat—Pete!" Pete's real name was Madeleine Clacton, and at the first reading of the play we began to understand Miss Porter's choosing her. Madeleine had a good clear voice; it would complement Mar-shall's stagey accent, which he called a blend of movie-south-ern-affected. She moved well too, stood without slumping, unlike most of her contemporaries, and her plain face was open and unapologetic.

Everyone was to be in the play; even the seductive Sylvia would act one of the guests at the house party. I was drafted to play St. John. "Because of your looks," Marshall ex-plained. "They can't have another ugly on stage. God knows it's not your talent. You're the worst actor I've ever seen, not forgetting those Republic westerns." Alice was to be the Gypsy fortune-teller. Posy was Mr. Rochester's ward and Jane's pupil. Judith played Rochester's mad wife and chilled us at every rehearsal with her maniacal laughter. After each outburst she would turn front and inquire anxiously, "Was that all right, Miss Porter?" Another "guest" was Celia, whose dramatic instinct was not keen. (I remember her say-ing after seeing a picture called *Vogues of 1938,* "Joan Ben-nett's pretty, but I don't think she's as good as Greta Garbo in *Camille;* do you?")

2 1 7

There was so much to feel that spring: love, hate, constant discovery, exultation, and fear as we anticipated the end of high school. We would be *grown*. The word filled me with sick panic. I was used to taking care of myself, but in desperation I could always be a boy. No longer; I would be a man, as Roland had proclaimed himself the day after his high school graduation.

With all that, the play rehearsals dominated our days. The cast was like another club. All were not called for every rehearsal, and the principals became a special club within The Club. Weekends and whenever we skipped a day rehearsing, we found that we missed each other. Out of context certain lines of dialogue became code jokes. We were thrilled by each other's performances, vastly pleased with ourselves, determined to give the best senior class play ever seen at Lanier. Beginning as the dark horse no one favored, Madeleine Clacton proved herself worthy and became popular. The day she managed to produce real tears in the confrontation scene with Marshall-Rochester, we all cried. Marshall, naturally, fell in love with her, and she enjoyed his offstage effusions with disarming jollity. Even I, not one for forgiving, forgave her early abrasiveness.

Marshall was in love with everyone in the cast, for we were *his* cast. Never did he forget that he was the star, and his self-assurance gave his performance authority. Both he and Madeleine were good; the rest of us were as proud of them as they were pleased with us. Any hint of criticism from Outside was rejected. We loved even our faults.

The night of the show—there was to be but one performance—was the only time I did not supervise the ushers. Miss Hamilton herself took on the job of head usher for the evening. There was a large audience, and although they did laugh at Marshall's first appearance on stage, it was because they were used to laughing at Marshall. They were quickly attentive, caught up and carried along by the powerful story.

Marshall was melodramatic at moments, but right. Madeleine was strong and winning and, finally, moving.

Even in the brief scenes I had, I fluffed one line and transposed two others, a victim of stage fright; and I swore to myself I would never put foot on a stage again as an actor. It didn't matter. The play was a triumph, and there was proof of it in the review in the next morning's *Advertiser*, which declared that such professional acting had never before been seen by students in a senior class play in Montgomery.

Celia's mother gave the cast party, and we laughed a lot, affectionately quoting lines from the play that had come to be favorites for one reason or another. In the manner of actors, everyone hugged everyone and swore to be friends forever; but it was the last time we were all together.

40

WHEN HE did not get a phone call from the Theatre Guild in New York, Marshall complained that it took a lot of time for word to get around. Otherwise, he found life good enough. Opening the bottom desk drawer in the Ushers Club room, he groped about for the small mirror no one but I knew was there. Holding it on his palm he said, "When I was little, I tried to glue one of these on the toe of my shoe and look up girls' dresses."

"It wouldn't surprise me if you still did."

He sniffed. "I could never work it." Looking into the glass, he leered. "Time to get up, Bela Lugosi; the moon is rising!

—Pimples almost gone. Let Bette Davis try to match those eyes. I think I'm going bald."

"Stop picking at yourself."

He replaced the mirror at the back of the drawer, leaned his head forward, and pulled hair aside with both hands. "Naked scalp."

"Everybody's scalp shows when they do that."

"Don't offer me comfort." He took a comb from his pocket and practiced parting his hair different ways. "Does it look better this way—or?" I shrugged. "Nothing helps, huh? I'll never forgive God if He makes me bald. This look sexier?"

"What's sex got to do with hair?"

"Innocent child. Sylvia holds on to mine when I kiss her. I had to stop using grease so she could get a grip. Everything has to do with sex."

"I wouldn't know."

He affected surprise. "Isn't Alice coming around?"

"No."

"She was at rehearsals even when she wasn't called. She's hardly out of your sight all day."

"She won't see me without Posy or Madeleine. She came to rehearsals because she and Madeleine are thick, and they take turns now driving each other from Maxwell Field."

"Try Madeleine. I bet you could. Better for you."

"I don't like her that way."

"Chaucer says all cats are gray in the dark."

"What does he know?"

"I saw a picture of George Eliot in the library. Madeleine looks just like her, change her dress."

"You go to hell."

"Bad temper is a sign you're not getting enough."

"I'm not getting anything."

"Who is? If I didn't have hands, I'd be a virgin.—Listen! You've tried everything: asking, begging, sulking, sighing. Surprise her. Lunge at her the way you do your food."

The following day he came to school ecstatic. Sylvia's fa-

ther, yielding to a long campaign of persuasion, had agreed
to let her go to the University of Alabama next fall. "I'll have
both my women—Sylvia and Mama! I'm so happee, Daddee,
I could sing like Shirley Temple: 'Pollywolly doodle all-a
day!'—No, God doesn't like to hear that." He dropped on one
knee and gazed upward. "Just having a little joke, Sir, making the best of things. I'm not happy. I'm just a mizzable sin-
ner needing grace and favors. Make me handsome. Make me
rich. Make the Theatre Guild call me. I've got plenty of talent like I got plenty of nothing!" He lifted both hands.
"Lawd, have mercy!"

I had tried before; I tried again.

Alice said, "I don't want to go to the university. I've been
set for Bennington for years."

"Change your mind. All they'll teach you there is how to
walk with a book on your head and keep your stocking seams
straight."

"I'm going to Agnes Scott," Madeleine said.

"At least that's a serious school," I said. "Are your grades
good enough?"

"I cheat."

"I'll probably never see you again after graduation," I
said.

Madeleine smiled. "That's right."

Ignoring her, I continued to Alice, "You could at least go
to the senior dance with me."

"I've told you—"

"Why not?"

"No!"

Madeleine said, "Tell him why.—She can't go with you
because she promised to go with Lieutenant Gerald O'Brien."

Alice glared at her and ran away. We had been strolling
and arrived at the fish pond by the side of the school. "Is it
true?"

Madeleine picked up a pebble and threw it into the pond.
"Is it?"

"You're so dumb! Can't you understand she's never going to like you the way you want her to? Why do you think she'll suddenly change? She won't."

It was my turn to go, but I walked.

"Okay!" she called after me. "Leave me feeling like a goon!"

If the world smiled for Marshall, it had no smile for me. After supper that night, Roland followed me into my room, where I always withdrew to study or read or write. As he closed the door behind us, I said, "Is anything wrong?"

"No." He sat down on the side of the bed. I took my chair. He made himself smile the way people do when they are about to tell you something you won't like. "Matter of fact, I'm happy about it.—*We're* happy. Heaven's going to have a baby."

I put on a smile too. "Congratulations. Both of you."

"It's not going to be easy, the expense and all."

"You'll manage, I'm sure. People do." I picked up a book.

"That isn't all." I looked questioning but said nothing. "You're set to graduate in a couple of weeks." I nodded. "That's sort of, uh, the end of it."

"More the beginning," I said.

"The end for us." I looked at him attentively. "That's what we agreed we'd do, keep you till you made it through high school."

"You talked to Uncle Grady?"

"He doesn't live here any more. All his things are at John Brown's. He comes by only when he remembers something he forgot to take."

"It's still his house."

"It's Heaven's and Mama's. They keep it."

My mouth was so dry when I tried to swallow, I almost choked. "What does Aunt Belle say?"

"She understands."

"You want me to get out."

"I think we've done enough."

"I'll be going to the university in the fall."

"How?"

"Somehow!"

"Heaven's word is my law in this. She says she'd feel funny having a teenage boy around the house this summer when she's going through her pregnancy."

"Okay."

"They have cheap rooms at the Y."

I had never been inside the YMCA, only walked by it downtown. It was a gloomy building that looked dark inside, and when the door was open, it smelled stale. The only people I saw go in and out were middle-aged men with lonely faces who looked as if they never spoke to anyone except to buy a cup of coffee or a package of cigarettes. But it wasn't the gloom of the place I was thinking of; it was the expense of a room there, when I needed to save every penny I could. However cheap it might be, I knew it would cost more to live at the YMCA and to eat at counters than to go on living at the Benedict house on Morgan Avenue.

Roland got up from the bed. "You can stay till you graduate. We've always done right by you. You can keep your job at the warehouse this summer, unless you come to your senses and decide to forget college and look for a real job. I hear Pillsbury needs a new salesman to work the road between here and Selma."

"I'll be going to college."

He paused at the door. "Like you said about us and the baby expense: you'll manage."

4I

IT WAS a shock to be told to go.

I hadn't been welcome since Beatrice left and Georgette moved in, but habit is as strong with the young as it is with the old, and I'd looked upon Morgan Avenue as home for five years. Embarrassment gave way to resentment. I had been insulted. I didn't study, or read, or write that night. I thought of rude things to say to Georgette in the morning; I imagined making my going a fine gesture, a matter of principle. While it was natural for me to reject old wisdom and ways because I was young, it hurt for *me* to be rejected. Anger wore down, but I festered, reviewing all my wrongs. When I am unhappy, my body forgets small skills. I cannot untie a shoelace without making a knot, or remove my pants without stumbling. As I undressed for bed, the very room seemed to be through with me.

There's something I've left out and almost forgotten. I never go to bed without wondering what will happen tomorrow. Hope is too soft a word for it and dread too hard; but the day never ends, however bad, the day never dawns, however uncertain, without the question in my mind: What comes next?

It was not for Georgette to evidence embarrassment when we met at breakfast. We ate that meal in the kitchen, and when I entered, I found her singing a hymn with the radio. When the program ended—her snapping off the radio before the news came on was the signal that we were allowed to speak—she said, "Roland has told me you're leaving. That will become mother-in-law's room." She patted Aunt Belle's hand, almost upsetting the cup of coffee in it. "We'll take hers because it's bigger and we need it. Too big for her now. Ours will be for Baby. It's all agreed, you see. Oh, I have so many plans! I even know what Baby's name's to be."

"What?" asked Aunt Belle.

"Angel."

"Not if it's a boy, surely."

"Angel, whichever. The Spaniards call boys Angel. I read it."

"I never knew that." Aunt Belle frowned. "Would you want a name that sounded Spanish, people might mistake?"

"I think it's perfect," Roland agreed loyally. "If I wasn't lucky enough to be married to Heaven here, I'd be out there fighting with the Abraham Lincoln Brigade."

"That suitcase they gave you for your birthday will come in handy," Georgette said to me. "When do you think you'll want to leave?"

"Graduation and the dance are on a Friday night. Saturday?"

If I thought they'd protest at the hurry, I was wrong. Georgette nodded and said to Roland, "We can change everything around Sunday while you're home. After church. I wouldn't miss church. We all have a lot to be thankful for."

I tried to catch Aunt Belle's eye, but she only nodded and sipped her coffee. "I'm all for the Ethiopians against the Italians," she mused. "Still, I wouldn't want to name a child anything that sounded Ethiopian." For the first time I noticed that she was beginning to grow a mustache. It was faint, but there.

When I mentioned moving to Uncle Grady, I could tell Roland had spoken to him. He wouldn't look directly at me, but said, "That'll be best, I reckon. Give her the house. That's what she wants, and she was bound to get it one way or another. I was never inside the Y, so I don't know, but it can't be much worse than living under the same roof with

Georgette.—Oh, I've heard queers hang around there some-times. Be on guard when you go to take your shower. They watch for nice-looking boys. So they say," he ended, denying knowledge.

They gave me a room by myself on the single rate because they weren't full, but said they might have to make me share "if more applied." The room was on the second floor at the back, showers and toilets and washbasins being half a long hall away. It had two metal beds, two lockers, a big wooden table, two straight chairs. The single window looked toward Dexter Avenue onto business buildings, and privacy was provided by a cracked green roll-up shade that was dusty when I touched it. The desk man showed the room to me, and I was satisfied because I wanted it to be ugly so it would seem temporary. I paid a week's rent and said I'd come back with my things Saturday morning if that was all right. He said that would be fine.

Beatrice hadn't much to say when I let her know I was moving. I made it sound like my idea, but she knew better. She invited me to supper with them Saturday night, which made me feel good.

Marshall paid little attention when I told him; he was busy thinking of his own plans. He and his mother would move to Tuscaloosa next week, having already been assured by Miss Eustace that their house was ready and waiting. They were packing. Marshall would take his first courses this sum-mer. He'd be a university student ahead of me. That stung for only a moment, because I still hadn't figured out how to go, knew only that I must. I would take the advice I had once given Roland: *Go*.

We cleared out the desk in the Ushers Club room and took down the clippings from the bulletin board. They had seemed important when we pinned them up, but after brief hesita-tion we threw them into the waste can. It was as if we'd never been there; we'd leave no sign of our passing, not even as much as the carved initials of earlier generations on the classroom desks. Miss Hannah watched from the open door as we carried our books away. She had already chosen next year's president and vice president for the club, boys who would be more amenable than we'd been. It was hard on us to see anyone glad we were leaving, so we pretended gladness ourselves.

The school yearbook had been distributed, and we'd asked friends and acquaintances to sign their pictures in it. Many had written a comment.—"Those were the days!"—"Will you ever forget Miss Pears???"—Neither Marshall nor I liked our own pictures, but we took some pleasure in the list of accomplishments under them. I was described, after the list of clubs and offices held, as "Lanier's Poet-Laureate, well-read, Marshall's friend, hard-working." Marshall was set down for the ages thus: "Witticisms, Charles Laughton, Sylvia's steady, infectious laugh." We thought whoever wrote us up might have done better. In response to the graduation announcements I had sent out, and I'd sent out fewer than most, I was given mostly ties and handkerchiefs. Beatrice and Harvey presented me with a table radio, off-white plastic with a good tone. Uncle Grady bought me a blanket, an alarm clock, and a train ticket to Tuscaloosa, and Uncle John gave me a reversible belt with a silver buckle. Aunt Belle surprised me by handing me a twenty-dollar bill. "Don't tell Roland," she whispered.

Whatever she felt, I never heard Aunt Belle complain of Uncle Grady's desertion of her—perhaps "living away" is a better way to put it, for he continued to superintend the broker business and to provide every need she had of him except his company, and he had never given her much of that. Acceptance of what came, without resignation or approval, was her customary reaction to life, her grace and her vital flaw. I never heard her praise Uncle Grady or blame him. Wise or not, she kept her own counsel.

Not so Georgette. To family and neighbors she trumpeted the speculation that Uncle Grady and "Storekeeper Brown" wallowed in liquor and whores and that the Lord had His eye on them. It was true that Uncle Grady still had drinking bouts, but they were less frequent, less sottish, and less prolonged than they used to be. As to whores, I never knew him or Uncle John to refer to women in any way that was not respectful and distant. To suppose them patrons of the local harlotry was a fantasy of the daughter-in-law.

Although I invited him, Uncle John did not come to my graduation. Uncle Grady did, arriving on time and sober and sitting with Beatrice and Harvey. A row away were Aunt Belle and Roland, between them an empty seat I had reserved for Georgette, who chose at the last hour not to attend. From my place on the stage I found all of them and saw the empty seat on which Roland had placed his jacket. It was a hot evening and he had sensibly removed it. Marshall was still alphabetically beside me, and Celia near, as we had been together in Mrs. Noble's classroom at Baldwin. But we ignored each other, Celia, paler than ever, giving her due to the awesomeness of the occasion, and Marshall and I never more separate than when we were together in company.

Aunt Belle, as she had done at Roland's graduation exercises, fanned herself with a pleated paper program. I sweated and steamed in rented cap and gown, aware of what was going on without caring about it, responding only when my name was called by stepping forward to receive a diploma from the principal who had not so long ago accused me of dishonesty and threatened to expel me.

Afterward, I found the family members together in the hallway outside the auditorium, which smelled of wilted flowers and sweated talcum powder. Their words and mine were mechanical; handshakes were awkward clutches. They left. I turned in cap and gown and went to the dance in the gym.

42

I HAD decided that if I could not take Alice, I would ask no one to go with me, so I was not only alone but on my own. I'd never gone to high school dances, nor had Marshall. He was with his mother now, and Sylvia with her father, they having decided to make it parents' night. When I entered the gym, bold and nonchalant and no one caring, the orchestra was playing "Bei Mir Bist Du Schon" with extra pizazz because there was no dancing yet and they hoped to encourage couples to take the floor. Instead, the early arrivers ignored the music, sat or stood on the sides of the gym, and behaved as if they didn't know each other, or where they were, or why they had come.

"Mark!"

I turned gratefully to see who had called my name. It was Celia, and she stood with a stranger who was presently introduced to me as, "A relative of Mama's from Nashville, Norman Brigham. He's here on business and brought me." Celia was not a girl to mince matters, and suddenly I was very fond of her. She explained me to Norman, a plump man about twenty-five, I guessed. "Mark is going to the university next fall, and I wish I was too." Celia's mother had decided to keep her in Montgomery and enroll her at Huntingdon College.

"Oh!" Norman said. "Of Alabama? I hear they have a good business school."

"I don't know," I said. "I'm an English major."

Norman grimaced jovially. "I never could spell cat."

"C-a-t," I said.

"Plan to be a teacher?"

"No!" Celia defended me. "I told you Mark is a writer."

The grimace unlocked. "Oh, this is that one."

"Well!" I said to Celia to get out of the dead end, "We made it, didn't we?"

"I'm sorry it's all over," Celia wailed. "School days are the happiest days of your life."

"Oh, I don't know." Norman tried a leer.

Ignoring him, Celia continued, "I'm going to be here all summer, I expect, if you want to play tennis or anything."

"What's *all over? Which* happiest days?" It was Posy with a boy named Bill Darby whose family was rich by my lights and sending him to Sewanee. Instead of either of them paying attention to the questions, the two girls embraced and began to cry as if they were best friends who hadn't seen each other for twenty years. It might already have been a class reunion. Catching themselves up after a few moments, they dabbed at their eyes, opened compacts, and praised each other's dresses.

Finishing "Bei Mir Bist Du Schon" the band went without a pause into "You Can't Stop Me From Dreaming" and I asked Posy to dance. There were now a few couples making the motions, and without excusing ourselves from our companions, although Posy did smile at Bill Darby, we moved into the rhythm of the ballad. I said, "I didn't know you— uh—him."

Posy gave me a ferocious smile. "How do you feel?"

"Fine! How do you feel?"

"Fine! Do you feel grown?"

"I'll say," I said facetiously.

We fell on each other with laughter, ignoring music and dancing, and then, without signal, became solemn and danced as woodenly as marionettes. During the second chorus, a party of four entered the gym: Alice and Lieutenant O'Brien, Madeleine and another lieutenant. Posy broke away from me and ran toward Alice, who left her party and ran to meet her. They shrieked and shrilled, behaving as they had never done before, "the way girls behave," I later told Posy. I shuddered like a wet dog shaking himself dry and sauntered over to Madeleine, who smirked at me and ignored her date. But after a minute's chat, the purpose of which was to proclaim our intimacy and exclude anyone who might be listening, my conscience made me say, "Evening, Lieutenant O'Brien."

He stared at me until recognition came. "You're the boy who didn't want to ride."

" 'They all laughed when I sat down to play!' " I cried, and he laughed as if Jesus was cracking the jokes.

"How do you think of things like that?" Madeleine asked. "Without thinking, I mean."

I said, "My friends wonder what I see in you."

"Tell them it's just sex," she replied. Her lieutenant jutted his chin but smiled, the gestures canceling each other. She patted him on the cheek. "Just hot-blooded American youth, you know. Mark Bowman, meet Ace Walton. You have nothing in common, believe me."

I said, "Do you think there's going to be a big war, Lieutenant?"

He looked at me suspiciously. "Sure."

"You'll be in it then, won't you?"

"So will you," he said, indulging me from the heights of his lieutenancy. "You going to try for the Air Force?"

"I don't think so." I had considered, as had every boy of my generation, going to war and being killed, but I had not dwelt on any idea as routine as choosing a branch of service. "Navy probably." I said it reflexively, because of Margaret Torrence's brother Charles. Walton squared his shoulders as if I'd issued a challenge.

"Doesn't he look clean-cut?" Madeleine said to me. "He

tongues when he kisses, though." I laughed and the lieutenant blushed. "Oh, loosen up, Reverend Dimmesdale," she said to him before turning to me. "You see, I *have* read a book, just not the same one you read. Which funeral parlor furnished the band? Come on, Ace, let's shake our fannies. If you think Daddy bribed you to take his daughter to some kiddies' matinee, you're wrong. Those jungle drums are driving me mad."

They moved away, and I looked at Alice and Posy, heads together whispering. Lieutenant O'Brien said, "It's not as if they don't meet every day and talk on the phone half the night." I wondered how he knew; was he that much in the Remington house? "Come on, Alice. I want to dance."

Alice, who hadn't yet spoken to me, gave me a brilliant blank smile and allowed herself to be embraced for dancing. I was about to take Posy's hand when the number ended and Bill Darby came up. "Me next. Go find your own girl, Bowman."

I had never imagined Posy's being anyone's "girl," and the notion that she might be disturbed me a little with its assumption that we were all now adult. Across the floor I saw Judith Cohen and Morris Beckman. They weren't dancing, and fleshy Morris was sweating profusely. The gym was getting crowded. After greeting them, I said to Judith, angling my arms into dancing position, "Care to be defiled by a Gentile?"

Morris growled, "Easy, fellow," and laughed to show he was a good sport. Judith actually looked to him for permission. He winked and nodded. "Don't forget I'm watching."

As we moved away from him, Judith said, "I'm heartsick at things not working out between you and Alice."

"How do you mean?"

"I know she came with somebody else," she said with friendly candor. "They passed right by us and didn't speak. Is the Air Force against Jews?"

"Not that I know of," I said. "Actually, I was just talking

to Alice and her party, so it doesn't really mean anything, her not coming with me. I waited too late to ask her, that's all."

"Oh, I'm glad," she said warmly. "Glad it doesn't mean anything, I mean, not glad you asked her too late." We danced and didn't talk.

Afraid she'd think I was brooding, I asked, "Where is it you're going to college?"

"Randolph-Macon."

"Where's that?"

"Lynchburg, Virginia. Morris is going to the University of Virginia to make a lawyer."

"Pearl Buck went to Randolph-Macon," I said.

"Did she?"

"I think so."

"Did you like *The Good Earth?*" I answered that I had and asked her if she'd read it. She said she didn't think so.

When the music ended, Morris was there to claim her; and that's the last time I saw either of them.

I wandered around, not knowing what to do with myself because I wasn't used to dances. I cut in on a few girls, but there were "no-break" dances during which I found myself on the sidelines watching with the sneering stags. Mostly I watched Alice. Mainly she danced with Lieutenant O'Brien. She wasn't popular the way Posy and even Madeleine were. Having avoided dances, I'd never seen my classmates so dressed up. The boys in their dark suits looked more or less their usual selves; but the girls in long dresses, cut to show off shoulders and bosoms (Marshall would have been hysterical) made them appear really grown-up to me for the first time. Although I watched her, I shied from asking Alice to dance, afraid it would seem begging and jealous.

The third time I cut in on Madeleine she didn't joke. She said, "I have finally seen someone actually eating his heart."

"Who?" I said dully.

"You."

Lieutenant Walton tried to cut in. "Scram," she told him,

"we're closer than the Curies." She frowned to concentrate. "If you hadn't been lost to her, I'd have gone for you, and I bet I'd have got you."

"Is she really close to O'Brien?"

"He wants her, and he's a catch. Family money. He won't stay in the Force to make a career. What I don't understand is why you act afraid to touch her."

"How could I compete with him?"

"What's great about him? So he can do handstands on a horse. You're smarter than he is, and better-looking, and sexier. He's about as sexy as a Kewpie doll. *And* you're going to be somebody and he isn't. He'll go into his father's business, New York real estate. They own blocks of Harlem. That's what you're giving her to."

"If that's what she wants."

She frowned again. "Have you considered the possibility she may be stupid? I'm not saying she is, but I wonder sometimes. Looking like Hepburn does not make her an Alberta Einstein."

"I don't care if she can't count her toes."

"Men!—as Sadie Thompson says. You haven't danced with her yet." I shook my head. "Look. I'm going to cut in on her and O'Brien, so you come back of me and take Alice. If she isn't a fool, she may still grab you like a piece of pie, even at this late stage."

She did what she'd said, and I found myself dancing with Alice. My arm trembled on her back; I didn't talk. When the song was over, I held onto her hand and asked her to dance the next dance with me. She shrugged and tried to take her hand away; I held tight. The music started, and I took her closer to me than I'd held her before. She tugged away, making space between us again. I looked at her so hard she had to look at me, if only in irritation. I managed to say, "I love you." She looked away resentfully. "I said I love you," I repeated.

"I heard."

"Well?"

"Well?"

"Don't you care anything about me?" I begged shamelessly and shocked both of us by kissing her on the mouth.

She pushed me back angrily, and O'Brien was there to take her from me. "Did Alice tell you about us?" he said as he cut in. "We're getting engaged. We'll be married at the end of her first year at Bennington."

They danced away, and I made for the door.

43

NOT SINCE my mother died had I known anyone so finally lost to me. I went home—it was the last time I would think of the Benedict house so—and packed my clothes. Aunt Belle had told me it was all right to leave things in the closet until I knew what I was "going to do about college." Suitcase ready, I looked around the room without affection. I could leave with no regret; for since Beatrice married and Georgette became its mistress, the house had held no warmth for me.

There is, they say, an audience for pain, but there is none for breast-beating, and "Woe is me" became a comic line long ago. Yet, if there is discretion in passing over suffering, there is dishonesty too, and I have promised myself to tell the truth in this account. Soon I might be able to think of Alice Remington with healing anger and of myself without contempt, but not that night. That night I despaired of us both. It did not matter that we were an unsuitable pairing or that we had remained unknown to each other. Love does not require knowledge to be real, and mine was no invention.

I rose early the next morning and went to the warehouse on North Court Street to work until noon. Then I returned for my suitcase and took a taxi to the YMCA. To unpack required ten minutes, after which I took a shower (no lurking strangers, Uncle Grady) and went out to eat a sandwich or two, feeling more cheerful.

Tomorrow I'd telephone Margaret Torrence and ask to see her next week. I'd missed her last night in the crowd. Tonight there was dinner for me at Beatrice's. Meantime, I walked about downtown, which could be done thoroughly in an hour, and returned to the Y. Strolling through Montgomery Fair, I had thought of buying a book and remembered I could not afford it. I was no nearer knowing how I was going to manage college, but I must save money anyhow. In the room again I put my typewriter and composition books on the big wooden table and sat savoring the squalor of my first home alone.

At five o'clock I took another shower, because it was hot and I sweat. After dressing in cotton pants and open-necked shirt, I walked down to Dexter Avenue and waited for the Cloverdale bus that would take me close to Harvey's house. I found Lucius and Roy as noisy as ever, but having arrived at the ages when brothers hate each other but need each other's company, they were off in their room most of the time. The baby was asleep. "She sleeps through thunder," was Beatrice's brag. Harvey was agreeable and easy; we were comfortable together now as we had not been at first, giving on trust some of the credit we saw only through Beatrice. Beatrice was in and out until we finally followed her to the kitchen and stayed leaning and talking, dodging as she set things on the table. Eulabelle came only mornings.

The boys were called when the steaming bowls and platters were on the table. There was country-fried steak with onions and thick gravy, rice, field peas, the first new corn and tomatoes of the year, and a bowl of "slaw" as we called it, though it had a lettuce, not a cabbage, base. There were biscuits and corn sticks, iced tea to drink with the meal and hot coffee after banana pudding with whipped cream.

Even Lucius and Roy admitted they were tight as ticks and went off to their room again, giggling and whispering over a secret no one cared about. I followed Harvey into the living room, where he turned on the radio and we sat down to listen to the Hit Parade. When Beatrice came in from the kitchen, she brought a sealed envelope, which she handed to me with mysterious uncertainty. More puzzling: she looked at Harvey, and together they returned to the kitchen, leaving me alone.

Opening the letter, I recognized Margaret Torrence's ugly handwriting.

My dear Mark,
Now that you have finished school, we are practically con-
temporaries, so I think you had better call me Margaret. We
shall continue to be friends; we both know that. Why a
letter? Because what I have to tell you will be easier for me
to write and you to read, and I don't want you to interrupt.
Knowing the problem you were facing, at least one of them,
your cousin Beatrice and I formed a committee of two to do
something about it, and we have. We approached three
others who are unknown to you and wish to remain so. The
five of us agree to make up the sum of twenty dollars a
month. That will be easy, even in these times, only a dollar
a week, you see. You will receive a check on the first day of
each month. Don't argue and don't feel grateful, or our little
gesture will stick in your craw. You are in no position to
refuse—remember that. You are not just any young man. You
are important. Come and see me next week? Friday for din-

ner and an evening of our good talk. Aunt Sally wants to feed you; she scorns my appetite.

Affectionately,
Margaret Torrence

I gave myself a minute and then went into the kitchen, where I found Beatrice and Harvey drying dishes. Making it jokey, I said, "As Georgette-Heaven puts it: 'Don't we all have a lot to be thankful for!' " I thought that would save me, but it didn't. When Beatrice gave Harvey her dish towel and touched me, I bawled.

44

SUMMER IS the longest time. I hated hot weather, always seemed to be waiting for something to happen in the fall. Summer 1938 was one of the worst. I worked, and some weekends I spent at the lake place with Beatrice and them. I played tennis with Celia, but neither of us was much good at it or cared to be better; we did it for something to do and for company. A few times Celia had me come out for supper. Her mother had given up on me, but Celia did more as she pleased than she used to. Once words passed between them I wasn't supposed to understand that told me Celia had made a bargain with Mrs. Cantwell: she'd see the favored cousin if she could ask me over now and then.

I saw Margaret Torrence when she wasn't visiting her brother Charles and his wife, and those were my best times because of the talk. Nothing fed me like Margaret's talk, but I loved Aunt Sally's cooking too, and she enjoyed cooking for somebody she said, "with a nice appetite." Aunt Belle saw to it that I took a few meals on Morgan Avenue, and even Roland asked me twice, both times on Sunday as sequel to church. The only times Georgette could tolerate me was after I had been sanctified by sermon.

I accepted any and all invitations to eat a meal, knowing it would save a quarter. Sometimes I made myself go a little hungry to save a dime, but more often I'd buy something cheap and big like a package of rolls and a jar of peanut butter. That filled me up, God knows, with or without a pint of milk.

I had letters from Marshall, but they were sketchy. He was too busy to tell me more than that he had a lot to tell me. I read. The Carnegie Library was only a couple of blocks away, and I was an old, known patron. There weren't any paper-back books then. I cut down on movies, rationing myself to a single second- or third-run a week. I wrote, but not much. My mind was on college.

Skipping buses when I could, I walked to save a nickel. After supper at a counter downtown I usually walked because, however hot, outdoors was cooler than my room at the YMCA. One night after such a walk I was standing on the steps to put off going in and found myself talking to a man who had wandered out the door. I didn't know him. He spoke first and I answered a time or two, but he began to make me nervous because I could see that he was becoming nervous. As I turned to go, he said in a low voice, "I'll give you a dollar." I knew; I can't say how. When I didn't continue inside, he said, "Not here," and motioned with his head, walking away.

After a minute I saw him stop and look back, so I followed and caught up. "What do I do?"

He took a dollar from a money clip and handed it to me. "Not much."

He walked. I walked alongside him. It was dark. He slowed down when we were in front of the closed library, and after a sharp look up and down the sidewalk, climbed the steps quickly. Again I followed, and he led me onto the grassy side of the building that was darkest. "Just sit on the ground and unbutton."

The first time, he played with me until I came, but the second, and from then on, he mouthed me. We didn't talk to each other, but when he got excited, he'd talk to it. "It" was me, so it was like being talked to, a little. It happened from then on two or three times a week. By the end of the summer he'd paid me twenty-seven dollars. I never touched him or said anything, just took his dollar and let him do it. He always wiped me with his handkerchief afterwards, explaining the first time, "I carry two."

One night I told him it was the last, because I was going away. It was the only time we talked. He thanked me for telling him I wouldn't be around and asked if I felt he was bad. I did, but said no. He said, "Well, don't feel bad about yourself either. You're not the first nice boy to make a dollar with his dick."

That surprised me to laughter. "Hope you don't mind my saying I'm glad I'm not queer."

That made him laugh. "Buy you a Coke?"

"No thanks."

"College?"

"Uh-huh."

He took out his money clip again and gave me another dollar. I handed it back, but he wadded and stuffed it into my shirt pocket. "You good to me, I'm good to you."

Uncle Grady and Uncle John took me to a big meal at Morrison's cafeteria, which was my favorite place in town to eat. I said goodbye to Margaret Torrence and Aunt Sally, who gave me a quart of fig preserves to take off to college with me. I said goodbye to Celia, who cried. I'd been seeing none of my other schoolmates since the graduation dance. I said goodbye to Mrs. Noble, who told me to make her proud. I went to a last supper at Beatrice's.

I said goodbye to places: the gold star on the porch floor of the Capitol, houses I'd liked in passing for reasons and no reasons, streets like Dexter Avenue, and Madison and Monroe, Kress's and Silver's, where I'd first seen Marshall. I took the long walk up Montgomery Street hill to Five Points, then along Goldthwaite to Mildred Street, past Morgan Avenue and on to the cross made by Mildred and Mobile, then left to Day Street with its hills and vales and windy alleys and dead ends, its black faces and black voices I was trying to catch on paper. I didn't want to write about "the Negro question"; I wanted to write about *them*.

I even went out to Memorial Cemetery again. Unable to visit my own dead, I stood one afternoon by Geraldine's grave and thought of her and all the dead around me. I was alive and life was before me. Poor Geraldine, poor baby.

The final Sunday came, and I'd been asked to midday dinner, Georgette insisting, "Come early for church." To church we went. One of the hymns was "Onward, Christian Soldiers," and I sang loud and lusty as any, until Georgette, seated with Roland in the pew in front of Aunt Belle and me, turned and frowned remonstratively. Dinner included the toughest old baked hen I could remember. Even Georgette allowed that it would have been better if the sermon hadn't gone on so long. The week before classes were to begin, I said goodbye to Montgomery, telling myself that from then on I'd be a visitor when I came back. With my still-new suitcase, I boarded the train for Tuscaloosa, using the ticket Uncle Grady had given me.

45

I STEPPED off the train to another world, carrying the new suitcase and holding a cigarette between my lips which I'd waited to light until the train stopped. And there was Marshall, a freshly lighted cigarette in his hand. When we saw each other, we laughed; and I lost the cigarette and stepped on it, pretending I'd dropped it deliberately. We weren't friends who touched, so I didn't set down the suitcase, but yelled, "Hey!" and got "Hey!" back. "When did you start?" I then asked.

"It's something I may have to do in a play." He shrugged. "Actors have to know how to do everything. I'm reading Stanislavski."

"To learn how to smoke? Girl I used to know named Beryl could show you how, and she never read a book, unless you count *Photoplay*."

He smiled wearily. "You haven't changed."

"I've had a lot happen this summer," I challenged him.

He forgot weariness. "You don't know nothin'! Wait'll you hear what-all *I* been doin', Kingfish!"

"Is there a taxi?" I looked about as I imagined Noel Coward might have on arriving in a town unknown to him.

"That all you got?" He used his Rathbone sneer on the suitcase.

"My books and other things are in a footlocker," I lied carelessly. "I'll send for it later."

Although it carried us only to Woods Hall, the oldest dormitory at the university, the cab route revealed much of my new world. I sweated in the brown winter suit I'd worn to save having to pack it. Marshall wore a gray suit I'd never seen before. "Sharkskin," he explained and touched a finger to the collar of his orange shirt. "Tabless-tab."

"How can a tab be less?"

"Don't be a clown," he begged and hunched forward in his seat, pointing. "That's Pug's, where you'll eat, having rightly skipped the college dining hall."

"I figured I could eat cheaper than they charge."

"Any place that feeds you is playing a loser's game. That's called the Supe Store, Supe for Supply. Books and note-books and Cokes. All overpriced. Everybody goes and hates it because the profits go to the football team, which no one loves but the cheerleaders and alumni. Post office is back of it to make sure everybody goes through the Supe Store at least once a day; ten times is more like it. You'll have to rent a box or wait in line."

"What were those big houses back there?"

"Fraternities. Around the corner are the sororities. The rich pussies and the rich peters are conveniently located. They're too dumb to find each other if they have to turn more than one corner. That's Denny Chimes and there's the library—they're going to build a big new one on the Quadrangle to ruin it. That's Morgan Hall, where the theatre is and most of the English professors.—There's old Miss Gorgas. She didn't build the Canal, but everyone thinks she did because she's so old. Shy, not seen much, never goes anywhere but the library from the Gorgas house, reads a lot of mysteries. And there's Woods Hall, ta-da!"

"It looks like a jail."

"It's the loudest, roughest, most beat up of all the dorms."

"Hence the cheapest."

"Hence," he agreed.

We found the room I was to share with a boy from New Jersey named Albert Pappas. That was all I knew about him and almost all I was to know. That he was from the North made him of potential interest to me, because I thought everyone from the North was sophisticated; but he turned out to be a simple boy with no bad habits and no liveliness of spirit. From movies I recognized his accent as lower-middle-class "New York vicinity." He had acquaintances but no friends and studied business administration. We were polite for the year we shared the room, but he had little to say and rarely smiled. Even Marshall was unable to make him laugh.

Marshall sat in one of the room's two straight chairs, feet on desk, and talked as I unpacked. When I'd showered and dressed in lighter clothes, he took me home to see Mrs. Blake and to have supper with them. The four room-and-board boys were there, two of whom were in law school, one in commerce, one in chemistry and pre-med. The only interesting thing about any of them, Marshall later told me, was that the commerce student had a false eye he put into a glass of fluid beside his bed every night. Mrs. Blake made it clear in a nice way that my having supper with them was to be only an occasional event, and indeed I don't think I ate more than half a dozen meals there during Marshall's college years, and those at special times like Thanksgiving or a birthday.

After supper we walked again, and walked. Behind those dark windows in the buildings we repassed until they were familiar to me were rooms where, I imagined, wise men and women would stand ready to share their knowledge with me.

"When does Sylvia come?"

"The day before registration. She'll live in a sorority house. She's got a connection; her mother was tri-Delt. I've, uh, been seeing another girl this summer. Nothing serious. We just go to the cemetery and neck. A tombstone can be a right-nice thing; the Second Richard wasn't so dim after all. I'll probably drop her when Sylvia gets here unless I keep her for, you know, sex stuff, so I won't be a threat to Sylvia."

"What's her name?"

"Agnes Egan; everybody calls her Baby. She's a little

plump and giggles when I kiss her, but she's got lips like a suction pump and the hottest tits north of hell."

"What's she studying?"

"Art, of course. The dumb ones all take art, and Baby is dumb. She doesn't know her right hand from her left, but she likes to keep them busy. She works on sets for the plays. That's how I met her."

"Poor Sylvia."

"A man has to take care of himself."

Not for the first time I was a little awed by him. Yet, what would he say if I told him about the nights on the library grounds in Montgomery? I would never tell him that, I decided. He was my best friend, but could I tell him anything, ever? At the back door of Morgan Hall, Marshall impressed me further by producing a key to what he said was the stage door. Earlier, he had told me of his acquaintance with a married graduate student named Hugh Weatherhead, who served as an instructor in the Speech and Drama Department while studying for his doctor's degree. Hugh had arranged for Marshall to make his NYA job working in the theatre instead of the main library, where he and I had been assigned.

After he turned on the office light, I followed him through the wings onto the stage, where he snapped on a bare standing light. He held his head over it a moment for the grotesque effect of light and shadow. "A heath, thunder and lightning.—'Poor Tom's a-cold.'—'Croak not, black angel; I have no food for thee.' "

I walked to the edge of the stage and looked into the dark auditorium. "I'm going to write a play," I said.

"Watch out," Marshall warned in his own voice. "You could fall into the pit."

Still playing guide-host, a role I would allow him only that first evening, he walked me back to Woods Hall, saying good-night downstairs and going home. Voices echoed back and forth from the floors above, calling, cursing, cawing, sometimes laughing. When Marshall was out of sight, I left the dormitory and walked again.

I found the cemetery, a little way off University Avenue, which led downtown. I stopped at Pug's for a cup of coffee at the counter and a piece of the lemon chiffon pie that was to become a favorite and a drain on earnings and allowance, for I often found that I wanted something sweet at night before going to bed. I made myself saunter past the fraternity houses, telling myself I was as good as they were. Last, I walked the four sides of the Quadrangle, needing to do it alone to make it mine. Denny Chimes was a sound I already loved by the time I undressed and lay in bed, head in cupped hands, awake and dreaming.

46

I BOUGHT meal tickets at Pug's at a small discount. One was supposed to last about a month, but didn't because of my late-night hunger for chiffon pie. Breakfast was fifteen cents, lunch thirty or thirty-five, dinner forty, no tipping expected or given. They were substantial meals, but I was never un-hungry.

At the library I learned the Dewey decimal system of filing and finding books and didn't mind the work. Classes were not exciting; all seemed a review of what I knew. I even made A's in trigonometry, which I could do without understanding it. The pleasure of being called Mr. Bowman instead of Mark by the teachers subsided after a week. Freshman English, taught by a graduate instructor working for her doctor's degree, was boring and made me remember how stimulating a teacher Margaret Torrence had been. The big books discussed in class were *The Return of the Native* and Strachey's *Queen Victoria,* which I'd read years before; and the oafs howled with merriment on discovering the cuteness of Dorothy Parker. I missed Margaret Torrence as a friend and waited for better teachers. The only thing I really hated was military training, obligatory for the first two years. Its only use to me was the uniform that saved wearing out my own clothes. Students were allowed to cut fifteen class periods a semester. I took most of my cuts in ROTC, a few in biology laboratory because the smell of my pickled frog turned my stomach.

The university was sports-minded; I was not. Marshall and I ignored the football games, although our Student Activities card would have admitted us to the local games free. On home-game days we repaired ostentatiously to the muddy woods bordering the Black Warrior River, a volume of poetry tucked under my arm, Stanislavski under Marshall's. On the day of the homecoming game and celebration we abandoned the university grounds altogether and spent long hours in the three movie theatres downtown. The sight of the fat, happy old graduates sporting their chrysanthemums and crying in each other's arms was too much for us.

Now that he had more or less free access to Sylvia, Marshall's appetite for her grew tamer, I thought; although to hear him talk, it did not. "She's possessive," he would complain smugly. He was forever discovering new girls. Agnes Egan, alias Baby, gave place to others whom he saw briefly and cautiously. "Just walking dates. After we pass the last streetlight, they take a handkerchief and wipe off their lipstick. For twenty minutes on a dark stretch we eat each other up. They're hungry as Siberian wolves. Then suddenly it's ten-forty, and they have to be back in the dorm or sorority by ten forty-five, because it's the law. Have you ever had to run with a hard-on?"

Aside from classes there were concerts and visiting lecturers and plays. Marshall played Sid in O'Neill's *Ah,*

Wilderness! "Because I look like a middle-aged drunk," he said, and one of the soldiers in Irwin Shaw's *Bury the Dead.* I came to know, through Marshall, who liked his friends to be friends, the Weatherheads, Hugh and Buffie. Hugh was a fat man about thirty with a big laugh as metallic as a thunder machine. I had the feeling he had developed it and thought it bold and masculine. Buffie was younger by five years, lighter by a hundred pounds, blond, pale, watchy. She watched me, frowning. She seldom joined in the talk. She watched authoritative Hugh and deferential Marshall as they discussed Clifford Odets and the Group Theatre. Sometimes she sketched our heads or her own hands, and sometimes she went to sleep with the sketch pad on her lap. Then she would wake and frown and watch again. I felt sorry for her without telling myself why. I wondered how she and Hugh managed sex; it must be awkward with his fatness. Often I followed her to the kitchen and helped her make the gallons of cocoa we all consumed with marshmallows and oatmeal cookies. Once or twice when we stayed on, she made a tuna casserole with a lot of cornflake filler for the four of us.

If I found classes boring, I loved the life of school and didn't understand those who complained of regimentation. Every day there was for me a glorious waking to be my own man. I didn't resent the obligation of class attendance or the hours worked in the library. There was time for everything, and people, always people eager to talk. I was approached by two fraternities during Rush Week ("Looks and grades," Marshall dismissed it briskly), but they dropped me when I told them I couldn't afford to join them. I wished I'd said I didn't want to join them, which was true, but I hadn't. There was a strict line between fraternity and nonfraternity boys. For all our ridicule of them, Marshall envied them their cars and clothes and girls, and I envied them the assurance that nothing but money can buy.

One night in November, a week after the production of *Ah, Wilderness!,* I was in my room studying, as I generally did a couple of hours each night if there was no special event and if I did not have to work in the library, which stayed open until ten o'clock. Albert Pappas was at his desk, I at mine. We had not said anything to each other since opening our books. We were both good at ignoring the yelling and the radios always turned to high volume in Woods Hall. Marshall came in without knocking, ignored Al, on whom he usually tried a funny greeting, and said, "You're to come with me." Even Al looked up, surprised. Marshall's face was dead white. I pulled a sweater over my head and followed him. We walked three blocks before he spoke.

"Henry the Eighth had his women beheaded for less."

It wasn't a quip, and I knew better than to treat it as one. But when he—by design or natural drift, I knew not—led the way into the cemetery and found a dark, cold tombstone for us to sit on, I did say, "This where you and your girl friends come?"

"A hit, a palpable hit." He laughed bitterly.

He said nothing more, but I heard his breathing grow more agitated. "I'm your friend, not anyone else's. Say on."

"Sylvia is pregnant."

"God!"

"Not by me. I never did anything to her. I didn't even do some of the things I told you I did. I always respected her. I know I've neglected her, but I was rehearsing, and working, and studying."

"And walking out with Sally-Jane and Emma-Sue," I said.

"You said you were my friend," he reminded me sullenly.

"Who is he?"

"A Yankee. I know him; he's in my Freshman Problems class. He's uglier than I am, a nose like Hiawatha's canoe, and sly bitty eyes. Black hair slicked down, black heads, greasy ears, round shoulders. He looks like he could die of TB before he's thirty."

"Evidently he can fuck."

Again he laughed, but this time it was real, hard-edged

but healthy. "I always think you're innocent; it's because you remind me of Wayne Morris. I hate her. You know why?"

"What will she do?"

"Oh, it's all settled. We had a short date tonight after supper, a walking date she arranged, so she could tell me. They're getting married Saturday. She has the distinction of being the first preggie pledge at tri-Delt this year. She had to tell her father, and Mr. Patterson came up and talked to the boy—I can't make myself say his name, because it's going to be hers. He's agreeable to marrying and so, surprisingly, is his family. They run a delicatessen in Corona, Long Island; respectable, Italian, Catholic."

"How come you hate her?"

"She saw him without telling me and saw me without telling him. She's going to quit school and keep house for him while he continues. Mr. Patterson will help with the money. I'll have to watch her get big—Sylvia! He had her on their first date. Two weeks ago she and I were on this very tombstone, Clifford Danziger, beloved husband of Rachel, died September 23, 1923. She tried, I swear she did, to get *me* to do it. We had this marble hot as a frying pan. She's as sly as he is! So she could have two choices maybe if he wouldn't buy? So she could flip a coin, him or me?"

"Would you have married her?"

"I'd have had to, wouldn't I?"

"So, virtue has rewarded you. You don't have to get a job at the A&P."

After a pause he said accusingly, "You never liked her."

"No."

"How did you *know?*"

"I didn't know anything; I just didn't like her."

"I did. I talk big, but I loved her. The worst thing—I feel so goddamn stupid.—Stupid! Goddamn it! Goddamn it!" He cried, and I let him alone. It took a few minutes to taper off and stop. He blew his nose and then sat still.

"I'm hungry," I said.

"You shit."

"I get a craving this time every night."

I got up to go, and he followed. "You're the only one ever saw me cry."

47

THE LIES we tell are probably necessary, because they allow us to live together. The truth is often dull or offensive, and besides, it is always changing. What are we to do but lie, adjusting the lies with little, bearable truths?

I was young and afraid of seeming young, so I pretended to be more knowledgeable than I was. To admit that I was lonely, to say I didn't know—unthinkable. The small recognitions, so gratefully received, can throw self out of balance. The only antidote is silence, that sometimes destroyer of souls, sometimes healer.

I liked myself, but I was not in love with myself, and self-deception early gave way to self-examination. No thought was safe, no sentence I wrote inviolate. I was forever changing my mind, and if I appeared impatient of others, it was a small part of a greater impatience with myself. I did not love deception, I only practiced it. Yet I was sometimes harsh and rude too.

I knew I wanted to be Somebody and that it mattered to me, but not very much, who got hurt in my quest for a place in the sun. I acted diffidence, postured sincerity; and my reward was to be believed. I knew that Marshall was selfish and intolerant and one of the thorough cowards of the world. I knew too that he was brainy and openhearted and that he could be fearless. I could have recited the motives behind the behavior of acquaintances as easily as the multiplication tables, and I didn't learn them from Psychology One, which always seemed to be about mice. I scorned religion and prayed alone in the dark.

I'd been afraid I'd have no place to go at Christmas when Beatrice, to my vast relief, asked me to come-stay with them. She was at the station, Margaret at her side, when I came into Montgomery from Tuscaloosa on the train that was so slow the students called it the Doodlebug. Surprised at the intensity of my own gladness at seeing Beatrice, I picked the baby up, pretending affection I didn't feel. The child stared at me and said, "Mark."

"I taught her," Beatrice said. "She's going to be smart like her Uncle Mark, not dumb in school like her mama." I hugged her then, and she took the baby from me and set her on her feet.

I was proud of being given the guest room, although I found it less comfortable than my battle-scarred half a room in Woods Hall. It was so feminine no man could have walked into it without wanting to walk right out again. Harvey was friendly, but happiness made him dull. He wasn't interested in anyone but Beatrice and his children, and when for politeness he pretended to be, his eyes had the look of glass. Lucius and Roy were newly awed (I was a *college* man) and as boring as ever with their boyish concerns and pointless questions. Part of the reason I didn't like them was that they had Beatrice; the other part was my awareness that they were curious about me but disappointed by the answers I made them. I wasn't evasive, but I couldn't give them what they wanted.

Aunt Belle struck me as scattier, but not unhappy. Yet a remark could startle. "I tell the bridge club I'm the only woman they know whose husband left her for another man. I'm a widow without the insurance money." Roland was get-

252

ting bulgy around the middle, which ill suited his hawky face and boney behind. Speaking of the brokerage business, he said "I" more often than "we." And Georgette—the three came out for supper the first Sunday evening I was there—moved with the ponderous importance of a new ice age. She was close to what she referred to in whispers as her "time."

I telephoned everyone I knew, except Celia, who had telephoned me five minutes after I entered the Briggs house, having discovered from Beatrice the time of my train. There were parties at which most of us (not Celia) pretended to see more change in each other than we did. Posy was, however, almost a stranger, her cheeks chipmunk fat; why? We used to know as friends how to dove-tail thoughts and remarks (the thing Marshall was jealous of). We didn't any more. Everyone bragged, clearly considering his or her school superior to others, except Celia, who said of Huntingdon, "It's all right. I don't care. I go." Everyone laughed as if she'd made a joke, knowing Celia never did.

Margaret Torrence was the best one to see again, and we had two good evenings in a row; and then Aunt Sally scolded her into bed for four days with one of the headaches she had been afraid was coming on. I saw her when she was well again, but she hadn't got her energy back, and I thought of her for the first time as vulnerable, almost fragile.

The truth was, no one was "satisfactory" any longer, except Beatrice and Margaret Torrence. My best times with Beatrice were the mornings when Harvey had gone to work and the boys were out of the way with their own concerns. Eulabelle still came to clean house, but Beatrice was clearly the mistress and kept the kitchen as her own. There she and the baby and I spent the mornings, Margaret gaining my approval by occupying herself contentedly in her pen most of the time. I loved watching Beatrice prepare food, not only because I was greedy, but for the pleasure of watching anyone do what he's good at. She usually had a cigarette lighted, in lips or hand or saucer, but I never saw her drop an ash, not Beatrice. I didn't enjoy smoking but sometimes I'd ask her for a cigarette and light it to be companionable.

I saw Uncle Grady at the warehouse, where I worked during the Christmas rush. Mrs. Bush still kept the office with her hoard of rusty paper clips and weak rubber bands and her ice-pick filing system. One night I was invited to Uncle John's for supper, which was a big pot of beef stew and a tray of bakery rolls. When Uncle Grady was in the bathroom, Uncle John told me he hadn't had a drink of hard liquor since the night of my birthday last February when they'd taken me to the Paradise for fried chicken. "We have a beer before supper, that's all." He was proud of him. I didn't mean to watch, but I suppose I did, because I was aware that they never touched the way people do casually when they are in the same room, or passing in and out. Yet there was a thing I could sense, there was a bond between them— that link between any two people who have come to some agreement, and which makes a third person an outsider.

The day before I was to take the Doodlebug back to school, Celia came to Beatrice's in her mother's car and asked me to ride with her. I didn't want to. I was finishing a short play that had started as a free-verse monologue. It was called *Wreath Without Laurel* and had only two speaking parts, Death and a soldier, although a dozen other soldiers were to mime the battle scene that opened the play. *Bury the Dead* had made a strong impression on me. I didn't care when Celia said she had something important to tell me, but I went with her. She asked me where I'd like to go that I hadn't been this time, and I surprised her by answering, "Day Street." She knew the way generally, but I had to direct her turnings. She parked where I asked her to, and we walked. She was puzzled and, I was gratified to see, a little impressed that I should want to be in the Negro section of town.

When it started to rain, we went back to the car, but she

didn't start it. She folded her arms and looked ahead through the windshield. "You remember Norman Brigham?"

It took me a moment. "At the graduation dance; your cousin."

"Distant."

"Nashville?"

She nodded. "He says he wants to marry me."

"You don't know him!" She glanced at me quickly, then turned her eyes again to the windshield. "I mean, you have to go to college."

"I don't have to finish because I started. Lots of girls go for a year and get married. I'm not very—intellectual, I guess you'd say."

"Do you want to get married?"

"I hate school, and I don't want to get a job, and he lives in Nashville; that's where his daddy's construction business is."

"Nashville is a long way."

"That's why. I'm sick of Mama. I've been sick of Mama all my life."

"Is that a reason to marry him?"

"It's the best I can think of."

"Do you love him?"

She looked at me and shook her head. I knew what she wanted me to say and do, and we both knew I wouldn't. There were tears in her eyes. She put her head on the steering wheel and cried. All I could do was pat her back. Pride stopped her. She found a handkerchief in her pocketbook and dried her face and drove me home. We were silent until she stopped the car in front of the house.

"I couldn't help it, Mark. I had to see how you'd feel about it."

"I guess we're grown up," I said inadequately.

She shrugged. "You can't help yourself. I know it. I can't either."

I sought words. "Celia, I'll always—" That was as far as I got. I sounded so phoney to myself I had to stop.

"You'll always fall in love with someone else. It wasn't just Alice."

I stepped out of the car and closed the door, irritable with her and myself. "Are you going to do it?"

"I'll finish my year at Huntingdon. He wants me to. It looks better if your wife has been to college a year. It establishes the fact that she's nice but not a bookworm. Then I'll do one last thing Mama wants: I'll let her plan my damned wedding." She drove away, and I went into the house thinking: A bridge is on fire behind me; the wind is blowing ash on my back.

For a day I thought of Celia more than I ever had before, because she'd cried over my not loving her. But I could not say I did when I did not, and I wouldn't have changed anything.

48

"IT WON'T act," Hugh Weatherhead said. "It's closet drama."

I knew it would act, and it did. Marshall directed *Wreath Without Laurel* and played Death in a tailcoat on a battlefield. I played the soldier, forgetting my stage fright in *Jane Eyre*. It was done as a workshop production, using R.O.T.C. uniforms and the black cyclorama instead of a set; but the afternoon audience we showed it to was enthusiastic, so it was put on again in an evening of one-act plays in March, with O'Casey's *Pound on Demand* and Chekhov's *The Bear*. Everyone said it wasn't a play and shouldn't "work." Nevertheless, it did. Conviction can make all the difference. That is why we are disconcerted when it doesn't.

It was a good spring of the year 1939. I was a man. I was a writer. I had a long way to go as both, but I was starting.

For all its gaucherie, *Wreath Without Laurel* had a human pulse. The next short play I wrote did not. I called it *These Silent Hills,* and it was a farm-family tragedy owing much to my having rediscovered Eugene O'Neill after thinking *him* gauche for a couple of years. When the Drama Department politely declined to mount it even as a workshop production, I myself became dissatisfied with it and turned it into a story. What I wanted was to be allowed to read it as a sort of audition to Victor Ward's writing class.

Professor Ward's class had achieved some recognition nationally. Novels by four of his students had been published by commercial publishers in New York. How was I to get in? I approached my English instructor, a Miss Ball from Wisconsin, who was sympathetic. She had read a few of my poems, which I had chosen carefully out of a hundred. She'd praised the language and control of forms and criticized a tendency to slip over into sentimentality. Cultivating the interest of teachers is something ambitious writers do, because they are the next step. It isn't cold-blooded, because creation, bad or good, is never cold, and getting an audience is part of creation. It is no more self-interested than learning how to run if you want to catch a rabbit. No English teacher I've known has been stupid, and none has refused the role of patron and helper. I've even heard Victor Ward described as "the mid-wife of southern writing."

I learned later from Ward himself that he invited me to read a story to the class because of my brashness, although he had been assured by Miss Ball that I did have "some talent." I was to read the story I still called *These Silent Hills* in early May.

I was nervous and so was Miss Ball, and the way it came out was brusqueness with each other. The class members arrived by ones and twos. There were only nine that semester. Professor Ward had no settled number. He would admit two or twenty. There were no formal entrance requirements. Acceptance or rejection depended upon his assessment of one's talent; his yes or no was final. The nine were all kinds. Three considered themselves bohemians. One of them, I discovered, wrote pretty good imitation Cain-Hemingway. There was a rich town woman in her thirties, pretty, a little plump. Her accent sounded English to me (she'd been to school there) ; but she was midwestern before she married a Tuscaloosa businessman. Belying the proper-lady look of her, she was to reveal a robust sense of humor that made us friends. If she was the wife of business, she was also, to a degree, the Wife of Bath. Another girl, small-town southern by accent, was thin and pale with fine facial features and rough-skinned hands. Her clothes were fussy verging on funny; yet she had an eye for detail and wrote a plain prose I envied and learned from. So much for books and their covers. The other students made little impression on me.

Professor Ward came in and sat at the head of the table around which we had collected in a downstairs room of the main library building. He told the class who I was, and two of the bohemians exchanged glances and slumped into their chairs as if they resented their being chairs and were trying to deny their contours. Mr. Ward explained to me that I wasn't to be distracted by the making of notes as I read. That was their method, if they had one; and everyone was free to say what he liked in comment or criticism when the reading was over. "We are not here to compliment each other." He smiled charmingly, and I remembered the warning that he was a little theatrical in his manners. "Unless compliments are deserved. Begin when you are ready."

I don't know where I found voice, I was so scared. I couldn't look at anyone. I felt on fire. I must have read badly, but it didn't matter. For the first couple of pages the class was still. I was aware of occasional, then frequent scratchings of pen and pencil. I began to read more quickly, until Ward interrupted me to ask me to slow down. He was the only one other than Miss Ball who did not make notes. (Miss Ball had already given me a cautious opinion of the story.)

Once I heard a laugh. Every sentence I read seemed to be wrong. I thought of stopping and saying I was not well and must be excused, but I could not. At last I finished, but kept my eyes on the title of the pages I had tapped together to straighten.

"We'll start with Mr. A.," Ward said.

"Well." It was one of the bohemians. He gave a short laugh I recognized as the same I'd heard during the reading. "There's no question that Mr. Bowman has read *some* O'Neill and too much Thomas Wolfe." The laugh came again and was echoed by a female student I had not noticed before. "I suppose—." Mr. A. for all his supposing did not sound doubtful. "It may as well be said right off that the story is awful. Is Mr. Bowman sure he needs to write?" There was a pause no one offered to fill. "I made a lot of notes, but they probably aren't worth going into. I stopped making them because I couldn't write fast enough. Is there any point?"

Ward said easily, "Give us what you have. Mr. Bowman read his story so that we might tell him what we think of it in small as well as large ways."

Mr. A. went through the list he'd made. The conception was imitative, the construction amateurish, the execution crude. This word was hackneyed, that one false to a character—not that the characters were not themselves false as well. The dialogue was wooden, emotions mechanical. I thought he would attack every word before he was done. I had never hated anyone as much, because I understood what he meant and could agree with most of what he said. When he said no more, I looked up at him stonily; he returned my look and shrugged.

His was the longest analysis of what I had written. As the

others explained in checking notes they'd made, "This point has been covered." There were new points, and familiar criticisms were made again and emphasized, as if the speaker could not rest with Mr. A.'s gentler judgment. No one ridiculed me. No one found anything good to say. In the case of the dowdy southern girl and the smart town woman, the criticisms were more politely spoken, but they were unequivocal in their condemnation. The worst of it was my feeling that nothing I'd ever done could have been good. To condemn my work condemned me. I had not felt so bad since I was in Savannah.

The session had begun at noon. When Denny Chimes sounded one o'clock, Mr. Ward dismissed the others with a wave of his hand. They left without haste, talking of other things.

Miss Ball whispered as if she were in a sick room that she must hurry to her office before meeting someone for lunch and then had a class at two o'clock; but if I wanted to talk to her, she'd be working in her office from three until four.

No one was left but the professor and me. I knew I must say something. "Thank you for letting me come." He looked down the table. "I wasted everyone's time. I'm sorry."

"What was said was true enough," he said. I nodded stiffly and got to my feet. "Cruel, some of it."

"I don't mind that," I protested.

"Well, there's this. You may never have a worse hour about your writing, but you'll never make those mistakes again."

"Maybe I won't make any. They say I'm not a writer."

"Do you think you are?"

"Yes sir."

"So do I." He smiled, enjoying himself.

49

THE SCHOOL year ended, and I returned to Montgomery to stay at the YMCA and work at the warehouse until September. I had put off leaving Tuscaloosa as long as I could. Marshall was already in summer school, and middle-aged high school teachers from all over the state had arrived in print dresses and white shoes and stockings, to take classes toward higher academic degrees that, they hoped, might in time bring them higher salaries. Celia had written a letter to me on her last day at Huntingdon, before her first day as Mrs. Brigham of Nashville. She wrote from the reading room of the college library, "the only place Mama doesn't follow me these days with a tape measure and pins in her mouth."

Back in Montgomery, I saw no old Lanier friends. Posy telephoned Beatrice trying to find me to tell me she was leaving the next day to be a bridesmaid at Alice's wedding to Lieutenant Gerald O'Brien. More ashes of the past, I told myself, and wrote a poem, and tore it up. It was another summer to work and wait while others went and did.

I had the company of Margaret Torrence once or twice a week, except for what had become the annual visit to her brother wherever he was. I had Beatrice's company and cooking, although she would spend most of her time at the lake house with daughter Margaret and the two stepsons, Harvey joining them week nights when he could, weekends always. Uncle Grady and Uncle John took me to supper at Morrison's cafeteria on Commerce Street and to wrestling matches at Crampton Bowl "for something to do." I saw new and old movies. One Sunday a month Aunt Belle insisted that I be at the house on Morgan Avenue for noon dinner. "You are my dead sister's boy." But, duty done on both sides, it was easy for me to leave after eating the inevitable dry chicken and pretending to admire Baby Angel, who had been born a girl, so the name was only precious instead of blighting. It was odd being a guest in the house I'd lived in for so long. Roland, who had no trouble giving me orders at the warehouse during the week, suddenly made conversation. "I suppose you must study a lot of interesting things at the university." Had I detected any feeling about his own lost ambitions, I'd have felt sympathy; there was none.

Most evenings I worked in my room at the Y. I was not so lucky the second summer as I'd been the first; I had to share a room with a young man who worked for the gas company. However, he slept most of the time he wasn't on the job and spent every Saturday and Sunday with a married sister in Eufaula. He said he didn't mind the desk light, and his snoring bore him out, for it was louder than the sound of my old typewriter.

I had been asked to write a framework for the autumn variety show of the dramatic society at the university. It was less an honor than a chore; no one was eager to do it, and the job usually fell into the hands of a nonwriter. The traditional framework for the event was an old-fashioned melodrama, the real show being the interpolated magic acts, tap and adagio dances, girl singers, group singers, boy accordionists, and xylophone solos by both sexes, sometimes on roller skates. I jumped at the chance. I was spinning like a top that won't stop.

I had the more serious project of writing what would be my debut reading as a *member* of Ward's class. I'd show Mr. A., the son of a bitch. Although one was supposed to write what he pleased how he pleased, Mr. Ward discouraged the doing of plays. I assumed this was out of deference to the Drama Department until he offered another reason. "It's harder to get a good first play produced in New York than it is to get a promising first novel published." The composition of stories was encouraged; it was a time of healthy magazines. There was a good deal of talk among class members of "literary" and "slick" and "pulp" fiction.

I picked as the subject of my first novel a boy's first year at college. Without a shred of logic, I believed everyone would be interested. My title was suggestive of the approach: *Wolf in the Wilderness.* Dickens might have made it funny. Dostoevski might have made it tragic. I made it boring, but I had to wait to be told that. Margaret Torrence offered once that it might be best to wait a few years for perspective on the subject, to which I replied that I had to do it *now.*

The slighter project was the more successful. I called it *Hellcat Hattie,* and it was about a Mae West type who ran a saloon in a cow town "in the late nineteenth century." It used to good effect my accumulated knowledge of bad movies, and it had some funny jokes, although I hadn't learned that what is funny on paper is often not funny on a stage.

Marshall wrote me that Sylvia had gone with her husband to have their baby in Corona, Long Island. In my antic mood I wrote back, "At least the kid won't want for salami and pickles," which Marshall in his next letter told me was in bad taste. That letter contained the first reference to a freshman football player named Carl Marek who had, surprisingly, agreed to do a small part in Aristophanes' *The Frogs,* which Hugh Weatherhead was to direct after Christmas. "We're trying to get more athletes, thinking the apes will look amusing in little dresses, but so far only Carl has agreed."

Having lived at Woods Hall and the YMCA with roommates, I made up my mind not to have another if I could help it; so one weekend I hitchhiked to Tuscaloosa to look around. Mrs. Blake had been able to find only three boarders for the summer and gave me her fourth bed free for a night. Nor would she let me pay for meals, knowing how it was with me. I found and reserved for the fall a single room at a place upstairs over several stores in a section of University Avenue that housed dry cleaners, lunch counters, photographic and record shops, and a bowling alley. The place was called the Spanish Inn, I never knew why. The room was as plain as a cell: single bed, oblong table with straight chair, metal lockers, and—the one indulgence—a big, stout rocking chair that filled all the window side overlooking a filling station across the street.

After supper Saturday night I read *Hellcat Hattie* to Marshall, who was the perfect audience for it; and he told me about his summer amours. "You should be here. Nobody has trouble. All these older women who teach gym in hick town high schools are hot. One, Myra's her name, has a pussy like an electric chair."

"You mean you have to be strapped in?"

He yawned. "Things dull in Montgomery?"

"Yeah," I said. "I just haven't had a piece of pussy the last day or two."

Around ten we went to Pug's for pie and coffee (my treat), and Carl Marek stopped at our booth to be introduced. He was a big, square-faced boy with black hair and pimples between thick eyebrows. "You're the writer Marshall's told me about," he said with so clearly admiring a smile I moved over to make room for him. He stayed only a few minutes. I was surprised at the way Marshall treated him. He made fun of him, told him he was dumb, asked him if he could count backwards from ten to zero in three minutes—all of which Carl took with a good-natured smile. When he left, I told Marshall he was showing off, behaving like a lion tamer to prove he was better than athletes, whom he'd been afraid of ever since Baldwin Junior High School.

"Well," Marshall said, "he *is* dumb, so I make him pay for being in the company of genius."

"Mightn't he hit you?"

Marshall shook his head. "He thinks artists are gods; don't

ask me why. He'd like to be one but knows he can't. A real freak, but he's nice to Mama. She knows him because he followed me home one day and stayed so long she had to ask him to supper. You should have seen him eat, worse than you. Both things, admiring artists and being nice to mothers, maybe they're the immigrant background. Second generation means he's the first one in the family to speak English without an accent."

"What's his family?"

"Polish, Lithuanian, I don't know. He likes to hang out backstage, but I don't listen to him. From Philadelphia on a football scholarship."

"Can he act?"

"All Hugh will ask him to do is stand up straight and look Greek. If I had a body like his, I wouldn't care if I couldn't do anything, let alone act. I wouldn't care if I was a leper."

"Lepers don't have very good bodies."

"You'd think they would. I mean, *some* compensation. For all that having to ring bells, and scratching, and things falling off."

I left next morning and was back in my musty room at the Y a little after noon. Having had a cheap trip with free almost-everything, I went to the Paramount with its upped Sunday prices. The picture was *Beau Geste,* the Gary Cooper one.

Summer passed. World War II began. School opened.

My debut reading the first chapter of *Wolf in the Wilderness* was not acclaimed. Ward himself had little to say. (He rarely said much in class, acting more as referee than lecturer.) The comments of the others were, I decided, fretfully resigned. Mr. A.'s remarks were the most outspoken. "Nobody has ever written a good novel about going to college," he said. "Nobody." Mr. A.'s name was Ash, I discovered.

We took turns reading, although sequence was not rigid. There were no requirements about size of production. Work went well or poorly, and Mr. Ward understood that. Therefore the same student might read twice in a week and another not read for a month. One of the reasons for the success of his method while so many other creative writing classes foundered in self-appreciating amateurishness was that Mr. Ward treated all of us like professional writers. We were assumed to be because we had been admitted to the class, although its purpose was to learn to be professional.

One day I read a new chapter and Ash's comments were particularly virulent; he did not shrink from insult. I couldn't pay him back in kind, because I often admired what he wrote, without wanting to do it his way. The closest I came to criticizing him was to accuse him of reverse sentimentality, which I declared as false as sentimentality. Every adjective he used created an ugly image. A bus could not be simply a bus; for Ash its lights at night made it "a dirty yellow blob." He had a fetish, I told him, of seediness and called it truthful observation; I called it cheap despair.

After that the severity of his attack became something of a joke in class. People anticipated it when I read, even as they disassociated themselves from it, as they might a fight between stray dogs in the street. I could admit that often what he said hit the mark. He said some things others were too polite or too bored to tell me. It would have been all right had he not relished it so, aping the snappy sadism of the critics of the day. I finally answered, "Thank you, Mr. Ashhole." It was the first remark I made in class that got laughter. Even Mr. Ward smiled before he reprimanded me and, looking at his watch, which he always kept before him on the long table, dismissed us for the day.

Ash was waiting for me outside the library. "Get smart with me again and I'll reach across the table and slap your face in front of everybody."

"You do and I'll kill you in front of everybody, Edward G."

I never understood why killers are surprised to discover that their victims hate them.

50

I LOVED the cell at the Spanish Inn; it was my first deliberate home. I set up a bookcase with three boards and bricks I'd stolen at night a few at the time from a construction site. During Beatrice's summer at the lake, which as she said mostly consisted of sitting on the screened porch and listening for sounds of trouble from the children, she had knitted and pieced together for me a many-colored afghan. I used the afghan as bedspread; it and the books gave the room all the color it needed. I hung a bulletin board too and pinned up a few postcards and a portrait from *Life* magazine of Tallulah Bankhead as Regina in *The Little Foxes*. We were all proud of her; Margaret Torrence's prediction that she would be a great actress had come true. In the rocking chair by the window, book or writing pad on lap, I was happy.

The inn was impersonal; I made no friends there. Most of the others were graduate students, and they generally looked worried, or at least preoccupied, for time was bought dearly by those young men, and they knew they must make the most of it and get on with their lives. I saw them only in the hall or the shower room. No one locked his door, and Marshall, my one frequent visitor, would stop by and leave a note on the bulletin board. ("Coming to rehearsal? Hedy Lamarr says maybe for Saturday night. Brother, can you spare a dame?") To Marshall's relief, Sylvia and her husband had not come back to Tuscaloosa. Maybe they attended a school closer to Corona, Long Island.

I went on stubbornly with the novel, but it had begun to

bore me as much as it did my fellow writers. Professor Ward said nothing to encourage or discourage me. Looking for approval anywhere, I showed a few chapters to a girl in English history class who had been flirting with me. She said when she gave it back that it was the best book she'd read in her life, including *Gone with the Wind,* so I dropped her. I was taking another class with Ward, Shakespeare. He gave fine readings of *Lear* and *Antony and Cleopatra* and *Othello,* and his explanations were more illuminating than any others I have since read. Casual he might appear to be with the writing class, but he was not with Shakespeare. He gave probing and difficult final examinations.

Hellcat Hattie was a success, variety acts and all. For once, I was told, audiences thought the "connecting tissues" were funny too. Hugh had the idea of casting a big, plain, shy, nervous farm girl from South Alabama as Hattie, the Mae West role. In costume, her inhibitions fell away; she was ebulliently funny, and her country accent was right. There were some mild double meanings in her dialogue with the cowboys whom I used to parody the overmanly westerner of the movies I'd seen, and was rooster-proud when I heard that the Dean of Men had stalked out of the show in disgust at the "dirt."

During autumn and early winter Carl Marek was busy with football practice, but when he saw Marshall or me, or anyone in the "arts" he knew and admired, he'd go out of his way to say hello and chat. We were amused because his athletic companions (they usually went in groups) were puzzled and suspicious of us. Hugh rehearsed *The Frogs* after Christmas, and with football season over, Carl had more time to hang around and become a nuisance. Wherever we were, he wanted to be. Marshall and I tried to ignore him, talking to each other in our usual way about love, life, and the humanities. But if there was a pause or a silence, Carl would say something so adulatory we'd laugh. He didn't mind. He ate with the other athletes in the dining hall, but sometimes he'd look for me in Pug's, knowing I ate at odd hours to avoid the crowds. It was a popular restaurant. He'd seat himself opposite me and order a glass of milk or a cup of tea, seldom anything to eat. He'd sit and just look at me. At first I found his gape disconcerting, then irritating, and finally fell into Marshall's way of saying rude things. He was unfazed. It was part of my being an artist, he reasoned—*he'd* seen those movies about musicians and painters.

In *The Frogs* he did what he was given to do earnestly, and the girls backstage and in the audience let out squeals when they saw him in costume. I was a walk-on-and-walk-about in the play too. ("Only," Marshall pecked, "because we couldn't get enough real tarzans." I reminded him that his own legs looked like a mosquito's.)

Carl took to walking back to the Spanish Inn with me after rehearsals and then performances. To escape him I'd say I was on my way somewhere else, or that I had to work in the library. He'd come to the inn uninvited. I liked time alone, to write or study or sit thinking, so I installed a bolt on the door. When someone knocked and got no answer, he usually went away, but sometimes turned the door knob. Privacy was my right, I told myself, but I felt furtive sitting and watching a moving knob and not answering to the call of my name.

At two o'clock one morning in January a knock woke me. When it came again, muted and urgent, I asked who it was.

"Carl."

"What do you want?" I turned on the light and saw the clock. "Do you know what time it is?"

"Let me in, please."

He was dressed in heavy pants and sweater against the cold night, but they looked like the first things he'd grabbed, and he was usually a careful dresser. He had a heavy beard, and his eyes were bloodshot. He was apologetic. "I'm sorry. I *am*."

"What's wrong?"

"I had such a nightmare. I've had it before, but this time I couldn't go to sleep again. I felt like if I did, it would get me and kill me."

"What 'it'?"

"I don't know."

"Well." I hesitated; he was clearly troubled. "Maybe if you talk a little."

"No, Mark." Gratefully, he made for the rocking chair and sat down. "Go back to bed and turn off the light. Let me sit here the rest of the night. I'll be all right with you in the room."

Not flattered, but sorry for him, I talked to him a couple of minutes more, told him it was all right, gave him my extra blanket, and went back to bed. I didn't know if he slept, but he was quiet. I woke at dawn to see him standing by the chair. Carefully, he folded the blanket and placed it on the seat of the rocker. Then he tiptoed to the door, opened it and slipped out.

After that he assumed that I was his friend; and having to endure his company, I listened to him now and then. I didn't encourage him, but he talked to me about his family. He loved his mother. His father was a brute who had worked in a coal mine until he was crippled in a cave-in. Now he was a janitor. He had two sisters and four brothers, all older than he. All of the family except his mother had picked on him and pushed him around. That's why he'd gone into athletics, to get strong enough to push them back and make them leave him alone. If I thought I'd been poor, they'd been sure-enough poor. Supper was sometimes nothing but fish-head soup full of potatoes and seasoned with ketchup one of the brothers had stolen from a diner. He, Carl, was the only one to finish high school and think of going to college; and his only chance had been a football scholarship. He went to Mass with his mother, and they both feared God.

"You go to Mass here?"

"Sure. You want to come?" he asked eagerly.

Like many southerners born Protestant, I felt a draw toward the forbidden Roman Catholic ritual; but I shrugged. "I don't get up in time." (A lie, I was always an early riser.)

"We can go any time. They have more than one. You say when."

I went with him the following Sunday at nine o'clock, thinking that I must remember to drop a careless mention of it into conversation next time I saw Georgette. I'd never been into a Catholic church before, so I observed everything, without making an attempt to enter into the forms of the ritual, although some were familiar from movies. I found myself surprised and touched at the sight of the big boy beside me going through his motions so seriously and humbly.

When we left, he stretched and shook himself like a dog, and then began to strut as if to rid himself of religion. I asked him if he went to confession often.

"People not Catholic always want to know what you tell the priest."

"Well," I said, "do you tell him everything?"

"I don't always get too particular."

"You just say, 'Father, I have sinned—'"

"I get more particular than that. But like—you ever have your dick sucked, Mark?"

"What the hell makes you ask that?"

"Well, you know, girls like to do it. They say it's so they won't get pregnant. Maybe it never happened to you because you're not Catholic and didn't grow up in a Polish neighborhood." He laughed. "So, if it's something like that, I wouldn't tell the priest *exactly;* I mean, out of respect, I wouldn't draw a picture."

I didn't go with him again, but he considered my going that time another tie between us. Sometimes when he came around, I made him leave. One day after I'd told him to go so I could do some work, he lingered, trying to tease me into amiability. I lost my temper and shouted, "Get out of here, you ape!"

He was instantly grim. "I am not an ape—don't use Marshall's word on me."

"I'm sorry," I said, "but I'm tired and busy."

"You have time for everybody else. You have plenty of time for Marshall."

"I've known Marshall all my life. Sometimes when he's here I don't even know it. Besides, he's funny. He makes me laugh. You don't."

"I want to be your friend."

"Okay, we're friends," I said casually, "but I have to work now." He looked at me intently, an asking look I wanted to deny I saw, so I said, "You ought not to scratch those things between your eyebrows. It leaves bloody scabs."

He thought about it and smiled. "That was nice. You are my friend because you care whether I scratch or not. I'll go now."

51

JOURNALISM WAS one of my minor subjects, and I was writing a movie review that had been assigned when a messenger came into the classroom and whispered to the instructor, who told me I was wanted in the Dean of Men's office. Puzzled, I went directly to the administration building. There was a bench outside the Dean's office, and when I hesitated, one of the two boys sitting there said, "He sends for you when he's ready." A few minutes later a student secretary opened the door and summoned the one who'd spoken. He was in and out quickly, and so was the other boy. I sat so long I thought I'd been forgotten, but when I knocked, the secretary told me the Dean knew I was there. Twenty-five minutes passed before I was told to go in.

The Dean, a lanky man in his thirties whom I knew by sight but had never had occasion to meet face to face, was looking at his desk top and continued to do so. He was not reading but staring at the large brown blotter that nearly covered his desk. My nervousness increased. Could I have done something wrong without knowing it, infringed some rule I was ignorant of?—Or was someone at home dead and I was about to be told?—I shifted from one foot to the other. I tried not to clear my throat, but did so, whereupon the Dean snapped his eyes directly to mine. His were icy. "Mr. Marcus Bowman."

"Yes sir."

"You write plays, I believe."

"I've done a couple."

"And I have seen them. I cannot say that I was impressed favorably. The western thing in a saloon I considered entirely unsuitable for performance at a university. It might indeed have made the animals in a stable blush." I didn't answer, but I set my face as hard as he'd set his and looked back at him as coldly as he was looking at me. "However, that is not why I have sent for you; you are here for a more serious purpose. You have held an NYA job in the main library for three semesters. I assume that you needed that job when you got it last year and that you still need it?"

"Yes sir."

"Really need it?"

"Yes sir."

His smile was small and belied the words he next spoke. "I am sorry to say the job is no longer yours."

Surprise became panic. "I can't do without it—"

"That, I fear, is your problem, not the university's. Those jobs are for worthy students, and they are not to be kept by those who show themselves to be irresponsible."

Anger was added to panic. "I can't see that writing a play—"

He waved a hand. "Nothing to do with that. One of your subjects is military training—ROTC. Right?" I nodded. "You have consistently, I may say arrogantly, cut a great many of those classes."

"We're allowed fifteen cuts a semester," I said.

"That is the maximum, yes, but they are not to be considered paid holidays. For a poor student—I shan't call you a charity student, but you are feeding at the public trough—"

"I'm paid thirty cents an hour for work that needs to be done, and I earn it."

"Silence when I am speaking!"

We glared at each other.

"Whether you have earned it or not, and I've had no complaint on that score—" He opened his hands on the desk top and shrugged to show fairness. "NYA jobs were created by the Federal Government at the instigation of Mrs. Roosevelt to enable poor, earnest students of high moral character to attend college. I do not consider you a shining illustration of that definition. The job is no longer yours. That is all."

"But, sir, please—"

"I said 'all,' Bowman; there is no use begging." He looked down again for the first time since he'd looked up. Opening a side drawer, he took from it a sheet of paper and a fountain pen. The paper he placed at a careful angle on the blotter. He unscrewed the pen and dated the sheet of paper. I went out.

My first anger was soon over; my second would be with me forever. In the exact, desperate meaning of the words: I didn't know what to do. I cursed myself for a fool. I might think the Dean a monster of inhumanity, but he was right, I had no doubt, from his point of view and the university's. I *had* behaved in a lordly manner cutting classes. I had taken it as my due, as did the other students. I was learning that the powerless have no rights. I had not appreciated my security, and it was gone.

I had no backlog of money. I lived hand to mouth. It hadn't mattered as long as I knew that once a month I'd be paid for my NYA job and receive twenty dollars from my friends in Montgomery. I did two things, cut unnecessary spending (no more movies, no pie and coffee in the evenings) and looked for a job. There was none to be had. I went the rounds of shops and stores asking for fill-in work, willing to do anything for any wage offered. I read ads in the local newspaper. I sounded out poorer acquaintances for leads.

Nothing.

I discovered something I hadn't known I possessed, or that I had taken for granted: pride. I could not write to Beatrice or to Margaret Torrence and tell them what had happened. I could not even tell Marshall. He would find out in time; meanwhile, I let everyone assume that I still worked at the library.

I did without dry cleaning and washed all my clothes except shirts. When my monthly meal ticket at Pug's was used up, I bought weekly ones and eked them out by skipping a meal a day, keeping in my room bread and peanut butter and the cheapest apples I could buy. This was noticed by my two regular visitors. Marshall joked about greed. Carl helped himself to the apples and criticized their quality. I hid food after that, but rats and roaches I hadn't known were there found it.

Dread of hunger induces and aggravates hunger; I found that out. With all my economies the day came when I hadn't a nickel left. I knew I could appeal to Beatrice, or tell Marshall and his mother; but pride would not let me yet. I was hungry before I had reason to be; and then I was truly hungry because I had nothing to eat. How could I say, "I'm hungry," to a friend? Make a joke of it?—a *joke?* How would they look at me? I could imagine Marshall, at first laughing, then slowly understanding I meant it.

That day I had no breakfast. I thought it would not be so bad and went off to attend classes as usual, but every place I passed threw out smells of morning food—bacon, sausage, toast, coffee. As I went by the fraternity houses set back on deep lawns the members used for throwing footballs or base-balls back and forth, I conjured up images of the big break-fasts being eaten inside and indeed could hear the clink and clatter of plates and silverware. Arriving at my first class early, after checking my mailbox in the post office behind the Supe Store (a surprise letter, cookies from Beatrice, a check from God?)—I watched the other students drift in. I held a book open before me, but I was looking at them, each one, and telling myself, 'He's eaten; she had only fruit juice and coffee because she promised her mother she'd go on a diet.' Even a diet seemed a feast to me. Their faces, calm or trou-bled, but not troubled about hunger, were an affront. They had eaten.

I simply, literally hated all around me because I knew they had eaten if they wanted to. I did not have the solace of being busy, because I had no job and only morning classes, having arranged my schedule to keep afternoons open to work for the library or to go back to the Spanish Inn and study or write.

After classes I went home, again down University Avenue past the fraternity houses with the rich boys idling on lawns and porches, waiting to sit down to a meal they would no doubt complain of. I went by Pug's, already noisy with its noon crowd, past humbler counter places, to my room. Know-ing I had missed nothing, I again searched pockets, turned out cuffs of pants. Then I sat in the rocking chair and, after a while, went to sleep.

I woke hungrier than ever, drank a lot of water, and felt weak. I tried to write. Nothing would come. I tried to study,

I tried to read. I could think of nothing but being hungry. Late in the afternoon I made myself go for a walk; and I found myself looking everywhere at, or for, food. A garbage pail with a loose lid—I wanted to look inside but was afraid of being seen doing it. I walked faster; but eventually I had to go home, and to do so meant passing the fraternity houses and the restaurants and diners again.

I took a shower and dressed, turned out the room light and sat in the rocker looking out the window. I tried to be stern with myself. Holy men fasted; it purified the spirit. It did no such thing to mine; it filled me with anger, self-pity, and hate. I could think of no one I knew without feeling anger and envy because, without its even occurring to them, they had the choice of eating or not; I had none, I slept again. When I woke, it was dark, but the lights and noise of University Avenue came up to me through the closed window. I felt weak and lonely and, standing, discovered that I was dizzy. The thought came calmly: kill yourself. Then, suddenly aware and horrified at the idea of being no more, I sat down on the bed and cried.

That was over and I had gone back to the rocker to look down again at the passersby on the night-lighted street when a knock came at the door. I ignored it. It came again, followed by, "Mark? Wake up and let me in. I've been by twice today and not found you. I know you're in there or your door couldn't be bolted."

Even as I pulled the bolt and Carl came striding in, my thought was that he smelled of food; he had been inside a warm place where people were eating.

"Jesus," he said, "don't even have the light on; you been asleep? You're not the kind to be hiding a girl, are you?" He knew where to find the light and turned it on. Glancing at me, his voice changed. "Hey, you look funny; you sick?"

I shook my head.

"What then? Something's wrong."

I sat on the bed to leave the rocker for him, and I didn't

answer. I hated him too, even as I knew I was glad he was there.

"You got to tell me, Mark."

"I'm hungry, you bastard!"

It was easy to say it then; I told him all that had happened beginning with my session at the Dean's office. I yelled and cursed and marched up and down the small dimensions of the room, but a few minutes exhausted me.

"Jesus. All that and you didn't come to me. I told you about rotten fish-head soup, but you—! Forget it. You're coming with me now."

I submitted to his pulling a sweater over my head and poking my arms into the sleeves. He took me to Pug's. The supper menu was over, but he ordered a steak and french fries and salad. "And a big glass of milk while we wait. Two."

I drank them both, and when food came and I began to eat, he looked less anxious. I didn't notice him again until I'd eaten the steak and potatoes and salad and all the bread from the basket. He had a cautious smile for me. "You know, Mark, all that shit about starving genius, it's shit."

I nodded, smiled back.

"Why didn't you come to me? Listen, I got money all the time. Those fat alumni types, they're always coming around. It's not only the free room and board and tuition I get; they can't leave without stuffing a twenty in your pocket. They like us guys to be grateful. It's like the scene in *Julius Caesar* you explained, when Antony is running the race. They think it gives them luck to touch us and leave a bill in the pocket. I think it's the only way some of them piss-their-pants, you want my opinion. But don't you ever—you hear me?—ever get hungry, long as I'm alive."

"Okay."

"Promise." He was dead earnest.

"Promise."

He walked me back to the inn. Downstairs he shoved something in my pants pocket I later discovered was a week's meal ticket he'd bought at the cashier's desk at Pug's when he paid the bill. "You'll want to be by yourself maybe, but I'm coming tomorrow. I got an idea. You're crazy, you know. Jesus." He grabbed me and hugged me and pushed me away. "I'm Polish, we get emotional!" He was gone.

52

CARL'S IDEA was simple. "Who do you know here's got the most push and shove?"

"Nobody." I thought. "Professor Victor Ward."

"Tell him you need a job."

I did, after giving him a calmer account than I'd given Carl of my interview with the Dean of Men. He told me to wait in his office; and when he returned half an hour later said, "You're going to grade papers for one of the instructors in freshman English. The pay is the same as NYA. Can you manage?"

"God yes."

Pride in myself revived; I was more than zero. I thought of the Dean with healthy, satisfying anger. The mail brought a package of cookies from Beatrice. I bought half a dozen of the best apples I could find, and Carl ate two the next time he came to the Spanish Inn.

However, there was a new worry, because I had made myself acknowledge a far more important development in my life than having lost the NYA job and done without a few meals. Folklore said the obvious remedy was to go to the right woman, and the only one I could think of who might help was Buffie Weatherhead. My friendliness with the pale, watching wife of the speech instructor had yielded an awareness that she found me attractive. I was not conceited, but there were looks and casual touchings I could not mistake. I telephoned Buffie and told her I had a problem I wanted to talk to her about, alone. She sounded pleased and said Hugh was in Birmingham for the afternoon (I'd called on a Saturday) and why didn't I come over anytime.

I took a bath and dressed as carefully as if I planned to commit hara-kiri. At three o'clock in the afternoon she let me into their apartment, gave me a glass of sherry, lighted a cigarette, and asked me what was the matter.

"I have begun to doubt my masculinity."

"Ah." She looked thoughtful and proceeded to lecture me on the need we all have to fulfill ourselves in physical ways—as well, of course, as intellectual and spiritual. She understood. I was not, in fact, the first young man to come to her with the problem. My friend Marshall Blake—but she would not tell tales out of school. She had considered it the duty of a concerned older woman. "We who know the way must help those who do not. As Emily Dickinson puts it, 'If I can help one fainting robin to its nest—' "

"That's beautiful," I said.

I shall not speculate on which of us was the more earnestly dishonest; enough to say that she had smoked only two cigarettes and I had hardly sipped from my sherry glass when we were naked and on the floor. Not for her the niceties. I had bathed. She clearly had not. Nor had she got around to shaving recently. Her legs were bristly, her chin unexpectedly rough; but what made it almost impossible for me to prove myself was the fact that there were several stiff hairs growing between her breasts. The Varga art in *Esquire* magazine had not prepared me for that. She also wore a dirty corn plaster that was coming loose.

She directed the whole sequence with the assurance of one to whom it is not a novel experience, and when she had frightened me half to death with her gasps and moans and I had driven faster and faster to put them out of my mind, she groaned the groan of a dying dinosaur, and I came from sheer terror. After a minute during which she squirmed a little more, she licked her tongue around my lips and said, "That was nice. No question, you're a boy."

She got up briskly and went to the bathroom. I didn't know what to do. I knew what I wanted to do—run, but it didn't seem polite. I found my handkerchief and wiped myself. It was a cool day, but I had sweated. I mopped face and armpits with my undershorts and put on the rest of my clothes, at the same time listening to the strange sounds from the bathroom. The only one I could positively identify was the flush of the toilet. She returned wearing her husband's bathrobe. I'd seen it many times on a hook on the bathroom door; it smelled of Vick's Salve. She was smoking again after putting on fresh lipstick, and cigarette paper came off on it.

"How do you feel?" she said with a wise look.

"Great."

"Some of my best talks have been afterwards."

"I'm too—I don't know what to say—happy, I guess."

"You go then. Hugh said he might get back for dinner." (Oh, God, I thought, French farce and Restoration comedy!) "You know where to find me, and you know I care, that I'm concerned about you."

Back at the Spanish Inn I took another shower, alternating between feelings of exhilaration and despair, because finally I was certain. Returning to the room, I found Carl. It was almost as if I had expected to.

"Hey! Your door wasn't bolted. That was a long shower. You going somewhere?" I said I wasn't. "Good. I thought— eat at Pug's maybe and a movie? I'm tired of the dining hall. It's Saturday night and I'm a free man. How about you?"

"Freer than I've ever been."

"Yeah?" He looked at me quickly and then went to stand at the window to watch the lights coming on and the people passing as I dressed. We had a good, big supper and lemon chiffon pie for dessert and then walked the mile downtown on University Avenue. The Bama Theatre was showing a murder mystery with Wendy Barrie, and at one point Carl grabbed my arm and squeezed. We were back at the inn by ten, and he followed me upstairs. Lights on, sweaters off, he said, "I could eat something," and I remembered Beatrice's cookies. As we finished them, I told him about her. That led to my telling him about Montgomery, and that led back to Savannah. Sometimes he asked a question.

"This Alice, pretty hot number, was she?"

"A cold number as far as I went."

"What the hell, it's just as well. You might have wound up doing handstands on a fucking horse. You know, you sound like somebody hasn't had a lot of experience, unless you left things out."

"Only things that would make me look bad."

"Still, I know you better now. I think I know you better than I know anybody. I wanted to be your friend a long time. It took some doing. You weren't interested in a cluck; why should you be? I think I'll write the Dean of Men a thank-you note for making you starve. That'd surprise the son of a bitch."

I laughed and he saw me look at the clock. There was a long pause. The thing that could happen was like a presence in the room. Both of us knew; neither knew the other did. He got up from the rocking chair and pulled down the window shade—"Just helping you get ready for bed."—then reluctantly picked up his sweater from the bed without putting it on. He was frowning, looking for a way and suddenly finding it. His face lighted, but he kept his voice flat. "I don't know. After that scary picture and eating up the cookies, I think maybe I'm going to have my nightmare. I'll probably bang on the door at three o'clock in the morning."

My mouth and throat were like glue; I could hardly get words out. "I wouldn't mind your staying if there was another bed."

He clapped his hands. "I can sleep in the chair. I've slept in chairs before. When you grow up the youngest in a big poor family, you learn to do a lot of things." He turned his back politely as I began to undress. "I got another idea. It'll be more comfortable if I take off my clothes and sleep in your bathrobe. You mind?" I shook my head. "That and Beatrice's afghan and I'll do fine."

We went to the bathroom down the hall separately, each in turn wearing the bathrobe. I got into bed, and Carl turned off the light. I could hear him settling into the rocker, and presently my eyes adjusted enough for me to make out his outline in the chair. He gave the sigh we sometimes make before we go to sleep. But neither of us went to sleep; we lay in the dark waiting. It seemed forever and may even have been ten minutes before I saw him leave the chair. He came and stood by the bed. "I know you're not asleep."

"No," I said.

"Mark, I can't stand it."

I flipped the covers back to let him in. I remember what it was like; they're wrong who say we don't remember joy. It was a time of trust and sharing, of learning to love for both of us. We slept a little but not very much. At some point I told him about the afternoon date with Buffie. And then, the classic cliché—the bed fell. As if it had never happened before in the history of the world, we howled, we wept with laugh-ter. Carl said, "Us fainting robins fucked our nest right out of the sky!" Then we turned on the light to set it right.

"I know how," Carl said, pushing me out of the way. "Slats and springs were always falling at our house. I know everything about cheap beds." When he'd fixed it, he turned, and it might have been the first time we looked at each other; we touched as tentatively as man might set foot on another planet. "Will you come to Mass with me tomorrow? I won't go to confession, but I want to be there with you."

53

IT BOTHERED me that I had not gone to football games, but Carl laughed. "If you'd come to every one, you might have seen me five minutes altogether; and if you looked away or left early, not at all. I'm no big star, you know." I did know. He was, I'd heard people say who'd watched him practice and play, a good player who might get better if he developed the killer instinct all great contenders in any field are supposed to have. He told me, "I'm sent in to substitute at the end of the game when the score is safe. It's to try me out and let the stars rest if they just broke their backs or something."

"It was arrogant of me never to go."

"So come and see me train, if you want to. I'll be playing baseball this spring in some of the go-easy games."

It was truth mixed with modesty, but he was not putting himself down. He was a strong, dependable athlete with pride in his abilities, but he had no desire to beat others. There was no question about my watching spring training, because so many did, both students and faculty. When the season opened, I went to all the games played on the home field. It was a new, baffling, delightful experience to watch Carl. I picked him out easily from any distance; I knew his body as well as my own. Watching him was akin to watching a good company of dancers when your body, unwilled, shares and responds to movements on the stage and you become one of the dancers. I hadn't, in fact, realized how much I knew about Carl. I gave myself the luxury of marveling.—The player who bunted the ball and made it to first base, though he had to slide, getting up now, safe, adjusting his cap and hitching his pants, spitting dust and glaring at the pitcher back on the mound after trying to throw him out—that boy is mine.

We were cautious without having to remind each other to be, careful not to be seen together more than we were with other people. Like all lovers, we had secret words we could speak in front of strangers—and friends, for no one must know about us. For either to call the other Robin (everyone had half a dozen nicknames, and they changed) meant "I love you." Sometimes he'd see me and wave from the training field. When I wondered about this, he said, "There's a hundred of you watching. How do they know I'm waving to you? It could be Arline Judge." He'd heard Marshall and me joking about college movies.

One day when we were killing time in Pug's, Marshall said, "How come this new interest in sports?"

"A writer ought to learn about everything."

He studied me casually. "You're in Carl's company more than you used to be."

"We get along okay."

"You don't think he's so dumb any more."

"Not dumb at all, different. Not everybody's dumb who can't tell you the pictures Toby Wing and Sir Guy Standing acted in together." Fear of my oldest friend led me to try a bluff. "You figure us for a couple of queers because we say hello, or did you catch us holding hands in public?"

He put on a parody-pansy lisp. "Mrs. Patrick Campbell said *she* didn't care what you fellows did as long as you didn't do it in the street and frighten the horses."

I smiled. "I picked up something funny about you recently. You and a certain instructor's wife."

There was no reaction at first. Came the dawn and a look of relief with it. "God, Buffie's had you finally! That woman's insatiable. Happened with me so long ago—she was my first, you know."

"No, you didn't tell me, although you always expect me to tell you."

"A gentleman doesn't fuck and tell."

"Better than telling and not fucking."

"Well, she's no gentleman in spite of the hair on her chest. You plan to keep it going?"

"I don't think it's a good idea," I said. "Do you?"

"Probably not. You might get crabs. She fucks anybody—the postman, the delivery boy, the cop on the beat, and probably Seeing Eye dogs in need of a little character building."

"How can Hugh help knowing?"

"He knows," Marshall said, "and doesn't care. It keeps her off him; and he's got a few smokey things going on too."

"But he's fat," I protested.

"Believe it or not, some women get their motors running for fat men."

"So they front for each other. A veritable design for living."

"And pimp for each other. After all, Hugh introduced *me* to *her*. And she keeps her ear to the ground for him at the teas faculty wives give each other."

"Surely they don't talk about screwing when they're knocking back the Tetley's. For all I know you're in the game too. You introduced *me* to her."

"It was time you lost your cherry."

I'd have to take a chance. "Cherries remind me of robins."

Marshall laughed. "Did she do Emily Dickinson for you? Of course she would, you a writer."

"Very high-class crowd," I said. I'd have to warn Carl. But before I could, Carl came into Pug's, saw us in the back booth, and joined us. He sat by me and ordered a glass of milk when he saw the individual teapots before us. Busy at meal times, Pug's was empty during the middle hours of the afternoon, and students spent idle time there. It was cheap and a place to talk out of the weather. Our talk was scrappy for a few minutes as it opened to include Carl. Newly self-conscious, I was careful not to be very friendly, but my caution backfired by making Carl anxious. He turned to me and said in what he considered an offhand way, "So, how you been, Robin?"

Marshall almost broke in two laughing. When he could, he gasped, "Him too!"

Carl blushed and looked the guilty lover, which Marshall interpreted his own way. But soon after, Marshall had to go to Morgan Hall to do some work backstage, and I explained to Carl. Instead of being relieved, he was annoyed. "I don't like it that you been with a pig like her. I could have had her too, you know. She volunteered to shave and paint my legs when I was in *The Frogs.* If you wanted a girl, you should have had something better."

"I didn't want a girl."

"I could have a hundred!"

"I know."

"I don't want 'em."

"I was trying to find out if I was queer."

"Well, you found out." He worried a minute, and I wondered about what. "I can't call you Robin any more, and I like to. What can I call you so you know what I mean in public?"

"Call me what you like."

"I can't call you Babe." He did sometimes in private. He shook his head. "*Marco?* It's still you but more—" He winked.

"Okay, Carlo."

"Hey, like we're a couple of Guineas in a gangster movie! Hello, Marco, how you been?—That means I love you."

"Sh."

He lowered his voice. "It means I'd like to kiss you right now till your lips bleed. It means I want to take off your pants and blow you out of this booth." He smiled. "I bet you got a hard-on, my saying that, huh?" I nodded. "Me too. Ain't love grand?"

Although I kept up my studies, I all but stopped writing for a while. I didn't merely abandon *Wolf in the Wilderness,* to the relief of Professor Ward's class, I denounced it.

Carl couldn't understand.

"It's bad work," I told him.

"You worked so hard on it. How can it be bad?"

"It's dishonest and self-pitying."

"What do you mean 'dishonest'? Your hero steal an apple or something?"

"It's not the end of writing, only like—chopping off the limb that offends me."

"Oh yeah? Well, you check with me first."

"As soon as I've destroyed it, I'm going to start something new and it'll be good, I bet you. You know why? I've got you; and you're too good for me to turn out crap any more and call it my bleeding Art."

He looked pleased, "Hey, you really feel that way?"

"You are my friend of the Sonnets, 'the onlie begetter.' And you're going to be my witness; we'll do it right."

I made a ceremony. Almost every day we managed to meet across the railroad tracks beyond the college buildings and walk and talk privately in the woods by the Black Warrior River. The next time we met there I carried the manuscript of the novel, and when we came to the muddy bank of the river, I struck a match and put it to a few pages, adding more when those burned down. Carl watched quietly. "When I think what it takes me to do a one-page English theme."

The first new thing I wrote I showed no one but Carl because it was a poem for him. It was better than any love poem I had written before, and he was proud of it; he carried it in his billfold from then on.

I helped Carl with his studying as I used to help Beatrice, and he began to make better grades. I never wrote themes for him, but I corrected their mistakes and made him copy them over before he handed them in. No moral qualm kept me from writing them for him. Themes were something I was good at and he wasn't; but I knew that any intelligent grader, let alone instructor, would see the difference.

"You're a good teacher," Carl said. "How come you're so good?"

"Because I'm antsy for the student."

"Yeah, well, couple of my real teachers give me a funny look now and then too, but they don't teach so good."

"Goddamn queers."

"Tell 'em, Marco."

He helped me too. It had bothered me that I didn't know how to throw a baseball or make that casual spiraling pass of a football every fraternity boy could do, and spent hours each day doing on the lawns of those fraternity houses I had to pass. Often someone supposed to catch missed. A ball landed at my feet on the sidewalk, and there was nothing for it but to throw it back. I was ashamed of the clumsy way I did it.

"Is that all?" Carl snorted.

We went back to the woods and found an open dry stretch where the trees had been cut. Carl had brought both a baseball and a football, and he showed me exactly how to hold and throw them. He worked with me for a couple of hours. He was very patient. I was exhilarated over my new accomplishment and tried to get a compliment out of him.

"Tell you, Marco, I don't think they're going to offer you an athletic scholarship." He was unable to teach me how to catch. "I've seen fox terriers that could catch a ball better than you can." It seemed to me that if a thing was coming at you fast, the only logical thing to do was to sidestep it.

It was a unique satisfaction to be able to laugh and hug in the open as we did before heading back to the college. Neither of us liked secrecy. We were open people with no talent for sneaking and pretending. But we knew we had to, that the expression of our love was against the law as well as against social acceptance. Had we been discovered, we doubted anyone would have tried to put us in jail, but we'd have been expelled.

Carl might have been saying it for me when he told me, "All my life I wanted somebody who'd let me love him." Our hearts were the same, and we needed and gave each other a lot of physical loving. Certainly our minds were different; what two are not? But we were never bored by each other.

Discovering the pleasures of sharing, we talked about everything. No thought was too small to exchange. I had been alone my whole life, and suddenly I had Carl to talk to. Miracle! Every childhood memory revealed a meaning or wonder when we told it. We reveled in similarities and marveled at differences.

I knew Carl worried about his religion. He tried to talk about it. "I feel close to God, but there are *those* between Him and me, and who am I to say I know better than the priest and the Pope? I figured it this way: God doesn't tell them everything either, and when He had my clay in His hands, He was feeling good so He said, 'This one I'll do for Marco to show him I love him.' "

54

WITH MORE than either of us had ever had, we could not be satisfied until we lived together. We talked about the difficulties. The first was money; it would have to be cheap. Most boys at the university had a roommate, a few shared apartments with one or more; but for an English major and a boy on an athletic scholarship with quarters already provided to decide to live together would raise questions. As we talked, we invented some answers we thought hilarious before getting down to sensible ones.

"How come I never knew you're a funny man?" I said.

"How could I be funny with you looking at the clock and waiting for me to leave? Marshall doesn't think I'm funny."

"Marshall doesn't think anybody's funny but him."

"He laughs at what you say."

"Only so I'll laugh at him," I said.

"Some way to talk about your best friend."

"You're my best friend."

"You really like me better than Marshall?"

" 'How do I love thee? Let me count the ways.' "

"Jesus, another quotation."

"One you should know. Elizabeth Barrett to Robert Browning."

"I seen a picture of him over in the library. He looked like a rabbi."

"A good-looking rabbi, maybe."

"Forget him. Nobody's good enough for you except me."

One of the bonuses of love, I discovered, is that you begin to think well of yourself.

We agreed that during times of strict training Carl would have to sleep in the quarters provided by the university, but he would be able to exaggerate the truth of his needing help to keep his grades up by sharing a place with someone who'd give him personal tutoring. ("I'll say," Carl interjected.) If anyone became nosey, Carl would then "confess" that living with me was a blind to hide the fact that he was involved with a widowed woman in town who had to be careful because of her job and family considerations. Several of his fellow athletes, he told me, had "outside arrangements."

We found no leads in newspaper ads or on the bulletin boards around the campus that often held cards of rooming houses. There was a side street off University Avenue we sometimes walked because it led around a curve to the railroad tracks across which were the woods and river bank we liked to wander. One day when I was coming home along that way, I saw a new sign on one of the houses near the end of the street. "Apartment for Rent."

I knocked at the door. A white-haired woman in a wheel-chair opened it; and when I asked about the apartment, she said I must talk to her son who wouldn't be home until six; but she didn't think he'd rent to students. I could come back if I wanted to.

I returned at seven-thirty when I thought they'd have finished their supper. I was met by the son, a thin, frosty-faced man in his forties, named Lester Mock. He repeated his mother's reservation about students. I told him who I was and explained my friend.

"A *football* player?"

"A very quiet one," I said, "who needs a very quiet place to live and study, just as I want a *very* quiet place to study and write."

"I don't mind if you look at it, I suppose." His thoughts seemed to be elsewhere from the way he frowned. "We made the last tenants move. Two ladies, or we believed them to be when they took it." He shook his head and let me inside the hallway. "It has its own entrance at the side-and-back, but we can go to it this way." He led me down the stairs at the back of the hall which opened directly into a large room. The house was on a slope, I then saw, the back of it facing a ravine with tall pines and a brook at the bottom. The apartment had been made from a half-cellar. The room we'd entered contained a big bed, a pair of stuffed chairs, floor lamps, a long library table, curtains, no pictures. It was clean and shabby; everything in it looked like a discard and this its last use before the town dump. There was a small bathroom and a small kitchen. Windows looked down the ravine. I couldn't hear a sound. It was private.

"Is it expensive?" I asked.

"Twenty-five dollars, lights and gas, and I have to be paid the first of each month, no waiting."

I said I liked it but that my friend would have to see it. Then, trying not to hope too hard, I said, "We couldn't take it until the fall, with the school year almost over." Instead of looking at him, I went into the kitchen and made myself busy turning the water taps.

When I came out, he said, "That might be all right if we settle other things."

I breathed easier. "Like what, sir?"

"An absolute promise of quiet. No use moving in otherwise; I'd only have to ask you to move out."

"We've been looking for quiet."

He hesitated. "I work for the city and am gone all day. My mother has arthritis and is housebound. She keeps her chair at the front window to see whatever is going on, but near the end of the street as we are, there isn't much passing. She gets lonesome. If one of you could look in for a minute, say once or twice during the day when you're coming or going."

"Glad to." I swallowed and waited, knowing from his face that he wasn't done.

"I've seen what students can be. There must be no drinking."

"Neither of us. He's always in training and I don't."

"And no girls."

"Solemn word."

"I don't mean if it's a real lady on a strictly friendly visit in the daytime, but no roughhouse and nobody overnight."

"Yes sir, I understand."

"Well. You look like a nice boy or I wouldn't have showed it to you. Bring your friend to look at it, and we'll talk. I assume you can give character references, or maybe I can call the Dean of Men."

My heart sank. "Of course, sir. Mr. Marek's reference would be the priest at St. Joseph's and mine is—Professor Victor Ward."

Some of the frost melted. "I've heard Professor Ward speak. Are you in his writing class?" I said I was. "He's quite well known, even in New York, they say—articles in the papers and so on." He was leading me back up the stairs after turning off the lights in the apartment. "Maybe you'll be a famous writer one day and I can say I knew you when." He laughed to be sure I knew it was a joke. "I write myself, a little poetry. I don't mean professional—no expectations."

We said goodnight after agreeing that I would return the next evening at the same time with Carl.

Lester Mock stared at Carl severely as they shook hands, then turned to me as if we were friends. "I had a few words on the phone this morning with Professor Ward. He speaks highly of you. I was a little hesitant about asking the priest because I'm not a Catholic, but if you'll vouch for your friend? Show him around. I know it's easier to talk things over if the landlord isn't standing there." He made himself laugh again.

I led Carl downstairs and turned on the lights. Unlike me, he checked everything, and he knew where to look and what to look for. I watched him prowl, but I didn't follow. Finally he came back and stood with me at the window where I was looking down at the ravine. It was almost dark, but I could see the brook.

He said, "Everything's terrible but I can fix it. I wish we were moving in tonight. The robins have found a nest."

After questions and answers, and cautions repeated and promises made upstairs; after Carl was presented to Mrs. Mock and charmed her in seconds; we left. It was understood that we'd return within a few days with a month's rent as deposit, but that it would pay for September; and we'd be free to leave our things there over the summer and to come in and out—not living there, of course—if there was "any little thing" we wanted to do before school ended to "improve" the place.

Outside we walked toward University Avenue. It was indeed a quiet block. There was a single streetlight in the middle. After we passed it, Carl took my hand, pressed it against his leg, and held it as we walked along. I tried to let go, but he held tighter.

"Somebody could see us."

"Fuck 'um."

55

LETTING PEOPLE in Montgomery know about the apartment would present no problem, but I knew that I must tell Marshall before leaving Tuscaloosa; otherwise, when he found out, he'd go, "Oh-ho! Oh-ho!" I waited until his mind was on summer school. By continuing classes with almost no holidays he'd complete the requirements for a Bachelor of Arts degree a year from now. His reaction to my announcement was mild; he made no comment on the matter of sharing, no reference to Carl, "I think Mama knows Mrs. Mock." I repeated the address. "It sounds like her."

Marshall was working hard. He planned sets—they weren't exactly designed—and helped build and paint them. He found props. He knew which of the home-furnishings stores in town would lend furniture in exchange for a program notice and from which graves he might steal the freshest flowers. He had long ago thought of approaching florists and funeral parlors to beg for leftovers. Only after they replied huffily that there *were* no leftovers did he resort to what he called his Burke and Hare act.

About lighting, he knew all he could learn from the light board backstage at Morgan Hall. He taught himself makeup. In two years he had become, to my surprise, a reliable director. I'd not thought he possessed the patience for it, his main interest being his own acting. As to that, he was a sturdy Dr. Gibbs in *Our Town,* and his performance of the title role in *Mr. Pim Passes By* was charming, though tricky and over-eccentric, which he did not like my telling him.

I was increasingly involved in Victor Ward's writing class. Toward the end of that year I produced little, but I learned by listening to others read their work and by the class criticism, in which I was now taking a constructive part. To say that something is bad in a way that gets a laugh is child's play; to go beyond into true criticism is man's work.

Marshall's and my activities being different, it was inevitable that we saw each other less often than we used to. Now and then, because we realized we were no longer the intimate friends of adolescence, we'd take an afternoon off from everyone else and go to whatever was playing at the Bama Theatre, making the same noise eating the same orange and lime Life Savers we had at theatres in Montgomery; afterward, walking back to college, making the jokes we'd make in the old days.

We would always care about each other; we'd helped each other grow up. But we would never again be best friends. We didn't talk about it, itself proof of the gap, but we knew and resented it, and so at times resented each other. If Marshall had become, consciously or instinctively, careful in his references to Carl, so had I in mine to a girl I knew he was seeing more than any other. She was a nice girl, but I couldn't understand why *he* liked her, or for that matter why she liked him.

Doris Bisbee was a sophomore, as was I, studying art as a major subject. "But she's not dumb," Marshall was quick to say. Her family were farmers, and how she came to her interest I don't know. I never asked Marshall how he'd met her or why he'd become interested. I think it must have been a gradual thing, not a lightning flash. She was a plain girl who could seem pretty. Her clothes were ever fresh and starchy, her hair clean and neat. Her face, with never much and sometimes no makeup, was serious. She had none of the sloe-eyed green velvet glamour that had made Marshall a slave to Sylvia Patterson. Doris was no ugly duckling, no swan. She had little conversation and no witty turn of mind, which probably suited Marshall because of his liking stage center. She was a girl who, I learned, could suddenly be unconventionally beautiful and amusing. She was what Miss Hannah Hamilton would have called a *good* girl. Marshall had chosen well for himself, although I didn't then know it. Not knowing, I made remarks about her plainness until I became aware one day that Marshall was looking at me with cold fury. That was when I realized he loved her. I thought about it and still didn't understand. Well, I saw more in Carl than he did.

In such ways we drifted apart.

Carl left Tuscaloosa before I did. He had a job arranged by alumni, doing road construction work on a highway in northwest Alabama, along with half a dozen other scholarship athletes. The job would last until August, when he'd make a short trip to Philadelphia to see his family before returning to the university to begin fall training. He left on a truck after spending the night with me at the Spanish Inn. When he returned to Tuscaloosa, he would do things to the apartment while I was still in Montgomery.

The summer of 1940 stretched on, dull and uneventful. I crossed off the days on my Dr. Pepper calendar in the YMCA room I shared with a salesman for Ballard flour who was in the process of learning a new rural territory and trying to find housing he could afford for his wife and two children who were staying in Kite, Georgia, with her mother and father until he could. "Sell very little Plain flour these days; it's all Self-rising; that's what people want. Won't even dip their chicken in Plain to fry them, much less do biscuits the old way." We got along well enough, but conversation was limited, and he thought I was stuck-up when he discovered that I didn't plan to go on working at my uncle's food brokerage after college.

After a week in Montgomery I lost Margaret Torrence's company until late August. Her brother had been sent to Hawaii for his next tour of duty, and invited her to visit. She went by train to San Francisco, by ship from there to Honolulu. Mrs. Bush was impressed when I told her. "Trip of a lifetime," she said.

I saw no old friends my age. High school seemed a decade ago, and Celia was no longer there, the only one I could always count on wanting to see me. I visited Mrs. Noble a couple of times. Harvey asked for my help in writing up two cases for a law journal and insisted on paying me. Both Beatrice and Georgette were pregnant, a coincidence Georgette viewed darkly. She didn't like children and wanted no more, I gathered from Roland. After naming her firstborn Angel, she ignored her when she could, leaving Roland to play the doting parent. Beatrice and I speculated on what they would name the new child. There had been no announcement from Georgette. I plumped for Rainbow, whatever sex; she liked Cloud. Carl and I wrote to each other. His letters were stilted, mine glum. It's bad not to value a day until it's yesterday, but that's how I felt the summer of 1940.

It was a time we all began to take the war seriously, the war that had cast a shadow so far ahead, and then when it came, the year before hadn't seemed like a war. Nevertheless, all Western Europe except Britain was now Hitler's, or neutral. Roosevelt decided to run for a third term; his draft bill, the first in peacetime, would soon be passed. We all knew we were preparing for war, but when it would come was still a vague "sometime." So we went on living very much as we had. I could think only of September, school, Carl. I didn't write very much, but I kept a notebook and set down in it short descriptions and fragments of overheard speech from solitary walks that more often than not carried me to Day Street. I can't say why the Negro area drew me, but it did. I had no strong feelings about race. Perhaps it was the unself-consciousness of the people. It was their territory, Day Street, but a white man was ignored if he kept on walking, and many of the people now knew me by sight.

I had only two evenings of talk with Margaret Torrence after she came back. She was full of "the islands," which she loved, and of the sophistication of Navy life there. "We had cocktails before lunch as well as before dinner!" When I told her I was going to live in an apartment with a boy named Carl Marek, she said, "Good."

Although he knew the time of my train, we had decided to meet at the apartment. Carl wrote, "God knows what I might do." I paid the taxi driver and, seeing no one, went around the house to the outside entrance of the apartment. The door opened as I stepped up and closed after I went in. Carl said, "Put it down," and I set the suitcase on the floor. He tackled me and then held me to keep me from falling.

A long time later as we lay on our backs, he slapped the mattress. "Some bed, huh? Solid. Elephants could mate on it. I took it apart and put it together again good."

"Thank you, Jumbo."

"Do I look different?"

"Yes. Do I?"

He shook his head. "It's because I been working outdoors."

"You're black as Bojangles."

"Were you afraid I'd *be* different?"

"No," I said. It was true; it hadn't occurred to me.

"Your hair stinks from train smoke. Go take a shower."

When I'd washed myself and dressed again, we talked, try-ing to say everything at once, repeating ourselves, exaggerat-ing, adding details—at last able to sit for moments and look at each other and say nothing. He showed me what he'd done. He'd taken the rugs outdoors to beat them, scrubbed floors, washed windows inside and out, and bought a hundred small things. When I tried to pay my share of what he'd spent, he said, "My house gift." In spite of her arthritis, old Mrs. Mock had made new curtains for the windows; and he had made tests. "It's really private. Nobody can see in unless they walk on stilts. I even went around to the street across the ravine. They can't see because of the slope. Is it okay if we stay home for supper?"

He'd bought six pork chops, and when I said that was too many, he said, "So you're the butcher in the family. You do the shopping and cooking from now on. I'll do the work." He stood by me beaming as I admired the pantry shelves he'd stocked with groceries. When I said, "Two boxes of salt?" he said, "Okay, you take over."

Doors bolted and windows open to let in cool air, we were asleep before midnight, but later I woke in alarm. The bed was shaking and Carl, who had rolled away from me, was making strangled, protesting sounds. I grabbed him and he woke, startled to silence. As I kissed him to comfort him, he began to relax. He swallowed and moaned, and as soon as he could, said, "It had me."

"What?"

"I couldn't find you. I was looking for you. I tried to call. It came closer and got me."

"No it didn't; I'm here."

He tightened his grip on me. "Don't go."

"No."

He put his head on my chest, and I fitted my chin over it. "I missed you," he whispered. Presently, his breathing told me he was asleep, and I relaxed my hold but kept my arms loosely around him. I was wide awake, Tarzan protecting his love from all the beasts of the jungle.

56

It was, however, Carl who was to become the home guard more than I.

The day after I got back, I brought Marshall in to see the apartment, while Carl was at football practice. I didn't plan it; we'd met on University Avenue. The Mock house was between the campus and the Blake house, and Marshall took to stopping by casually, as he'd done when I lived at the Spanish Inn. I didn't mind, but Carl did. He'd come home, glance around, and say, "Marshall's been." They were friendly enough when they met, but Marshall was not careful with people for whom he felt no basic sympathy, and Carl was one of the enemy merely by being an athlete. He began to behave again as he had when he first introduced me to Carl, as if he and I were the friends and Carl the outsider. I knew Carl wouldn't put up with that for long. He didn't care about Marshall's good opinion; he had mine. He said nothing, but one day when he came in limping from field practice and found Marshall, he exploded. Marshall made himself comfortable wherever he went; on entering anyone's room at school, he usually made straight for the bed and flopped on it as he continued to talk. "Marshall! I made up that bed *neat* this morning! I don't want you wallowing on it. Go sit in a chair."

Marshall looked at him as a king might look at a courtier gone mad. "I'll sit where I please."

"You won't sit on my bed."

"It's *his* bed too," Marshall said, drafting my support.

"Okay," Carl said, "it's *our* bed, but it's not your bed, so get your ass off it."

Marshall looked at me, and I simply looked back at him. "You heard the man."

He got up and left, and I didn't stop him. He'd been wrong. He and I made it up, but he and Carl were always on guard with each other. It was surely Marshall who mentioned the apartment to the Weatherheads, because I now saw them only in passing. Marshall enjoyed mischief, and it would have been like him to put the idea into Buffie's head. One afternoon when I came home a little later than usual, I found Carl in the kitchen starting supper. He said offhandedly, "Oh, your girl friend was here."

"Who?"

"Buffie Weatherhead." I must have looked surprised. "Yeah, came to see how we were getting settled. Heard what a sweet little place we had and could she look? 'Ooo, you've got a kitchen!' she says, woopsing all over. 'Ooo, you've got a bathroom! Ooo, you've got a broom—and a mop—and ooo, you've got a big bed!' So I said, 'Yes ma'am. We do our own cooking and our own cleaning and our own fucking, so why don't you barrel-ass out of here?'"

"You didn't say that."

"She got the idea. I don't think she'll be back. I *did* say Mrs. Mock was anxious we shouldn't give the place a bad name by having girls in and out."

I wasn't sorry that Carl was possessive about the place; it pleased and amused me. We had few visitors, but some. If they stayed what he considered too long, he'd become sulky and finally just sit there staring at them until they got up and left.

"It's *our* place."

"You're jealous."

"Do you blame me?"

"Nope."

"Just don't give me cause."

"Nope, I won't; and don't you growl at me."

"Hey, Marco, you mad at me?"

"Nope."

"Then say more than fucking nope!" He glared at me.

"Okay. I love you."

"When you say that, Mark, I could come all over you and me and the whole world."

It's truly said that you never know anyone until you live with him. I was tidy because I'd learned that it was simpler than not being. Whatever he saw me do, he would thereafter do exactly the same. The way I hung a towel or a pair of pants was the way he did it from then on. The way I did anything was the right way. It bothered me and sparked the only thing like a quarrel we ever had.

"Carl, do things your own way, for God's sake! I don't want you to be me!"

"But you *know*. I don't. My family are Polacks. You're American, you know the way. I don't speak a word of Polish —I never listened when they spoke it at home. I wanted to be one hundred percent American, just like you."

It hadn't occurred to me that he felt vulnerable because his family was Polish. No one had ever called me American, and it hurt that he saw me as being different from him. He relaxed when I told him I'd been annoyed because he had no reason to copy anyone. He was incapable of awkwardness or thoughtlessness. His language might be rough, but it was never false. He was sensitive. Our squabbles were light ones, usually about whose turn it was to do something, because we'd agreed to share everything. I learned that what Carl meant by sharing was that he would try to do more than I did. It was the only way we were ever watchful of each other. I wasn't really serious when I said one night, "People who love each other are supposed to have fights, you know. Everyone says so; it's in the books."

"Yeah?" He was working at the library table on a graph about measles for one of his classes in physical education. It was expected somehow to prepare you to be a better physical education teacher in grammar school.

"Yeah. They say if you don't fight, you don't love each other."

He didn't look up. "What a load of bullshit."

Conventional in some ways, I took a while to get used to Carl's casual nudity. He'd finish a bath and pad around the apartment naked, doing things. When I mentioned it, he shrugged. "Athletes don't think about their bodies; they're bare-ass half the time. You know, locker rooms and all."

"Do you ever look at them?"

He snorted. "You should see them! Bruises, plaster, tape. Only a Florence Nightingale could get a hard-on looking at them. Besides, I'm the only good-looking one."

"Well, put some clothes on anyway," I said mildly.

"How come? It's our place and the door's bolted." He looked sly. "You mean I get you going?" He reached to my crotch. "Yeah!" I slapped his hand away and pretended to read again. He sat down in the other armchair and examined the soles of his feet, picking at dead skin. His thoughts went a couple of other places before he frowned. I watched him as the frown became brooding. "Mark, do you love me?"

"Yes."

"You're the only one in the world ever did."

"Everybody else is straight. I'm queer."

"What a guy."

My share of the apartment rent was more than I'd paid at the Spanish Inn, and that was more than I'd paid at Woods Hall; but I was able to come out even on the difference in food costs. I was a careful buyer for us; I hadn't forgotten what I'd learned as a butcher boy in Savannah when I bought food for the family and prepared our meals. On school days breakfast was cold cereal with fruit, toast and milk and coffee. Weekends one of us cooked bacon and eggs, and few evenings passed we didn't break our studies to make fried egg sandwiches. Carl ate his lunch at the dining hall with the other athletes; I'd usually come home for bologna or peanut butter sandwiches and milk. Dinner, or supper as even Carl called it following local custom, we almost always ate at home. We ate good-cheap: meat loaves, pork chops, big stews, big salads. We cooked and sat down; we didn't stand eating out of cans. I was the better cook, but Carl was comfortable in the kitchen too. He liked doing what he called his messes: whatever meat I'd bought, simmered in a big deep skillet with tomatoes and onions and garlic and almost any other vegetable he felt like throwing in. We ate at the library table we also used for studying, and I for writing.

I had a notion that turned out well. We invited Doris Bisbee to have supper with us (after telling the Mocks we were going to) on the night of the first performance of *The Man Who Came to Dinner,* and the three of us went to the show together to watch Marshall strut his stuff, although his strutting was verbal since his part compelled him to sit for most of the play. Doris *really* liked our apartment; she and Carl *really* liked each other, and I began to like her. Marshall was at his best during the play and afterward holding court backstage. Carl's greeting was, "Hey, Marshall, you were okay; a wheelchair suits you."

I went to all home games now, but I couldn't afford to travel to the others. I was glad Carl's chances to play were few, because I was afraid he'd get hurt. Baseball was different. I enjoyed watching his concentration and speed in a baseball game. It was, anyway, more of a game. Football always looked to me like mass murder.

Beatrice kept us supplied with cookies, and Aunt Sally with preserves. Pug's got few of our quarters for chiffon pie. In letters Beatrice always asked about Carl, which pleased him. He got short letters from his mother once or twice a month, nothing from anyone else in his family. Three weeks before Christmas, Beatrice wrote asking both of us to stay with them. Carl was anxious about it. Would he be all right? There was no question of his going to Philadelphia for Christmas with his family.

He was shy at first because of the size and comfort of the Briggs house, but Beatrice was quick to like him and make him easy. She was a woman he could understand and appreciate, a family woman; and they discovered the bond of having felt "dumb" at school. Lucius and Roy worshiped him. To him he might not be a football star; to them he was. Bringing him home with me was the first thing I had done the boys seriously approved of. Having heard me talk about her, Carl was wary of meeting Margaret, and I can't say the meeting was a success. They were too different. It was the only time she and I found ourselves uncomfortable together.

A surprise moment occurred at the big Christmas dinner. I helped Beatrice in the kitchen that morning while Carl attended Mass with Harvey and old Mrs. Briggs and the boys. Beatrice had invited everyone. She believed in family gatherings, no matter how dreadful they promised to be. And so they came: Harvey's mother, Aunt Belle, Uncle Grady, Uncle John, Roland, Georgette, and of course the children. Eulabelle's main job that day was to look after Angel and Margaret, now called Mag.

Georgette provided the surprise, her first since Candle Salad. After fruit cake and ambrosia we sat on at the table with second cups of coffee. She had craned her neck out over her large pregnant body to find me down the table. As if we were alone she droned, "I like your new friend better than that sissy Marshall Blake you used to know. He may be a Yankee, but he's a he-man, and maybe he'll make you one too." There was nervous, general laughter. Carl, across the table, beamed at Georgette and smiled broadly at me. I could have killed them both.

It was a fine Christmas, and I made Carl walk Montgomery with me, because I wanted to show him my life. He was interested, but he couldn't understand my fascination with Day

Street. To him the people and their ways were incomprehensible. What did I see?

When we left, Beatrice drove us to the old train station, Roy and Lucius insisting on accompanying their hero and carrying his suitcase. The train was full of students, many drunk and still drinking beer. We found a seat at the back of a coach and pretended to be sleepy and cold, spreading our coats around us so we could hold hands unseen.

It was good to go home together and be alone. Carl examined the apartment while I paid our respects to the Mocks, and then we closed the door against the world.

We were reading, each in his armchair, and had been quiet for some time when Carl began to laugh.

"What?" I said.

"You, Shakespeare; it had to be the library!"

The tour I'd given him of Montgomery had included the YMCA and the library nearby; I had told him about the man who'd paid me to let him do me the summer before I entered college.

"At least I told you," I said. We'd talked about many things: past and present, the future; but he'd never been able to tell me about his first "experience," and I hadn't pressed him.

I went back to my book, but I could feel him thinking, so I turned my back to give us both privacy, swinging legs over an arm of the chair. When he spoke, his voice sounded timid. "I'll tell you, only don't turn around. I was eight years old. One of my big brothers took me in the bathroom on a rainy day when everybody was out of the house and told me to suck. He said I had to or he'd beat me up. I did and he beat me anyway. Maybe he felt bad; he hated me worse after that."

"What about girls?"

"I did it. The first time, same year; not again till I was sixteen and every boy I knew had done it, so I had to. I did it as much as anybody, but it was always like it wasn't me. I got nothing against girls, but I never wanted them." I heard him leave the old chair and come around to my side. "It's not such a big deal, is it? You rubbed it all out. The bad dream don't come any more, you notice?" I nodded. "You and me, Mark?"

"You and me," I promised.

"I don't mean to be crude at such a tender moment, but could you use a fried egg sandwich?"

"I'm starving."

"I'll make 'em."

He brought them out a little later with glasses of milk, and we began to talk. He talked eagerly about everyone he'd met in Montgomery and about all we'd done there. He was discreet about Margaret. "Everybody doesn't have to like everybody. She's your friend, and I'm glad she is, but she's too brainy for me." I let him say nice things about Roy and Lucius without telling him I found them boring and intrusive. We praised Beatrice with great mutual satisfaction. "She is some girl, some *woman!*" I refused to admit that Georgette was human; he thought she was funny. I took empty plates and glasses to the kitchen and rinsed them, leaving them in the sink. One of us would wash them in the morning. Tomorrow was not a school day; we had come back a day early.

We returned to our books. He was trying to read *Tono-Bungay* for a report, and he said it was dull as owl shit. I was yawning but wanted to finish a story in *Obscure Destinies* before bed. "Hey, Mark," he called softly. I ignored him. A minute or two went by. "Mark?" He was smiling, Mr. Happy. "We got a home."

57

CARL WAS the center of my life, but life was busy for both of us. He had classes to attend, training and practice, then games to play. I had classes, work as a grader, my writing. Each of us saw other friends for minutes or an hour, but we spent most of our time together. We were usually doing different things, but we were together; we could look over and see each other, we could speak, and we knew we would go to bed together.

He might interrupt my studying, as I did his, to tell me something or merely to make a remark; but he never interrupted my writing. He asked to read everything, and he praised everything. I could smile and know the truth, but his trust helped me. I was beyond being a talented boy. I was a man trying to write well. I could conceive of no greater occupation, imagine no keener satisfaction when it went right. It had nothing to do with vanity, but was the opposite of vanity in its combination of surrender and control.

The stories I wrote were getting better, but nothing seemed good enough. One of them I called "Doomsday Trumpet." It was about Negroes on Day Street, not the first I'd written but the first I read to the class. Professor Ward, who sometimes contradicted himself for good reasons, thought there was *too* much dialogue. It read like a play and —he looked at me sharply—had I written it as one and then turned it into a story? I had, but I said no, feeling stubborn rather than dishonest. I was suddenly angry with him. My process was none of his business. I knew it was good. So did the class. There wasn't much praise, but there wasn't any bad comment. A fat, middle-aged, politically left-wing woman from Mississippi (Ward's students were all kinds and came from anywhere) pointed a finger at me and said aggressively, "I'll tell you what I like about it. It's not lofty and pretentious. It's not about 'Negroes'—" (She had fluted her voice into parody.) "It's about *niggers*. It hasn't the social awareness it ought to have, but I can hear them, I can see them, I can smell them; and so, by God, could any black man or woman who read that story. They've got their character, not ours, if indeed we have any."

It was one of four stories from the class Ward submitted to a competition *Atlantic Monthly* was having to choose the best story by a college student in America. The prize was to be fifty dollars and publication in a special supplement of the magazine. A few weeks later I learned that my story had taken first place in the contest. Everyone was surprised, even that good, wise, intelligent, noble, near-Communist fat lady from Mississippi. But I had won! Years, years—belief in myself teetering from zero to a hundred and sometimes vanishing altogether, the kindness of Mrs. Noble, the stimulation of Margaret Torrence, the money she and Beatrice had raised to give me college—we had not been wrong; I did have some ability. I had become twenty-one in February, but this was my coming of age.

Ward's class met now in an upstairs seminar room of the new main library on the Quadrangle facing Denny Chimes and University Avenue. I heard the news there, and at one o'clock when I was free, I galloped down the stairs and all the way to the dining hall where I knew I could find Carl eating with other team men. I caught him going in the door, to his astonishment and theirs, grabbing his shoulders and blurting out my triumph. Oh, how he yelled and yahooed his pride and joy! I thought he would hug me to death. It was so open and clear, the others understood and crowded around us. Athletes love and are ready to cheer any kind of victory, and they joined in mine. They knew vaguely that I was a friend of Carl's from seeing me around with him, but now I had "won," and that made me really "okay."

Carl left them, throwing over his shoulder, "We're going to Pug's to celebrate!"

So we did. We laughed; we couldn't stop, except to eat, but we managed to eat hugely. We said the same things over and over and never tired of hearing and saying them. By the time we left the restaurant we had decided to cut afternoon classes and go home, where we went straight to bed. Later, side by side, sweat drying, we looked at each other. He said, "Hey, didn't I tell you? I said what a good story it was." He laughed. 'Can I pick 'em!"

I went out and telephoned Margaret, who was emphatically pleased, and Beatrice. She was pleased too, although I had to explain what it meant. She would tell everyone in Montgomery, she vowed, as soon as I got off the phone; and indeed my high school graduation picture (the only one she had) appeared the following day in the Montgomery *Advertiser* with a paragraph.

Returning to the house, I stopped at the front door to see Mrs. Mock. It was after six, and Lester had just come home. Both were excited for me and insisted that I come in. "You see?" Lester exclaimed. "I told you one day I'd say I knew you when!" He brought out a bottle of sherry. "It eases Mama sometimes; doesn't it, Mama?" They toasted me and I toasted them, declaring that I couldn't have done it if they hadn't given me the perfect place to write.

Downstairs I found Carl in the kitchen, stark naked and singing the Toreador Song from *Carmen*. He had been out to buy steaks, come home and had a shower. He'd also bought four bottles of beer from another athlete who lived off campus and kept himself supplied with the (in that county) illegal beer. No one ever had a better coming of age.

As I went to sleep, I remembered: I hadn't told Marshall. I was at the front door of the Blake house first thing next

morning. Mrs. Blake answered my ring; then Marshall came
in his bathrobe and smiled at me bitterly. "I heard. Congratulations."

58

Marshall took his Bachelor of Arts degree in June, but by
then had decided to continue at the university another year
to win his masters. The Mocks didn't charge Carl and me
rent over the summer, but let us leave our things as they
were. Lester said, "We wouldn't think of renting to anyone
else when we're getting you back in the fall." Mrs. Mock was
up early and on the porch in her wheelchair to wave Carl off
the morning he left for another summer of road construction
work. As the truck pulled away, she began to sniff into her
handkerchief. "I can't help it; that boy is so good to me." I
wanted to pull out my own handkerchief and tell her,
"Ma'am, you don't know"; but instead I went back downstairs and fell across the unmade bed and cried my heart out.

I saw more of Uncle Grady and Uncle John; I even went
fishing with them, which bored me, because I liked being
with them. I saw less of the rest of the family. The household
on Morgan Avenue was occupied with its new baby, named
at his father's surprise command Roland, Junior. Beatrice
had also given birth to a boy, two weeks after Georgette. "I
tried my best to have it sooner," she told me, lighting a cigarette and waving smoke out of her son's face. "For the rest of
my life I'm going to have to hear her say, 'Our boy is older
than Beatrice's!' We've named him Peter Joseph Briggs, and

Harvey already calls him Joe. It was all I could do to keep him from naming him Saint Peter Saint Joseph Briggs."

The best of the summer was that Margaret and I had the chance to come closer. She would not go to see her brother this year; the trip was too long and expensive. We needed each other's company, and we had it two or three times a week. Occasionally when we'd made no date, she'd be waiting for me in her car at the warehouse when I finished work, and take me home with her for supper. Miss Friede and Miss Bartley were in New York attending Teachers College sessions at Columbia.

"With only me to cook for, Aunt Sally would leave me," Margaret said.

"Aunt Sally will never leave you."

"No," she agreed, "not until one of us goes to her grave."

I had the idea of making a book with a series of sketches about Negro life in Montgomery. One evening when she'd read my new work and we'd talked about it a little, she said, "Why are you afraid of it?" I denied that I was. "Don't you see where all this points, including your *Atlantic* story? You want to write a novel, but you won't admit it to yourself."

We sat in silence for a time, and when I said I must go, she let me. It was early. She and Spot walked with me through the late twilight to my bus stop. The next time we met I told her that she had been right. "I was afraid. I still am, but I'm going to do it. I'm going to write a novel about them and call it *Day Street*. Here's the first chapter. The last chapter may use pieces from 'Doomsday Trumpet.' Can I do that?"

"You can do anything you want to," she said so absently it seemed the greatest compliment she'd ever given me, taking the pages from me. We had known each other too long to be self-conscious about work. She read with me sitting there and when she finished it, said, "Hooray. You've made a start."

By the time I went to Tuscaloosa in September I had four complete chapters. I was returning for my senior year, Carl his junior, although he was only six months younger than I. He had become twenty-one in early August.

"I thought of something just before my birthday," he said. "From February when you hit twenty-one until I did, they could have put you in jail for interfering with a minor. Now all they can arrest us for is—which is sodomy and which the other?"

"I can never figure out from the dictionary," I admitted. "You think we ought to ask somebody?"

Our lives were busy and satisfying, but of course the war was there all the time. We talked about the draft and of how we might dodge it. We tried to make plans, but it was impossible, and easy not to. Then December 7 came, and we suffered all the emotions common to the day: disbelief, shock, anger, fear. To make a long distance telephone call was a major undertaking, but I managed to get a line late in the day and spoke to Margaret Torrence in Montgomery. She sounded hoarse and exhausted. "Yes, I've tried to reach Charles in Honolulu. I can't get through. I'll let you know when I do. Thank you for calling, my dear. And what about you?"

The next day no one attended classes at the time the President asked Congress to declare war on Japan for its attack on Pearl Harbor. Students and professors crowded around cars outside the buildings to listen to car radios. During the days that followed I felt increasingly that I and my generation had been betrayed. Grant the provocation; still, how could our elders make such a complete about-face? They had preached peace to us, and we'd believed them. Most of us considered ourselves pacifists. Now everyone screamed, "War!" I followed the logic; I told myself I understood; but an essential part of me felt betrayed.

Carl and I went to Montgomery again at Christmas, and this time he was going back to visit friends; but it was very different from last year. Already we were looking on those days as innocent and lost. I went to see Margaret only once;

she wouldn't let me come again. She'd learned that her brother was killed in the raid. She looked like a sick, old woman. When I told her I had signed to go to officers training school in the Navy, she patted my hand, but she didn't care. I asked if I might see Aunt Sally and found her in the kitchen.

"Mr. Mark, she won't eat a thing; can't you make her?" I shook my head and put my arm around her; she hugged me. Then she wiped her eyes with the back of her hand and spoke firmly. "I tell her what she must now do is write Mr. Charles's widow-wife to bring herself and their baby to make a home with us. Don't you think that's right?"

"Yes, I do."

"I heard you say you was going in the Navy."

"Next summer, unless they call me before."

"Don't you get killed; hear me?"

"I won't, Aunt Sally." As I said it, I knew I wouldn't. I had promised Aunt Sally.

"You staying for supper?" I said no. "I'll make something and send you at college." She lowered her voice. "If you see any them Japs, kill the shit out of them, honey."

Briefly, Roy and Lucius tried to make a Navy hero of me, but they rightly did not see me as hero material and switched their attention back to Carl. What they really wanted was parades, the sound of guns and tanks, and for everyone to march off to war, themselves included; or, lacking that, at least an air raid. Eventually, the war happened to everyone, but it was not to disrupt the Montgomery families. Roland was a married man with children. Uncle Grady, Uncle John, and Harvey were too old to be drafted.

Back at school in the new year of 1942, we lived our lives much as we had done before. I went on with my novel and school work, Carl with his school work and athletics. I'd heard and read about a new show in New York called *Lady in the Dark,* with Gertrude Lawrence and music by Kurt Weill, some of whose earlier work Hugh Weatherhead had introduced us to. We bought the records and played them over and over, falling in love with Miss Lawrence and with Broadway musicals. Our time together had always been precious, but now we were aware that it was coming to an end.

Carl didn't want to be drafted, and he didn't want to follow me into the Navy; there was no reason to, since we couldn't stay together. He joined the Marines. They would let him finish the school year, as I was doing, before he went to boot camp at Parris Island, South Carolina. It suddenly became important for us to make plans for *after* the war. Carl would finish college. If my work was successful, I could write and live wherever I chose.

"I choose you live with me," Carl said.

59

In March I won another national story contest, this one sponsored by *Mademoiselle*. The fashion magazines then prided themselves on their interest in "quality" fiction, and my tale of a poor farm boy whose rabbit dies was soon to be sandwiched between glossy pages of ice-maiden models showing new clothes and makeup. When I later showed a copy of the magazine to Aunt Sally, she said, "Sugar, these women look to me like hardened criminals. You stay away from them."

My reward was five hundred dollars. For the first time in my life I had spending money. There was no use buying clothes; I was going into the Navy. I bought a bottle of capers, but we didn't know what to do with them, so we sprinkled them on our fried egg sandwiches. I also bought a small can of pâté de foie gras because I'd read that rich people ate it. Eagerly we spread it on slices of bread, expecting a treat. Carl said, "It looks like a cross between peanut butter and cat shit, and it wouldn't surprise me if it is."

Harvey and Beatrice left Roy and Lucius with their grandmother and brought the younger ones with them in the car for graduation exercises. As I maneuvered to kiss her around the babies, she said, "Well, I finally got to college." No one else from Montgomery came, although they sent presents and messages. Margaret wanted to see me as soon as I "came home" but was busy getting the house ready to receive her sister-in-law and young nephew. Roland and Georgette sent a tie. I took a look at it and dropped it into the wastebasket.

There was an alumni banquet to congratulate outstanding students on their achievements. I was invited because of my prizes last year and this, although I was not an honor student in the Phi Beta Kappa sense. The Dean of Men had to read out my accomplishments and then wait while I stood up to acknowledge the applause. It was a nice moment.

A bigger event at the end of the school year was Marshall's marrying Doris. There was a Sunday wedding at the farm, which was forty miles from Tuscaloosa. With my new wealth I rented a car for the day so Carl could drive. Doris had pressed him to come too, so there we were in the hot, clean, country air brushing away flies and bees and hearing good old Marshall make solemn vows. It was touching in that it was his worst public performance. Doris spoke clearly, but Marshall mumbled and hung his head.

He revived when we gathered on the screened back porch around the punch bowl. Under the din of happy relief that follows all ceremonies we even managed to say a few private things. It was the time to remember long years of friendship and exchange sentimental hugs. Marshall had other news. He and Doris would live with Mrs. Blake until they saved enough money for an apartment. "Also, I can claim Mama as a dependent if the draft gets too close. I have a tricky knee, you know." (I didn't.) He had an instructor's job in the speech-drama department for next year. The Weatherheads were moving on to the University of North Carolina at Chapel Hill. There was no mention of Broadway and Hollywood. Goals change.

Carl and I were singing and joking as we drove back to Tuscaloosa with the top of the car down.

"Do you suppose straight people enjoy it?" I said.

"Nah; how could it be fun?"

"Maybe they're all sick."

He slowed, pulled the car over to the side of the road, and stopped. "It makes you feel outside, doesn't it?"

"A little."

"Well," he said, "we are outside; but I tell you this, Marco. I don't need roses and hound dogs underfoot and crying mamas to marry you. I marry you here and now. I, Carl, take thee, Mark, forever." We kissed hard and sweet and long; and then he started the car again.

"Hey," I said, imitating his voice. "What if somebody had passed and seen us?" Together we said, "Fuck 'um!"

The biggest event, though, was orders that came next morning for Carl to report to Marine boot camp on a day just two weeks away. We had hoped to have a vacation to-gether. I had finished my novel and given it to Professor Ward, who'd offered to show it to publishers he knew. Now there was only time to close the apartment and for Carl to go to his family. "My mother would never forgive me if I didn't."

We had a week, and he was gone. I stayed another night and left in the morning on the Doodlebug for Montgomery. I had already said goodbye to Mrs. Mock, but Lester came downstairs before he went to work to tell me goodbye.

"I may never see either of you again," he said.

It was an odd thing to hear from him. We'd been friendly but not close. "Old grads always come back, don't they?" I didn't believe I would, but it seemed the right answer.

"It's been nice for Mama having you boys, all the things you did. And just having you here. It was nice for me too.—I could think of you and feel less alone. I never had anyone, I never dared. Also, there was Mama to take care of, and I wasn't good-looking, and now I'm getting old." He laughed. "I guess you could say I've got to the age where every man pleases and only prospects are vile." We shook hands. Something in my expression led him to add, "Didn't you guess?"

"I never thought about it."

He nodded, reassured, and left.

60

CARL WAS killed on an island in the Pacific called Kwajalein on 31 January 1944. When I heard, I died; but Lazarus is strong in all of us. A long time after, I met someone else, and someone else, and someone else.